LOCKHART'S NIGHTMARE

WAYNE BARTON
AND
STAN WILLIAMS

A TOM DOHERTY ASSOCIATES BOOK
NEW YORK

This is a work of fiction. All the characters and events portrayed in this book are either products of the author's imagination or are used fictitiously.

LOCKHART'S NIGHTMARE

Copyright © 1998 by Wayne Barton and Stan Williams

A Forge Book
Published by Tom Doherty Associates, LLC
175 Fifth Avenue
New York, NY 10010

www.tor.com

Forge® is a registered trademark of Tom Doherty Associates, LLC.

ISBN: 0-812-57196-7
Library of Congress Catalog Card Number: 98-2878

First edition: June 1998
First mass market edition: June 2000

Printed in the United States of America

0 9 8 7 6 5 4 3 2 1

Forge Books by Wayne Barton and Stan Williams

Fairchild's Passage
Lockhart's Nightmare

In memory of
Stan Williams

Home is the sailor, home from sea,
And the hunter home from the hill.

—Robert Louis Stevenson

LOCKHART'S NIGHTMARE

1

The big Union Pacific loco-motive swayed into a curve with its wheels squealing in noisy protest, coming to the end of the forty-mile downslope run into Sacramento. Inside the Pullman Palace at the rear of the train, the five rail drummers threw in their cards and stood pat while they saved their after-breakfast coffee from spilling.

"Last round, brothers," Melvin Baker said in his clipped Vermont accent. He gathered in the cards and began dealing out a new hand. "Sacramento in five minutes. I ain't getting even this trip."

James Lockhart grinned at him. "There'll be another time, Mel. We spend half our lives riding trains together."

"More." Baker gave a fractional nod to indicate the inside of the car. "Far cry from the old days. These new-fangled Palaces feel just like home."

"Home," Lockhart repeated.

Baker gave him an anxious glance. "That's to say, they're comfortable. Like a—well, like a palace."

Lockhart nodded, trying to hang on to his lighthearted mood. Mel was right. The new Pullmans were a treat to ride, far different from the dirty and crowded coaches he'd known in his first days on the road, back fresh from the Rebellion and newly married to Martha.

Today, the long car was almost empty except for the five of them gathered at the round saloon table in the near front corner. A woman sitting by the window had turned round to watch the card players, as if, Lockhart thought, she'd like them to deal her in. Because she was pretty and because she couldn't see his hand, he didn't mind her scrutiny.

Across the aisle a tall, leather-faced man with prematurely white hair and penetrating blue eyes had also taken an interest in their game. Lockhart couldn't see him without turning, but he felt those eyes watching. Two or three rough-looking characters sat further back, darting occasional glances toward the five men at the table. In the old days, Lockhart might have worried about his shipment of bank-notes, bound for the Merchants' Bank of Sacramento. But the notes were safe in the express car up forward and the idea of train robbery seemed ridiculous in this day and time.

"Cards, brothers," Baker said.

Catching himself up from his thoughts, Lockhart fanned out his cards one at a time. Jack–king–queen of spades, a nine, and a four. Practicing his poker face, he looked at the other players.

"Lord of mercy," Lysander Thompson complained. "If it weren't for the sociability of the thing, it wouldn't hardly be worth playing. Give me three."

Mel Baker peered at him through rimless spectacles. "That how you got all those chips, Reb? Being sociable?" He chuckled as he peeled off three cards. "Three for Brother Thompson."

"Two," Ed Givens said. The word made him cough. Whatever Lockhart thought of his own performance, it was Givens who had the real poker face. The oldest of the five players, he hid behind an unfashionable hedge of grizzled brown beard. What Lockhart could see of his expression was stony, and his flat midwestern twang gave away nothing.

"Two for Brother Givens. Opportunity?"

Opportunity Knox frowned at his hand. He was the baby of the group, still in his twenties. His boldly checked seer-sucker trousers and gold vest proclaimed the brash confidence of a young man on the make—not much different,

Lockhart thought, from his own attitude almost twenty years before.

"I'll stand on these."

Baker raised his eyebrows. "Well, well. Brother Knox stands pat. Don't try betting any of your stock in that new-fangled aero-whatever-it-is."

Knox grinned. "Aerobat. The Kendrick *Air Traveler*, and I tell you, it'll revolutionize transportation. All these Pullman Palaces will be dead as the dodo. Now, it happens I still have a few shares available."

"Not likely." Mel Baker's eyes, sharp and amused behind the glasses, cut toward Lockhart. "Jim?"

Lockhart discarded the four and the nine. With the king, queen, and jack of spades, he had a fair shot at coming up with a high pair, a distant chance at a straight or flush. Trying to look like a man comfortable with three queens, he said, "Two cards."

"Two for Brother Lockhart."

The train came out of a curve with an opposite lurch and began to slow toward the Sacramento depot. Suddenly, Lockhart was impatient for their arrival. Mel's chance mention of home had set him thinking, and thinking too much was always a mistake these days. He had tired of the game. What he needed was a bath and a good dinner and a couple of drinks. Maybe Mel or Reb would join him.

"Jim? Your bet."

Lockhart realized he hadn't even picked up the two cards Baker dealt him. He reached out for them. As his fingertips brushed their backs, a heavy hand slammed down to pin his wrist to the table. By instinct, he jerked backward, but he might as well have tried to move the locomotive. Looking up in surprise, he stared into the muzzle of a revolver held by the leathery man who'd been watching the game.

"What the hell!" Reb Thompson demanded. He started to rise, but one of the rough-looking passengers pushed him back into his seat. The leader paid no attention. His cold blue eyes fixed without question on Lockhart.

"James Lockhart?"

"So. It is a holdup."

Lockhart put down the cards in his left hand. The robbers no doubt planned to take his samples, might even think they could force him to have the express coach opened. He was carrying a Colt's New Line .38 in the inner pocket of his coat. He might get to it if the big man didn't notice.

The big man noticed. He shoved the muzzle of his gun into Lockhart's neck.

"Hands flat on the table, Lockhart, if you want to live to face the hangman. Martin, disarm him."

One of the other men reached over the seat, rummaged in Lockhart's coat, yanked at the Colt. Lockhart felt the hammer spur catch on something. Cloth ripped.

"Listen," he said, "that's a new suit."

The blue-eyed man released Lockhart's wrist, took the little .38, glanced at it with a nod of satisfaction, and dropped it into his coat pocket. From that same pocket, he withdrew something and held it out. Lockhart tore his eyes away from the icy blue stare and looked. It was a brightly polished silver badge.

"James Lockhart," the man said in a voice that seemed to go with his size and self-assurance, "I'm United States Marshal Rance Henson. These men with me are officers. You're under arrest."

Ed Givens half-rose. "The hell you say, sir!" he interjected. "By what right?" It cost him another cough.

The blue glare shifted to him. Henson said, "What's your name?"

Givens wasn't an easy man to stare down. "Givens," he snapped. "Edward P. Givens, sir. By trade a traveling representative for the—"

"A drummer, eh?"

Givens set his jaw. "By trade, I say, a traveling representative for the Gibraltar Safe & Lock Company of Chicago. By nature, I'm a friend of Mr. Lockhart, who certainly has committed no crime."

"You've been traveling with Lockhart?"

"All the way from Denver, this time." He gestured at the others. "We often ride together, all of us."

"Then you'll come with me," Henson said without rancor or question.

"The hell you say."

"The hell I say. Sir." Henson penetrated Givens with those eyes, pinned him to the seat. Then he looked at each of the others in turn. "The rest of you had better come along, too. We'll have some questions."

"Listen," Lockhart began.

Henson wasn't listening. The woman who'd been watching their card game had risen without haste, brushing the wrinkles from her deep red polonaise walking suit. Gathering up a hatbox and a large flowered bag, she started for the door at the far end of the car.

"Ma'am," Henson said in the same tone he'd used on Lockhart. She gave no sign that she'd heard. Raising his voice a trifle, although Lockhart thought it plenty loud already, the marshal tried again.

"Marian Taylor!"

Although his thoughts were racing among possible explanations for the marshal's error in arresting him, Lockhart couldn't help watching the woman. Again, she made no acknowledgment of Henson's call, continuing her stately way along the aisle. The marshal gestured to the officer who'd torn Lockhart's coat.

"Martin. Get her."

She paused, turned her head, looked at Henson out of the corners of her deep brown eyes. Touching her bosom with one gloved hand, she said, "Pardon, sir, but were you addressing me? I don't believe I've had the opportunity."

"Is your name Marian Taylor?"

Lockhart watched as she turned more fully toward the marshal. He guessed she was in her mid-thirties, her oval face unlined, seven or eight years younger than he. Ever so briefly she let her big dark eyes flicker to meet his questioning gaze. Then she nodded in answer to the marshal's question.

Her voice had been cool, pleasant, distant. Her nod was the same, barely enough to move her smooth dark hair. It seemed to say, *Yes, I'm Marian Taylor and that's all you need to know about me.*

Henson put away his badge, produced handcuffs for Lockhart, and said to the woman, "I'll ask you to come along with us."

Immediately, Marian Taylor said, "And if I'd prefer not?"

Without looking at her again, Henson said, "Up to you. But I wish you'd come without a fuss. Else I'll have to chain you to this cold-hearted killer here."

Fear flashed in Marian Taylor's deep brown eyes.

"This *what?*" Lockhart blurted.

"And drag the both of you along." He waved the muzzle of his revolver at Lockhart. "Stand up. Slow and easy."

"Marshal, there's some mistake here. I haven't done anything."

"Hands out."

Henson snapped the handcuffs onto Lockhart's wrists. Two of the other lawmen caught Lockhart's shoulders and hauled him out into the aisle. He heard his coat rip again.

"Marshal, is it your misguided intention to chain and drag us all along in your entourage?" Givens demanded.

"That'll be up to you. One way or another, you're all coming along." He looked at the others one by one. "Any objections?"

Opportunity Knox was staring as though Lockhart had turned into the hippopotamus from Barnum's circus. He managed to close his mouth long enough to goggle at Henson. "No. I guess not."

"I've been a prisoner of the Yankees before," Reb Thompson said, "and lived through it." He frowned at Lockhart's chains. "I judge I'll go along to see what I can do about all this."

"Who are you?"

"Lysander C. Thompson, of Colt's Patent Firearms Company. Late of the Fifteenth Tennessee—"

"That'll do." Henson glared at Baker. "You?"

"Melvin Baker. I'm in wholesale dry goods."

"All right. Come along."

"Arresting us, are you?"

"No," Henson said. "You aren't under arrest."

"I can't go, then," Baker said. "Got an appointment in San Francisco first thing tomorrow. Scarcely make my train as it is."

Lockhart looked at his closest friend Melvin Baker and saw a man he didn't even recognize. *Sure you wouldn't like to kiss my cheek, Mel?*

"Whatever Lockhart may have done, I've had no part in it."

Henson said, "I'm detaining you. Carries no mark of Cain. But you'll come with me. The only question is how."

They looked at each other. None of them seemed to want to meet Lockhart's eyes. Marian Taylor was the first to answer.

"Peacefully," she said. She braced herself against the makeshift poker table, and palmed two cards as the train braked hard on its final hundred yards into the depot at Sacramento.

She was not the first to leave the Pullman Palace when the porter put down the folding steps. Two of the lawmen came out first, searching the platform with alert eyes. Carrying their own bags, the disgruntled salesmen stepped out. Then came the woman, Lockhart in his chains, and the marshal, who herded them with no more than looping motions of his arms. No one strayed. Two more officers trailed behind.

Standing against the station wall, two men waited for the group. One was middle-aged, blue-uniformed, portly, his red face shaded by the narrow brim of a tall gray police helmet, his mouth and chin hidden by a vast, drooping mustache. The second man, in checked suit and derby hat, might have been another drummer.

"Chief Biddle?" the marshal asked, extending a hand as he approached.

"Marshal Doom, I mean Henson, sir. I got your wire. Did the men perform all right?"

"They did, and I thank you." Henson almost smiled. He inclined his head toward Lockhart. "As you see, we got our man."

"Not every day we're asked to assist the government. I would have come myself, but for the press of duty."

"Don't worry, Chief. Your cooperation will be recognized in my report. Now, if we could find a room."

"Marshal Henson!" The second man thrust himself halfway between Biddle and Henson. "Marshal Doom, I should say! Clyde Darrow of the *Sacramento Daily Union*. A great honor. It's always a pleasure to meet a lawman of your standing."

"Thank you. Now if we could have some privacy."

"If you could answer just one question, sir. What are your feelings on capturing the most dangerous miscreant since Jesse James?"

"Not me," Lockhart said.

"Yes you, Lockhart. They say you're a respected man in Ohio. A hero of the late war. What made you turn to a life

of crime? What lust for bloodstained gold led you down this
path?"

Lockhart merely looked at Darrow, who then returned
his attention to the marshal. "How'd you find this villain?"

"All part of the job," Henson said.

"Did he put up a fight?"

"Not enough to notice."

"Watched us like a snake from the second we set foot on
the train at Roseville," Martin interrupted. "Looks innocent
enough, but you could see by his eye he was a bad 'un."

"Martin," Henson said.

"Never took his hand off that little hideout Colt. Not off
his guard an instant, but us and Marshal Doom was too quick
for him."

"Martin."

"You can see where he tore his coat trying to draw on us.
And the woman tried to slip off, but I caught up to her."

"Martin!"

Martin blinked at the marshal. "Yes, sir?"

"Shut up."

"Yes, sir."

Chief Biddle cleared his throat. "I think that's enough for
now, Clyde," he said to the reporter. "We'll see you don't lose
out on your story, but we'd better get these prisoners over to
the station."

Mel Baker said, "Prisoners?"

"You can use my office for the interrogating, Marshal. I'll
give you plenty of privacy. The wagon's waiting outside."

"Lead on," Henson said.

"Marshal?" Clyde Darrow cried to Henson's back. "Marshal, is it true you've brought in over a hundred men and
never lost a prisoner?"

Henson halted with a big hand on Lockhart's shoulder.
He looked back at Darrow.

"Chalkline straight, I've never. And I don't propose to lose this one." He gave Lockhart a shove. "Get along, you. The hangman's waiting."

Walking beside Lockhart into the station, Marian Taylor slanted her brown eyes his way. "I've seen you before," she whispered. "Several times."

He liked that. "Have I seen you?"

"Oh yes."

"I don't think I'd forget seeing you."

"I was someone else when you saw me," she said. Before he could analyze the riddle, she added, "But I remember you. You're the last of your crowd I'd take for a killer."

"Thank you."

"Are you?"

It was a pleasant autumn day above Chickamauga Creek, but the dark woods seethed and stank with powder smoke. The larks that had sung at dawn cringed in their nests amid the ripping crash of massed rifle fire. Above the din, Captain James Lockhart, his new bars shiny on his coat, heard Cleburne's division howling their battle cry as they came on. He saw the tattered hedge of Rebs break cover and trot toward the log breastwork where his own men crouched, saw a volley rip them, saw the rest surge up and over the logs and into the ranks. He felt the jolt through his arm and shoulder as his sword countered a bayonet thrust and struck down the man who'd made it.

Lockhart blinked, swallowed. Marian Taylor was staring at him. With pure will, he pulled away, put it all aside. Twenty years. Twenty years, this coming September, and it was still as fresh as paint.

"Anyone's a killer," he said, "if the time is right. But I'm innocent of whatever they think I did."

"You don't sound very convincing."

Lockhart smiled. "I swear!" he whispered.

"Here's a gift, then."

"What?"

Marian Taylor tripped, let out a short cry, and clutched at Lockhart for support. Marshal Henson made a grab for her, and for an instant she clung to both men. As Henson helped her upright, she slipped two playing cards into Lockhart's manacled hand as slick as a carnival grifter slipping a pea under a walnut shell.

"Thank you," she said to Henson. He growled something and steered her away from Lockhart.

While Henson's attention was diverted, Lockhart looked down at the ten and ace of spades in his hand. He snorted, began to laugh, made a great noise of it, and couldn't stop until Henson jabbed an elbow into his ribs.

"What the hell's the matter with you you can't be your age in public?" Henson rasped at him.

"It's—" He choked, coughed until tears came to his eyes before he could finish. "It's just—aha—it's just my lucky day!"

The police station itself was square and squat, a cube in white stone with one black iron door and grilled windows at the front. Lockhart didn't like the looks of it at all, but he kept his mouth shut. Until he better understood the charges against him, he wasn't going to give Marshal Henson—had Biddle called him Marshal Doom?—the satisfaction of a heated denial. He could deny it, of course. He hadn't done anything. But Henson wouldn't believe that.

Chief Biddle produced a big ring of keys, led the party down a long hallway and into a creaking, crowded elevator. It opened on the third floor. Beyond an iron door ran a hall lined with bars at the fronts of opposing cells.

"Here's your home for awhile, Lockhart," Henson said, and unlocked his handcuffs.

"Listen. Could you tell me what I'm charged with?"

"You'll have your turn to talk presently. Chief?"

Biddle made a great bustle of opening the cell door; the reporter was busy taking notes, Lockhart saw. Henson thrust him inside, and Biddle slammed and locked the barred door.

Mel Baker said, "Is this it, then? Are you going to put the rest of us in these other cells?"

"We'll only need one more," Henson said. He opened the door opposite Lockhart's. "Mrs. Taylor, if you please."

Marian Taylor drew herself up. "Marshal, I demand to know why I'm being treated like this common criminal." She waved a hand toward Lockhart, who was watching her through the bars.

Henson sighed. "For now, you're charged with intent to defraud. We'll see about the rest later. If you'd like to add disturbing the peace and resisting arrest, I can fix you up."

She stared at him, bit her lip, and swept into the cell. As the door clanged behind her, Officer Martin said, "And we ain't forgetting that Lockhart's supposed to've had a female accomplice, either." He winked at the reporter. "Them two tried not to show it, but I could see how thick they were."

"Martin," Henson said.

"I never saw him before," Marian protested, her eyes wide.

"Ain't what you said on the platform," Martin said.

"Martin." This time it was Chief Biddle. "Shut up."

"Gentlemen," Henson growled, leaving it unclear whether he included Martin, "if you'll come with me, we can get this business finished and you on the next train." With Biddle's help, he herded them back toward the elevator. "Just a few questions, that's all."

"Listen," Lockhart said with as much force as he could gather, "I want to know what you think I've done." The heavy iron door clanged behind Henson.

"Doesn't pay a lot of attention, does he?" Marian Taylor asked with irritating good humor.

"Not a man to doubt his own convictions," Lockhart said. He slammed a fist into the door. It hurt.

"Oh, we're not convicted yet," the woman said. "Though

the good marshal seems to have that pretty well settled in his own mind, too."

Lockhart looked at Marian Taylor. She was smiling as if the whole thing were a great joke on them both. He decided she was very pretty indeed. "I'm sorry they put us in separate cells," he said.

She raised her eyebrows. "I believe I feel safer over here."

"Well, so do I, as far as that goes," he said, stung. "After all, I don't know what crimes you've committed."

"I? I haven't done anything at all. Not anything!"

They don't arrest innocent people, Lockhart almost said. Then he looked at his own situation. He had no inclination at all to laugh. "Neither have I."

She looked as if she were about to voice his thought. Unlike him, she had the grace to smile again. "Oh sure. Then what is it your so-called friends are in there testifying to right this minute?"

"How do you know they aren't testifying against you?"

An hour later, U.S. Marshal Rance Henson came back through the iron door, closed it behind him, and walked straight to Lockhart's cell. For a moment he stood facing Lockhart as if waiting for the prisoner to take the initiative.

"Are you going to tell me the charges?" Lockhart asked.

"We've had our talk in there. I've gathered enough evidence from your friends to hang you six times." Again, he waited, his coat open to expose the gun hanging by his side.

"You're mistaken," Lockhart said at last.

"Am I?" Henson's face went dark, his hand fell to the revolver. He brought it up with a single practiced motion, pointing the muzzle at the middle of Lockhart's chest. "Lockhart, I gave you your chance to draw, and I wish you'd done it. Now's your moment. Call or fold!"

Lockhart stared at him. "What?"

"I warn you, I'm not a man to trifle. Hand it over before I imagine to three or, by the ghost of Julius Caesar, I'll shoot you down where you stand."

"Why, Marshal," Marian Taylor said in a bright, sociable tone, "I had no idea you knew Shakespeare."

"Keep out of this, ma'am," Henson said. The pistol didn't waver by as much as a hair. "Last chance, killer."

Lunatics, Lockhart thought wildly. *I've fallen among lunatics. He's as mad as she is!* "Marshal, I don't know what you want."

Henson cocked the hammer.

Lockhart didn't blink.

The Taylor woman sighed. "Is this what you're looking for?"

Henson froze, apparently uncertain whether she would shoot him in the back if he remained as he was or whether Lockhart would shoot him in the back if he turned. He turned.

Marian Taylor was holding Lockhart's nickel-plated revolver out to him, butt-first. Henson crossed the aisle in two strides, grabbed the gun out of her hand.

"You black-headed minx. You've sunk your own ship. I was more than half minded to believe you really weren't mixed up with him. But not now. I'm taking you back with Lockhart on the six o'clock train to stand trial right beside him as his accomplice in those murders."

"What *murders?*" she and Lockhart demanded together, but Henson paid no attention. He turned like a plowhorse in its furrow, went back through the door, and slammed it behind him.

Lockhart stared at Marian. "Minx indeed," he said. "How did you get my pistol?"

"While he was keeping me from falling."

"Why'd you do it?"

"I thought it might be useful." She shrugged. "Truth is, I've always been prone to act on impulse." For a second, her mouth made a tight line, but then she smiled again. "Taking the pistol out of his pocket wasn't a very good idea."

Lockhart smiled back. "Just our lucky day, I guess." Neither laughed.

The iron door flung open and banged against the wall. Rance Henson came through the door like a hard wind, stalked without a word to Marian Taylor's cell, and thrust out his hand. She started to speak, then instead dropped five nickel-plated cartridges, one at a time, into his open palm.

2

Marian Taylor took a graceful pose on the hard cot in her cell. Her effort was wasted. Lockhart had lost interest. He slumped on the opposite bunk, his head bent over his two cards as if they were keys to the jail door. Easing herself into a position with less grace and more comfort, Marian lowered her lashes and watched him without his knowing.

For two or three months, off and on, she had watched him without his knowing. Their paths had crossed often, although he had never noticed. He had given her something to think about, a daydream while she'd tried to ignore what was going on between her husband and Sissie. She'd noticed him in the theater audiences, watched him on shared trains, once seen him laughing and chatting in a restaurant with some of his clients.

James Lockhart. Jim, the others called him. Older than she. Handsome, in a way, although too thin. She knew he was married, certainly, because all the good ones were. But he hadn't mentioned a wife. No womanizer, anyway; at the theater, he was always alone or with one of his drummer friends. War hero, that Darrow man had said. Salesman. Traveler. Gypsy, like herself.

Thief? Murderer? She didn't know. From what she'd seen, Lockhart seemed more stable, possibly more honest than the run of men she'd known. On the strength of that, would she bet her life he wasn't a killer? God knew her judgment was nothing special where men were concerned.

Forlorn in his cell, Lockhart seemed the very picture of an innocent man downcast by injustice or of a guilty one overtaken by doom. Marian was still trying to decide which when Marshal Henson came back into the compound and opened Lockhart's door.

She didn't trust Henson at all. For that matter, she reminded herself, she mustn't trust Lockhart. Lockhart was another *man*, like the marshal, like her father, like June, for God's sake! She'd trusted June—Junius Brutus Taylor, her worthless excuse for a husband—and he'd managed to leave her to foot the troupe's unpaid bills while he ran off with Sissie. Men were always managing things like that.

"On your feet, killer," Henson said. When Lockhart didn't respond, the marshal grabbed his coat and hauled him up. Marian heard the coat tear. She didn't like the way Henson shoved Lockhart against the bars.

"Right there, killer. Stand pat." The marshal snapped one shackle of his handcuffs onto Lockhart's right wrist and anchored the other end to the bars of the cell door. "Just you entertain yourself while I see to your lady friend."

"I'm not his lady friend," Marian said. Then she gave it up. Henson was not a man to doubt his own convictions, Lockhart had said.

Henson crossed the hallway in two strides and unlocked the door to Marian Taylor's cell. She stood very still. "You don't want to make this hard on yourself," Henson said. "Step over here beside the killer."

She eased past him warily, waiting for him to grasp her arm or to touch her the way men tried to do after performances. She was puzzled when he didn't. "Do you propose to shoot us both, as you threatened earlier?"

"Not yet." Henson removed Lockhart's other handcuff from the bars and turned toward Marian.

"Wait," she said, truly alarmed as she saw what he meant to do. "You can't chain me to him."

Henson snapped the link around her wrist. "I believe I can," he said. "Chief's got indoor plumbing down the hall. Either of you got any business, you'd best say so, because we're about to travel."

Henson was as good as his word. In less than ten minutes, they'd checked out of the jail and boarded a police wagon for the depot. An eastbound passenger train lay beside the platform, its green Pacific engine simmering with steam. Henson herded them to the iron steps at the rear of the third car. When Lockhart hesitated, Marian boarded ahead of him. The chain pulled tight, wrenching his arm.

"Watch it."

"Move along," Marian snapped, pitching her voice to Henson's tone. "Can't keep the hangman waiting."

She saw Lockhart grin. The dozen passengers in the car turned to stare. One man muttered something to his seatmate and both laughed. A woman gathered her young daughter closer to her skirts. With a bright smile, Marian stepped to the rear seat and turned her back to her audience. Of necessity, Lockhart sat beside her. Henson wedged himself into the seat facing them, his knees all but touching Marian.

"Give your lady friend some room," he growled. Taking

the cuff off Marian's wrist, he motioned Lockhart over to his side and chained him to the rail next to the window.

Marian lowered her lashes. "Thank you, Marshal," she murmured. "That was very gallant."

"Don't reckon you'll run. Not off a moving train, anyway."

The train was chuffing out of the station. Henson gave the conductor three tickets, showed his badge, growled a few words of explanation. The conductor, a rotund, gray-haired man, seemed properly impressed.

Lockhart said, "It's kind of you to give us a free ride."

The marshal laughed. "Onliest thing you'll have to pay for is a lawyer, if you can find one who'll bother," he said. "Everything else is free. The trial and the hanging and even a new casket."

Lockhart started to answer, then bit it back.

Marian saw his face darken with anger. *What had he said about being a killer? Any man's a killer if the time is right?* "Where are you taking us, Marshal?" she asked in a soft voice.

Henson said, "Denver. It's the handiest from here. I reckon it won't make much difference where the trial is."

Lockhart released a long breath, and his voice was calm. "I'd appreciate it if you'd tell me what I'm—what *we're* charged with."

"In a case of this kind, I figure you've done a sight more than you're yet charged with. I'd allow you really want to know which of your crimes have caught up to you."

"Have it your way. Any objection to telling me?"

Henson frowned, as if trying to think of a reason. Finally he drew a battered black leather notebook from his pocket.

"Lockhart," he muttered, turning the pages with a moistened thumb. "Lockhart. Four counts of robbery. Two of murder. Most recently in Fort Worth."

"Who in hell said so?"

"But the one you'll hang for is E. F. Murdock in Denver the twelfth of June."

Lockhart's indignant question died in mid-word. Marian saw his face lose its color as he twisted toward Henson.

"Murdock? Elvin Murdock's dead? How? My God, I saw him just last month."

"Just last month is exactly right," Henson said. His voice was the purr of a big cat. "June twelfth. Want to deny it?"

Lockhart stared at him.

Marian heard the murmur of the other passengers talking, the clank and rattle of the car on the rails, the deep note of the locomotive's huffing as the train ground up from Sacramento's valley toward the mountains. To break the tension, she said, "And what is it you think I've done, Marshal? Whom did I kill?"

Henson waited a moment longer. *He wants Lockhart to break*, Marian realized. *He's trying to shock him into a confession. Maybe his proof isn't all so strong after all.* Then Henson shrugged and turned to her.

"What I *think* you've done is help Lockhart every step of the way," he said. "What I *know* is that you and your husband sashayed out of Cheyenne without thinking to pay the bill for yourselves or that bunch of so-called actors you run with. Left a crowd waiting in the opera house, they say. Same story in Jefferson City three weeks earlier."

She saw Lockhart's eyes move to her face, puzzled. Resolutely, she kept to the marshal.

"A few bills. That's hardly a matter for the hangman. Or for Marshal Doom."

"It's enough to hold you until we get more facts. Want to deny you were in Denver in June? That you were in Elvin Murdock's bank?"

Now he's trying it with me! "I asked for a loan. I didn't get it." She pouted, looking at him with injured innocence.

"That wasn't on the twelfth. We were playing Virginia City on the twelfth."

"Left a slew of bills there too, I shouldn't wonder."

"What if we did? Does the government have so little for you to do that you need to worry about that?" Marian stopped herself short. That wasn't the way. She lowered her head, sniffled, dabbed at her eyes, and turned to the window as if to hide her tears. The train was pulling the first long slope of the foothills, making slow work of it. Almost even with their car, a boy on a bony white horse loped along beside the tracks, easily keeping pace with them. Marian watched him for a moment, wishing she could trade places. Then, weak and hesitant, she looked up at Henson.

"I just don't understand these things, Marshal. Junius always handled all the business matters. I was only a member of the troupe."

Henson snorted. "Junius Taylor couldn't handle his own—" Whatever image the marshal had started with, he decided not to finish it. "I know who handled the business matters. The assets were in your name."

For all the good that did me! "You should know, Marshal, a woman must be loyal to her husband."

Henson laughed. Then, like a bulldog worrying a bone, he went back to Lockhart. "How about it, Lockhart? Even now, it might help if you made a clean breast to the judge. You're a clever devil, I'll give you that. Truth to tell, I think you'd have gotten away with it, but for me."

Lockhart shook his head.

"You're clever, like I say. Four robberies in four months, spread around the country. Chances are, the local law would never have realized it was all the work of one man. I got onto it just after the Denver job. Well, right away I saw it had to be you."

"Why?"

"Deduction. You were in the right place every time. I'm only sorry I couldn't catch up to you in time to save that poor feller in Fort Worth—Stanley was it?"

"Stanley?" Lockhart demanded. "You mean Stanhope? George Stanhope? My God!"

"When we follow up, I expect we'll find receipts at your hotel and some local witnesses. Right now I've got the sworn depositions of your four friends that you were at the scene of every crime."

Lockhart shook his head. Marian thought he looked dazed.

"How would they know?" she asked.

Henson looked at her with disgust. "Hell, *they were there too.*"

Marian Taylor laughed. "Then I'll give you my deposition the four of them were there too," she said.

"I just told you that!"

Lockhart raised his head. "Then you have four more suspects. How do you know one of them didn't do it?"

Marian laughed again. "*I* don't know that any one of the five of them did it, because I wasn't there!"

Lockhart said, "Thanks a lot."

Marian said, "I'm not even sure you didn't do it, Marshal."

"You're a funny pair. I'll remember to laugh at your hanging."

The boy on the horse went past them again as the laboring locomotive covered their view out the window with a thick cloud of smoke.

"It wasn't me," Lockhart said, sitting straighter. "It was one of them. It had to be. We work the same routes, cross paths all the time. It's one of them because I didn't do it."

"Nice try," Henson said, the cat purr back in his voice. "Smart man like you might get away with that, if he gets a dumb enough jury. Trouble is, there was *some* of your friends where each crime was committed. But you're the only one we can put at the scene of *every* crime."

"Damn it, Henson."

"Well, listen to you, now. You could be violent. Especially if you had a club and got around behind an elderly man sitting at his desk." The marshal raised a hand to cut off Lockhart's outburst. "Lucky for you, it doesn't much matter what I think. My job's to bring you in for trial. You can count it like money in the bank I'll do my job. May as well spend your worry on the judge and jury."

Marian saw Lockhart's eyes go dark, not sad or frightened but ugly in a determination she didn't understand.

"Have you ever brought in an innocent man?"

Henson was ready for the question. "Never have. Brought in a hundred as swore they were innocent. Two or three the courts let off. But I and the Almighty knew better."

"I see."

Lockhart turned his attention out the window where the boy had stopped his horse and pretended to be sleeping until the train caught up to him. Looking at Henson's stony face, Marian understood why people called him Marshal Doom. The way she had it figured, the chances were eight to five that Lockhart was guilty. The chances were three to one he would be convicted whether he was guilty or not.

The odds didn't please her. If Henson wasn't fooling about accusing her along with Lockhart—and he didn't seem a man to joke much—then Lockhart's odds were her odds, too. No one would believe the fact that she had not been at the scene of the one crime nor ever even met Lockhart before he was arrested. If only she hadn't embarrassed Henson by taking the gun from his pocket! Bruised his pride. Maybe that would be the way to get to him. Boost that male pride. Play up to him.

She rearranged her skirts and crossed her legs so that

she brushed against Henson. He noticed. She smiled at him. He did not return the smile but neither did he frown. It seemed to her that he relaxed his arrogance a bit. "Did you see the boy on the horse?" she asked.

Henson nodded. "He can have his fun for another mile or so. Then we'll be at Roseville and the country'll be too rough for foolishness."

"Will it? I'm afraid I didn't notice before."

"Turns to scrub brush and rocks not fit for anything but goats, sheep, maybe."

"That's fascinating," she said. "You must know the whole railway system, being a United States Marshal." She tried the smile again.

"I know my part of it." He sat taller. "Having to cover my territory, I ride the cars pretty regular."

"Just think, these rails weren't even here twenty years ago." She remembered something she'd overheard during Lockhart's poker game. "And now they're even talking of flying machines! Isn't it exciting to live in such a time of—of discovery?"

"Don't figure the Almighty meant folks to fly." Henson's tone suggested the Almighty would surely have consulted him first. "Too fast. Too busy. Too many people hustling around now."

"Yes. It makes me dream of a house on a lonely farm or ranch, away from all the noise and bustle."

"Lonely'd be the word for that."

"It would depend on who else was there in the house, would it not? I mean, I've found that a person can be in a busy city or in a crowded Pullman car and still be very lonely." She looked at him without smiling, willing softness and feeling into her face so that he would know she was not making fun, not trying to batter his pride. She felt Lockhart's eyes on her and hoped he would keep quiet.

After a term, Henson nodded ever so slightly. "I suppose

that's possible." It seemed to be a new idea he would need to ponder.

"But I see what you mean," she said. She thought he liked that—though he might be wondering what he had meant. "One person would be even more lonely in such a remote house as in the midst of a full congregation at church." She was proud of that last touch. She'd been about to say "crowded theater" or "court." But she needed to keep their conversation away from such things. "You meant that two people need not be lonely no matter where they were."

Henson said, "I believe you meant that."

"Did I?" *Blush. Lower your eyes. Stare at his badge.* "I must have found the thought in your words." *Now look in his eyes again. Tilt your face a bit like Juliet. I haven't played Juliet in years.* "Or your thoughts."

Lockhart coughed.

Let him choke on it!

"My thoughts?"

"Yes." *Twist your hands a little. Look down at them to draw his attention.* "Didn't you picture a little house with a porch across the front?"

"No."

The man has no imagination at all, and you've made it show! Marian smiled brightly. "You see! No one can know what another person is thinking. But I wish you'd tell me."

"I was thinking of a square brick building with two stories above ground and porches all the way round at both levels."

"Were you? And where did you see it?"

"In Denver. It's the city jail. You'll be seeing it soon enough."

James Lockhart stared out his window at the dark-skinned boy kicking his white horse past their window at a gallop, at

the boy whose sombrero was hanging down his back by a
strap, at the boy whose freedom was not threatened by false
accusations and false arrest and relentless lawmen. The locomotive emitted a long wailing whistle. It sounded lonely to
Lockhart.

Two minutes later the train looped out to the north,
gained strength on fairly level ground, and rolled into Roseville. *Not even a water stop*, he thought. *We won't be here very
long*. He was right, but once they curved back west they made
no more than a mile before chuffing to rest on a siding while
a long freight slid past downhill on the main line toward
Sacramento.

The sun was going down when their train stopped for
water at Rocklin. Lockhart had kept his peace, trying to remember his last meeting with Elvin Murdock.

*I went to the bank at four o'clock. He smiled, shook hands, of-
fered me a drink. But we didn't have a drink. Talked maybe thirty
minutes, more about his family than about business. His daughter
had just gotten engaged. I left fifty thousand dollars in new banknotes with him to be signed and issued. He walked me to the door,
shook my hand, told me to take good care. I said I'd stop by to see
him on my way back east.*

He'd said it casually, the way people did. He hadn't even
suspected he'd never see the banker again. If he'd known, he
would have thanked Murdock for his friendship, congratu-
lated him on a beautiful family and a full life, wished him
well. But he hadn't known.

You never know in time, he thought. *Like in the war. Like
with Martha. That day I left for the office, who would have
thought—*

Turning to Henson, he said, "What the hell do they
think I stole from Elvin Murdock?

The anger in his tone surprised the marshal, who leaned
away to see him better. "Close to fifty thousand in newly
signed banknotes. You should know, you'd just delivered

them. I been waiting for you to bring it up. It might go a little easier for you if you tell us where you hid it."

Lockhart snorted. "Easier? How's that? You'd only hang me once?"

"How about you?" Henson asked the woman. "No need for you to hang. He hide all the money in one place or each bundle of it close to the place he took it?"

She did not reply.

"Or maybe it was your job to hide the money, seeing it wasn't in either one of your luggage."

She said, "You had no right to go through my things."

"Every right in the world. They'll never hang a woman pretty as you. Chances are you'll get off with twenty, maybe thirty years. Even at that, all those frilly things in your trunk will be out of fashion by then, nor they won't do much for a woman the age you'd be."

Lockhart saw pure hatred in the stare Marian Taylor gave the marshal. "We've neither of us taken or hidden any money," he said, wondering why he felt called to defend her.

Henson ignored that, kept his gaze on Marian. "On the other hand, if you divulge the whereabouts of all that money, I'll put in a good word with the judge. You'd get, say, ten or twelve years at worst. Maybe less."

"A tempting offer." Marian's voice was cold as an Ohio snowstorm. "It's too bad I have nothing to confess."

Lockhart watched her with admiration, mixed with a nagging curiosity. He should know her. Her face, her voice, were hauntingly familiar, but not quite right. She was calm, now, though. Cool in a crisis. Tough.

And maybe a killer.

The thought surprised him. He looked at it. It was possible. Henson thought she'd been involved. Maybe she had been. For all he knew, she might have been the killer's female accomplice.

But not mine.

" . . . sing a different tune when we find that husband of yours," Henson was saying. "Once he tells all he knows."

"He won't tell."

"Ha! Don't think he'll risk his neck to protect you. Else he wouldn't've run off."

Marian Taylor laughed. It was a low, eerie sound. Her expression startled Lockhart. Her eyes were wide. The skin of her face seemed to have tightened over the bones, and her smile showed too many teeth. Even the marshal hesitated, broke off what he was saying.

"He'll never talk," Marian said in a whisper that somehow carried to half the car. She pointed a long-nailed finger at Lockhart. "Lockhart killed him!"

"What!"

"By the ghost of Julius Caesar."

"Mabel, did you hear?" a shocked male voice asked from a row or two ahead.

"Oh, I helped," Marian went on. "I laid their daggers ready! He could not miss 'em. Had June not resembled my father as he slept, I had done't myself."

"What in hell?"

Lockhart laughed. "So *that's* who you are!"

"And that's not all, Marshal!"

Marian leaned nearer Henson, who unconsciously drew away. Conversation in the car had died. The woman paused for a moment that seemed endless. Lockhart sensed that everyone within earshot was straining to hear.

"And after that—" She broke off suddenly, then said in a different tone, "Yet who would have thought old June to have had so much blood in him? Here's the smell of blood still: all the perfumes of Arabia will not sweeten this little hand." She stared at Henson again. "And after that, Marshal . . . "

"Yes?" Henson said into the expectant hush.

" . . . we boiled him and ate him!"

The silence hung on for a stunned second, then broke in

a great roar of laughter from the passengers. "That's the ticket, sister," a man across the aisle called. From his clothing, Lockhart thought he might be another drummer. "You really had him sold. You can peddle my corsets any day."

Henson's broad face flushed brick-red, until Lockhart thought the lawman might have a seizure on the spot. Marian leaned toward him.

"There's one of *my* little tricks, Marshal," she said in a normal tone. "Now why don't you take your little tricks and go to hell."

For a moment longer, Henson struggled for breath. Then he came out with a bellow of laughter that startled Lockhart more than anything else the marshal had done.

"By the ghost of Julius Caesar, you're a pair to draw to," Henson said. He shook his head with something like admiration. "Truth to tell, I'll be right sorry to see the judge send you up." He rose from his seat. "Tell you what I'm going to do, so you can see that I'm a fair man, I'm going to leave you two to talk it over while I have a smoke."

The woman looked at Lockhart, said, "Don't leave me alone with him."

The marshal said, "I don't intend to leave you on your lonesome, Mrs. Taylor." He unlocked the cuff from the seat. "Take a seat over here. Put your arm over the seat and back through to me. You do the same, Lockhart."

Lockhart put his arm over the seat and through. The empty cuff hung on the seat rail. Henson was freeing it when the woman got her sleeve caught, cried out in pain, wriggled her slender arm loose, and presented it beside Lockhart's. "There," she said. "Go ahead and do it. People are watching."

Marshal Henson laughed. "They are, are they? Didn't mind it awhile ago, when you were playing me for the fool." He snapped the cuff on her wrist, tipped his hat, and went out the door toward the rear of the train.

As soon as he was gone, Lockhart looked at Marian Taylor. "That's who you are," he repeated. "Lady Macbeth. I saw you play in St. Louis."

She pulled her hand back through the opening between the seats, yanking at his wrist with the chain. "Hold still." She smiled at him. "Took you long enough to remember. That's right. Lady Macbeth, Desdemona, Calpurnia. All of those."

"You're the Prairie Rosebud!"

She made a face. "June's idea, my husband's. Named me after the Jersey Lily. But I've bloomed, and he wanted one still in the bud. Hold *still!* Look out the window or something."

Lockhart had no idea what she was doing, but he looked out the window. The setting sun had given way to low heavy clouds as if the train had rolled out of the world of sunlight into a dark world of doom. *If those clouds don't bring rain, there's no justice.* Then he laughed. "Of course, they won't then," he said out loud. "God knows there's no justice in this world."

"Hush," the woman said without moving her lips. After a minute she whispered, "Think of someone besides yourself for a change."

"You?"

She didn't answer. Lockhart looked down into her face. Her hat was loose and crooked on her head. Her dark eyes—almost black, he saw from this distance—were fixed in concentration. A streak of lightning lanced the brushy slope a mile out to the south, and almost immediately a boom of thunder rattled the window next to Lockhart's ear. Rain began to fall hard and fast.

"That's better," Marian said. He glanced back at those eyes, then down to his manacled hand. Her hand was nowhere in sight. "Pull your hand back. Slowly! Don't attract attention."

Lockhart slipped his hand backward, waiting for the chain to hang on the seat's center brace. It didn't. The two of them were sitting side by side with their arms dangling behind the seat. "How the hell'd you do that?"

"Hush. Very slowly now, raise your arm with mine. Good. Over the seat and down between us." She moved closer to him so that their freedom from the seat would be less obvious.

Lockhart took a deep breath of cool moist air mixed with acrid smoke from the straining locomotive. "Listen," he whispered, watching the passengers in front of them. "We've got to go while we have the chance." She looked at him as if he were a slow child, then nodded.

He moved against her. They slid together until she was at the edge of the bench. Then they stood, stepped into the aisle, and turned to the door. Behind them someone said, "Look, Herbert, they're loose." Lockhart did not wait but opened the door and thrust the woman through it onto the rocking platform.

He had no more than gotten the door shut when a conductor came out of the next car and met them face-to-face, stared at them from his platform. "Say, what you two doing? You're not supposed to be out here."

Lockhart said, "Yes we are. We've got to find the marshal. Have you seen him?"

"Find the marshal?"

"There's a man in our car attacking a woman!"

"The hell you say!"

"Where's the marshal?"

"He's two cars back on the last platform, smoking, but we won't need him for this. Where's the man?"

"He ran out the front of the car!" Marian said.

"Come with me," the conductor said. He stepped past them, opened the door, and dashed along the aisle through passengers who tried without success to stop him.

Lockhart peered through the rain at the shadowy rocks and brush gliding past on both sides. "Which way looks best?"

"We can't," she cried. "The train's picked up speed."

"No it hasn't."

"He's behind us. He'd see us by the tracks."

Lockhart had been thinking about that problem. He saw a thick patch of brush coming up on the south side of the tracks. He dragged her to that side.

"No!" Marian screeched. She grabbed the safety rail, clinging to it like a drowning person. "You can't. We'll be—"

Lockhart didn't take time to argue. Gathering her against his body, he broke her grip on the rail and flung them both into the rushing darkness.

3

The thicket was past before they hit the ground. They fell on the rocky slope of the embankment and tumbled downward in a tangle between patches of brush. Considering the damage he felt from lashing branches, Lockhart figured they were lucky to have missed the thicker stuff. He finally got a heel into the rocky dirt and dragged the two of them to stop. Without taking time to pant, he slung the woman off him and dragged her as far under cover as he could.

"Be still," he said. "He might be looking off the other side."

"Be still!" Marian moaned. "Listen, you—you *man!*"

"Shut up!"

Much too quickly, the last car rumbled past their hiding

place. On the rear platform, Marshal Rance Henson stood out of the rain smoking his cigar. If he saw them in that second before the car passed, Lockhart couldn't tell it.

After a moment, he got up on one bruised knee and peered through the brushtops toward the retreating train. Henson blew out a big cloud of smoke. But he made no other move. *Is it possible he didn't even see us?*

Marian groaned, jerked him down sharply with the chain. "Are you crazy?" she demanded. "Why don't you wave a flag at him?"

"I wanted to know how fast we'd have to run. If he saw us."

"Did he?"

Lockhart peered again, lifted his head higher, saw the conductor emerge onto the platform waving his arms. Henson threw his cigar into the rain, took the man by his lapels as the train rounded a bend out of sight.

"He didn't see us, but he knows we're gone! Can you walk?"

"Walk? I'm broken all over. I can't even move. Ever again." As she complained, she was getting to her feet, shaking down the battered traveling suit, trying her weight on her ankles. Her dress was torn in ways that Lockhart might have found interesting at some other time. "All right. Quit staring at my bodice. Which way did you plan to go?"

"Away from here." Lockhart wasn't entirely sure his own left leg wasn't broken, and he didn't want to see what the rocks had done to the arm he landed on. But he intended to put some distance between himself and the rail line. It even crossed his mind that the rain might hide their tracks after a time.

"Brilliant."

"Better than nothing. And after that trick with the handcuffs, Henson will want you worse than he wants me. I'd still like to know how you did it."

"Later. Get moving."

In the distance Lockhart could still hear the train grinding at the long slope. But Henson would jump if he had to and run them down on foot. He glanced at Marian, saw a tomboy determination in her eyes, a somber recognition of the truth that Henson would see her hang if he caught them. "He'll see where we landed and know we were headed south."

"Tell me tomorrow," she said. "Let's go." She tried a step, whimpered, and tried another.

"Wait a minute. Let's try it this way." He tried to put his arm around her, but that only folded her own arm behind her back. He led her across the rocky clearing where they had fallen, bidding her step on the larger rocks so as to leave no more trail than necessary. Then within the fringe of the next heavy brush, they began to climb toward the tracks. The rain fell in heavy, slanting sheets all around them.

"What are you doing?"

"He'll figure we went south. We're going the other way."

They kept to the largest rocks they could find, crossed the tracks bent over to stay beneath the brush. They could still hear the train, but its rear lantern was out of sight in the gloom of the rain. After another moment, they could no longer hear the sound above the noise of the storm. "They've stopped," the woman told him. "He'll be back in no time."

"I don't think so."

"Now I know why I took that gun out of his pocket. I'd give a hundred dollars for it right now!"

"How about fifty thousand dollars? That's what Marshal Doom thinks we're hiding."

"That's just from one place. You were a busy little bank robber."

"I wasn't. You were."

They kept up their pace, not bothering to step on rocks any longer because water was already draining down the slope to wash out their tracks. The other edge of that was that Henson might not know which side they jumped off and guess at their direction. That would give him a fifty percent chance to be on their trail in spite of their subterfuge. But no. One of the passengers had probably seen them jump.

"Slow down. My ankle's killing me."

"It isn't your ankle that's going to kill you. It's Henson."

"Did you mean you thought *I* took that money?"

"Just teasing." And he had been teasing, coaxing her on, keeping her mind off her injuries. *But I can say it as easily as she! I don't know that she didn't do it.*

"We don't have time to tease. Watch where you're going! Wait a minute. I'm stepping on my skirts."

A net of sheet lightning delineated them clearly in the brush. The long skirt of her dress had torn loose at her waist. She hiked up the mass of heavy wet fabric and held it in her free hand. Then he tugged at the chain and led her on across the brushy slope, heading north as best he could tell.

The rain and low clouds had melted into a gloom almost as dark as night. Lockhart wasn't sure if they were lucky to have the fairly frequent glare of lightning to keep them on track, or incredibly unlucky in that the next bolt might split them in two. But the danger of lightning did not stick in his mind. Instead, he worried about Henson somewhere behind them, about the cold rain that lashed at them, about the woman who was not moving nearly as rapidly as he wanted her to. He looked round and saw her by the distant electrical display in the clouds.

"Why are you holding the chain?"

She was looking back into the gloom. "The cuff hurts my wrist. Go a little faster if you can."

Lockhart would have smiled if he hadn't been hurting all over. Only the cleansing rain kept his eyes free of the blood that ran down his face from a cut somewhere on his scalp. The pain suggested to him that the cut reached clear through his skull. His left arm did not work as well as it should, and there was no identifiable spot anywhere that did not hurt. Of course, the woman was probably as banged up as he, and she was urging him forward. He went faster.

They had been struggling through the dripping brush for almost an hour when a lightning flash showed something angular and gray down to their left and perhaps a hundred yards away. *Hell, everything's gray*, Lockhart thought, but the object had not reminded him of a tree or a boulder. The part of it he had seen was clean-sculpted.

"This way."

Marian followed him blindly downslope in the direction he remembered. They were only slightly off course and ten yards past it when the next lightning flash gave him another glimpse. *Another minute and I'd never have found it!*

"There!" he told her. "There's something over this way."

"What kind of something? I don't see it."

"I think it's a shed." With his next long stride he walked smack into a wall of vertical planks. Marian stumbled against him before he could warn her.

"Did we find it?"

Lockhart rubbed his nose. "It found us."

"What is it?"

"Light a lantern and we'll see."

He was feeling his way along the planks, tugging her with him as he tried to keep his footing in the mud. He came to what might be a door, but found no latch, no handle, no bar. Finally a flicker from the fading storm showed him the latch. He lunged across to it and lifted it. Man and woman leaned through the opening off balance and fell in a tumble. The dirt floor was relatively dry.

Marian Taylor said that she wouldn't have believed it could be any darker inside than it was outside. Lockhart asked her to move off his leg.

It might have been a hay shed or mine opening or lion's

den. Lockhart reached out as far as he could stretch to be sure of the floor.

"Seems solid."

"What about snakes?"

Lockhart snatched back his hands. "We need some light," he said.

"Do you have any matches?"

"Yes. They ought to be dry by Saturday."

"I have some in my hat."

"You don't have a hat."

She reached her free hand over her head and felt aimlessly. "I had it when we jumped."

"I had skin on my knees and elbows when we jumped." He sat up, put out another tentative hand, and leaned on it. Outside, the rain was falling steadily. Lockhart found it comforting. No one was likely to be out in it—no one except Marshal Doom, and he wasn't likely to find them any time soon.

Not unless he can see in the dark. But maybe he can. Brought in over a hundred men and never lost a prisoner. He is not going to be happy!

"What?" Marian Taylor asked.

"I wish we had a light."

"There's something over here by me. A table, I think." He heard her patting around on it. "Yes. And a chair."

She tried to stand, reached the end of her tether with a jerk that he thought would tear his arm out of its socket. Instead, the arm held and caused her to fall back across him. "What are you doing?" she rasped at him.

"What I'm *not* doing is trying to get my arm broken. Get up. No, wait. Let's do this together." On the second try, they made it up to their knees together, put their hands on top of the table, and levered themselves up. "Here's a chair. Have you found one?"

"Yes. Could we sit?"

"As long as we don't fall." They sat in the dark and put their elbows on the table. The rain stopped. They were left with little more memory of it than was afforded by a leak that dripped between them for awhile onto the tabletop. Fifteen minutes later a bright moon peeked around the edges of the door and a shuttered window they hadn't been able to see before.

"Light," Lockhart said.

"Maybe we could open the window, if we don't fall over ourselves again."

"Let's try. I'm beginning to get the hang of this."

Lockhart found the latch and opened the shutters to flood the little cabin with more light than he'd ever expected to enjoy again. When they turned, they saw the square table, two good chairs, and a third with a broken leg. A two-tiered bunk stood in the back corner.

"A real bed!" Marian said. She took a half-step toward it, dragging Lockhart along. " 'Faintness constraineth me to measure out my length on this cold bed.' "

"I don't know that one. Anyway, it's impossible, unless you want to share the lower bunk."

Even in the moonlight, he saw the rebellion on her face. "*Midsummer Night's Dream*. And not damned likely. But nothing's impossible. Maybe there's something like a mattress. Two mattresses."

The two straw ticks hardly merited the description, but with three-armed clumsiness, Lockhart and Marian finally got them laid in a clear space on the floor.

"Just close enough together for a handcuffed couple to recline without impugning their reputations," Marian said with satisfaction. Then she cast a wary look at Lockhart. "Another awkward question arises. As our missing friend the marshal tactfully put it, I have some business before retiring."

Lockhart nodded. "I'd been thinking the same thing. Let's look out back. Maybe there's something like a privy."

"With something like a door." Marian shook her wrist, shaking Lockhart's as well. "The next time they handcuff me to somebody, I hope they use a longer chain."

Lockhart stirred, half awake. The tent must have leaked because he was wet and uncomfortable. He would give that damned dog-robber of a sergeant hell for carelessness, but right now it was still dark, probably an hour before daybreak. He could still catch a few minutes' sleep before reveille. He rolled onto his stomach and stretched out to finish his rest.

Immediately, he was awake. He couldn't possibly roll over. He had gone to sleep on his back, his chained arm outstretched toward Marian Taylor, the handcuff chain slack between them. Shaking memories of the long-ago war out of his head, he stared at his arm. The handcuffs were still attached to his wrist, but Marian Taylor was not. Where she had been was only an empty shackle, still closed.

He felt a second of pure panic, but before he could leap up, he heard the creak of the door's hinges. All right. She had gotten free again somehow, had gone outside for a moment's privacy, and was coming back into the cabin. Lockhart relaxed a bit, waited for his heart to slow back down to a race, and rose to meet her at the door.

"You're full of tricks," he was saying as he opened the door to stare into the angry face of Marshal Rance Henson.

"You know a couple yourself, by Godfrey!" Henson pointed his big revolver at the middle of Lockhart's chest. Lockhart could see three horses tied to a scrubby tree forty yards from the cabin. "But truth to tell, my old horse did most of the tracking. What've you done with the woman?"

Too dazed to think of a better answer, Lockhart shrugged. "She's gone."

"I just about expect she is. What'd you do, knock her in the head and cut off her hand?"

"With what?" Lockhart was dizzied by the very idea.

Henson raised the gun's muzzle an inch. "Step back, killer. We'll see about this."

He followed Lockhart inside, striking a match with his free hand and peering around the small room. His eyes fell on the head of a hatchet Lockhart hadn't noticed before. Only a couple of inches of splintered wooden handle remained.

"Most likely with that." He said it more to himself than to his prisoner. "I knew you'd brought her this far, else I'd have found her body on the way. Where'd you put her?"

Lockhart thought about his situation, measured his chances. *The woman is gone. The marshal doesn't care whether he brings me in alive or dead. I've got to have time. Time to think!* He remembered Marian's charade on the train. "There's a well out back," he said.

"What?" The marshal's eyes narrowed, his color deepened, his grip on the gun tightened. "You'd not only kill a woman but poison a well with her body!"

"I wasn't thinking."

"God have mercy."

"I think she's floating."

"You what?"

"We can pull her out."

"What about her hand?"

Lockhart trembled. "It's out there," he said, trying to think. "I couldn't touch it."

"Couldn't touch it! You killed your consort and threw her body down a well and stuck at picking up the hand? I ought to kill you right here!"

"I'll show you. We can get her out. Maybe she isn't dead."

"Not dead'd be a crime against criminals!" Henson said. "Get out there ahead of me in a hurry."

They went out, Lockhart looking for an opportunity to try for the gun and Henson mumbling bitterly behind him. The area behind the cabin was choked with brush.

Henson said, "Hold up a minute. I don't see any well." Then he went perfectly quiet as a rifle hammer locked back with a crisp click behind him.

"I didn't shoot you last time," Marian Taylor said in a flat voice. "But I damned well will this time unless you put down that revolver. It's your rifle. That's the muzzle you feel tickling your back."

Henson said, "Let go that Winchester or I'll shoot a hole through your partner."

"You shoot him, I'll shoot you. It's all the same to me, but it'll make a big difference to you."

And to me, Lockhart thought, but kept quiet. He could feel Henson tense. Marshal Doom wasn't going to throw in his hand without a fight.

"I'm not letting the two of you loose again. We'll settle it right here."

There was a way to deal with somebody who had a gun to your back. Lockhart remembered it. He'd done it before, and his life had depended on it then, too. But now he was twenty years older, twenty years slower, twenty years more afraid to die.

And Henson knows it, too! he realized, and moved.

The marshal was already starting to turn when Lockhart spun to the side away from the Colt, swept one arm down to knock Henson's hand aside, drove his other fist into the marshal's face. The Colt roared, its big bullet slapping into the plank wall of the shack and blowing out a chunk the size of Lockhart's hand. Henson staggered back. Before he could recover, Lockhart was on him, tripping him and coming down hard on top, grabbing for the pistol with both hands. Henson swore and clubbed at Lockhart's head with a big fist, then froze as the long barrel of the Winchester punched him in the chest.

"There, now," Marian Taylor said, leaning over Lockhart's shoulder to smile at the marshal. "I knew we could work this out peacefully."

For one second, Lockhart thought that Henson meant to fight it out. But even Marshal Doom wasn't that stupid. With a disgusted grunt, he relaxed beneath Lockhart's weight. Then he opened his hand and let the Colt drop.

"Damn you," he said, mostly to Marian.

Lockhart scooped up the big revolver and scrambled to his feet. Henson sat up more slowly. The handcuff chain had slashed across his forehead when Lockhart hit him. He touched his hand to the cut, looked at the blood on his fingers, looked at the two of them.

"Damn you both. I've brung in some of the meanest, dangerousest, most low-down hombres that ever lived. It's a damned disgrace to end up killed by a damned sissified drummer and damned fancified tart."

"Marshal!" Marian Taylor's tone was as steady as the Winchester. "You might want to stop right there, or you're likely to end up just as killed as you say." She waited a moment, then nodded. "Much wiser. Turn out your pockets."

He made a show of refusing but in the end swallowed his pride and emptied some change, his wallet, a fountain pen, and a knife onto the ground beside him. "Damned petty thieves."

"Vest pockets."

He took out a watch, undid the chain, and stretched it out to Lockhart, who accepted it carefully. "It's a good Waterbury," he said, "but it'll tell on you. It was give to me in a ceremony and has my name engraved on it."

"Other vest pocket."

"Nothing in it."

"Turn it out."

Henson tightened his mouth, glared at the woman, produced a small key. Marian laughed.

"Marshal, you could've saved us a world of trouble if you'd done that first. Get up, slow and easy, and let's step back into the cabin."

Inside, Lockhart took up the key and tried it in his handcuff. It fit. He flexed his hand, then made to fling the cuffs and chain out into the mud.

"No, idiot!" Marian cried.

"Listen, who are you calling . . . ?"

Marian spoke as if explaining to an especially slow child. "Keep the key. Give the handcuffs back to the marshal."

Feeling foolish, Lockhart pitched them into Henson's lap. "Put one on your right wrist," he said. Tight-lipped, Henson did so. Then Lockhart wrapped the chain twice around the iron frame of the bunk and snapped the other cuff on Henson's left wrist.

"You're not going to leave me here to starve? It may be a month before another rider comes up to this cabin."

Lockhart said, "We're not going to kill you," intending the words as much for Marian Taylor as for the marshal. "We can't turn you loose, and we can't take you with us."

"I was going to take *you*. There's three horses."

Lockhart laughed. "Marshal, I'd rather travel with a nine-foot rattlesnake. You'll get loose before long, and we'll leave you your horse. I'm counting on you to catch up to me."

"You'd do better to dread it."

"But not until I've done your job for you."

"Nobody does my job for me."

"And found whoever murdered Elvin Murdock."

Marian Taylor said, "God in heaven, why don't you draw him a map to follow us by?"

Lockhart looked at her. "Why don't you go check the horses. Hobble his and take the bit out of its mouth." He was surprised when she gave him no more than a long look before she turned to do as he asked.

Henson said, "Don't do it, Mrs. Taylor. If you and him leave me here, it won't be just a matter of arresting you. It'll be a purely personal matter, and I'll come a'shooting."

"You'd shoot a woman?" she asked.

"You're damn right I will!"

She said, "I'll pray for you," and went out to see about the horses.

Henson turned his attention back to Lockhart. "I'll give you one more chance to do the right thing here before I add assault on a federal officer to the charges against you." He saw Lockhart was going through the wallet. "And another of armed robbery."

"Planning to have them hang me twice? Let's call it a loan." He took the cap off Henson's pen and wrote out a brief note. "There. I owe you twenty-eight dollars."

"Twenty-eight dollars, a Winchester, two good horses, that forty-five in your belt, and my good gold watch!"

Lockhart grinned and laid the Waterbury on the table. "You keep the watch. See you again, Marshal."

"By the ghost of Julius Caesar, you can bet the farm on that!"

Marian Taylor was already in the saddle, waiting for him. He thought she had chosen the better horse.

"I still want to know how you got out of that cuff." He urged the horse and they went off at a fast walk in the mud.

"The same way I got out of it on the train." She held up a slender hand and waggled her fingers. "Tough as he is, Doom didn't cinch them tight enough to hurt a lady. How'd you think we got loose from the seat?"

"I thought it was more of your sleight of hand. But you slipped the handcuff back on before I noticed you were loose. Why did you tie us together again?"

"I was afraid you'd leave me with Marshal Doom."

"You're more afraid of him than me?"

She laughed and gave him a sideways look from her dark eyes. "More certain, anyway. I *know* where I stand with him. With you, I'm not so sure."

4

Had he been a deeply reflective man, Marshal Rance Henson might have pondered James Lockhart's strange behavior. Judged by all Henson knew, Lockhart was a heartless, remorseless murderer. Judged by all Henson knew, Lockhart should have killed him at the first opportunity. He'd had all the opportunity he could ask for at the cabin. Any halfway sensible criminal would have shot Marshal Doom dead, removing a relentless pursuer from his trail. Instead, Lockhart and his woman were riding off, leaving Henson angry, sore, and trussed like a Christmas goose, but still alive.

Feeling every inch a goose, Henson listened to them ride away toward the south. He didn't spend a lot of time on reflection. In twenty-odd years as a lawman, he had observed that very few outlaws were halfway sensible. Many, in fact, did things that were outright crazy. It even seemed to him that the craziness had steadily increased over the years.

Things are going to hell all over, he thought as he turned his attention to getting loose from the handcuffs. *Don't even get the class of criminals we used to.* Maybe he was getting too old. He'd twice been outwitted by Lockhart and his woman. He was glad Chief Biddle wasn't around to see him threatened with his own rifle and helpless in his own handcuffs, nor

Martin, nor that gadfly of a newspaperman. Maybe it was time to retire.

"Like hell," Henson said. He owed Lockhart and Marian Taylor something for hurt pride and humiliation. If he had to chase them until he was stumbling over his long white beard, he would pay out that debt. *Then I'll retire.*

He wasn't surprised they had ridden south. For all Lockhart's big talk about finding the killer, they would run for the border. But they had a good long way to go, and he would catch them before the day was out. Two or three miles away a train was braking down the grade. His prisoners might get across the tracks ahead of it, but that wouldn't matter much.

The extra key to his handcuffs was safely tucked in his hip pocket. Because Lockhart had wrapped the chain around the bunk rail, Henson couldn't reach that pocket. He strained and twisted himself like a circus clown until he felt the blood pounding in his throat from anger and frustration. No use. Working his knees up onto the lower bunk, he grasped the upright with his bound hands and leaned over as far as he could in the hope of causing the key to fall out of his pocket.

Craziness accounted for Lockhart. As for the woman. He couldn't tell about women. *Never could!*

"Full of tricks as Barnum's monkey," Henson said. His knees slipped on the edge of the bunk. He lost his balance and fell, landing solidly on his head on the dirt floor. "Damnation. That's another entry on your ledger, Lockhart."

Lying on the floor, Henson cursed fate and himself and the handcuffs and his prisoners and the conductor who had let them escape and all railroads since the invention of the steam engine and himself again. As if he had not suffered enough indignity for one day, he drew himself up close to the bunk and fumbled at his belt buckle. When he had his pants undone, he let them fall. He couldn't get his hands down far enough to reach them, so it took him ten more maddening minutes to jockey the key out of the pocket. Finally it dropped free, bounced, and skittered under the table.

"Lord in heaven," Henson said, resigned now. With his pants around his ankles, he dragged the bunk a half step at a time across to the table. He went down on his knees, making himself a solemn promise never again to kneel on account of any man or woman. He couldn't reach the key with the toe of his boot. Out of patience at last, he yanked the bunk over, allowed it to fall half on him and half on the tabletop, and leaned far enough down to fetch up the key with his teeth.

To his complete surprise, he made it back to his knees and dropped the key into his anxious right hand with no more miscues. He unlocked the left cuff, tore himself loose from the bunk, found his hat, and scooped up his knife and watch from the table. He unlocked the other cuff on his way to the horse.

They'll have hell to pay now, and I'm keeping the books! Then he glanced upward in silent apology to the Almighty. He'd used up a six months' ration of profanity in a single short morning, and more than half the day was still to come.

Marian Taylor had hobbled his horse, all right. She'd also taken its bridle. "Whoa, boy," he said to the horse while he was getting the hobble rope around its neck. *Where the hell would the little minx have put it?* He spent terrible, valuable minutes looking around in the brush. Finally, he saw that someone had opened his saddlebags. "Hell," he said, starting on the next six months.

The bridle was not in his bags. Neither was Lockhart's little nickeled .38 hideout pistol. He looked for the leather notebook in which he had kept the charges against Lockhart and the deputations from his pals. It was gone as well.

"Mexico's not far enough, Lockhart. Better head for Peru."

But no. Chances were, the woman was the brains of the operation. Lockhart so far had seemed not quite bright enough to get his boots on the right feet.

Bright enough to chain you to the bedpost like Aunt Tillie's bulldog! he reminded himself.

"Not Peru. Maybe the South Pole."

He would get all those things back. *Just calm yourself, old horse,* he mused. *You'll get it all back, horses and guns and book. And God Himself can stay your hand if He wants the man and woman to stand trial!*

He tied the ends of the hobble rope to the handcuff loops, eased the chain into his horse's mouth for a bit, and stretched the contraption up each side of the animal's jaws. The horse didn't like it much. Henson didn't blame him. Nearby, a train let out a mournful wail of its whistle. From the sound, it was pretty nearly south of the cabin. Henson noted the information, but he didn't propose to catch the train, not today.

Satisfied with his makeshift bridle, Henson stepped into his saddle and leaned out almost flat to get a grip on his foolish reins. The horse didn't like that, either. "God of Granny Johnson," Henson told the horse, "you should just be grateful there's nobody here to see us like this. Let's go!"

The morning was clear and cloudless with a bright sun raising steam from the wet ground, but the mud was too deep for any gait much faster than a walk. Henson started in to curse the mud, then stopped. He couldn't afford another six months of arrears in profanity. The way this thing was shaping up, he suspected he would need all he could buy or borrow before he brought in Lockhart and Marian Taylor.

At least the mud fell on the just and the unjust alike. The two fugitives couldn't flee any faster than he could follow. Leaving his horse to pick its own way, Henson delved into his saddlebags again. Lockhart had left him his cigars. He selected one, found his matches, and settled in for the long haul.

Fifteen minutes later, he guided the laboring horse onto the railroad's roadbed. He had crossed it to the south before he saw that the deep hoofprints he'd been following had disappeared. He looked along the tracks but saw nothing besides the dissipating cloud of smoke from the westbound freight he'd heard going past. *Did they get up here and run the ties?* He didn't believe it, but it made sense.

They'd sure enough make better time, especially if they went downhill, but would they be going west or east?

A train was coming from the east, the passenger local from Reno, screeching downgrade with its brakes locked. Its whistle spouted steam to hoot him off the tracks, but he wasn't yet ready to choose a side. Why had the prisoners' horses quit leaving tracks on the north side of the rails? *Because they went upgrade and got off to let the freight come past!*

He counted it pure luck a minute later when he followed the backtrail down to the brush. This time, he saw the marks leading west into a thicket tall enough to hide the horses. To his complete surprise, the horses were hidden there, tied off to branches and snuffling at the rocky ground for something to eat. He would have heard them whinnying at him if the train hadn't made so much noise.

Was it Lockhart or Mrs. Taylor that had the bright idea of making a mess of their trail up to the rails and then backtracking to the brush again to hide the horses? And where in thunder are they?

Only when the train had passed and the horses had begun to nicker at him did Henson realize that his former prisoners could have killed him easily if they had been hiding with their mounts. They still might be lying in wait for him at the end of their own footprints, which he saw running generally south and west toward the roadbed.

They're surely the dumbest pair I ever threw a loop around! Though maybe not dumb enough to hunt two armed killers with nothing but a pocketknife.

That was it! They never suspected that he'd come after them, unarmed as he was. Well, that would work in his favor. He smiled to himself until he saw that the footprints ended on a rocky shelf near the glistening rails.

"Damn it all to—" he said before he remembered. He drove his horse up the muddy bank again. The fugitives weren't there. He saw the reason for the shelf. He even remembered seeing a handcar sitting on it the day before, left on purpose or through the sloth of the repair crew. There was no handcar now.

Henson shook his head. Not even Lockhart and Taylor would have been stupid enough to try to saw a handcar uphill. For that matter, no one except the two of them would be crazy enough to ride it downgrade. *Not if they knew a train was coming!*

The marshal twisted to stare downhill. A mile below him on the switchbacked rails, the locomotive was spouting like a tea kettle. A few seconds later, Henson heard the long drone of the warning whistle as it drifted back to him.

Is it possible? Could my birds have flown downslope? He laughed. "Out of the frying pan into the fire? Well, if that's it, I'll need a bushel basket to gather up the pieces. Being careful not to miss an ear or a hand!"

Marian Taylor looked past Lockhart as they flung round a hard left curve. The blunt black nose of the locomotive was getting larger behind him. Given another half mile, the train would loom above and around him without her having to lean out or wait for a curve to see it.

"What were you thinking?" she screamed at Lockhart.

He shook his head. "Save your breath," he panted, though he thought it a particularly silly question. He was winded, his arms aching, his backbone threatening to unwind like a spring toy. "Pump!"

"It's gaining!"

He didn't try to answer that.

"It's ten miles and more to the next town."

Twenty! he thought, but he saved his breath.

"We can't make it!"

"We'll have that—carved on—your stone." All the same, he turned to look over his shoulder. The train, in spite of a muted throttle and brakes bolted down to dead lock, was slithering down on them like a snake after a snail. Swinging his eyes back into Marian Taylor's, he nodded. "We can't make it!"

"Brilliant!"

"We'll—have to—jump!"

"Going—too fast—to jump!"

"Right!"

"Damn you," she moaned, gasping for air, "we'll carve—*that*—on *your* stone."

It won't take but one stone for the two of us, Lockhart thought. *One coffin—or one sewing box will probably do it. They won't even be able to sort us out.* "Get on that brake!" he yelled.

"We can't stop." She freed a hand to wave behind him. "That's a *train*, you idiot!"

He quit pumping. "Get on the brake!"

"We *have* to go faster!"

"We'll run off that curve." He pointed down the track. Then he began to drag at the brake.

She looked, then turned back to Lockhart with a fear in her face that almost paralyzed him. Apparently she realized as he did that the car would flip over if they maintained its speed. If they didn't, the train would mince them when it caught up.

"Now. The brake."

She began to help, keeping her eyes away from the train, which seemed to be coming toward them as fast as a falling guillotine. "I would have loved you," she said. "After awhile I know I would, even if you *are* a killer."

He looked at her, and set the brake with all he had left. The handcar squalled to a stop in the middle of the curve, almost catapulting its riders into the canyon. Stopped, it stood its ground as boldly as a cricket before a stampeding elephant.

"Now!" Lockhart cried. "Jump!"

"Oh, Lord," he heard her moan. "Not again! My poor dress." But by the time he reached for her hand, she had already flung herself over the side. He saw her tumbling down the slope in a tangle of skirts, heard the elephant-bellow of the whistle almost in his hip pocket, and leaped after her.

The rocks of the embankment slammed out what little breath he had left, scraped away and skin he'd missed the first time he'd jumped from a train. Brush and trees and sky wheeled past in wild alternation as he tried to stop his downward slide. Above and behind him, the locomotive gave one last piercing scream, and then there was a mighty *scrunch!* The handcar cartwheeled past him down the slope, shedding pieces as it went.

"Look out!" he yelled to Marian, though he wasn't sure what she could do beyond praying. She had fetched up in some bushes. He saw her face, all wide eyes and open mouth as fragments of the handcar sleeted past her. Then he slid into the brush beside her.

"Quick!" Lockhart told her.

"Quick what?" But he was already half-dragging her back up the long slope. "Where?"

The locomotive was a hundred feet past, still roaring its wrath out the whistle spout. The train had slowed dramatically in the curve. Instead of answering her questions, Lockhart hauled her up the slope, slipping on its sheet of egg-sized rocks, reaching two steps up, sliding one step back.

"Why?" she insisted.

"Free ride," he rasped. His breath was coming in harsh, shallow puffs, his heart racing to avoid being drowned in the rush of blood it had already pumped.

"Ride? We can't get on that train!"

"We can't do anything else. Come on!"

They ran. Over the crest onto the roadbed, along the narrow right of way beside the caboose, up even with its rear platform as it threatened to outdistance them. He kept a hand on her until she got a grip on the railing and began to hoist herself to the step. Then he took hold and dragged himself up beside her. For a long moment they sat there panting.

He was just about to ask her what she'd meant in that last moment on the handcar when a heavy voice behind them said, "Well, now, what have we here?"

Lockhart turned to look up at a brakeman wearing greasy denims, a striped cap, and a genuinely nasty expression. Hanging from his right hand was a length of chain.

"We can explain," Lockhart said.

"No need. The lady can stay. But I think I'll let you set right there until we pick up enough speed so's it's interesting to watch you bounce when you accidentally fall off the train."

Marian Taylor put her face in her hands and began to cry in great trembling sobs. "Oh, my poor baby," she wailed. She drew herself to her feet and put out a hand to the brakeman. "Did you see my baby? She was on that handcar!"

"Your baby?" Before the brakeman could finish, Marian's foot slipped and she tumbled into his arms. He caught her out of instinct. "Did you say 'baby'?"

He hadn't taken his eyes off Lockhart any longer than the second when he was catching the woman, but that was long enough. Lockhart whirled, got a knee onto the platform, and thrust the muzzle of Henson's big Colt into the brakeman's stomach. Marian pushed away to lean against the wall of the caboose beside the door.

Lockhart said, "Drop the chain. No, not over the side. There on the platform. Don't make me say everything twice because I've had a rough morning and I might accidentally shoot you right off this train to watch you bounce."

The brakeman let the chain go, listened to it clatter on the platform without glancing down. If the shift in his situation had improved his disposition any, Lockhart couldn't tell it.

"There's a track that goes north out of Roseville," Lockhart said. "How far are we from there?"

The brakeman shook his head. "I wouldn't know."

"Go inside."

"I don't believe I will. Don't believe you'll shoot me neither."

"You're right," Lockhart admitted. He took a step vaguely between the man and the woman. "It's hard for me since I get sick if I see blood and since I'm really rather afraid of firearms." Then he took a half step toward the brakeman and ground a boot heel down sharply on the man's instep.

The brakeman's expression changed. He bent over reaching for his foot but unable to get Lockhart's weight off it. "You've broke it!" he screeched.

"You needn't apologize. As long as there's no blood, the lady won't be offended and I won't get sick."

"You son of a bitch!"

Lockhart stood aside, keeping the gun trained on his adversary. "The whole trouble here is you've made me say it twice that I'd like you to go inside the caboose."

Marian Taylor whimpered. "Please, mister," she said. "It gets just awful if he has to say something that third time."

The brakeman went into the caboose, sat on a side bench, and bent over to hold his foot in both hands. Lockhart reached back through the door and dragged in the chain.

"Mrs. Taylor?"

"Let's take it we've been properly introduced. Call me Marian."

"Marian, then. I wonder if you'd hold this pistol on our railroad friend here?"

"My pleasure."

She took the Colt from Lockhart. The brakeman raised his head, tensed his hands on the edge of the bench. Plain as print, his flat face showed that he believed he'd gained an advantage.

"Don't think about it," Marian told him. "He doesn't like the sight of blood, but I think it's very attractive. Move, and I'll paint the inside of this car with yours."

Lockhart was looping the chain around the man's wrists. He started to tie it off to a stanchion toward the rear of the bench, but the brakeman pulled back. For the first time, his face showed some real emotion.

"Hold off, mister. Less'n you really aim to kill me, that is. When old Newt up in the cab stops this train, I'll get flang about everywheres if you tie me to that."

Lockhart considered, imagining the forces that would be generated when the cars started slamming together. He saw what the brakeman meant. "Can you think of any reason I should care?" he asked, but he was already dragging the man forward by the chain. He lashed it securely to a heavy steel pipe against the front wall. "That better?"

"Pauper's handcuffs," Marian said.

"Paupers can't be choosers." To the brakeman, Lockhart said, "Where's the first point we can catch the rails rolling south?"

"South?"

"Mexico."

"There's a line goes south out of Sacramento, down Modesto way. But it don't get to Mexico. You got to go plumb to the coast for that, clean to Vallejo." The brakeman shifted himself against the car's wall. "I'm telling you true, mister. You played square with me."

"Thanks."

Out on the rear platform with the door closed, Marian said, "Mexico?"

Lockhart smiled. "We'll head north at Roseville," he said. "We'll just hope our new chum will remember to tell Henson we went south to Mexico."

"Fine. Just so long as I don't have to jump off the blessed train again." Marian hesitated, then said, "Listen, I said something just before we jumped off that handcar."

"The whistle was too loud," Lockhart said quickly. "And I was pretty busy. I guess I didn't hear."

He looked away. He was a terrible liar, Marian realized. She knew he had heard, and that it was all right.

"Good," she said, and the relief in her voice was real. "If you didn't hear, then it's all right."

5

"You're crazy."

"Possibly. But I need my trunk."

"We can't go back to Sacramento. Everybody in town is looking for us—the police and that reporter and Marshal Doom himself."

"They aren't looking for us in Sacramento. They're looking along the way to Mexico or Canada or back in Omaha or wherever you said you were going."

"Denver."

"Denver, then. I need my trunk, and it's in Sacramento."

"What's so important about a trunk?"

"We can't be ourselves. They're looking for us, so we have to be someone else. And all my other faces are in my trunk."

That wasn't quite true, James Lockhart thought. She'd had a couple with her. He stared out the passenger car window toward low rolling hills speckled with patches of verdant foot high grass. What he saw was the reflection of a stranger in the glass. The stranger needed a shave. He wore Lockhart's brushed and patched clothes, a makeshift mustache, and hair too black for his skin coloring.

The car itself was a second-class coach, about half full. None of the other passengers seemed to see anything odd about Lockhart. Many looked at least as seedy as he. In a window seat across the aisle, Marian Taylor hid behind half-lens reading glasses. Her long hair, now grayed, peeped out around a man's felt fedora shaped into something like yesteryear's feminine fashion. The seams and hem of her dress would not have passed close inspection.

She gave the conductor her ticket without looking up, hiding what seemed to be bone-deep sorrows etched by a lifetime of grief. Lockhart hoped she wasn't overacting to the point of making herself memorable. But she was the actress.

The conductor averted his face from her picture of woe as quickly as a Levite passing a victim in the ditch. Pleased by the man's lack of Good Samaritan blood, Lockhart offered his ticket. He thought of the seven dollars left in his pocket and smiled across the aisle at Marian. She instantly turned away. Again he admired her ability to transform herself into another person so completely that her own bright soul did not show, even in her eyes.

His role was to pretend he didn't know her. He opened the thin folder which was all of his luggage and removed a leather notebook. Henson's hand was a puzzle. Although the marshal made his notes in legible schoolboyish print, he'd devised a system of shorthand and abbreviation all his own. After a little study, Lockhart began to cipher out their structure.

Each entry was dated, but the notes were not a diary, not in any personal sense. He leafed through the book to the end of the printed pages, then back to the last dated entry: *Tu, Jl/26/83.* Underlined notations at the left margin were followed by text in Henson's curious glyphs.

Arr. James K. Lockhart o/ch murd, a/r, I/S fl to av. Sacramento CF. See sheet/Denv, Co, Jn/12/83 re JKL. Adl ch att esc Sac CF Ja.
Arr. Marian J. Taylor o/ch fr/fl. Sac CF. See sheet Jl/10/83 re MJT. Ad ch/consp/JKL o/ch murd, a/r, I/S fl. Ad ch att esc Sac, CF Ja.
Det/Ques JKL's Trav Companions: Opportunity Knox(?!), Edward P. Givens, Melvin Baker, Lysander Thompson re. topics of JKL
1. Dep/OK(?). Reg. JKL: dn't kn wl, good comp, lkd & trstd by others; no knl acts in Denv, FtW, EP, Hnbl.

Half-understanding that, Lockhart thumbed a few pages looking for Mel Baker's evidence. Instead, he found a folded sheet interleaved in the book. At the top, he read: ARREST WARRANT. Dated July 10 at Denver, Colorado, it carried his own name on the line labeled *Subject* and detailed the charges without abbreviation: *Armed robbery, grand larceny. Murder.* A federal judge named Steele had signed it. The sheet on Marian Taylor wasn't in the book.

From the front of the car, the conductor swayed along the aisle in that gait which years of walking on moving trains had taught him. "Sacramento in ten minutes. Ten minutes. Connections to Fresno and points south, Reno and points east."

None of the passengers seemed much interested. The man paused toward the middle of the car and repeated his cry, then came on to the rear. Lockhart watched him above the rim of the marshal's notebook.

He's looking at Marian. Does he suspect? Does he know? Without thinking, he felt for the grip of the Colt revolver hidden under his coat. He lowered his eyes as the conductor turned toward him.

And now he's looking at me. He must know or think he knows. Has some dog of an informer turned us in? Is he deciding whether to take us himself or wait for help? Is Henson, Doom himself, waiting at the next stop?

Lockhart fought the urge to look across the aisle, gazing instead out the window until the conductor opened the car's rear door and went out onto the platform. After that he didn't need to look at Marian Taylor, didn't even want to. The conductor was just doing his job, looking over the passengers.

It came to Lockhart that the situation he'd feared would have struck him quite differently a week ago. Reading it in the newspaper while he rode west in a Pullman Palace, he would have felt gratitude for the sharp-eyed informer, admiration toward the brave and dedicated conductor, a warm glow of satisfaction that the inexorable Marshal Doom was on the job of running down lawbreakers.

"Funny," he murmured, loudly enough to draw a quick glance from Marian. As usual, he didn't feel like laughing.

Instead, he went into his memory, pondering the days before his arrest. He and the other drummers had an odd, hit-or-miss companionship. Often, he stayed overnight in a city while one or more of the others moved on to another stop. Equally often, any one of his sometime companions might stay over for a promising client while Lockhart went ahead. Sometimes business would take them far apart, but because they worked the same basic routes, their paths always intersected again before long.

Opportunity Knox was the least predictable, ranging far and wide to sell shares in his outlandish *Air Traveler* and other speculative stocks. Mel Baker, like a bespectacled donkey on a treadmill, plodded a well-worn rut of big accounts in big cities. He was as dependable as the sunrise. Thompson and Givens—and Lockhart himself—moved where business took them.

Now Lockhart tried to remember who had been on which trains on which days. In particular, he tried to remember who had stayed behind in Denver. He knew he hadn't. He frowned, trying to picture the card games. Who was in the first game out of Denver? Who wasn't? *I wasn't. Sick from the oysters night before. I lay in the upper berth until noon.* Hell. If only he'd kept a journal, the way Reb Thompson did.

Behind Lockhart, the conductor came back into the car. Resting his hands on the backs of the empty aisle seats separating Lockhart and Marian Taylor, he stood swaying with the motion of the train. After a moment, he glanced down at Lockhart, hesitated, then dropped into the empty seat beside him.

Not quite whispering, he said, "Your mustache is slipping."

Lockhart lifted a hand to his mouth, found that the mustache was indeed loose on one side. He pressed it back into place with unsteady fingers.

"Thanks."

"My pleasure." The conductor smiled and put out a hand to shake with Lockhart. "Abe West. I know you. All these others would as well, but for the mustache. Keep it straight!"

"I'll make every effort."

Keeping his eyes on the other passengers, West said, "You're the only honest man in our legislature. I just wish I didn't have to ride this rattler on to San Fran. I'd rather be on the front row to hear your speech tonight."

Daring to breathe again, Lockhart patted the leather notebook. "Wish you could be there. I know it would improve the audience." He clasped West's hand again. "By heaven, it's good to know my work is appreciated by a man like yourself. You'll be in my thoughts tonight."

He watched Abe West lift himself back into the aisle to continue his rounds with a fresh I-know-something-you-don't bounce in his gait. Lockhart made a point of looking straight ahead, though he could feel Marian Taylor's eyes burning into the side of his face. He could play a role too, if need be. And need there clearly was. He had a mountain of work ahead if he hoped to clear himself of the charges in Henson's notebook.

Who was on the train, and who wasn't, that first day out of Denver? Marian Taylor would remember, but he couldn't ask her before they reached Sacramento. *You can't even get started without looking to her for*—But of course! Marian Taylor wasn't there either. *We were playing Cheyenne that day*, she'd told Henson, and Henson had confirmed it.

Lockhart hadn't known her name then. So far as he could remember, he'd never seen her offstage and out of costume— though she had recognized him. Why? Why had she taken notice of him?

I would have loved you, she'd said. *After awhile I know I would, even if you* are *a killer*.

She hadn't been on the train from Denver. But she had visited Elvin Murdock a few days before he was killed. For a loan, she said, a loan she didn't get. But she was a good liar. He'd seen her lie, to Henson and to others—probably even to him. She was an actress. She lied for her living.

What did it mean that she had known Murdock? Henson thought she'd somehow prepared the way for murder and armed robbery. Was the marshal right? She and some accomplice might have contrived evidence against Lockhart.

Maybe she had been on the train from Denver, hiding behind some disguise? Was she on this train this moment to help him or to help the law capture him?

If she's here to help capture me, she's doing a damned pitiful job of it!

Closing his eyes, Lockhart drew a deep breath. His heart was pounding and sweat lay cold along his ribs and shoulders. Worst, his thoughts had turned crazy. He wasn't making sense, even to himself.

It was like that before Chickamauga. It was like that behind the breastworks in Franklin, watching the Rebs mass in column of brigades, watching them deploy across those open fields, watching that Alabama boy run himself onto my saber straight as Brutus dying on his friend's sword. Waiting does it, waiting and not knowing. But once the action started, I did all right.

Lockhart glanced at Marian Taylor for reassurance. She sat perfectly still, studying her intertwined fingers as if to discover some pattern of order in her sad life. Lockhart smiled. The actress was very good, good enough to make the woman behind her worth knowing.

If a man could dig down through the layers to the real woman. But how could a man be sure? How could he ever be sure he'd found the woman and not just one more role? He shook his head. *Worry first about Abe West! Who the hell does he think you're pretending not to be?*

Surely enough, Conductor West made a point of nodding to him as he stepped off the train in Sacramento. "Give them a good one," West said with a conspiratorial wink.

"I'll give them hell."

Lockhart hastened away, concerned about the attention West was calling to him. A few yards down the platform, he saw Officer Martin sitting on the high, flat bed of a baggage wagon as if he lay in wait there to meet every train. Lockhart put a hand to his unreliable mustache, kept his eyes on the policeman, wondered again why he had been stupid enough to come back through Sacramento.

Officer Martin paid Lockhart no more than a glance. He was staring instead at Marian Taylor, just then making her sad, tired way down the iron steps with the aid of Abe West. It occurred to Lockhart that people might remember her handsome dress, even in its present state. Martin gave every evidence of a man who remembered the dress or the woman or both as he eased down off the baggage cart and started across the platform toward her.

With a long stride, Lockhart kicked a chock away from the cart's iron wheel. A hard shove with his shoulder set the unwieldy vehicle grinding along the wooden platform after Martin. Still pushing the wagon while making a show of trying to stop it, Lockhart yelled, "Look out!" in a high, wavering voice, then stumbled and went down.

Abe West abandoned the old lady, echoed Lockhart's cry, and dashed toward policeman and wagon just as Martin was turning with dignity to say, "What the hell?"

His brisk, authoritative question ended in a near squeak as he saw the baggage cart thundering down on him. He leaped aside, then grabbed the wagon by its yellow tongue and hauled backward to stop it. It dragged him along, dignity and all, until Abe West arrived to help.

By the time Lockhart got to his feet, the two men were wrestling the wagon to a stop at the very lip of the platform. Marian Taylor was nowhere around the Pullman steps.

West said, "It's great to see you, Lucius, but this is a hell of a welcome!"

"Welcome, hell. That fellow must have pushed it. Disrespect for the law, that's what. Go to help an old lady, and some jackass tries to play you a trick. Where'd he go?"

"Who? Only fellow I saw was you sitting on that wagon proud as a pig in church. Likely you moved the chock when you got down. But look yonder, there's that *Daily Union* newspaper snoop."

"Not him. This was a tall hombre. Gray suit, tweed sort of. Black hair. Mustache."

"Aw hell," West said. "You know who that was?"

Marian Taylor said, "That was a good job you did with the wagon. I'm proud of you."

"Thanks."

"I was especially taken with your choreography in the stumble and rollover. It was very convincing."

"It should have been." Lockhart bent to rub his shin. "That wagon tongue went between my feet and tripped me. I could have broken a leg."

"My hero!" She laughed. "I've been dying to know who the conductor took you for."

Lockhart paused, scanning the sidewalks in both directions as he and Marian came out the far end of an alley a hundred yards from the depot. He offered his arm.

"*Whom*, I believe."

"What? All right, *whom!*"

"I wondered that myself. An honest man in the legislature was what he said."

"That should narrow the field. Wait, slow down for those people. Remember I'm your mother, damn it."

Lockhart glanced at the couple they were meeting. "Gee, Ma," he said, "alls I remember is he thought I was making a speech here today."

"Idiot."

"They weren't listening to us. They're in love."

She smiled. "We'll remember that act for later, Sonny."

"Maybe. Right now, Ma, let's worry about your trunk. We know our friend the marshal looked in it. We're pretty sure he didn't have our luggage when he put us on the east-bound yesterday. So, where's the trunk now? Chief Biddle may be sitting on it down at his office."

"It's in the depot."

"What makes you think so?"

"I saw it. Through the depot window before we boarded the train with Henson. It's a blue trunk, back in one corner of the baggage room."

"Unless he's had Biddle send for it."

"We'll worry about that if it's happened. Not so fast! Im too old and frail to trot along beside you."

Lockhart escorted her to a bench in front of a mercantile store, motioned her to sit. The storekeeper, sweeping off his section of sidewalk, nodded to them and went about his work. They watched a freight wagon lumber past, its deep bed piled with beer kegs.

"How will we get it?"

"We'll stroll around until they've forgotten us at the depot. Then we'll go back through the alley."

"And what? Break out the window? We can't do something as silly as that."

"Horace Rainwater," Marian said.

"Pardon?"

"Horace Rainwater." She pointed to a pale pink paper poster pasted to the store's front wall. The photograph of a lean-jawed man without a mustache beamed back at them. "You do look a bit like him."

"A bit, if I were ten years younger." He read out the poster: " 'Hear State Senator Horace Rainwater speak. Tonight only, seven P.M. at the Eagle Theater.' So. It's nice to know who I am." He thought again of stripping away Marian Taylor's costumes and makeup and colors of hair until he got a glimpse of the real woman. "Given the choice, however, I'd rather be myself."

"You're Horace Rainwater in disguise, and your mustache is slipping again. You don't *have* a self. Not until this is over." *If it ever is* showed in her dark, troubled eyes as she looked at him. She smiled—with some effort, Lockhart thought—and said in a lighter tone, "I don't know that I like it, your being in disguise. I haven't known you long enough to be certain who you are when you're yourself."

"Nobody special."

"Everyone's special," she said with such assurance that he wondered at it. She smiled again, then looked down and became a forlorn old lady as two men passed, chatting. "I'll bet your wife would say you were."

Lockhart started to answer, found that he couldn't. He turned his head away. The woman misunderstood.

"It's all right. She won't believe what Doom says about you. Maybe she'll even forgive your hiding out with an abandoned actress when she knows what really happened."

He shook his head. "It's not that. It's—"

"What?"

"She died." Even now, it was hard for him to say. "No, it's all right. Two years ago. It was very sudden."

"I'm sorry." For a moment, she was silent. She patted his hand, an elderly mother bowed with years of sorrow. Then she looked up and he saw the real woman in her eyes again. "That's why you went back on the road."

"How did you know I was ever off?"

She looked down the street, then hobbled briskly to her feet. "Not now. Policeman coming. Let's see about that trunk."

Ten minutes later, the man who looked like Horace Rainwater and the woman who looked like his mother walked quietly along the alley loading platform behind the downtown depot.

"There. That window," the woman said.

The man was about to look through the open window when he heard voices just inside the room. He put his back against the wall and gestured to Marian.

"What?"

Lockhart put his finger to his lips. "Shhh. Listen."

" . . . can't rightly do that, Clyde. Old Biddle told me particularly."

"I shan't take a thing. I'd just like my look."

"You don't have no look coming. You don't even have no right being in this room with me, seeing I'm on official business."

"Damnation!" Lockhart heard Marian Taylor mutter. He shared the sentiment if not the wording. Too late, and just by a whisker.

"Then why did you call me, Lucius? I'm here on an errand of great urgency, I was led to believe."

"Aw, hell, Clyde."

"Something about your courage and awareness, I believe, that I might mention in tomorrow's paper. Something like, 'Police Officer Lucius Martin knows more than he's willing to tell about a certain matter.' Wasn't that much the way you put it?"

"I never put nothing like that in my life. Only thing I said was Marshal Doom left a pile of luggage as might've belonged to them escaped desperados."

"You raise an interesting point."

"I do?"

"What, one must wonder, is the feminine form of desperado?"

"Deceitful bitch."

"Perhaps. But my esteemed editor wouldn't wish to inflict such a term on the delicate eyes of our readers, Lucius. I might devise a more palatable appellation."

"Huh?"

"If I could only have one small look into her luggage."

"Anything you'd find in it's evidence. That's the rightful property of the state, and you'd have to leave it in there."

"Lucius, I'd never dream of disturbing evidence! All I ask is a momentary glance to pique the interest of our readers." Darrow's voice dropped. "What do *you* suppose is in there? A tiny costume or two, some lacy undergarments?"

"Undergarments?"

"One would think. What sort of fancy flimsy underthings would an actress wear, Lucius? Wouldn't you like to know?"

"I would."

"Well, then."

"But I dassn't."

"I dast. Just you go out in the front room a moment."

"If old Biddle ever knew of such a thing."

"Old Biddle will never know a thing." Paper crinkled. "You've stood a long watch, Lucius, on difficult and hazardous duty. A credit to our police force. Why don't you go for a little refreshment, while I take your place on guard."

"Marshal Doom—"

"—is far away. And likely not so high and headstrong now that he's lost his first prisoners. I fear some of our gentle readers might think to laugh at the good marshal."

"Best they don't laugh where he can hear them, if they does. And if he finds out you've been fiddling around that there trunk, he'll hang you his own self."

"I'm willing to take that ugly risk my own self. Here's my offer, Lucius, one man of the world to another. You take this ten-dollar note and do as you will. I'll remain here. In due course, I'll pay a Chinese to take the trunk straight to Chief Biddle."

"Sounds fair to me."

"You can trust to my discretion."

Lucius Martin laughed very loudly. "What I trust is we ain't got no key to this blue trunk!"

"I'm wounded by your suspicions, Lucius. Just help me drag it out on the rear platform where my man will collect it."

Lockhart motioned to Marian. They jumped off the loading dock and bent beneath it just as the station's back door opened above them. The building itself was three feet above the ground. At either end, the walls came all the way down, and at the front, a set of steps came to the ground on the ticket office end. The rest of the front extended near enough to the tracks to permit the loading and unloading of baggage and freight cars. Dust filtered down between the floorboards as the two men dragged a small blue trunk through the door onto the platform. Then one of them went back into the freight room and closed the door behind him. The other knelt before the trunk and began picking at its catch with a penknife.

"You son of—" Marian Taylor whispered. Lockhart put a hand to her mouth to quiet her. Almost immediately, they heard hinges creak. Clyde Darrow opened the trunk. Marian trembled in Lockhart's arms, and it took him a moment to realize her emotion was not fear but anger. *What the hell could be so important?* he wondered again, but he couldn't ask.

A few moments later, the reporter finished rummaging, put a packet inside his coat, and closed the trunk's lid. Lockhart listened until the reporter's footsteps faded toward the front of the office. By the time he heard the door close, Marian had pulled loose from his grip and climbed onto the platform.

"Do you have a key?"

"Of course." She tugged a necklace out of her blouse and used the key at the end of it to open the trunk. "Why else would I be here with you? Oh, that *dirty* son of a—"

"Will you keep your voice down? Let's get out of here before Darrow gets back with his freight man or Martin changes his mind."

"Darrow won't be back. Listen to me now. How much money do you have left?"

A moment later, Marian Taylor emerged from the alley and searched the street for pedestrian traffic. A hundred feet away, Clyde Darrow was talking to a Chinese porter with a handcart.

All right, you're sending him to get my trunk. Now what else is on your crooked little mind?

She lifted her skirt until the hem showed her ankles, put away her glasses, and strode rapidly along the muddy street toward the reporter. The porter passed her halfway, bowing low. With a gracious nod to him, she fell in behind Darrow, who was walking rapidly in the direction of the police station.

When it became clear that she couldn't catch him without running, she called out his name, stopped, and waited for him to come back to her. *Fine. He hasn't recognized me yet.* She turned away, listened to his steps coming closer. *With any luck, he won't know me at all.*

"Why, how nice to see you again!" Darrow's voice held the same half-contemptuous amusement as when he'd been talking to Martin. "What a happy coincidence. Mrs. Taylor, isn't it?"

6

- - - - - - - - - - - -

Clyde Darrow smiled at Marian Taylor, unable to believe his luck. He'd hoped to find a story in the Taylor woman's trunk, some shattering new revelation that would put his byline back on the front page. In that he'd been disappointed. He'd had to settle for a scrapbook of clippings, hoping they might yet provide a lead, and for the packet of money he'd found. But now, both scrapbook and money faded into insignificance. He had the woman herself, as good as in his hands.

He could picture the headline: ALERT DAILY UNION REPORTER CAPTURES DESPERADESS—damn Lucius Martin—CAPTURES MURDERESS. And that would be only the beginning for him.

Momentarily mazed in his dream, he almost missed what the woman was saying.

" . . . Marian Taylor. Thank God you remember me."

"I remember faces rather well, actually. Forms and figures even better. I'd've recognized you at a quarter mile."

She took off her reading glasses. Behind her attempt at disguise, Darrow saw that she was an attractive woman. No longer quite young, but entirely presentable. Her dark eyes were remarkable, though now they were wide and filled with fear.

"I believe I'm flattered," she said, giving him a tremulous half-smile.

No, you aren't. You're frightened. And you should be.

"I'm in such terrible trouble," Marian Taylor went on. "And I've been so afraid. You look like an honorable man. I do so need to speak with someone I can trust. I had hoped you might take the time to hear my story."

Darrow swept off his hat and bowed slightly. This was going much better than he could've imagined. *Confession of the Murderess! From Her Own Lips to* Union *Reporter!*

"It is I who am flattered, dear lady, that you would think to repose your trust in so unworthy a vessel as I." He worked to make his tone soothing and sincere. "You may rely entirely upon my discretion. No doubt you've been misunderstood."

Marian Taylor dabbed at a tear. "That's exactly why I'm so grateful to find you. I had taken you for the sort of gentleman who might offer a moment of comfort, an understanding of my poor life." She sniffled. "The ugly chronicle of my misadventures, of those men who have taken advantage of me."

"No doubt." Darrow shot a quick look up and down the street. It would be just like that jackass Martin or some other officious fool to show up and cart the woman off to jail before she had time to speak. He had to avoid that. The game was his if he could keep his head. "Tell me, where have you left James Lockhart?"

"That's the most important part." Her eyes darted this way and that, as though she feared Lockhart might spring from the pavement. She gave a shudder and whispered, "He might be watching us. He really doesn't like you at all. The things you said when he was arrested, I think. And he's such a *vicious* man. You should've seen what he did to that poor trainman—with *chains!*"

Darrow thought he might shudder himself. *Further Outrages by Bloodthirsty Killer. His Accomplice*—no, too commonplace—*His Paramour Tells All.*

"Perhaps we should go somewhere less—ah—public. We could have a cup of coffee, and you would be at liberty to speak freely."

"In a public café?" She watched his eyes.

He watched hers. "I live not far from here."

"Do you? Oh, it would be so nice to feel safe again, safe from the police, safe from—from *him*." She gave a cry of gratitude, threw her arms around him, then just as quickly let him go and looked away in embarrassment. "I—I put myself entirely in your hands, sir."

That's not a bad idea, either. Darrow smiled. Older, yes, and obviously none too bright. But a deucedly attractive woman. And an actress. *Entirely in my hands, she said.* He offered his arm.

"This way."

By the time they reached his rooming house, Marian Taylor's composure had evaporated. She clung to his arm while she constantly looked behind her. If Lockhart was responsible for her terror, Darrow thought, he must be something truly remarkable in the way of criminals.

Attila of the Plains Captured. Daily Union *Reporter Responsible for Apprehension of Ohio Bluebeard.*

He whisked the Taylor woman up the stairs quietly, avoiding his ogre of a landlady. She would certainly have too many questions. What Darrow wanted was a few hours alone with Taylor, long enough to get her story and whatever other rewards he might reap. Then he would need a sufficiently public way to turn her over to the law.

Even inside his rooms, she stayed with him as closely as possible. He couldn't find a moment to slip into his bedroom and hide the money. She cloyed him with attention.

"Coffee? Or would you prefer tea?"

"A cup of tea would be heavenly."

He put on a pot of water, then shepherded her to the parlor. She looked at his easy chair, then chose, with a glance at him, to sit on the sofa. He sat beside her, and she immediately turned toward him, taking his hands.

"Oh, I'm so thankful. You can't imagine the relief a poor woman feels at having a strong, reliable man to look after her. And after all I've been through with that beast." She looked at him through lowered lashes. "Mr. Darrow, I just can't properly express my gratitude to you."

"Perhaps you could do it improperly."

"Pardon me?"

"I've done nothing for you yet, dear lady. But as you've seen, I have some small influence with Chief Biddle and others. I'm sure your difficulties can be arranged. Perhaps if you'd tell me the whole story." He let the words hang there until the scatterbrained baggage seemed to collect herself.

"Oh, of course. I'm such a goose at these practical matters. But you're so forceful, so decisive." She put up a hand as though to touch his cheek, then hesitated and rested it instead on the breast of his coat. "Aren't you warm?" she asked.

Darrow almost laughed, so transparent was Taylor's pathetic attempt to seduce him. *But don't worry, my dear,* he thought. *I have every intention of seeing that you succeed! Oh, but the packet, still in my coat! This won't do. She might find it. This won't do at all.*

He cleared his throat. "As a matter of fact, I am. I'll just remove this coat." He stood to take it off, backing away from her. "And while I'm up, I'll see to your tea."

"Oh, let me do that!"

Playing right into his hands, she jumped up and bustled to the gas hotplate where the water was boiling. Darrow hastened to carry the coat into the bedroom. When he looked, Marian Taylor was already coming back toward the sofa, supporting two cups of tea. Darrow looked toward the heavy paneled wardrobe, then settled for hanging the coat on a hook behind the bedroom door.

When I get her in here, I'll keep her too busy to do any snooping. And at some point along the line, I must persuade her to stop nattering and tell me about Lockhart!

He felt much more comfortable when he returned to the sofa. *More romantic. More intimate, one might say. My luck has indeed taken a turn!* Perhaps after all he should delay asking about Lockhart. She might be in a better mood to talk afterward. He sat beside her and casually draped his arm across the back of the sofa.

"Could we make a plan?" she asked, sipping her tea.

"Rather than just let things happen? I like that," he said. He let his hand slip down onto her shoulder.

"I know where he'll be at a certain time."

"Who?"

"That beast. Lockhart."

Damn the woman. She'd cackled all around the subject

before, but at a moment like this, she chose to start making
sense. He turned toward her, but kept the hold he'd gained
on the shoulder.

"Yes, of course. Where?"

"Let's agree on our plan."

"When will he be there?"

She lowered her eyes again. "It's so difficult for a woman
to be sure about a man," she said. "Yet I feel I can trust you."

"I don't know that you can," Darrow murmured. He put
his cheek closer to hers, breathed on her ear. "I mean alone
here with me."

"No, I mean not to turn me over to the authorities once
he's dead."

"Dead?"

"Oh, yes. He's sworn he'll never be taken alive."

"I see." He touched his lips to her cheek. "How can I
persuade you of my devotion?"

*If I play it right, I can have her and then claim the reward for
her afterward, along with Lockhart. And I haven't even had the
pleasure of counting the money from her trunk as yet!*

"I have to be there. Otherwise he mightn't show himself."

Darrow pulled back. "No doubt. But where are you to
meet him?"

"First, you must agree to let me out of it."

"I've given you my word already, dear lady." *There's no
bond of honor between an honest man and an escaped felon.*

She smiled at him. "I believe you. And in my disguise, the
police won't notice me. They are hardly so observant as you."

"I'm sure you're right." *Fortunately, they'll have me to point
you out.*

"So. When he shows himself, you and the police can fall
upon him and take him."

He began to suspect her. "I don't suppose you'd want a
share of the reward?"

"Why, how sweet of you to think of that!" She was apparently quite unconscious of his irony. The idea seemed a new one to her. "It *would* be only fair, after all the unspeakable things I've suffered."

She broke off, leaving Darrow fighting the urge to shout, "What things?" *If Lockhart's such a desperate murderer,* he thought, *why in hell hasn't he strangled this trollop? God knows she's tempting me to it!* But he concealed his impatience behind a hungry smile as she went on.

"But of course, I couldn't dare wait for it. I know! You can mail my half to me at my mother's in Oregon. I'll leave you her address after we part."

That last word and the look that went with it held a world of promise. Feeling that he'd again found his way after wandering in a desert, Darrow squeezed her shoulder.

"Very well." *Very well, indeed!* "Then we must prepare our trap. Where are you to meet him?"

She looked a long time into his eyes as if making up her mind. A bit of hope showed in her face.

"I believe I'll be more relaxed when I've confessed to you. We're to meet on the steps of the state capitol."

"Great Scott!" *Murderous Felon Apprehended on Statehouse Steps.* Daily Union *Foils Possible Murder of Governor!*

Marian Taylor lowered her long lashes. "There, I've told you all. I'm in your power now. Does it make you happy?"

You have no idea! Aloud, Darrow said, "It does indeed. We've nothing left to worry about now." He toyed with her hair, then touched her shoulder again. "Except how we should while away the hours until it's time to set our snare."

She took the hand he had on her shoulder, held it tightly, staying its downward progress for the moment. "I shall leave that to the imagination of my host," she murmured.

"Indeed!" Darrow rose, taking her hand. "Then perhaps we would be more comfortable in the other room."

"We'll have plenty of time. I'm not to meet him until three o'clock."

"If we stepped into my . . . I beg your pardon?"

"I said I'm to meet Lockhart at three o'clock."

"Great Scott!" Darrow shot an agonized look at the wall clock, frantically checked it against his watch. "It's twenty minutes of that now!"

"Is it really? Why, how foolish of me. I must have misread the clock."

Daily Union *Reporter Slips Up. Legislature Massacred.*

"You addlepated little—" Darrow broke off, reining in imagination and tongue with difficulty. "Ah, that is, we must be quick, my dear. If you'll remain here, I will set our plan in motion."

Surprise and hurt showed in her eyes. She inclined her head toward the bedroom door.

"But don't you want to step into your other room?"

"No! I mean later. Later, dear lady, when we have time to savor the moment. I must leave you for a brief minute. No, sit down. Finish your tea. Wait here. I'll be right back."

"Why, whatever you say, Clyde dear. Shall I make you another cup of tea?" He let the door slam behind him.

Twisting the key in the lock to hold her there, Darrow tore down the steps and pounded on the landlady's door. *Deaf old biddy! Always around just when I don't need her. Where in hell has she gotten to?* He thundered at the door again. *Reporter Waits at Rooming House Door During Bloodbath.*

"Damn it, Mrs. Warren, hurry up!"

"Who's there?" She opened the door a crack and peered through it with nearsighted malignity. "Mr. Darrow. I might have known. I'll tell you one last time, this is a respectable establishment."

"Mrs. Warren."

"And I won't tolerate such language from any tenant."

"Mrs. Warren!"

"Least of all one with such questionable visitors."

"Damn it, *shut up!*"

For a moment, she actually did. Then she sniffed and demanded, "Have you been drinking?"

"No, but I intend to be before very long. I have to use your telephone."

"I smell lilac water. Do you have a woman in your room?"

"Yes, but it's all right. She's locked in. The telephone, please."

"Mr. Darrow, this is a respectable place. If you force me to summon the police, I will."

"It's the police I'm trying to call!" He shoved the door open, carrying her with it. "The telephone, woman!"

She blocked his way. "Ten cents."

You hear it well enough when it means money, don't you, you old harridan? Flinging a handful of coins at her, Darrow pushed past and lurched down the dark hallway. Some piece of china bric-à-brac crashed down behind him, bringing another wail from Mrs. Warren. Darrow pressed onward until her reached the telephone. He spun the crank with sweat-slippery fingers. Daily Union *Reporter Held for Vandalism While Murderer Flees.*

"Operator, the police station, and hurry! Yes, it's an emergency. Hello, let me speak to Lucius Martin. Martin! Not there? Well, where the hell is he? All right, let me speak to that idiot Biddle."

"This *is* that idiot Biddle. What drunken lout am I speaking to?"

Darrow watched the clock on Mrs. Warren's mantel tick off two minutes while he hurried through an explanation, hastily tailoring some of the facts to fit a police chief's ears. Then he put down the earpiece, rushed past the still-remonstrating Mrs. Warren, and dashed back up the stairs.

Damn foolish rattlebrained woman! Have to hurry now. How to get her story? Or why does it matter? I can invent something better. But it's too bad to miss out—though she'd have to combine the charms of Helen of Troy and Cleopatra if one had to listen to her during the act!

Composing himself into something like calm dignity, he tapped at the door. "Dear lady?" No answer. She had seemed oblivious to the urgency of the moment, as to much else. "Marian? I'm coming in."

He saw that she had left the sofa, looked in the kitchen where the kettle was singing, called her name. Nothing. Could it be possible she was continuing her design of seduction? Was she even now waiting coyly in the bedroom, perhaps with that abominable dress off? He went in, half-expecting to find her reposing there. Instead, he found an open window leading onto the fire escape.

Oh, the deceitful bitch! After all her promises, she's run out so I don't get the reward on her? But no, that wouldn't work. I'd still recognize her, point her out for old Biddle. There remained the delicious irony that he had the woman's money, and he would soon have the reward for Lockhart. *Hell, even if she doesn't show at the plaza, I'll have the reward for her. I'll put them where to find her! Where's that Oregon address?*

There was a loud knock at his door, and then it burst open. Lucius Martin filled the doorway. "All right, you lying, cheating newspaper son of a bitch!"

"What's the matter with you? Have you spoken with Biddle? We've got twenty minutes to get to the capitol building."

"Where's the dad-damned blue trunk?"

"Trunk? I sent a freight man with it more than half an hour ago. Never mind about it."

"Never mind, hell. He must have got lost, because he's never came to the jail."

"The trunk can't be lost. I pointed it out for him, the way to the station. I tipped him! We have to get to the capitol."

"He never showed. And now I wonder will Marshal Doom let me live long enough to explain it wasn't me but you took the trunk. 'Cause if he's going to kill me before I have the chance to explain, I think I'll just bounce you down the stairs right now."

"Forget the damned trunk! We have to get to the capitol. Now. Immediately! Lockhart's going to be there."

Clyde Darrow stopped. He'd begun to take it all in. The coincidence of Marian Taylor's arrival just moments after he had been through her trunk. Her leading him away so that he wouldn't know the trunk reached its destination. Her mistake about the time she was to meet Lockhart.

"It's all right," he assured Martin. "We'll make up a story about the trunk. Right now, we absolutely must get to the plaza."

"Why?"

"You're about to recapture James Lockhart and make it all up to Marshall Doom!"

"I am? And that might make it up to him, mightn't it?"

"And I'm about to collect the reward. But we must fly. The woman has a head start on us!"

"Well, get your coat and we'll fly!"

It was, Darrow thought, a certain flatness in the word *coat* that suggested to him even before he ran into the bedroom that he might be missing yet another of his day's pleasures.

7

- -

James Lockhart stared at the vaguely marked brass badge Marian Taylor had pushed into his hand. "What should I do with this?" he asked.

"Pin it inside your coat, ninny. Hurry! You have to keep them from getting that trunk."

"But where are you going?"

"No time. I can't afford to lose him. Remember where to meet me."

"All right." But he was talking to her retreating back. He watched her hurry down the loading platform, lift her skirts to clear the mud, and set off across the street not at all like his mother. Shaking his head in resignation, he pinned the badge inside his coat lapel as she had told him.

He counted his money again and set aside two dollars for his present purpose. Then he sat on the blue trunk and waited. Before he had time to get comfortable, a Chinese man pulling a handcart trotted up to the dock.

"Pardon, honorable sir," the man said, bowing. "Many pardons, but I must take the trunk you repose upon."

"There you are at last," Lockhart said. "I suppose Mr. Darrow sent you."

"Don't know honorable gentleman's name."

"Proper talking sort? Nice new clothes? Told you to take this trunk to the police station?"

"Indeed yes. *Paid* me to take this trunk to the police station. Very agreeable gentleman."

"Good. I'll help you load it."

The porter was obviously hesitant about that idea, but went along when Lockhart stooped to lift the trunk by one end strap. Together, they placed the trunk on the handcart.

"Thank you. Must hurry."

"Just a minute." Lockhart pulled the lapel of his coat aside to give the man a glimpse of the badge. "Detective Hartlock here." *Damn. I'll have to do better than that before I try this on somebody who grew up with English.* "Mr. Darrow was mistaken. We've had a change of plans."

The porter straightened. "Ah?" His expression was absolutely blank, but his dark eyes were alert and curious.

"Yes."

"Honorable gentleman said take to Officer Martin at police station." The porter's tone didn't change perceptibly, but Lockhart still thought he caught a hint of an opinion about Officer Martin. "What is change, please?"

"Officer Martin left me here to tell you. He won't be at the station. We're to take the trunk down to the steamboat landing. I'll wait for him there."

"Ah."

"This is for your added trouble." Lockhart took the first dollar from his pocket and held it out to the deliveryman. "To make up for the change in plans."

"Ah!"

"Good. I'm to go with you so the trunk won't be out of official sight." Lockhart had another thought. "One thing, though. You wait here until I get back."

Lockhart ducked into the baggage room for a moment, came out again with a small leather case that he placed on top of the trunk.

"This goes too."

"Honorable gentleman follow. We find Officer Martin."

Lockhart saw that he had overplayed his hand a bit, but he had the duration of their walk to figure a way out of it. Turning their backs on the police station and jail, they hurried down I Street past Huntington's store, then turned on Front. The street was busy with people going about their own business in what seemed a terrible hurry. The porter trundled the cart through them at a smooth, rapid pace, and Lockhart, though much larger, almost had to trot to keep up. He felt as conspicuous as a cow in the parlor. No one seemed to notice.

The depot on the steamboat wharf was nearly as large and had once been far more ornate than the railway terminal. Now it needed paint and a few wayward shingles angled out of the roof like unruly locks of hair. Lockhart saw but one ship, a white sidewheeler with bright red trim. Faded gold lettering on the wheelhouses identified it as the *Cali-*

fornia Queen. Its two tall chimneys puffed columns of gray woodsmoke.

If she's building steam, it mustn't be long before she sails. "Nice river," he said, to make pleasantries with the porter. "Pretty water."

"Ah."

He started to ask if anyone ever fished there, then remembered he was supposed to be a local detective. Suddenly, he wanted to know. He'd often passed through Sacramento, but had never taken time to look at things like the river. Too busy. No, but that wasn't true. The real reason was that such things brought up the thought, *Martha would like that,* followed by the knowledge that Martha was gone. *Martha would have liked that.*

"Whaff."

At least that's what it sounded like. Lockhart came out of his study to find the porter looking at him, respectful, diffident, intelligent, curious, suspicious.

"Right. We'll just unload the trunk beside the gangplank."

"Officer Martin is there?"

"Where?" Lockhart almost said before he caught himself. He wished he'd been better at poker, better at smiling like a man with a pat hand.

"Honorable Officer Martin is probably on board talking to the captain right about now," he said, doing his best.

"We wait?"

"I wait. I'll be staying with the trunk until he comes on shore."

The porter unloaded the case and trunk onto the smooth-worn grayish planks of the wharf, setting down each as if it held a clutch of brood eggs. He looked at Lockhart.

"Honorable gentleman, he say see trunk into Officer Martin's hands."

"But Officer Martin said I was to pay you to leave the trunk on the dock."

"He say that?"

Lockhart hesitated, then drew a deep breath. *All right, Marian Taylor. We'll see who can act.* "You know good and well he didn't." Then, mimicking Martin's voice, he said, "He actually told me, 'Give that damned heathen this damned money and tell him to haul that damned blue trunk down to the pier chop-chop or I'll give him and you both a kick in the ass.' "

The porter didn't smile, but something in his eyes made it seem he had. "Ah." He took the other dollar that Lockhart held out. "Now you tell me truth. I go."

Lockhart sat on the trunk in the sun and waited. *I'm out here in the open like a snail on a hot anvil. Anyone could spot me. For all I know, that's what she intended. Suppose she's turned me in and sent Martin to arrest me. God knows she could do it without tipping her own hand!*

Then he saw her. Marian Taylor walked down the steep road, her skirts lifted almost to her knees to clear the mud in back, her gait a bit faster than she might wish, her eyes on the road in front of her as if she hadn't seen him at all. In each hand she carried a cheap new suitcase. *My saviour? Or a Judas goat?* He studied the background, straining to see among the buildings any sign of Martin or Biddle. *If they're there, they're very cleverly disguised as two young girls in pinafores throwing breadcrumbs to the ducks.*

She came on, still ignoring him, and walked past to the ticket booth. Having spent a moment there, she came straight to him, smiling, carrying her empty luggage.

"You got it. The trunk?"

"Yes. And this." He patted the leather case.

"What is it?"

"My samples. Doom had left all our luggage together. That'll give Darrow something else to dig through if he figures it out."

She made a face. "Let's get on board," she said. "We've only a few minutes."

Lockhart looked around for help, then noticed that she had taken up her end of the trunk. "It's too heavy."

"It certainly is, but I can carry my part if you can manage yours."

"Do people ever fish here?"

She stared at him, took the tickets in her free hand. "How on earth should I know? Hurry up."

He lifted his end by the strap handle, tested her a step or two, found that she was much stronger than he'd thought. *Or I've grown much weaker!* They stopped halfway up the wooden slope to rest and to give their tickets to a ship's officer. There Marian allowed the officer to help Lockhart with the trunk while she went back for the grips. Still they got their burdens on deck before the deckhands began casting off the docking ropes and taking up the plank.

"Where'd you get the money for tickets?" he asked her.

"It's mine. I didn't steal it, if that's your question. I worked hard enough to save it."

"No, I didn't mean that. I meant where *was* it?"

"In the trunk. I'll tell you about that when we're alone."

He pondered it. "If you already had it out of the trunk, why are we still carrying the thing around?"

She walked up toward the bow, trailing a hand on the rail. "I told you. All my best faces are in there. There are other things we'll need, too."

Lockhart walked in front of her, turned, made a stand. "I can't do this. I'm not going with you to San Francisco. I have to find the truth back east. Learn what I'm charged with. Clear my name." He felt the ship surge beneath his feet, heard the great paddlewheels churning up a mist that made rainbows in the air, saw the dock fading away behind them.

"You're not going to jump?"

He didn't know. "I'm not going," was all he could say.

"Very well. I shan't go either."

"*Shan't* you? How do you plan to get off?"

She took his arm, led him onto the bow, away from the noise of the engines. They could see the green water parting to feed into the great wheels amidships. "Did you think I'd left you?"

"No. I wondered."

"And do you think I won't go back east with you to find your truth?"

"I wonder." He looked into her face, saw the evening sun reflected in her eyes. "I don't know why you should. When I've cleared my name, they'll know you were never involved."

"But you don't know I wasn't."

It was true. He didn't know *who* committed the murders. "I trust you weren't." He laughed. "Trust! That's what made me a good salesman. My clients knew they could trust me. But that's all gone now."

"Not if you clear yourself."

"Even then. If I get a choir of angels to vouch for me, there'll still be people who think I'm guilty."

She took a packet from someplace in the bodice of her suit and put it in his hand. "I trust you. With this."

He realized what she had given him. *All she has in the world!* Saw that her giving it meant she was going with him. He couldn't think what to say. He bent to her and kissed her cheek. She did not draw away.

Instead, she murmured, "Tickets to Boone's Bend wouldn't have cost half as much as these to San Francisco, but then that big policeman would have known we weren't making the whole trip as soon as he asked the ticket agent."

"You never intended to go to San Francisco?"

She shook her head.

"You were willing to spend more of your money to throw off my pursuers?"

"Throwing off *our* pursuers should be cheap at the price, don't you think?"

He kissed her other cheek.

"But now we must take what we can from the trunk."

Not wanting to ask, he figured it out while they made their leisurely way back astern along the port rail. *She intends to fill those new grips from the trunk.* "It's a good idea," he said. "We'd have a devil of a time carting that trunk all the way back east."

"And the police can follow the trunk all the way to San Francisco. And your sample case, too, once you've gotten what you want from it."

He saw she was curious about the sample case, but he didn't want to talk about that yet. He had an idea, but it wasn't one he was very eager to put into practice. "While we shall've gotten off at Boone's Bend?"

"It was my thought," she said. Looking to see that their part of the deck was deserted, she opened the trunk and began sorting her things into the two cases, keeping out a fresh dress and an assortment of vials and bottles. "My last thought for awhile. Now you're carrying the money and leading the way. I'm fresh out of ideas." She looked at him a moment to gauge his mood. "Stay here. I have to go to the ladies' salon and change my face. Then we'll do something about yours."

In the pale yellow glow of a single lantern, Boone's Bend appeared to Lockhart to be little more than the name implied—a bend in the river. He looked at the woman beside him, not surprised to see a stranger. She'd come out of the salon looking thirty years younger, the gray brushed out of her hair—which was now a smooth chestnut color—and a fresh dress flattering her figure. She might have been a new bride to the man who stood beside her. He was another stranger, wearing an ill-fitting readymade suit she'd bought in Sacramento and sporting a rakish Imperial beard and mustache.

"Boone's Bend," he said. "I see now why you turned the planning over to me." Out on the dark river, he heard the *chunk-chunk-chunk* of paddlewheels biting the water, heard a deckhand swear at some bit of rope or rigging, saw the white swirl of foam breaking from the bows of the retreating *California Queen*. Of the man who had come in a surrey to meet the boat, he asked, "Why would the steamer stop here?"

The old man replied, "Why, son! What'd you say was your name?"

"James . . . Merriweather."

"E. G. Boone." He shook hands with great enthusiasm. "As I was about to tell you, Merriweather, Boone's Bend is the hub of transportation for this entire area. By river, road, rail, and . . . " He paused as if to be certain no one else could hear him, though Lockhart doubted there was another person within miles. Then he pulled a folded and creased piece of parchment from his pocket, opened it, and showed it to them. "And air," he said.

"Air?" Marian Taylor asked.

Lockhart looked at the parchment and smiled. "It's stock in Opportunity's *Air Traveler*," he told her.

The old man said, "Sure is. Revolutionize transportation, it will. Biggest advance since the horse. And I'm part owner in the venture."

"The fellow who sold you this, was he a young man, wearing a checked coat, maybe, and a bright tie?"

"That's him. Opportunity Knox!" Boone paused to laugh in a shrill cackle. "Get it?"

"That would have been yesterday or the day before?"

"Yesterday morning. He let me have it for ten dollars under the going price. Offered to give me back my money if the *Air Traveler*'s not a'flying through here before Christmas.

But I declined that offer. I intend to be part of the new age of air travel."

"Congratulations."

"Thank you. You got relations hereabouts?"

Lockhart said no at the same time that Marian said yes. "Well, not now," he amended.

"Where headed then?"

"East. Boone's Bend being the hub of this part of the world, how shall we get to the railroad you mentioned? To Bakersfield?"

"Bakersfield? Son, you could have took the train to Bakersfield out of Sacramento! Why'd you come off down this river 'fore you asked directions?"

Lockhart said, "Because we wanted part of our honeymoon trip to be on water and part on land. We'd take the rest of the trip through the air if you could offer us the *Air Traveler.*"

"Honeymoon?" The old man looked at Marian Taylor. "I see. Elopement, is it? I trust they's not none chasing after you."

"We trust," Lockhart said. "But we can't be sure." He led the old man aside a few steps, lowering his voice. "Truth is, the lady's got a husband who's likely to take this very bad. Married her for her money, held her prisoner, you understand. We're childhood sweethearts, she and I."

"Why, that's a right touching story. Just like one of them dime romances," Boone said.

"Pretty much. It would be a favor if you didn't mention us to anyone who might come looking."

"They couldn't torture it out of me."

Marian kissed him on the cheek. "Do you know of lodgings or a rig for hire?"

"Know of both, Mrs. Merriweather. Would love to have you lodge with me and my own dear wife. Must tell you true, however; if you suspect anybody might be following, you'd do best to go on. And if you want to make it to Elk Grove in time to catch the Bakersfield train, you need to go east in a hurry."

"You said you know of a rig."

"You're looking at it."

"How much?" Lockhart hadn't even looked at the packet of money, much less counted it.

"Well, let's see. I know the route and the distance well enough and it's worth four dollar, but there's two of you and two grips which would usual bring it to eight dollar, but then on the other hand you're fresh married and that makes you one in God's sight. Tell you what. Promise never to mention it to my Sally, and we'll price it by God instead of by Sally!"

"She couldn't torture it out of us."

"I wouldn't bet by God on that, but we'll hope she won't never have the opportunity. Say, you know that fellow Opportunity?"

"We've met."

"You buy a part of the *Air Traveler*?"

Marian Taylor said, "That's why we're looking for him."

"Well, you should've stayed on the *California Queen* for that. He's headed to San Francisco."

"Pity."

"He says that inventor feller, Professor Kendrick, is in San Fran. Going to maybe fly the *Traveler* out of there for Carson City."

"We'll hope to meet him there, after our honeymoon," Lockhart said.

"Throw them grips in the back and climb aboard, then, and let's fly. A-ha-hee-hee."

In Elk Grove, the station man was eating a late supper beside the telegraph unit. "Night train don't normal stop here," he said between bites of stew and corn bread.

E. G. Boone said, "Not without you get out there with your lantern and wave it down, which it is your duty to do when there's passengers waiting."

Lockhart thought he could hear the train coming. "We would appreciate it if you would."

"And I'd appreciate it if you people'd let me eat my supper lukewarm 'stead of stony cold. Besides, I don't know as there's any oil in that there lantern."

Boone took up the lantern and shook it. "Plenty for this job," he said. "Be you going to do it, Roy, or be you not?"

Roy chewed with thoughtful deliberation. "Being as you've got the lantern," he said.

"I ain't no dadblamed railroad employee."

"We'll hire you on temporary, just for this one time."

"Shiftless. Plumb sinful bone idle."

"Train's coming."

Boone walked out onto the unpainted platform and lit the lantern. In the distance, a locomotive headlight was driving toward the station. The train whistled its warning, its question. The old man stepped down beside the tracks and began to swing the lantern in a wide arc.

To Lockhart, it seemed the train was already slowing before Boone made his signal. He frowned. "Does the train only stop when somebody waves it down?" he asked the station man.

"Wouldn't know. My first day on the job."

"What?" Lockhart saw just the hint of a smile at the edge of Roy's mouth as he wiped at it with his napkin.

"That's the night local. Mixed freight and passengers. So it's bound to stop when there's people or parcels or whatever to pick up or deliver."

Lockhart looked at Marian. "So it stops for passengers arriving, too."

"Yep." Roy chewed another bite. "Now, that's six-two-one pulling it tonight, Brent Hoover driving. He'll stop for freight or passengers or sometimes just to visit. Was it your six-two-nine with Anderson at the controls, it'd be a toss-up. Awful hurried, he is."

Marian was picking up their suitcases. "I'll wait outside."

"Right. I'll get the tickets and join you."

Roy smiled. "Bet money old Boone charged you four dollars for the ride. Don't cost him no more to bring two than one, but he'll double that price ever chance he gets. But I can't make it up to you, got to charge you full price. Be the two of you to where?"

"Bakersfield. What time will we arrive?"

Behind the high counter, the telegraph key began to rattle. Roy picked up a pencil, jotted words on a yellow pad without interrupting his talk to Lockhart.

"Bakersfield? Take you most of the day to get there. She's scheduled to fetch up in Bakersfield a little shy of six, but it might be an hour one way or the other. Can't always tell with a local."

"Can we get a connection to El Paso?"

"If you're lucky, you'll just catch the Continental Cannonball coming through Bakersfield. Be in El Paso at dark tomorrow's a day gone."

"How much will it be for two to El Paso?"

Roy was listening, writing. When the chattering telegraph stopped, he looked at the pad, then turned it for Lockhart to see:

James Lockhart, early forties, 5' 11", clean shaven, brown hair and eyes. Traveling with handsome woman, thirties, dark hair and eyes. Report. Detain if possible. Armed and dangerous. Henson, U.S. Marshal.

Roy said, "Could almost be the two of you."

"Almost."

"That story old Boone told about you stealing the lady away from her husband. That about half true?"

Lockhart said, "About."

Roy looked at the remains of his meal, then wrapped the leftover corn bread carefully in a big bandanna. He opened a drawer beneath the counter and put it inside.

"You armed and dangerous?"

"I'm not going to shoot you, if that's what you mean. Nor anyone else unless it comes to life or death."

"Relieved to hear it." He closed the drawer. "Fare to Bakersfield's thirty-two dollars for the two. Being the Cannonball's a express, cost you a hundred and fourteen."

Lockhart counted out the money. With the remaining bills still in his hand, he looked at Roy. "Anything extra?"

The railroad man shook his head. "Nope. If I'm doing the right thing letting the two of you go, I don't deserve no extra pay. If I'm doing the wrong, don't want to be paid for it."

"Thanks, then." Lockhart hesitated. "Look, whatever you hear, I swear to you we've done nothing wrong."

"Better get along. Train's stopping."

Lockhart emerged from the station and found Marian in the shadows at one side of the platform just as a smartly dressed man swung out from the first coach. Lockhart pulled Marian deeper into the darkness.

Darrow! Henson ought to follow him; he could give lessons to a bloodhound. He touched the butt of Henson's .45, then remembered what he'd told the station manager. *It hasn't come to life or death. Not yet.*

E. G. Boone intercepted the reporter and asked if he might be of service.

"Indeed you might, if you know how to get me to Boone's Bend."

"I know the way."

"I'm seeking my sister," Darrow said. "A maiden lady. She's run off with a good-for-nothing drummer."

"Say, now, what's she look like? Pretty? About this high? Nice shape? Dark eyes as like to black as brown?"

"You've seen her! What about the man?"

"Tall? Hiding a badge inside a store-boughten coat?"

"Where, old man?"

"Boone's Bend."

Boone took out his *Air Traveler* certificate and held it in the light of the railroad lantern. "Were on the *California Queen*, same's the fellow sold me this."

"Has it already gone by, then? I'd hoped to catch it at Boone's Bend!"

"Sure has. Of course, be another boat in the morning."

"Can you take me there?"

"It's late. Wouldn't be no place to stay but with me and my Sally."

"Fine, fine. Let's go."

"Go? Why man, we'll about fly! Ha-hee. That's if you got four dollar for nighttime half-fare. 'Course now, tomorrow, should you need transportation, why the fare's not but six-fifty, for a newspaperman."

"Maiden lady!" Marian snorted as the two faded out of earshot. "That's not what he thought—"

She cut herself off short. Lockhart didn't notice. He was pondering the twin coincidences of Darrow's arrival and the wire from Henson. "Tell me," he whispered to Marian, "how did you know the price of boat fare to Boone's Bend?"

"I asked the agent," she said.

Lockhart nodded. "We may be having more company."

He waited until the surrey rattled into the darkness, then hurried across the platform toward a conductor who was looking at his watch and lifting his other hand to signal the engineer. "Just a minute!" Lockhart called out.

The train began moving out of the station before Lock-

hart found empty seats in the lone passenger car. He had just
gotten Marian settled and the luggage stowed overhead
when he looked toward the rear of the car. Slumped in a
double seat with a big white hat tilted over his eyes, Officer
Lucius Martin sat fast asleep.

8

- -

                                  Exhausted as she was, Marian
Taylor did not rest well. Lockhart kept watch in the seat beside her so that she could sleep, but it didn't help. People and
places had become a spinning whirl in her thoughts. Related
only to her, the people hardly seemed to know each other.
Repeatedly, she fell into a restless dream in which she was
walking beside a river that rushed and murmured like the
wheels of a train. She was well escorted, with a man on either
arm, and she found herself introducing them: *Mr. Darrow, do
you know Officer Martin? Marshal Henson, have you met James
Lockhart? Jim, this is Junius Taylor, my husband.* They would
shake hands and she would wake herself trying to run away.

"What's the matter?" Lockhart asked finally. "Can I get
you some water?"

"You go to sleep. I can't."

He argued, gave in, pillowed his head on his folded coat.
In five minutes, he was sleeping as serenely as if he'd never
heard of Marshal Doom. Marian sat staring out the window
into a darkness relieved only now and then by a passing light
along the way. She had made a schoolgirlish mistake in asking the distance and fare to Boone's Bend. Lockhart hadn't
said even a word about it, but she knew that he knew it, too.
She wished he had been angry. She was accustomed to anger

from men. She understood it better than she understood his silent acceptance.

"Damn," she murmured, then glanced over to see that Lockhart hadn't heard. He stirred in his sleep and mumbled something—Martin? Martha?—then fell quiet again.

Martin, probably. Officer Martin was still with them, hard to shake off as the family cat. Marian thanked God and her greasepaint that he hadn't recognized them during the seemingly endless ride to Bakersfield. Once there, he'd left the station while she and Lockhart waited for the Cannonball. They'd hoped he was gone for good, but Lockhart saw him again on the platform just as the train was pulling out, running with his big white hat in one hand and a carpetbag in the other. He was a car or two back now, and what in hell was he doing there? Had he been traveling with Darrow? If so, why hadn't they gotten off the train together at Elk Grove?

Lockhart opened his eyes. As if he'd been thinking the same thoughts, he nudged her arm and said, "We'll be all right as long as he doesn't come up to our car. Even then, he may not know us."

"Right! He's on vacation without a thought of us at all."

"Don't worry. If he goes anywhere, it'll be back to the smoking car, and that's behind us."

"So's the diner. Don't us fugitives from justice ever get a square meal?" She sighed and looked at him. "I thought you were asleep."

"I was. I keep having these dreams." Lockhart smoothed his false goatee. "When the boat was leaving Sacramento this afternoon, a man stood at the top of the road. Did you see him?"

"No. Was it Martin?"

"I'd seen this man before, but it wasn't Martin."

"Was he watching us?"

"He was watching the boat. Maybe it was Darrow." He

didn't sound convinced. She turned back to the blackness outside the window.

"It wasn't Darrow."

"I thought you didn't see him."

"Darrow was on his way to the capitol building. I imagine Chief Biddle and Officer Martin and the whole police force and maybe the Army were, too."

He sat up and cocked his head toward her, waiting. She'd been clever with Darrow, and she'd imagined it would be fun to tell Lockhart about it. Now she found that she didn't want to. Suddenly, her playing up to the reporter while he leered and pawed her didn't seem clever at all. He had taken her for a cheap slut, and she'd played her part well. Maybe she'd played it for so long that it was natural to her now.

Lockhart smiled, put out a hand to touch her cheek. "You don't have to tell me," he said.

Damn you, don't be so understanding! For a moment, she thought she'd spoken aloud. Then she told him. Told him about Darrow's theft, about going to his rooms, getting the money back, sending him on the snipe hunt to the capitol.

"Did you have to do it that way?"

"Oh, no, not at all. I could have killed him instead."

"You could have let him keep the money. Was it worth compromising yourself like that?"

She laughed. "If I hadn't compromised myself, we'd be broke back in Sacramento, waiting for Doom. Do you think it was worth it?"

"You could have let me handle him."

When at last she understood the anger at the edges of his eyes, Marian Taylor was surprised. *No man's been jealous of me for such a long time, I'd forgotten the signs!* She put a hand out toward him, then pulled it back. *No! He's a man, too, same as the others. Just because you've been nursing him along like he's a sick cat, don't go getting sentimental.* "I don't need help handling somebody like Darrow. I've had practice enough."

"Suppose he hadn't bought your story?" His voice was low, still angry. She couldn't tell if the anger was directed at her. "Suppose he'd wanted his payment right then and there?"

She turned her head back toward the window. "Then I *would* have killed him," she said.

By noon that day, she had not seen Lucius Martin again. She'd had time and opportunity to study the passengers in their car. Martin was the only one on the train to worry about, but from habit she catalogued the others: A young couple with a baby who cried too often not to be spoiled or sick. An older couple, probably the grandparents. Two women alone but not together, older, widows most likely, most likely going to visit grandchildren of their own. *Will I ever have grandchildren? I'd need to have children, first, wouldn't I? What kind of father would Lockhart make?*

"I have a daughter in Ohio," Lockhart said.

"What?" *Have I been talking out loud?*

"She's married now. He's a farmer. Baby on the way around Christmas. Don't know what they'll make of all this, if they hear the law's after me."

They'll hear, all right. That kind of news travels faster than Knox's flying machine! " 'Thus conscience doth make cowards of us all,' " she said aloud. It didn't quite fit, but it brought a smile from him. She pointed. "Look. Food!"

A homesteader family from Gila City—mother, father, and seemingly innumerable children—had staked out a quarter of the car, where they slept and played games and talked of visiting Grandma. Now the mother had hauled out an ample bundle and was spreading a feast that made Marian's neglected stomach clench with envy.

"Wish we could get in on that."

"You're the actress," Lockhart said. "Convince them you're Grandma."

"I might just do that, Buster."

Sharp-nosed and cleanshaven in his long robes, a Catholic priest read from a small black book, occasionally raising his head to bestow a fatherly smile on one of the homesteader brood. In a front corner of the car, but loud enough to be heard throughout, a man said, "Two pair, aces high."

"Well, if that don't beat all! I'd suspect you was cheating, if I'd thought you was smart enough."

"Now, gents, you behave yourselves. Your deal, Sol."

"Give me a little sip from that flask, Leonard. No point in carrying it over. Plenty of places to refill it in El Paso."

"Drummers," Lockhart murmured.

"How can you tell?"

The four had been on the train when she and Lockhart boarded, seats turned to face each other, playing cards on a sample case balanced on their knees. They had broken off their game to go smoke, to eat, maybe to sleep, though Marian couldn't remember when. But they'd always started it up again before long.

"Reminds me of the story about the Indian gal and the drummer and the buffalo. See, there was this—"

"They're more interesting than your group," Marian whispered to Lockhart. He almost blushed as the story ended and the four dissolved into laughter. Two of the homesteader boys nudged each other and grinned. The priest looked up, clucked his tongue, and went back to reading.

"Different routes. Different products."

"Different manners," Marian declared.

But still men, she reminded herself. And all men were alike—weren't they? *Look out when you start asking that question, sister. It's gotten you in trouble before!*

"What do you sell, anyway?" she asked Lockhart abruptly.

"Banknotes."

She stared at him. "What? Banknotes? They're money. How can you sell money?"

"It's only money after an officer of the bank signs it," Lockhart said. "I work for Western States Engraving in Cincinnati. They print notes for a lot of western banks. I deliver them."

"But people steal them." *Kill for them! That's how you got into this mess.*

"People have. But not from me."

"Not until now?"

He stopped, bit his lip, thought about it. "No, not even now. I made my deliveries clean and properly. As nearly as I can make out from Henson's notes, somebody must have followed me, learned my schedule. He—that somebody—stole the notes after they'd been delivered."

"How could anyone do that?"

" 'Ah, there's the rub.' "

When the train stopped at Tucson, Lockhart braved Officer Martin's possible presence to buy sandwiches and bottled water at the station. During the long afternoon, while the train crept across the bleak Arizona desert and the scarcely more hospitable plains of New Mexico, Marian busied herself with Marshal Henson's notes. Even with Lockhart's hints, the marshal's odd abbreviations left her a bit mystified, and finally she started copying out the pages, translating as she went, leaving blanks for words she couldn't fill in.

She understood the deposition of Edward Givens well enough, even through the dark glass of Henson's language. She could picture Givens's stern face, could almost hear his self-righteous voice.

Actress! Harlot, more likely. A harlot on steel wheels, follow-

ing the rail lines. Yes, I've seen her perform. In Kansas City, I believe. No, I can't recall the date. Yes, I'm sure Lockhart attended her performances. What of that? He's a great theatergoer. No, I never saw them together. Listen, Marshal, in my youth I myself was on the stage for a season. I know her kind all too well. I'm certain Lockhart had nothing to do with these crimes—but if he did, it was that abandoned woman that led him to it!

"Some friend," she muttered.

Knox and Reb Thompson admitted to attending some of her performances, sometimes in company with Lockhart. They'd taken no special notice of her one way or the other. Melvin Baker had never heard Lockhart mention Marian Taylor. He himself didn't attend theatrical performances, believing them morally questionable.

"Priggish little man."

Lockhart had already studied the details of the crime in El Paso, but she went over it again. Vernon Wilkes of the Lone Star Security Bank had taken a delivery of banknotes from Lockhart on April 9. He'd stayed late in his office to sign them. As he prepared to put them into the vault, he heard a noise. He took a pistol from his desk and went to investigate. Then someone struck him over the head. When his employees found him next morning, stunned and bleeding, the banknotes were gone. Nearby, stained with blood, was a walking stick presented by the Cincinnati chapter of the Grand Army of the Republic to Captain James Lockhart.

I figured he'd just left his stick behind and the thief used it, Wilkes had told Henson later. *But from what you say about the other crimes . . .*

Lockhart put a hand on her shoulder. "El Paso's coming up. I have our things ready. Let's try to be the first ones off."

"Off?" She closed the notebook, thrust it and her notes into her bag, turned her eyes to look for Lucius Martin. Then she went over a quick list in her mind until she was certain of the whereabouts of her luggage, props, money. "I'm ready."

We'll have to find a place to stay, then get an early start in the morning. If we can prove Jim's innocent of the crime in El Paso, it ought to mean something even to Marshal Henson.

He took her arm, guided her into the aisle. The baby was crying, its young father trying to quiet it. The priest rose and fumbled in the overhead rack for his bag. Carrying their own luggage, Marian and Lockhart made it past the others to the front of the car. Only one of the older women was ahead of them. Marian glanced behind but saw no sign of Martin.

Lockhart helped her down the iron steps and onto the platform. On the next set of tracks lay a passenger train taking on water, readying for a run to Denver. Passengers were disembarking from other cars along the platform. Thirty feet away, Lucius Martin stood holding a carpet valise and yawning. If he recognized either of them, he gave no sign.

"Don't look," Marian whispered to Lockhart, "but there's Martin."

"I see him."

"Well, stop looking! I don't think he's noticed us. Can't we get out of this light?"

"Come on," Lockhart said. He pulled her along by the arm. "We'll get out of sight first, then find a hotel."

"What if he's at the hotel?" She felt the pressure of Lockhart tugging her by the arm and tried to keep up. They made it out of the depot lights and into an alley. "Where are we going?"

"Out of sight. I believe we've made that. Now, let's see about that hotel."

"No need for that."

They turned to see Lucius Martin standing at the gloomy corner, a long revolver in each of his hands. "The county'll be glad to put you up, leastways until I can get old Doom out here." He gestured with the right-hand pistol.

"Just put down them bags nice and gentle so's we can get to disarming the two of you."

"Disarming?" Marian said. "Is this a holdup? Who are you?"

"I'm the man's going to shoot you both two or three times if you don't do like I'm telling you." He laughed. "Doom figured you'd be returning to the scene of your crimes."

"Because I told him," Lockhart muttered savagely.

"So he sent somebody along to watch for you. And I hit it lucky. Didn't see you anyplace on the train, so's I looked for a man and a woman getting away quick, and there you were."

"All right," Lockhart said. "We're yours."

"Damn straight you are. Now, shower down them guns I know you're holding."

Marian Taylor saw someone move in the shadows behind Martin—a man in a long dark duster or a robe. She would have thought it the priest from the train, except that he had a gun in his hand. "Look out!" she cried.

The policeman laughed again. "Put down them guns!"

The priest's gun roared, flamed, bucked. Martin lurched as if he'd been kicked in the back. He fired one of his pistols without lifting or aiming it, and the bullet tore at Marian's sleeve. The priest was raising his own gun, pointing it past Martin, pointing it, it seemed to Marian, straight at her. Even in the dimness, she could see his fatherly smile.

With a sound that was half cough, half cry, Lucius Martin staggered, giving way at the knees as he turned. His other pistol flared. Marian heard the priest cry out, saw him fire, felt the push of air and the jarring impact on the planks beside her as his shot went wild. Then Lockhart's left arm lashed out, slamming her aside as he leveled the marshal's .45 in his other hand.

Marian staggered, tripped over something, went to hands

and knees among the stones and broken glass of the alley as the night roared and flamed and crashed above her. Belatedly, she thought of the small pistol she'd taken from Henson's saddlebags. She clawed through her purse for it, gripped its handle, started to get up.

"It's all right." Lockhart's arm was around her. "You don't need the gun. It's over."

"No! He shot. Shot Martin. But he's a *priest!*"

"I doubt it."

She raised her head. Not a yard from her, Lucius Martin sprawled on the ground, his eyes still wide in shocked surprise. Blood, dark and wet, covered his coat and vest. Beyond, the robed man was a huddled shadow with the same liquid blackness pooling on the hard-packed dirt beneath him.

"Who was he?"

"Nobody I've ever seen before. He was on the train."

"Did Martin shoot him?"

Lockhart's voice was gentle. "No. I did."

She stared at him.

"Martin winged him, which is why one of us isn't dead right now. That gave me time."

"You?" She couldn't quite understand it. "You killed him?"

"Very little choice."

She scrambled up, getting tangled in her skirts. Her legs were shaky, but her mind was starting to work again. "We have to run," she said. Already, she heard voices from the front of the station, heavy feet pounding across the platform. "Those shots. People will come."

"Yes."

Lockhart stood like a man mortally wounded, staring at the fallen priest. A bolt of fear went through her.

"Are you hit?" When he didn't answer, she grabbed his arm, shook it. "Can you hear me? Are you all right?"

She saw him smile, but it was a different smile than she'd seen before. "I did it," he said. Then he bent to put Henson's gun beside Martin's body. He took one of Martin's revolvers and turned back toward Marian.

"Let's go! Bring the bags." She ran ahead, holding up her skirts and screaming at every step. "Help. Oh, help! Back there. My God, they're killing each other. Somebody help!" She met a man running toward them in the alley and dodged away when he tried to grab her. "No, back there. They're shooting!"

After that, she got past the others with less trouble. Lockhart caught up to her, led her out onto the tracks and around the rear of a motionless freight. They ran, intent upon putting distance between themselves and the dead men. At last they swung past the caboose only to find their way blocked by a second train on another set of rails. A conductor was calling: "All aboard. Rocky Mountain Limited to Denver. All aboard!"

Lockhart angled toward it and she ran with him. They swung up onto the platform at the rear of the last Pullman. The train was already moving.

"Come on," Lockhart said. He drew her on to the far side.

He was poised to jump when Marian Taylor said, "We can't stay in El Paso." He hesitated, looking back at her. "We can't," she repeated.

"I have to. If I can see Vernon Wilkes, maybe I can clear this up."

"All you'll see is the inside of a jail! Can't you see they'll blame us for this?"

He stopped, blinked, put down the suitcase he was holding. "Dear God," he said. Then he drew a deep breath, and she saw the strength come back into his eyes.

"No matter," he said. "Fortunately, we have plenty of other charges we can investigate elsewhere."

9

James Lockhart might have enjoyed the ride to Denver if his mind had not been so full. Darkness overtook the train in the grim expanse of rock and greasewood north of El Paso, but by daylight, it was climbing into the wooded hills near Santa Fe. Lockhart watched the sky behind the Sangre de Cristos grow bright with sunrise. He was tempted to wake Marian so she could see it, too. He didn't know if she liked things like sunrises. He didn't know much about her at all, when it came to that.

A pair of antelope bounded away from the train in long, soaring leaps. Lockhart thought of his own flight, which now included Marian Taylor. She might have been guilty of nothing at all before she met him. But she had become as much a wanted felon as he the moment Lucius Martin fell dead at her feet.

In his mind, Lockhart saw the man in a priest's robe raise his pistol toward Marian. He hadn't been conscious of drawing his own gun, but he'd seen the counterfeit priest jerk backward with its first shot, seen him try to recover in the instant before Lockhart's second bullet hit him, seen him drop with the loose flopping sprawl that meant a wound in the head or spine. Lockhart shivered. He had killed men on battlefields, and their memory still sawed at his soul after twenty years.

But he did not regret killing the man at the station. The man had killed Martin. In another moment, he would have killed both Marian and Lockhart. *But why?* Lockhart asked himself for the thousandth time. Who was that sharp-nosed little man in the robe? Why had he tried to kill them? Lockhart was certain he'd never seen that face before. He did not know whom he'd killed. He knew why, but that wasn't enough.

I want an end to it! There must be an end. But he wasn't sure who the enemy was, nor how to recognize him, nor what kind of trumpet would call him to battle. Worst, he could envision no Appomattox Courthouse waiting to conclude his new war. Only a gallows loomed in his visions, a gallows or Marshal Doom with a gun in his hand. *What then? Would I kill Henson to save myself?*

No. He faced that limit within himself. *Hang me or not, that far I will not go.*

Then he looked at the sleeping face of Marian Taylor and wondered how to protect her. In the moment when they'd faced death on the handcar, she had said she would love him. *Did you mean that? Could you love a man like me? Even so, could I ever love again?* He thought of his wife's grave mounded with flowers. Would Martha approve? Would she have married again if he hadn't come home from Chickamauga?

Beside him, Marian Taylor changed positions, resting her head against his shoulder. The train slowed, curved gently onto a siding, and waited. Had they stopped it to take him off the train and hang him right there?

"Ummm!" Marian waked, lifted her head away from him, fussed with her hair. "Where are we?" She leaned in front of him to stare out the window. "What time is it?"

"Daylight. Close to Lamy, I think. That's the station for Santa Fe."

"I don't see any station."

"We're on a siding."

"Oh yes, I hear it now."

"What?"

"The other train's whistle. We're waiting for a southbound to pass."

Lockhart sat taller in his seat as if he'd just been unyoked from a loaded wagon. "Of course," he said. "My ears aren't as good as they used to be." *Could you love a man like me?* "Before the war," he added to see if she knew he was that old.

"Artillery?"

"No, infantry. It was loud enough, sometimes."

She laughed.

"Do you find humor in that?"

"Your ears are all right," she replied. "I said it softly and I turned away."

"What?"

She laughed again. "That's good. I like that."

Lockhart smiled, too. It felt good to joke again. "I like you," he said. It was a start. "You've been a good sport about all this."

"Good sport?" She laughed again.

"More than that."

The other locomotive thundered past them so that he'd have needed to shout. He put his arm around Marian and kept quiet, enjoying a pleasure and peace and hopefulness he had not expected to know again. Wanting to kiss her hair, he turned instead to look out his window at the other train. There, framed in profile in a Pullman window, was a face he recognized immediately.

Marian said, "Wasn't that . . . ?"

"Yes," he said grimly. "Marshal Doom." *On his way to see Martin's body and fix himself on our trail.*

"Do you think he saw us?"

"No. He wouldn't be looking for us here. But it doesn't matter."

She thought about that for a moment, then nodded. "No. He'll need about two minutes to find out we were there and to guess we took this train. In three minutes, he'll be after us again."

"Maybe not so fast as that." Lockhart tried the smile again. It worked. "We ought to have one clear day before he can catch up."

"Will one day be enough? To find out what happened in Denver?"

"It had better be."

He worried about the telegraph all the way to Denver. If Henson thought to wire ahead, he might have a posse wait-. ing at the terminal. With that in mind, Lockhart insisted they disembark separately. Neither had any problem. He waited fifteen minutes before he approached her. Then they went to a restaurant for their first real meal in a couple of days.

"Heavenly!" Marian Taylor closed her eyes and inhaled the steam from a cup of coffee she held like a votive offering. "I'd forgotten how good steak and potatoes could be."

Lockhart used his napkin. "Nothing like running for your life to make you appreciate the simple pleasures."

Marian sipped the coffee, then set it down and looked at him. "We are running for our lives, aren't we?" she asked. "That man in El Paso, do you know who he was? A disgruntled client, maybe?"

"I'd never seen him before."

"But he knew us. A bounty hunter?"

Lockhart had been thinking about it. "Not that. Nobody halfway inside the law would have shot Martin. My guess is that somebody doesn't want us to start retracing my route to look into the robberies." In his mind he saw the priest bring his gun to bear on Marian. Why would he have done that?

"Somebody. The somebody who really committed them, you mean?"

He stirred cream into his own coffee, watching the white streaks feather into a smooth golden color. "Makes sense. With me dead, all he has to do is sit on his money until the commotion dies down. We were safer in jail."

"You mean with *us* dead. We need some safety now. We have to find a place to stay. For a couple of days."

Lockhart nodded. "And it must be a place neither of us has stayed before."

He fell silent when a plump, smiling waiter came to clear the dishes, to inquire how they'd enjoyed the meal, to offer a selection of after-dinner drinks for the gentleman and his guest. If they wished to retire to the bar upstairs, rooms were available for private parties.

"No thanks," Lockhart said. He was surprised when Marian put her hand on the waiter's. He was more surprised to notice she was no longer wearing her wedding ring.

Giving the man a confidential smile, she said, "Maybe you could direct us to a hotel that would be—ah—discreet about our accommodations for the night."

The waiter didn't quite smirk. "Oh, yes. I think the Continental would be just right for you. A nice place, you understand. Refined. Catering to ladies and gentlemen like yourselves. You can depend on them not to ask too many questions."

"Thank you," she murmured, with eyes downcast. "You're very understanding."

"My pleasure, ma'am. It's just a block south. Tell the desk clerk Jordan sent you."

"Thanks."

Trying to hide the anger in his voice, Lockhart rose, fumbled for bills to pay the check, remembering a generous tip. At the street, he said, "Damn it, Marian—"

"Shut up." She smiled sweetly at him, fluttered her ringless fingers, patted his arm. "Remember, 'All the world's a stage, and all the men and women merely players.' "

"*As You Like It.* And I don't like it much."

"Be a good sport, then. At least we have a place to stay."

Lockhart had to admit the Continental was all the waiter had promised. It looked the part of rundown respectability, and the desk clerk didn't twitch even an eyebrow when they registered as Mr. and Mrs. Merriweather. Lockhart waved away a hovering bellboy and carried the bags to their own room.

"You rest awhile," he told Marian as he set the luggage down. "I have to go out."

She came to him with quick concern. "Are you still angry with me?" She looked almost contrite, but a hint of mischief lurked at the corners of her mouth. "I'm sorry. I didn't mean to tarnish your reputation."

He managed a smile. "It's not that." *I want you to know I don't expect to share the bed with you,* he didn't say. Instead, he patted her arm.

"Aren't you tired?"

"I want to look around. There's nothing I can do about the bank until morning, but I might be able to pick up some other information tonight. I want to try." He shrugged. "It'll give you some privacy. When I come back, I'll rest."

Her face showed doubt. "But—you will come back?"

It was a moment he hadn't counted on, a moment when words wouldn't carry the load. He put his hands on her shoulders, hesitated for an answer in her eyes, saw it, and took her in his arms. Immediately he found the pleasure more than he could bear. He was about to move away when she reached up to him. Drawing his face down to hers, she kissed him on the mouth.

He became awkward then, clumsy as a boy, anxious and afraid at the same time. "Forgive me," he said.

She frowned, trying perhaps to understand his meaning. "Were there a reason, I might forgive you almost anything. Except not coming back."

Feeling himself at the edge of a chasm he wasn't ready to span, he said, "You've stuck with me—God knows why— and I'll stick with you." He took the packet of money from his coat, took out a bill, and put the rest on the bureau. "So you won't think I'm running out."

"I didn't think it."

"You'd've had to wonder." Then, daring his doubts, he kissed her. "I won't be long."

"Wait."

She put a hand to one long point of his mustache. Much the worse for the kissing, it came away in her hand. She giggled.

"First, we'd better fix you a new face."

Lockhart had grown accustomed to seeing strangers in his mirror. Most of them had been Marian's idea, but this newest one he'd chosen himself.

"I'm going to be talking to some tough people. Best if I look like one of them."

"Are you sure you know what you're doing?"

"No."

"Well, why change our approach now? Hold still."

She had equipped him with a patch over his left eye and a scar that might have come from a sword cut on that cheek. He hadn't needed a false beard this time. His own unshaven face, highlighted with a little dirt, had served the purpose. A patched leather coat and a Confederate forage cap crushed low on his head finished the outfit.

"Where on earth did you get this?"

"My trunk. We played *The Lost Cause* last time we were through Texas. Wasn't a dry eye in the house." She lifted the eyepatch, frowned, and reached for a jar of makeup. "Speaking of eyes, close yours. Your tough people might be suspicious."

"This'll get in the way if I have to wear it more than once."

"They won't look more than once. Hold still."

One-eyed, walking with a slight stoop, huddling his shoulders against a cold wind off the mountains, Lockhart skulked down to Market Street. The Row, they called it in Denver. The places at the upper end had a veneer of respectability—clubs, saloons with doormen out front, establishments that might have been boardinghouses.

As he strode along, the character of the place changed, always for the worse. The street itself grew darker and dirtier. The few streetlights gleamed like lighthouses bordering a dark ocean. In their occasional flickering glow, puddles of black water shone sullenly in deep holes in the street. The saloons too were darker and dirtier, the whorehouse less refined and more blatant. Passing one doorway, Lockhart caught the sickly smell of opium.

The place he was looking for was toward the very end. It was no more than a hovel, its windows boarded up, not even a sign to mark its existence. Smoky yellow light spilled out the batwing doors. When Lockhart pushed them open, he saw eyes gleaming at him from the gloom, as if he'd invaded a nest of bats or foxes. He paused by the doors, staring with a fierce one-eyed squint, until the eyes winked out and their owners went back to their drinks.

"Well?" The bartender was an old man, slope-shouldered and bearded. His eyes still gleamed on Lockhart, but not like a fox's. *More like a skunk, or maybe a weasel.*

"Beer." Lockhart put a nickel on the bar. "Put it in a glass that's been washed this month."

The barkeep swept up the money, drew a mug of darkish liquid from a wooden cask, and slammed it down in front of Lockhart. "You don't look that particular, mister."

"You don't like my looks?"

Lockhart hitched around so the butt of his big Colt

showed in his belt. The bartender muttered something and drew back. Turning from him, Lockhart took his beer to a table and sipped it, studying the other patrons from beneath the bill of the forage cap.

He'll look like a lumberjack, Colonel Billings had told him once. *So our operatives tell me. Wool shirt with the cuffs rolled up. Shoulders an ell across.*

Lockhart rose, went back to the bar. "Janks around?"

"Who?"

"Sim Janks. Big man."

The weasel eyes gleamed. "Don't know him."

"He comes here a lot."

"Don't know him. Don't know you. Drink the hell somewhere else."

Lockhart realized he'd become the center of attention again. That wouldn't do. He bit hard down on an angry comeback to the barman, muttered a curse, and turned away. It had been a long shot anyway.

Just as he reached the swinging doors, they opened inward. Half the portal was filled top to bottom by a tall, broad man in a plaid woolen shirt. His sleeves, rolled up to the elbows, revealed muscular, hairy arms covered with bluish tattoos. A three-inch-wide belt girt his waist, and his dark pants were tucked into big brown boots. He was grinning, talking down to a man comically smaller than himself. The smaller man wore a cap too large for his head. The two of them stopped when they found Lockhart in their way.

Still grinning, the big man said, "We're wanting in, you're wanting out, somebody's got to give." He made no move to give.

"I've come a long way to see you," Lockhart said.

"Have you now?" The idea seemed to amuse the big man, to seat the smaller one more firmly in his own suspicion and doubt.

"I have. On a matter of vital importance to both of us."

Then Lockhart stood aside to let them enter the dark tavern.

"Been asking about you, Sim," the barman piped up. "Asking lawman questions."

"Damned good for you, you sneaking coyote. Get me a beer. Rags, too." Janks looked down at Lockhart. "I don't know you."

"You're Sim Janks."

The big man didn't like that. "I know myself. It's you I don't know."

"James Moneytree. My friends call me Reb."

"Still don't know you. You're in my trail."

"You've room to pass. But if it suits you to walk over me, have your try."

The smaller man bristled, tugged at his cap, backed away a step and turned sideways, but Sim Janks grinned down at Lockhart. "Try, you say?"

Lockhart nodded.

"Well, now, I like that in you, Moneytree. Whatever it is is going to get you killed one of these days, but I like it. Come set at the table with us and say your piece."

"I've come to see you. Alone."

Janks thought about it before turning to the smaller man. "Tell you what, Rags, you run on down to the smithy and see has he finished shoeing my horse. Time you get back, friend Moneytree'll be gone or dead."

Rags said, "Ain't gonna."

Janks said, "Are," and the argument concluded. The smaller man gave Lockhart a dark glare, then turned and stamped out of the saloon. "That's my table back in the corner," Janks told Lockhart. They went back to the table and sat.

Lockhart took up his unfinished beer and sipped it. Janks said, "My God, don't you care who you drink after?"

"It was mine. I've been waiting for you."

"I'm going to tell you a truth. It rankles me to have a man

I don't know his name come up knowing my name and the table I set at. It don't scare me. It just rankles me all to hell. Now I want your story in a thimble and I want from you a better name than Moneytree."

"So do I, but I'm stuck with it. Here's the deal. I've got something I want to sell."

"I ain't no pawnshop."

"I don't want to sell it to you. I'll sell it only to the King of China himself in person."

He heard a sharp intake of breath from the bartender, who'd been replacing their empty mugs with full ones. Sim Janks changed color, looked quickly about the room. One big hand shot out and closed on the bartender's scrawny throat.

"You stay the hell away from here." Lockhart saw his fingers tighten, and the barman clawed desperately at his arm. "You keep your ears over there, or I'll nail them to that bar while you're still wearing them."

He shoved the man away and glared at Lockhart. "What's the matter, you crazy? You can't throw names around in the air like that. God Almighty. You talk loud's a deaf man."

Lockhart spent a moment worrying about his hearing, then went on. "I have the merchandise. The question on the table is whether you can make a deal."

Janks drank off half his beer, put both giant hands on the table, and said, "Just what sort of merchandise are we gabbing about?"

Lockhart took an envelope from his pocket, looked briefly at the rest of the men in the bar, and put the envelope down in front of the big man. Janks opened it and removed a single unfolded parchment. Hiding it behind the envelope, he pored over the fresh new unsigned bank draft, giving every indication that he could read. Finally, he put the note back in the envelope. "Given it's real—which I don't know— how many you got?"

Lockhart said, "It's real as gold but not as pretty. I have an unopened case from the printer. Sixty thousand dollars in fives, tens, twenties, and hundreds."

"Where are they?"

Lockhart laughed. "I'm crazy, remember, not stupid. The question is, can you make the deal?"

He saw Rags slip in through the alley door and stand at the rear of the bar. For a moment, he wondered if the eye-patch had been a good idea. It was easier to slip up on a one-eyed man. But it might give him an advantage later, if he lived until later.

"How'd you get 'em?" Janks growled.

"The question is—"

"All right. Hell. I might be interested. 'Course, I'd have to see them."

"Perhaps I'm not talking loudly enough," Lockhart said. "I'll show them to no one but the King of—"

As he'd done with the barkeep, Janks snaked a hand across the table to grip Lockhart's throat. "I told you about that name. You want me to kill you here and now?"

"Rather you didn't," Lockhart said with some difficulty. "You ever hear the story of the goose that laid the golden eggs?"

"No, I never. And if it's another yarn like you been spinning me, I don't need to."

"To the moral, then. You kill me, you don't get the notes. *Comprende?*"

"I'm going to let go your neck. You sing out that name again, I won't be so gentle. *Comprende?*"

Lockhart nodded. He put a hand to his throat in spite of himself and massaged his pinched arteries. "I like your flair for the dramatic. But since you don't seem able to make a deal, I'll have my note back, if you please."

It was Janks's turn to laugh. "What makes you think I'd give it back?"

"The gun I'm pointing at your belt buckle."

The big man stared at Lockhart, saw that he had one hand beneath the table. "If there's anything rankles me worse than a man knows the table I set at, it's a man points a gun at me."

"It may just rankle you all to hell when I pull the trigger."

"Mister, I been shot, stabbed, cut at with an ax, and run down by a steamboat. The steamboat I didn't take personal. All them other folks is waiting for me in hell. Best you think about pulling that trigger."

"Best you think about doing business." Lockhart leaned across the table to loom in Janks's face. With his left hand he took the envelope, put it back in his coat. "I wouldn't care to be in your place when I find the King and tell him you stood in my way. Besides, you won't get your cut."

"Just what the hell is it you want?"

"First, I want you to get Rags off my flank. Second, I want to see the man I asked you about. Or would you like me to call out his name again?"

"I don't know the man, myself, but I know better'n to go bawling his name in public saloons."

"Where is he?"

Janks thought it over, made up his mind. "No Man's Land. Oklahoma Territory."

"That doesn't narrow it down much."

"You'd need a guide. But you're making one big mistake. You go in there, you die and lose your notes, too. You deal with me, you stay alive, get your money."

"How about a compromise? You guide me there and I'll give you half my share."

"He'd be like to kill us both." But Janks was thinking it over, looking for holes in the offer since it seemed so simple and stupid. "I might risk it. Where can I find you, say tomorrow, when I've thought it over?"

Lockhart said, "I have a partner to deal with. I need time

to get the notes. I'll meet you right here day after tomorrow, ready to go."

"We could help you. Rags and me. Divide the work by three."

Lockhart smiled. "Day after tomorrow." He stood, let Janks see the gun, then put it in his pocket. "Deal?"

"Deal."

Lockhart turned to Rags. "Sit with your boss, little man. Be best if you didn't try to follow me."

"Ain't."

Lockhart stepped out into the alley, hurried to the street, cut into the first doorway, which happened to be a brothel. Shouldering his way through like a man with a mission, he found the back door, scampered down the weed-choked alley, and emerged into light and traffic at the far end. No one seemed to be following. To be certain, he circled a couple of business blocks, then finally made his way back to the hotel.

He knocked lightly on the door before unlocking it. Marian Taylor had been sitting in the wicker rocker at the window. She came quickly across the room to meet him. She had bathed, washed her hair, dressed herself in a warm blue robe. She did not kiss him but put her arms about him and held him tight.

"I'm sorry to be so long. Did you think I wouldn't come back?"

She shook her head. "I won't think it again." Then she kissed him.

"I thought we might go out to eat."

"I thought we might have something sent up."

"You have the better idea." He went to the window, stood to one side and looked as far as he could see along the street.

"Were you followed? Is it Henson?"

"Not Henson, no. Nor a lawman, though he's just as dangerous. I played a long shot, and I may have won."

"Won what?"

"A chance to meet the King of China."

Marian raised her eyebrows. "Is he coming here? I'm not sure even my trunk will take us to China."

"He's a criminal who deals in stolen goods. He's been known to buy banknotes. He has artists working for him, real artists at forging signatures on the notes."

"Wonderful. How does that help us?"

"Maybe he knows who sold him the notes I'm accused of stealing."

"And who killed the men you're accused of killing."

"That too."

"How do you know this King of China bought the notes?"

"I don't, but he's in the business. I've heard about him from the day I got into this line of work."

"I see. So it's your bright idea that we go wherever he hides out and find him."

"Not we, me."

"And you think he'll be only too eager to tell us everything."

"Not us. It's entirely too dangerous for you."

"My hero!" Marian laughed. "Gosh, and I feel so safe *here*."

He took her in his arms. "I am sorry."

"No more your fault than mine." Her voice was choked, but her eyes were bright and clear. "Am I to wait for you here in this little room?"

"Well, I thought you might."

"All right. I'll ask a few questions at the bank here. Then I'll get on to Fort Worth—that's the next place in your crime spree, isn't it?—and see what I can find out there."

"That's dangerous, too."

"It's that or take me to the King of China. Your choice."

Lockhart sighed. "Again, you have the better thought."

"Really?"

"At least you'd be a moving target. But we'd better plan a time and place to meet once I'm finished with the King."

Or he's finished with you. Lockhart read the thought in her eyes, but she didn't speak it aloud. He was grateful. He started to speak again, looked into her eyes, saw that he must keep quiet. He drew her in close against his chest, close enough to realize that she was wearing nothing beneath her robe. When he kissed her, he allowed himself to become lost in her soft strength. He knew when they sat on the bed that he would remember all his life the moment he drew the robe off her shoulders.

When he awoke, he was lying naked beside her. Lying in the dark, looking out the window, listening to the soft and trustful murmur of her breathing, he wondered whether he could live up to all he had promised her—not in words but in the bridge he'd built across that chasm between them.

None of those things disturbed him, however. What disturbed him was the figure of a man in the shadows across the street, a smallish man wearing a large cap and standing with the aloofness of a sentinel on guard.

10

The High Country Café was crowded. A motley gang of miners, travelers, businessmen, laborers, and others not so clearly identified jostled each other and jockeyed for seats and loudly exchanged the latest news. At a table in one corner, out of the mainstream of confusion, Marian Taylor picked at her biscuits and scrambled eggs and wished the other customers would be quiet and go

home. At least, though, she and Lockhart could talk without
fear of being overheard.

"We're going about this all wrong," she repeated.

Lockhart frowned as he buttered a biscuit. "I don't see
why you think that. I'm going after the money and you're
looking into the robberies. Where else can we start?"

"With the killer. It has to be one of your friends."

"That's ridiculous." His appetite that morning was dis-
gustingly good. He took a big bite of his eggs and smiled at
her with insufferable male smugness. "I've known those men
for years."

"Exactly."

"Exactly what?"

"Whoever implicated you had to know your schedule.
And he had to be in the same towns as you at the same time.
Who else?" She hesitated, wishing she could bite off her
tongue instead of finishing. But the damage was done. "Who
else knows that much about you?"

She read the answer in his eyes. *You do.* He was good
enough not to say it aloud. Instead, he drank the last of his
coffee and signaled the harassed waiter for more.

"There's something in that," he conceded. "But why
would one of them do it?"

"For money, of course."

He thought about it. "I don't know Opportunity that
well, but he doesn't strike me as the brains behind a bloodthirsty criminal venture."

She pressed her lips together while the waiter poured
coffee and bustled away.

"You don't strike me that way, either," she said then. "But
tell that to Marshal Doom."

"And Mel Baker's my best friend."

"I could tell that from the ringing endorsement he gave
when Doom arrested you. The only one who spoke up for

you was that polecat Givens." She frowned. "He visits banks, too, doesn't he?"

"Well, yes. He's a master locksmith, and he works for a company that makes safes and vaults."

"There was something in his deposition."

Lockhart laughed. "So that's it. You don't like Givens because of what he said about you in his deposition."

"Damned right I don't!" *And you shouldn't, either!* she wanted to cry out. She glared at him as he calmly spread jam on a biscuit. Maybe it didn't matter to him that Givens had called her a harlot. After last night, maybe he agreed. *An adulteress, at least. Why not a harlot?*

"That wasn't what I meant," she said. He paid no attention.

"You'd as well suspect Reb Thompson."

"Why not? He visits banks."

"Bank guards use guns. He sells guns."

"He certainly knows how to use guns."

"The murder victims weren't shot."

"And he's an ex-Rebel. Maybe he wants to get back at the Yankees."

"After twenty years?"

She clenched her hands and her teeth, drawing in a long breath, letting it out slowly to keep from screaming. "Maybe he has it in for modest, softspoken, know-it-all war heroes, then."

Lockhart raised his head, stared at her. "You're upset," he said.

"Brilliant."

"What's the matter?"

She didn't scream. "Nothing." She laughed the way Lady Macbeth laughed in the third act. "Nothing whatever. Every lawman in the civilized world is looking for us. But that shouldn't upset me."

"Shhh."

"And now you're going off the end of the earth to be killed by some crazy Chinese criminal, and I'm supposed to sit around on a velvet cushion waiting for you to come back for me."

"You'll be helping."

"If you even bother since you know I'm just a harlot and I already have a husband." She stopped just in time to keep from crying. Damned if she'd cry. In a level tone, she finished, "What could possibly be wrong?"

For a moment, he said nothing at all. Then he reached across the table and squeezed her hand. "Good. I was afraid it was something important."

She bowed her head, put her napkin to her lips, swallowed against tightening throat muscles. "Damn you, be careful," she muttered, clinging to his hand like a lost child.

"I lead a charmed life. What kind of jelly is that?"

"It's jam. Blackberry. Do you like it?"

"I love it. We'll plant a blackberry tree in our backyard."

"Blackberries don't—" She stopped. Raising her head, looked into his face. "What?"

"In the front yard, if you'd rather. Maybe I'll plant two."

"*Whose* yard?"

"Ours. Your and mine." He swallowed his coffee, glanced around at the other tables, looked directly into her eyes. "I would like that more than anything."

"But June, my husband. What will we do?"

"Marian, once we're finished with this business, a husband more or less is going to seem like a very minor inconvenience." Lockhart laughed. It was a pleasant, boyish laugh, and he sounded like he meant it. Then he looked at her, and his voice was entirely serious. "If you'll have me, that is."

She thought about the evening before, not the specific events so much as the feeling of warmth and security which had allowed her to sleep as she had not slept in years. "Yes. Oh, yes," she said.

He let go the smile to look at her with something like the seriousness and urgency of the evening. *Will he tell me now? Will he say what he could not bring himself to say last night?*

He opened his mouth, looked as if he would say something important, but made no noise. He nodded and put his hand on hers. Perhaps it was the best he could do.

She wanted more. She said, "I believe blackberries grow on vines."

"Do they? Well then, we'll have to live where they grow."

"I'd like that. A warm place where berries grow."

"It won't be long. We'll meet in Fort Worth. Maybe then we'll have this thing whipped and be ready to choose a place."

She decided that was the best she was going to get, at least for now. *It's as if he were going to war and didn't want to make any promises beforehand.* She had a third cup of coffee, wanting to drag out the moment as long as she could. But then, much too soon, it was time to go. "I'm ready," she told him. She waited for him to help with her chair, then took his arm and walked beside him into the bright morning.

"Are you all right?"

"I'm not going to cry," she said, feeling bright tears at the corners of her eyes.

"You're a tough girl."

"Not tough. Certainly not a girl."

"You have the thirty-eight?"

She nodded.

"I hope you won't need it. Could you use it if you did?"

Brightening, she said, "I'll shoot their eyes out at thirty paces." They had come to the hotel. On the way up to their room, she wiped at her eyes. *I might keep him another hour if I'm wanton enough.* Instead, she watched without comment as he checked his things and fastened his bag. She knew that she might yet tempt him to the bed, but knew as well that she must let him go, must make him go. She was looking out the window when he took her in his arms.

He turned her round to him and embraced her as she allowed her arms to hang at her side. "God knows it," he said, "so I may as well say it."

She stared at him, confused, lost in her own thoughts. "What?"

He kissed her, leaned back to focus on her face. "I love you." Then he kissed her again before she managed to get her arms free to put around his neck.

She pulled free long enough to whisper, "Thank you," into his ear. *One more kiss as a promise; then I'll let you go.* She drew away and gathered her spirits. "Well, then, take care of yourself out there among the heathens!"

"I'll shoot their eyes out at thirty paces."

She closed the door behind him, knowing she could have walked down with him. They had to make an end to it somewhere, and she chose the room. Even after he was gone, she did not cry but began immediately to change her costume.

For this role, she chose the elderly lady. With the makeup salvaged from her lost trunk, she transformed her face, darkening and deepening lines and wrinkles, graying her hair and twisting it into a tight bun. Then she struggled into a tightly corseted dark dress and arranged a veiled hat with a raven's wing at the side. Her grandmother would have liked it, she thought.

In the hotel lobby, the desk clerk bowed to her without recognition. Two matronly ladies chatting in the parlor glanced her way, smiled, and went on with their talk. On a settee near the main door, a huge, scarred man in a lumberjack shirt glowered at a newspaper. He looked up, saw her, and hastily rose, throwing the newspaper aside.

"Allow me, ma'am." With a funny half-bow, he held the door for her.

"Why, thank you, young man," she chirped. "It's wonderful to see such good manners."

Down the steps, she felt him looking at her with an animal frankness she had seen before. *In dogs and randy audiences!* But when she looked back, he was again seated with the newspaper held before him.

Walking slowly and rheumatically, peering at the world with shortsighted eyes, Marian went along Sixteenth Street past the Tabor Grand Opera House. She'd wanted to play there for two years, ever since its completion. But the only Denver booking June had been able to get was at the Palace, where the gambling wheels were a bigger draw than the stage and the men in the boxes took more interest in the wine girls than in the performance.

It's time to quit, she thought, wondering if she believed it. Time for that little house with roses 'round the door and blackberry trees—vines, bushes, whatever the hell blackberries really grew on—in the yard.

You've heard that before, sister. Wait and see. But she knew it was too late. She'd done it again.

She turned right on Larimer. Denver was busy, growing, half the street blocked with bricks and girders that would soon be another building. She picked her way fussily through the mess. A grinning young Irish workman directed her to the Rocky Mountain Consolidated Bank, and she tottered up the steps, still trying to get the character just right. Then she was on.

At the cashier's cage, she fussed over cashing one of Lockhart's banknotes from a distant bank. The teller was patient and polite, then only polite. Finally, he said, "Let me call Mr. Carter. Perhaps he can explain it to you, ma'am."

"Why, thank you."

Ralph Carter was a busy man. His brushed brown suit and clipped no-nonsense mustache and his calm rapid speech all said so. Nevertheless, he greeted Mrs. Merriweather— "I'm a widow, you know," Marian said—with tact and courtesy.

"This way, madam. I must ask you to wait just a moment. I have one bit of rather unpleasant business to conclude."

"Of course." She let herself be led to a deep leather-covered chair to wait outside Carter's office. She wondered whether James Lockhart had sat in the same chair. Then she wondered what she would say to Carter. It was easier when there were lines to learn. *But not as much fun*, she admitted to herself. *Maybe he's called the police and now he's stalling me until they get here.*

Then, hearing voices beyond his door, she realized that he already had a visitor. One of the voices grew louder as it neared the door.

" . . . would have been here to see you sooner but for the murder of a police officer in El Paso."

" . . . understand completely," the other voice, less loud, assured him. "Rest assured, Marshal, we'll keep our eyes open."

The bank officer's door swung open. Through it stepped a tall, wide, broad-faced, silver-haired man, just putting on his hat. Marian Taylor gave a little squeak, then clamped down hard on herself, fighting not to gape.

My God! Marshal Doom himself.

Perhaps hearing her involuntary sound, Rance Henson glanced her way. The marshal straightened. Hastily, he removed his hat again.

"Your pardon, ma'am." Then, to Carter, "Lockhart'd be seven kinds of fool to come here. But near as I can figure, that's just what he is. Remember, he's dangerous as the smallpox."

"No need to remind me, Marshal. When I think what happened to poor Elvin Murdock." Carter shook his head. "I'll look forward to your next visit, to any news on the case."

Marian Taylor studied the floor while Henson's boots walked past her without hesitation. She waited an anxious moment before she looked up again. The marshal was gone.

Beside his door, Ralph Carter stood reading a sheaf of papers brought to him by an attractive young woman. Nothing in Carter's presence suggested that he considered Marian more than a confused customer. "Mrs. Merriweather?"

"Yes?"

"Won't you come in and have a seat." He waited for her at the door, then went to a chair across from his desk and stood behind it until she was seated. The chair was still warm from Henson's presence. Marian adjusted her skirts and peered at Carter above the lenses of her half-glasses.

"My," she said before he could speak. "What a forceful man that was."

Settling himself into his big swivel chair, Carter smiled. "Yes, he is, rather. That was Marshal Rance Henson. Perhaps you've heard of him?"

"Why—isn't he the one they call Marshal Doom? How exciting!" She gave an exaggerated shiver. "Now that I've seen him, I certainly wouldn't care to have him on my trail."

"I hardly think you need worry," Carter said. "Now then, how may I help you? I understand you wished to cash this banknote."

"Yes. My nephew assured me you would exchange it for hard money. I'm so distrustful of paper money ever since my family lost the plantation in that unpleasantness with the Yankees."

"Quite. Normally, we'd be happy to help, ma'am, but you see, this note hasn't been properly signed by the officials from that bank."

He held the banknote out to her. She peered at it through her glasses. "Oh. Is that important?"

"I'm afraid it's vital."

"Oh, dear!" She clucked her tongue. "The carelessness of that boy! My nephew. It's his business. He wouldn't have misinformed me intentionally, I'm sure."

"Your nephew?"

"Yes, indeed." A bit of pride now, regaining certainty. "He delivers these notes to gentlemen like yourself. It's a position of trust."

"Indeed it is. But I'm afraid this time he's given you a sample rather than an actual—who is your nephew, Mrs. Merriweather?"

"Oh, of course, you may know him. His name is Lockhart."

"*Jim* Lockhart!"

"Yes, indeed. My sister's son. A fine boy, a fine young man." This with the knowledge that Carter was more Lockhart's age than the age she was pretending.

The banker's demeanor had changed. He leaned across the polished desk, looking at her more closely. In a quiet, careful tone, he asked, "Is he here with you?"

"Oh, goodness, no. I haven't seen him in months. Nearly a year." She leaned toward Carter. "Sometimes I think he may come through on one of his trains and never even bother to visit his old auntie."

"Quite."

"You young people are so busy nowadays."

"Have you heard from him lately?" Carter was as interested as she had hoped.

"Oh, no. But you are acquainted with him?"

Carter nodded. "We've met."

"Then perhaps you use his banknotes. They're printed on the finest paper."

"We do in fact use them. Tell me. When might you hope to see your nephew again?"

"Oh, I couldn't say. Why? Are you running low on the drafts?"

Ralph Carter laughed. "We're fresh out. And we are extremely eager to contact Mr. Lockhart."

"I had thought to ask you. I've no address now since he took to riding the trains back and forth across the country."

Carter shook his head. "I suspect, Mrs. Merriweather, that you've not heard about our situation."

"I beg your pardon." She turned her head to suggest she had a better ear. "Situation?"

"We've had a robbery."

"Oh my soul. What? Now, today? I should have known something from that marshal person."

"Now, ma'am, you're perfectly safe." He smiled at her. "I suspect Marshal Henson would be very eager to talk with you about Lockhart."

"Me?" She overplayed it a bit to suggest her need for attention. "Dear me, how exciting! But why would he want to talk about my James?"

"What was taken in our robbery was a shipment of the banknotes your nephew had just delivered."

Carter was conspiratorial now, telling her things she had no right to know. She had a chance.

"Was James hurt?"

"Why no. What would make you think he was present?"

"Was he?"

Carter hesitated. "I think perhaps you should speak with the marshal about that."

"Was the marshal here when it happened?"

"Certainly not."

"Then I must ask you. I will speak with your marshal, all right. But it would help me to know more of the matter. Was my nephew present or not?"

"Not being present myself, I really can't say with certainty."

"Oh my. But you think he may have been?"

Carter thought about it. "Your nephew was here. He came in after hours, as he had before, and delivered the shipment of banknotes to a gentleman named Elvin Murdock."

She leaned even closer toward Carter, showing her interest and concern. "I see. Then what happened?"

"We don't know. I myself saw Lockhart and Mr. Murdock together. Elvin locked the door behind me when I left. He and Lockhart were to put the notes in the vault and discuss some additional business. When we opened the next morning, both Lockhart and the notes were missing."

She hesitated, but she had to ask. "But what of this—this Elvin person? What did he say?"

"He didn't." In his turn, Carter hesitated. Looking at him, Marian judged that beneath his polished exterior was a kindly, rather sensitive man. He obviously didn't want to give Mrs. Merriweather the bad news about her nephew.

"Yes?" she prodded.

"He was dead, ma'am. Murdered."

"Dear Lord, how horrible!" Marian put her hands to her mouth. "But surely, you don't believe James . . . ?"

"No, ma'am, I did not believe it of James—Jim," Carter said. He shook his head. "Not at first. But there was absolutely no trace of anyone else about the premises. The vault was locked and the doors were locked. And the notes were gone."

"But if they were like this one—unsigned, you said?—of what value are they?"

"There are people who buy them for a discount and forge the signatures. But"—Carter hesitated again, then said—"but we think the killer might have forced Elvin to sign them before."

"Oh, no!" Marian put her head down. A few tears. "I hope—oh, please forgive an old lady."

"Of course, ma'am. Would you like some water?"

Carter came around the desk, so obviously concerned that Marian felt a creeping shame at the way she was imposing on him. His next words did nothing to make her feel better.

"Please believe, ma'am, that we didn't jump to suspect your nephew. It wasn't until we heard of the other crimes."

"Other crimes?"

"I believe you'd better speak to the marshal about that."

"Oh. Very well." Marian hesitated a moment, uncertain whether to push things further. But there was more that she needed to know. "There are some friends, business associates of my nephew's. They might know where he is. Perhaps you know them?"

"Well, that's possible. If you could give me the names."

"There's a brash young man, Mr. Knox." Carter scribbled the name on a pad and looked up. Marian went on. "Then there's a Melvin Baker."

"Why yes, he's been a depositor here."

"And a Mr. Thompson who sells."

"Firearms. Yes."

"And a perfectly awful person named Givens, Edmund Givens."

"Edward. Yes, he's worked on our vault." Carter held up the list, frowning. "Yes, I know all these men."

Marian licked her lips. There was no innocent way to ask the next question. "I was just wondering: Were any of them in the bank around the time of the robbery?"

Carter looked surprised. "Why, since you mention it, let me think." He stopped, and there was suspicion in the look he turned on Marian. "Why would you ask that, ma'am?"

"Oh, just an old woman's fancy. Maybe James was *not* the only one who might have had an opportunity to commit the crime."

"I see." Carter went back to his chair, chewed on the stock of his pen, and looked at her. "I think you'd better take that up with the marshal, too."

Gritting her teeth in frustration, Marian smiled at the banker. She'd almost had something there, but clearly she'd heard all she was going to from Ralph Carter. And as far as she could see, it amounted to absolutely nothing. Sitting straighter in her chair, she gathered up her banknote and bag.

"I shall most certainly speak to him. Where might I find him?"

"I'll send a messenger."

"No. If you please. I have other errands. If you wouldn't mind telling me where to find him, I will go as soon as I'm free."

"Very well, ma'am. But I would like to have your address, if I may, for future reference."

"Certainly." She took the piece of paper he pushed toward her, adjusted her glasses again, and wrote an address on it.

"And you will come back this afternoon in the event you've been unable to contact the marshal?"

She stood up. "I shall return in any event. I wish to know more about the whole matter." For a moment, she was afraid she'd have to run for it—no small trick in the hobbles of skirt and petticoat—but finally Carter nodded.

"Good. The marshal is staying at the Continental Hotel."

"Is he?" She hoped alarm did not show through her makeup. "What room?"

"Nine, I believe he said. First floor. But they can tell you that at the hotel. They may prefer to call him out to meet you in the lobby."

"I should certainly hope they would! Can you imagine a lady going to a gentleman's room unattended?"

"No, ma'am, I cannot."

Marian Taylor hurried to her hotel, worried that Carter might yet send a messenger to the marshal. She crossed the lobby, half fearful that Henson would suddenly emerge from the parlor or spring from behind a potted plant. In a far cor-

ner the same large man sat reading the same newspaper just
as if she had never left. This time he did not even look up at
her. At the desk, she inquired whether her niece, a Mrs. Merriweather, was registered.

"Oh good," she said. "I want to surprise her. But first I
would like to pay her bill."

"You want to do what?"

"Please be discreet, sir. I know she's short of money, what
with that ne'er-do-well of a husband. I want to surprise her
by paying her bill."

The clerk shrugged and looked in his ledger. "Hers and
her husband's room is paid through tomorrow," he told her.

"Well, good, good. I'll just slip around and visit her. I believe she said room seven."

"Room seventeen," he said, too loudly. "That means its
on the second floor."

She thanked him. *So you do love me. You paid the bill before
you left!* Upstairs, she stripped off costume and makeup. Half
an hour later, carrying her luggage, she emerged from her
room as an energetic red-haired woman in early middle age.
Looking good enough, she thought, to draw closer attention from the big man with his newspaper. With that in
mind, she went down the back stairs and into the alley. Down
on Seventeenth, she found a hansom cab just stopping to
discharge its passengers. Crossing the street, she waited for
a passing wagon and then mingled with a group of younger
men crossing from the other side. "Have you a fare?" she
asked the driver.

"I'm free."

"Union Station, then."

As far as she could tell, no one was following her. No one
even seemed to notice her aside from a gentleman who had
reached the other side of her buggy only a moment too late
to hire it. Sinking back into the cushioned seat, she tried to
gather her thoughts. The driver cracked his whip, more for

showmanship than to encourage his horse, and the cab plunged into the afternoon traffic.

From the moment she heard Ralph Carter's story of the theft from his bank vault, she had fought against the obvious explanation that he himself had committed the crime. Now she realized why that was unlikely. *Not because he's too nice a man to do such a thing—though he is—but because the theft is a bead on a string. It would be too strange a coincidence that Carter should have framed Jim; it would mean that the others had all done the same. No, Carter didn't do it. And he really believes that Jim did.*

"Ma'am?" the driver was saying.

"Yes."

"We're here. The depot."

She got out with her bags, paid him, and went into the station. At the window she purchased a ticket to Fort Worth. Some distance behind her and off to one side, a very large man strode beneath the pavilion, leaned against a pillar, and unfolded his newspaper.

11

There were no through trains where Lockhart was going. He bought a ticket on a Denver & Rio Grande local to Pueblo with connections with the Santa Fe. If all went well, the Santa Fe and its feeder lines would set him down in a couple of days at Liberal, Kansas. Liberal was the end of the line, in more ways than one.

Back in his Confederate veteran disguise, he settled in one of the coaches and spread a newspaper in front of him. He had sent most of his belongings on to Fort Worth with

Marian. He could have stayed with her a little longer. They might have ridden the same train as far as Pueblo. But it had seemed better to part—better because it was safer for her, since Lockhart was sure Rags had tracked him to the hotel, and maybe better for other reasons.

What have you gotten yourself into now? Weren't things complicated enough without falling in love with a—

A what? Lockhart looked inside his mind, couldn't decide how he ought to finish that sentence. An accomplished liar, as he'd seen more than once? An actress who was always playing a part? Maybe even, as Givens had said, a harlot?

No! A brave, loving woman who's helped you far more than you deserve. Who's shared her knowledge and her money and now her life with you when you were in trouble.

At least, that was what he wanted to believe.

He'd thumbed idly through the newspaper, using it mainly as cover for his thoughts. The headlines showed the usual mix of news, foolishness, and scandal: TELEGRAPH SERVICE TO BRAZIL COMMENCED; FAMED SCOUT CODY OPENS WILD WEST SHOW; STRANGE LIGHTS IN CALIFORNIA SKIES— PHANTOM AIRSHIP SIGHTED; CIVIL SERVICE INVESTIGATION SHOCKS WASHINGTON. Then a headline at the top of the third page caught his single eye. TWIN KILLINGS ON FRONT STREET, the headline ran in bold capitals, and below that in smaller type, *El Paso Shocked by Murder of Lawman. Theories of Marshal Henson on the Motive for the Crime.* The piece carried the byline of Clyde Darrow.

Squinting at the crowded type, Lockhart read through it. California Deputy Lucius Martin shot down. At first it appeared a priest had also been a victim.

"By outstanding police work, the renowned Marshal Rance Henson identified the second victim within 24 hours. The supposed priest was in fact Phineas Janks—"

Lockhart stopped dead, staring at the name. Janks. What

were the chances of a coincidence, the possibility that Phineas was unrelated to Sim?

"None," he said aloud, drawing a startled look from an elderly lady hobbling down the car's aisle. The next sentence of Darrow's story confirmed his judgment.

"—well known in Denver's sordid underworld as a purveyor of stolen property and a hired assassin. Whatever nefarious scheme he hoped to conceal beneath the sacred vestments of a priest was thwarted by the intrepid Officer Martin. . . ."

Janks. What were the chances that Phineas's attempt of Lockhart's life had nothing to do with Sim's interest in stolen banknotes? Again, none. Whatever was going on, it wasn't coincidence. There was a connecting link someplace, if only Lockhart could find it.

And if I can stay alive in the process.

Lockhart scanned further down the page. Great alarm and indignation. Much speculation as to the manner of the killings. Possible the two had shot each other. However—

"However, police officials hint that bullets from at least three firearms contributed to the bloody shambles in the alley. Local authorities and Marshal Henson have refused comment upon a Colt revolver found beside the slain deputy, and upon early reports that the martyred Martin's pistol was missing."

More of a mystery than I intended, Lockhart thought. *And maybe not such a good idea. But I had no idea Darrow would get his nose into this.*

"It is well known that Marshal Henson and the heroic Deputy Martin were engaged in the nationwide manhunt for James Lockhart, fugitive bank robber and murderer who escaped from the marshal's custody earlier this month. Speculation has it that Lockhart and Janks were partners in crime, and that Officer Martin inadvertently came upon a falling out among thieves."

"Oh, God," Lockhart muttered. "If ever there was somebody who needed killing—"

Staying alive just got that much harder. God help me if that big moose Sim finds out who I really am!

"Known to be traveling with Lockhart is Marian Taylor, herself a desperate character and a disgrace to her pure and delicate sex. A so-called actress and *doyenne* of the Cyprian sisterhood, Taylor hid her iniquities under the innocent sobriquet of the Prairie Rosebud, until . . . "

"Oh, God," Lockhart repeated, prayerfully this time. "Don't let Marian ever see this."

He folded the paper and jammed it into his coat pocket for later study. At the moment, he couldn't think beyond the impulse to hunt down Clyde Darrow and strangle him. But assuming there was a shred of truth in Darrow's screed, it gave Lockhart plenty of new things to worry about.

If he'd been followed from Denver, Lockhart couldn't tell it, but he took it on faith that Sim and Rags wouldn't let him off easily. He kept his one wary eye open each time he changed trains or moved about on a depot platform, and he took every opportunity to refresh his disguise as Marian had taught him. His beard had grown out so that he no longer had to depend on false whiskers. He looked pretty scraggly, but that accorded well with the character he was playing.

When the branch line's ancient American locomotive finally panted into Liberal, Lockhart felt an overwhelming sense of relief. His waiting was over. For better or worse, he would at least be *doing* something from here on out. Liberal seemed the quietest place imaginable, but Lockhart did notice an unusual percentage of the menfolk going about with firearms displayed openly. The border of No Man's Land was only a couple of miles away. From what Janks had said and from what Lockhart had heard elsewhere, he guessed that Little China was not far beyond.

The mercantile Lockhart chose was lined with dark wooden counters, dark floorboards, and dark walls. At the rear counter, an open skylight provided air and enough light to make out the merchandise. Framed in the square of light, a man on a high stool turned toward him.

"What'll it be?" The proprietor wore his dark hair in two long braids like an Indian, which he was not. Pale hawk's eyes glared at Lockhart past the high bridge of a beaked nose.

"Box of .44-40s." Two racks of rifles and shotguns stood behind the shopkeeper. "The ones on this side used?"

"Some. Most not much."

"I'd like to handle that Winchester carbine, second from the top."

He worked the action, sighted along the barrel, peered down the bore. Without speaking, the owner passed him a bit of white paper to reflect the light along the rifling.

"How much?"

"Eight-fifty."

"How much for a new one?"

"Thirteen-fifty."

If it were my own money, by Ned, I'd take the new one, but I owe it to the lady to be frugal with her money. Even with frugality, Marian's money wouldn't last much longer. If the venture to Little China didn't work out—*the money won't matter. You'll be dead.*

"That there carbine in your hand belonged to a farmer died the day he bought it. Never but one box of shells fired through it was by his invalid wife. Making noise to keep the buzzards away till some'n came along to fetch her husband's body out'n the pigsty."

"He died while slopping the hogs?"

"Way it was told to me."

"Always figured it to be a dangerous way of life, farming. I'll take the gun." Poking around the dark shelves, he found a saddle boot for the Winchester, a few cans of beans and tomatoes, and a slab of bacon. As an afterthought, he added a canteen. "That'll do. How much altogether?"

"Mought need nother box cartridges, moughtn't you?"

"Just mought."

At the livery, he bought a dun gelding that looked as though it might survive the day. His deal was for horse, saddle with bags, bridle, and full feedbag. When he had stowed his ammunition and gear in the saddlebags, he strapped the carbine and his remaining grip to the saddle and rode out toward the Cimarron.

For the first half hour he looked over his shoulder pretty often. After what seemed a long time, the church spire of Liberal fell out of sight below the gentle roll of the prairie. Lockhart crossed a dry creekbed and entered onto a plain unmarked by any road.

"Well, pal," he told the horse, "if we never find anybody or nobody ever finds us, we'll eat for a couple of days."

The gelding rotated its ears toward its rider long enough to absorb that information. Lockhart eased himself in the saddle. He hadn't been on horseback for a long time, and he'd never enjoyed it much. Already, he felt his legs and back beginning to knot from the unaccustomed strains.

Some hero. Some adventurer. If Janks or the King of China don't kill you, there's a good chance this swaybacked camel will!

It didn't seem so funny that night when he made cold camp beside a narrow creek. He was stiff and sore, and he knew it would be worse in the morning. But some of the kinks worked out as he went through the business of tending the horse and laying out his blankets. The days and nights of his Army years began coming back to him, good memories and bad, ways of living in the outdoors that he'd almost forgotten. He watched a golden prairie moon rise round and full, listened to a discordant chorus of coyotes off in the distance, wondered if Sim Janks was lurking somewhere out in the night. Finally, he went to sleep.

The next morning brought heavy clouds and a keen, cold north wind. It also brought the follower Lockhart had been expecting. He was cinching up the gelding's saddle and wondering if his bones would endure another day of travel when the horse nickered a warning. Lockhart turned, drawing the carbine from its boot. A rider was approaching from the north, a little man hunched in too-short stirrups on the back of a tall gray horse. Rags. Levering a shell into the chamber of his Winchester, Lockhart stepped out to face him.

"S'posed to meet you this time yesterday," Rag complained. He tugged the too-large cap further onto the bridge of his nose and huddled smaller in a fresh gust of wind. "Told Sim you'd about forget our appointment."

"And I figured you'd about forget which day."

"Ha. You're a funny one. Don't sound like a Reb to me, though, you don't." Rags straightened to his full height, such as it was, on the gray's back. Stretching out his skinny neck, he peered all about him. "Don't see your partner."

"Don't see yours."

Rags thought that was funny, too. "That's a fact, Moneytree. But he'll be along. I'm thinking we'll maybe both see our partners at the same time."

Lockhart didn't like that at all. Rags gave his cap another tug, then dropped his hand casually to the butt of the heavy Colt revolver that seemed longer than his leg.

"Don't," Lockhart said.

"No offense. Just worried about that rider over there." The little man made a wide gesture with his left hand, the one holding the reins. With his right, he gave a sudden twitch that brought the big pistol halfway out.

That was as far as it got. Lockhart grabbed the gray's bit, pulling its head down. His right hand thrust the carbine upward like a lance, digging the muzzle hard into the little man's stomach.

Rags let out a grunt. His adam's apple worked as he

stared down at Lockhart with round eyes. "Hey, listen, friend, that thing's dangerous."

"Listen, *friend*," Lockhart told him. "Unless you part with that pistol right now, I'm going to do myself and this horse and the world at large a favor by blowing your wishbone out." When Rags hesitated, Lockhart said, "Time's up."

"Hey, wait." With exaggerated care, Rags lifted the Colt from its holster, held it at full stretch, dropped it clattering onto the ground. "Trouble with the world today," he complained, "is nobody trusts anybody."

"Where's Janks?"

"How in hell'd I know?"

"Time's up."

"Listen."

"Talk."

"Ain't." Rags looked at Lockhart's face, changed his mind. "Following your lady friend. Told you, we'll see them together."

"You may not live to."

Lockhart understood without going over it that Rags and Janks had found him in Denver and had seen Marian. He felt a strong urge to go back and find her at once. It was part of the swamp of deep feeling he had tried so hard to avoid blundering into. But she was on her way to Fort Worth, depending on him to do his part. He would have to ride it out, have to trust her to take care of herself.

"Damn if it ain't like Sim," Rags said. The carbine seemed to make him more talkative. "Takes the easy job hisself, leaves old Rags to ride around in the cold, get shot by some crazy man. You don't want to shoot poor old Rags. Never find the King without he shows you where."

"Fair enough." Lockhart stepped back, though he didn't lower the carbine. "Start showing."

Rags shook his head. "Ain't time. I's to find you, wait

with you. We's expecting some company, a friend of the King. Come about dark."

Lockhart raised the carbine to his shoulder, centered the front sight on the little man's nose. "Come about dark, I intend to have my deal made with the King. Only question is, will you be there or not?"

"You're lost, not going anywhere without'n me." Rags sounded edgy again.

"That's my problem. Yours is staying alive."

"You can't just up and shoot me."

"Can't have you at my back. But maybe I'll just tie you up and leave you to explain to your boss that I've already made my deal and you two aren't part of it."

"Explain, hell! Why, he'd kill me."

"Or you can take me to see the King."

"Then him or Sim'd kill me."

"I figured you to be smarter than Sim. Figured you could strike this deal better than he could."

That seemed to be a new idea to Rags. "I might."

"Of course you could. Then I'd be happy, the King'd be happy, Sim'd be happy, and you'd be happy. We'd all have what we wanted."

"Maybe. But I'm s'posed to wait here."

Lockhart cocked the hammer. "Your choice."

"Wait!" Rags's right hand twitched, his face twitched. He weighed his choices. "Sim don't tell me what to do!"

"I thought not. I figured you for your own man. Let's go see the King."

"We have to go through the Roost first."

"Lead on."

Lockhart lowered the carbine, reached for the gelding's bridle. Then he turned suddenly, pointing the Winchester at Rags again. The little man's eyes widened.

"You said you ain't gonna shoot me!"

"Maybe. But a smart man like you's got a hideout gun someplace. Let's have it, just so you don't shoot *me*."

"Hell." Rags fished somewhere in his ragged coat and handed Lockhart an old cap and ball Navy Colt .36 revolver butt-first. "You don't trust a man much."

"I do now. You lead."

They rode south along the creekbed. By and by, a trickle of water oozed up out of the sand. The bed grew deeper, its sides lined now with taller grass and stunted live oaks. In the next hour, the trickle grew to a respectable little stream. The banks were taller than a man's head, the trees and brush along their crest too thick to ride through.

Lockhart said, "I'll still kill you if you bog us down in this canyon."

"You and your pretty horse can't take it, you just find your own trail."

Lockhart figured he deserved that. "Remember what I said." A hundred yards further, the stream emptied into an ancient sandy riverbed overarched with the limbs of oaks that must have been there when George Washington took the oath of office. Lockhart surveyed it. *A snake couldn't get up either bank and I don't see an end to this tunnel.* Rags stopped. Behind him, Lockhart said, "Is this where you want to die?"

Rags laughed. "Settle down. This here's the place a man lets his horse rest, if he's got any sense at all."

The horses were breathing from forcing their way through the sand. Tracks of other horses pocked the dry riverbed all around them. Lockhart eased his aching body in the saddle, needing the rest as much as the gelding did. Finally, they rode ahead, uphill this time. High stone walls rose sharply on both. At the rims, brush and boulders grew thick enough to hide lookouts.

Lockhart kept his eye on Rags. If lookouts on the rim wanted to shoot from ambush, he couldn't do anything about it. Rags was in no noticeable hurry, though he too glanced up at the rim now and then. The trek might have lasted a quarter of a mile farther. At last they came to a very narrow pass leading into a wider space.

Built above the floodline along the sloping walls of the canyon were a string of ramshackle wooden fronts covering the mouths of caves. Rags rode straight to one of the hovels, ignoring a couple of armed guards, who in turn ignored him. He swung down off the tall gray as nimbly as a monkey. Lockhart just behind him, he went through the low doorway into smoky darkness.

By the light of a few guttering candles, Lockhart saw three men at a table playing cards. Half a dozen others lined the walls or lounged at the massive wooden counter that seemed to be a bar. Rags took two steps into the semidarkness.

"Boys, I been kidnapped by this one. Probably a lawman!"

"Shut up, you little weasel," Lockhart growled. He jerked the heavy revolver from his belt and pointed it at no one in particular, waiting to see who would challenge him first. Screwing his face into what he hoped was a fearsome scowl, he said, "Anybody wants to take his word on anything, come on!"

One of the card players laughed. "Hell, Rags, he don't look like no lawman I ever seen." He shifted keen eyes to Lockhart. "What's your story, friend?"

When in doubt, tell the truth. The rule had served Lockhart pretty well over the years. Maybe it would work now.

"I have business with the King of China." The title had the same effect it had had on Sim. The room went deadly silent. "This gutter rat's supposed to be guiding me, but he don't seem too willing."

The card player pursed his lips. "Can't blame him for that, seeing's nobody hardly never comes back from there."

"Maybe they take another way out."

The man threw back his head and laughed. "That's the

truth of it, mister, it surely is. But I'm thinking it ain't a way you'll like." He shrugged and picked up his cards again. "No never mind of ours. You'll be wanting to bunk here tonight. Have a drink, if you're minded."

"I'm minded."

Holstering the revolver, Lockhart turned toward the bar. He met a pair of bright, beady eyes staring at his face. They belonged to a slope-shouldered bear of a man scowling behind a piratical black beard. Before Lockhart could decide how to react, the man's face cleared and the beard split into a wide, snaggle-toothed grin.

"Tarnation! You've changed a mite since the war, but that blind eye gives you away! Cap'n Jeb Ross, sure as I'm a foot high!"

The bear lurched forward, swallowing Lockhart in a smelly, bone-bending embrace. His beard scraped Lockhart's ear.

"Don't tell me you've forgot Sergeant Matthew Quint. Ain't seen you since that day old Bloody Bill was kilt!"

Trying to draw air into his flattened lungs, Lockhart felt an instant of panic. *My God, what do I do now? I can't swap war stories with this unreconstructed ridgerunner!* The bear's next words gave him his inspiration.

"Where you been, Cap'n? Last as I heard, you was riding with the Youngers, and the damn Yankees had a price on your head. Then somebody said you was kilt up Minnesota way."

When in doubt, tell the truth. "I ain't him," Lockhart said.

"Eh?" Matthew Quint stepped back, his low forehead wrinkled in perplexity. "Sure you are. You're a mite taller than I'd recollected, but—"

"Listen up, Sergeant." Lockhart wished he could wink, but the eyepatch spoiled the effect. "I ain't nobody with no Yankee price on his head. That Cap'n Ross must've been kilt right alongside Bloody Bill. I don't know nothing about the war, and my name's Smith."

Rags shrilled, "That ain't what he told me."

Lockhart spun on him. His draw was nothing special for speed, but at least he managed it without fumbling. He brought the Colt up ready and cocked an inch from the little man's nose.

Rags looked down the revolver's bore. He cleared his throat. "Now I think on it, that's just exactly what you told me, Cap'n. I need a drink."

"I'll see your money first," the bartender said.

The small man dug in his pocket, pulled out a heavy coin, and slammed it down on the rough unpainted wood. Sergeant Quint had been sorting it all out. Finally, he boomed a great laugh and slapped Lockhart's shoulder hard enough to dislocate it. Fortunately, Lockhart had already put the revolver away.

"By God, Cap'n Jeb always was the sly one. Come along, whoever you be, and let me stand you a drink." He waved an arm. "That feller shuffling cards is Texas Bob Evans, and me and these others, why we're kinda his helpers. Boys, meet Cap'n Smith."

Texas Bob nodded and lifted a hand. The others grunted in more or less welcoming tones. Lockhart took the drink that Quint offered, but he was careful not to finish another. The men in the bar seemed to feel the occasion called for a party. By the time Lockhart began to wish for supper, they were crowded around Texas Bob's table singing with drunken enthusiasm:

> "Oh, I'm a good old Rebel, now that's just what I am.
> For this fair land of freedom, I do not give a damn!
> I'm proud I fit against it, I only wisht we'd won,
> And I don't want no pardon for anything I done."

Because it was expected, Lockhart joined in. Inwardly, he was appalled. He'd met veterans, both north and south, who still carried a load of bitterness from the war. God knew he had enough of his own nightmares about his time in Georgia and Tennessee. But these men had stopped the clock sometime in those black days when Kirby Smith surrendered the last of the Rebel armies, and apparently they never intended to start it again.

> *"Three hundred thousand Yankees is stiff in southern dust.*
> *We got three hundred thousand before they conquered us!*
> *They died of southern fever, and southern steel and shot.*
> *I wisht it was three million instead of them we got."*

Looking away, Lockhart caught sight of Rags sidling toward the door. "Hey!" he cried. With a lunge, he grabbed the little man by the collar before he could slip out. Rags kicked and struggled, but Lockhart hauled him back to the middle of the room. The singing stopped.

"You oughts to throw 'im back, Cap'n Smith," Quint allowed. "Too poorly to keep!"

"I agree. But I need him." Lockhart grinned, wishing Marian could watch him. For an amateur, he hadn't done so badly, finding allies among these lost Rebels. "Listen, Sergeant, I have to get some sleep. Would you see this little weasel is here and alive to guide me come morning?"

Quint gave him a sloppy salute while the others laughed. "Damn straight we will, Cap'n. He tries to slip off again, we'll hamstring him and let him crawl, same's you did them Yankee prisoners at the Big Blue in 'sixty-four." Quint winked solemnly. "But I reckon you don't remember that."

The room was rank with smoke and the smell of bad whiskey. Lockhart felt a little sick, and not nearly so clever as he had a moment ago. "No. I don't remember that."

"Don't you worry, Cap'n. I'll stand you another drink before you turn in."

"Thanks, but not tonight." Lockhart smiled. "I'll have it when I come back from Little China, unless you'd like to ride with us."

Quint put up both hands and backed away. "Not me, Cap'n. You know I ain't afraid of hell nor nothing in it. But that road to Little China's one trail you'll have to ride by your lonesome."

Like the trail to death.

Texas Bob Evans laughed. "Do you come back alive from there," he said, "I'll be rightly proud to buy you that drink myself."

12

As always, Marian Taylor felt safer on the train. As always, she still didn't let her guard down. Marshal Doom was still on the trail, and based on her experience so far, might show up anywhere at any moment. And the big man in the hotel lobby had not seemed to recognize her but surely had been looking for someone. There was too much coincidence in that.

Neither was it lost on her that their real enemy, whoever he was, might not stop at one attempt by a hired killer.

Maybe that's who the big man is! But no, he has no reason to kill me. He was after Jim.

That at least had been their idea when they'd talked it over. Marian found she took little comfort in the idea—less, because Lockhart was somewhere out in the wilds of Kansas by now, looking for Little China.

Damn you, Jim, why couldn't you listen to me? If we'd started at the other end, we could at least be together!

She was more certain than ever that the killer—the mastermind, at least, no matter how many helpers he might have—was one of the other drummers.

But which one? Ay, there's the rub.

She thought of Lockhart again, bit her lip, bought a Denver newspaper and a bottle of water from a vendor passing along the aisle. Damn it, she would *not* cry. She would read the newspaper.

She found Darrow's story much faster than Lockhart had. Wide-eyed, she read it all. The name Janks meant nothing to her, but she noted that he'd been a hired killer, had disguised himself as a priest, had dealt in stolen goods.

If we could have caught him alive, he might have led us to the thief. We won't get many chances like that.

When she reached the part about herself, Marian smiled.

. . . so-called actress and doyenne of the Cyprian sisterhood, Taylor hid her iniquities under the innocent sobriquet of the Prairie Rosebud, until her involvement with Lockhart came to light. When the inexorable Marshal Doom swooped down upon the depraved pair, it was she who masterminded their escape.

Oh, my, Marian thought. *I believe I wounded Mr. Darrow's tender pride. Considerably.*

Lockhart, a widower and a veteran of the late war, had long held a position of trust with Western States Engraving of Cincinnati. Evidently, it was his liaison with the scarlet Mrs. Taylor that led him in time to a wanton betrayal of that trust. Now, with Marshal Henson hard upon his track, he cravenly attempts to flee just retribution for his misdeeds.

"My God," Marian murmured, half aloud. "Who taught that man to *write?* I hope Jim never sees this."

The authorities have posted a substantial reward for the apprehension of the pair, dead or alive, and for the return of the missing banknotes. We await further information on the killings, and anticipate an early arrest of Lockhart and his consort.

Reward—dead or alive!

Someone took her hand, tugged at it. Marian jumped, barely managing to strangle a scream. The hand holding her fingers drew back hurriedly. Marian turned, round-eyed, to meet the equally round eyes of a girl of four or five. Under Marian's gaze, the child lowered her tear-stained face, sidled back a step along the aisle, stuck three or four fingers into her mouth. Her other hand clutched one arm of a limp rag doll.

Marian could only stare. She looked around for the child's mother or father. No one seemed interested. The other people in the car were going about their business, reading, chatting, napping. In one corner, three drummers played cards under the disapproving eye of a black-hatted matron in the seat behind them.

"Miss," the child said around most of her hand, "where's Mommy?"

Marian found her voice. "Your mommy?"

"Do you know my mommy?"

"No, I don't believe I do."

A fresh tear glimmered at the corner of a large dark eye. Marian scooted hastily over and patted the seat beside her. "Sit here beside me and tell me what she looks like."

The child sat. Looking up at Marian, she removed the fingers from her mouth and wrapped them damply around Marian's hand. "She's very pretty."

"Is she in this car?"

The girl shook her head. Marian did not like to think of her crossing the open platforms between cars.

"What's your name, sweetie?"

"Ellie. What's yours?"

"Marian. What's your mother's name?"

"Mommy."

"Oh." Again, Marian looked around the car. Lost in the newspaper and her own thoughts, she hadn't seen Ellie enter, nor heard her crying. She must have cried very quietly. Marian realized she knew very little about children. "Is your daddy with your mommy?"

"My daddy's in heaven."

"Oh," Marian repeated. "Did your mommy go into another car?"

"She went to sleep."

"I see. Can you tell me what she looks like?"

"She has big pretty dark eyes like your eyes."

"Thank you. But I believe they must be like your eyes."

That brought a shy smile and a tightened clutch of the slippery fingers. "Thank you. Can you help me find my mommy?"

"I'd better call the conductor." Then Marian remembered the newspaper on her lap: "*a substantial reward for the apprehension of the pair, dead or alive . . . anticipate an early arrest. . . .*"

"Maybe not," she said. "Come along. We'll go find your mother." She stood, ushering Ellie ahead of her. "Which way did you come from?"

"I've forgot."

"Brilliant."

"Ma'am?"

"I said your mother has taught you very nice manners, Ellie." Marian looked both ways, guessed that the child had most likely approached from behind her, and turned toward the rear of the train. "Let's go this way."

Swaying with the car and drawing the attention of various passengers, they passed into the next car. "Do you see your mommy?"

"No." Ellie clung very tightly to Marian's hand. "I don't see her!"

"Do you see anything else you recognize?"

"N-n-no." Ellie's lower lip trembled. "Why isn't she here?"

Good question, kid. "She's just in another car, sweetie. Come on, we'll find her."

Behind them the Pullman door opened to let in a strong draft of wind. "There she is!" a woman's voice cried. Not sure whether the indictment fell on her or the child, Marian turned. The dozen passengers in the car, perhaps glad of a disturbance to break the monotony, also turned. As one of them lowered his newspaper, Marian met his feral stare squarely. Their eyes met for no longer than a blink before he raised the paper again, leaving her nothing to see but a pair of large hands around its edges. But it had been long enough for Marian to see a flicker of recognition there, long enough, she feared, for him to see the same.

Big man—big boots, big hands, big shoulders. Checked lumberjack shirt. The man from the hotel!

"Who are you? What are you doing with my baby?"

Marian felt Ellie snatched from her grasp. As furiously as a mother sparrow confronting a crow, a small, blond woman glared up at Marian. Behind her, the conductor tucked his thumbs into his belt and frowned.

"I'm sorry," Marian said.

"Where were you taking her? Conductor, I want this woman arrested."

"Now, ma'am, I'll handle this." Slipping his considerable bulk between Marian and the sparrow, the conductor said, "Mrs.—ah—may I have your name, please?"

"Miss," Marian said automatically while she tried to

think. She'd been caught with her guard down this time, and no mistake. What name had she used to buy the tickets? *Merriweather? Locke? Hartley*—that was it! "Miss Hartley."

"About the child, Miss Hartley?"

"She was lost. We were trying to find her mother."

"She was not lost!" The blond woman was kneeling in the aisle, hugging Ellie, smoothing her hair. "She was right beside me. Then I dozed off for just a moment!"

"Mommy!" Ellie wriggled around to point. "This is Marian. She was helping me."

The woman glared at Marian, unwilling to release the anger that had replaced her fear. "Help you where?"

"I see," the conductor said. Other passengers were starting to leave their seats. One or two voiced support for Marian; others wanted to argue. The conductor raised his voice. "I think we have a little misunderstanding here. Maybe we should just all go back to our places."

"I don't feel safe," Ellie's mother began, but the trainman was bending over her, helping her to her feet.

"Now, ma'am, you've got your little girl back safe and sound, and a fine, sweet child she is. Why don't we forget the whole thing? All's well."

The conductor went on shepherding mother and child back toward their places. Edging past as quickly as she could, Marian hastened back to her own seat.

Who is he? She pictured the face of the man behind the paper. She was certain he was the one who'd waited in the hotel lobby. Thinking about it, she believed he might have been at the Denver terminal, as well.

Brilliant! Of course he was at the terminal. He got on the damned train, didn't he? But who was he? She didn't for a moment believe his presence was accidental. *Lawman? Bounty hunter? Then what's he waiting for?*

Jim! That was it. He was waiting for her to take him to Lockhart.

"Pardon me, ma'am."

Again, Marian jumped. Ellie and her mother stood in the aisle beside her seat. Afraid the young woman planned to renew her quarrel, Marian said, "Yes?"

"I wanted to apologize for the things I said."

"May we sit down?" Ellie asked.

Marian gestured to the seat across from her. "Please."

The young woman sank down, Ellie scrambling into her lap. For the first time, Marian looked closely at her. Not much more than twenty, she seemed frail. Dark circles showed beneath her eyes, making her face seem even more pale. Her black suit was close to new, but shabbily inexpensive.

"The truth is, I went to sleep," she confessed. "When I woke, I couldn't find Ellie, and then when I saw her with you—" She shrugged and lowered her brown eyes. "Well, I blamed you, I guess. I'm sorry."

She sounded so miserable that Ellie turned and hugged her. "It's all right, Mommy. Don't cry."

"Yes, please don't," Marian said. "No harm done. Anyone might have thought the same."

The woman stopped and shook her head. "Well, thank you for taking it that way. Come on, Ellie. Let's go back to our seats."

"No! I want to stay here with Marian."

Marian quickly put out her hand. "Yes, do stay. You're terribly tired. If you'd like to nap, I'll watch Ellie." She smiled at the little girl. "I'm sure we'll find a lot to talk about."

"Well." Under Ellie's urging, the woman let herself be persuaded. "If you're sure it won't be an inconvenience. I'm Nellie North, Miss Hartley."

"Please. Call me Marian."

From Nellie, Marian learned that Mr. North had died four months before. She and Ellie had been in California for a couple of weeks, and were now returning home to Fort Worth.

"Oh. Were you visiting relatives in California?"

Nellie looked away. "Not exactly."

Later, while Nellie slept, Marian quickly exhausted the few games she knew that might be suitable for Ellie. "All right, then, I'll tell you a story."

"Good. I love stories."

"Then once upon a time, there were a boy and a girl named Romeo and Juliet."

Using the play's words where she could and fitting the rest to Ellie's ears, Marian whiled away the long day. By the time the train began to slow for Fort Worth, Ellie had adopted her completely.

"You'll have to stay with Mommy and me," she said. "Then you can tell me more stories."

"Well, thank you. But I couldn't."

"Why not?" Nellie, curled in a corner of the seat, smiled at her sleepily. "Please do. It'll be little enough repayment for your help. And Ellie and I are all alone, in that big house. Why not?"

"I really couldn't." Marian cut herself off. *Why not, indeed!* Doom and God knew how many others were looking for a couple or a lone woman. They would be watching the hotels and boardinghouses, asking questions at restaurants, watching for strangers. They wouldn't be looking at the North home.

Only, the lumberjack. I can't lead him to their door! Then, looking at the two young faces, she nodded. She would find a way to shake off the big man.

"Very well. I accept your most gracious offer, on the condition that you allow me to pay for a hack from the station."

"How sweet! We do live some distance from the station. A cab would be nice."

*   *   *

The Norths' home was a modest cottage toward the outskirts of the city. Marian felt certain that no one had followed them, going to such extremes of looking behind the
carriage that she'd finally called Nellie's attention to her concern. "Is something wrong?"

"Oh, no. I've just never been here before. I wanted to see
the city." She didn't think Nellie believed her, but the
younger woman didn't press the matter. "You live in a very
nice quiet part of it."

"A lonely part, usually." Nellie North caught herself and
smiled. "So we're doubly glad to have guests, Ellie and me."

She went through the small rooms, opening windows to
dispel the musty smell and straightening things. Marian
helped where she could, while Ellie kept up a stream of chat-
tered questions and observations. Marian enjoyed herself
much more than she would have expected, though she was
never quite free of worry about Lockhart.

After a cold supper, the three played games until Ellie's
head drooped despite her best efforts to stay awake. Nellie carried the child to bed. Returning, she stopped in the
doorway.

"I'll make us some hot cocoa."

"Oh, don't trouble."

"No trouble." The young woman looked thoughtfully
at Marian. "I know it's not my place to ask, but it seems to me
you're troubled. Is there any way I can help?"

"You have already."

"I haven't done anything."

*Only given me the first night since I first saw Henson that I
haven't felt hunted. Only given me something to think about besides Jim and what might be happening to him.*

Marian smiled. "More than you might think." For a moment, Marian was tempted to confide in Nellie North, to
tell her everything, to share her misgivings and her worries

about Jim. Then she pulled herself straight. *You know better
than that. You know better than to think about trusting anyone.
What's Lockhart doing to you?*

Putting on a bright stage smile, she said, "I'm just tired,
I suppose. And tomorrow, I must visit the bank here, City
National. Do you know where that is?"

"Oh, yes. I have a loan there." Nellie came and sat on
the arm of the sofa. "It's right downtown. I'm afraid you'll
have the expense of another cab." She hesitated, then said,
"A terrible thing. One of their officers—one I knew, George
Stanhope—was murdered just a few weeks ago. They're still
looking for the man who did it."

"How awful! Was it a robbery?"

"Well, some kind of a one. The newspapers haven't had
much to say about it, after the first few days. But it wasn't a
holdup or anything like that."

"Really? Did you know Mr. Stanhope well?"

Nellie blushed and looked down at her shoes. "No, not
well. He—ah—talked to me once about the loan. And—"
She stopped and pressed her lips together. "I know it's wrong
to speak ill of the dead, but Mr. Stanhope was no gentleman."

"Oh." Marian considered, then smiled at Nellie, a smile
of warmth and understanding that invited confidences. "I
believe I've changed my mind about the cocoa, Nellie. Can
I make it for us?"

The next morning Marian crept out of bed before anyone
else was awake. She needed a few minutes to herself to work
on her makeup, and she preferred that neither Ellie nor Nellie see her leaving. She kept the red hair, but brushed it out
and pinned it up into a more youthful style. Careful work
with face powder and rouge and a makeup pencil left her
looking younger than the first Miss Hartley, but noticeably
harder and more predatory. A green walking dress from her

bag just fit the personality she wanted. Finished, she slipped out of the house and walked a half mile along the tree-fringed lane until she began to reach civilization again.

At the Longhorn Café, she had coffee and a roll, then caught the horse car downtown. The City National Bank was a tall, narrow structure with three stories and a mansard roof decorated with gingerbread trim. Marian inspected it as carefully as any bank robber, taking special note of entrances and exits. With an hour to wait before the bank would open, she went on down Main, casting a wistful look at the newly finished opera house. On a bench across from the post office, she busied herself writing a letter to Lockhart, telling him where she was and what she hoped to do. She proposed two times and places they might meet. Then, having addressed the letter to James Merriweather, General Delivery, she posted the letter at the window.

"I forgot to ask," she said to the man behind the counter. "Have you a letter for me?"

The man looked at her, then put aside the letters he was sorting. He smiled, running a finger over his mustache. "I certainly hope so," he told her.

Marian smiled back, pleased at the tribute to her new character. "Marian Hartley," she said. She lowered her lashes and added, "*Miss* Hartley."

"General Delivery, *Miss* Hartley?"

"For the moment, yes. Until I find suitable lodgings."

"I believe I would remember such a lovely name, but let me look." He shuffled through a box of mail, looking mostly at Marian rather than at the envelopes. "No, no, I'm afraid not. But I hope you'll check with me again soon."

"Oh, I will."

At ten o'clock she went back to the bank. She handed a folded note to the young man behind the first teller's cage.

"Please take this to Mr. Grove. He's your president, isn't he? Yes, ask if he has a moment to see me. I'll wait."

It took considerably longer than a moment. Marian spent the time reviewing in her mind what she'd learned from Henson's notebook. The story was much the same as the one Ralph Carter had told her in Denver. Lockhart had arrived not long before closing, had gone in to make his delivery to Stanhope. Lockhart had then left, but several witnesses overheard him making an appointment to meet Stanhope for supper. Around midnight, a janitor found Stanhope dead in his office. The time lock on the vault was undisturbed, but the banknotes Lockhart had delivered were gone.

The Fort Worth robbery had been the last of the crimes, a month after Denver. No suspicion had fallen on Lockhart until bank officials learned of the others from Henson. But they couldn't imagine anyone else who might have persuaded Stanhope to open the bank again, nor any reason Stanhope might have returned there alone.

I can help you with that one, Marian thought grimly. Her mouth was dry. She hoped someone would offer her a cup of tea inside, or at least a glass of water. Of course, they might offer her nothing more than a pair of handcuffs. The approach she'd chosen was risky, but nothing else had gotten them anywhere.

"Miss Hartley? This way, please."

The teller opened a section of counter and ushered her through, leading her back through a door with a frosted glass pane. Two men waited in the office beyond. The one behind the desk looked like a banker, plump and graying and satisfied, though Marian didn't miss the worried quirk of his mouth. The second man was darker, leaner, younger. He leaned against the frame of an inner door, keeping his hands in the pockets of his dark suit. *Lawman!* Marian thought, but there was nothing for it but to go straight on.

"Miss, Hartley, is it?" The man behind the desk rose and gave her a courtly bow. "I'm Thaddeus Grove. This gentleman is Leo Pritchard, our vice president for operations. Please sit down."

Marian took a large leather chair across from him, even though it left Pritchard behind her. "It's very kind of you to see me," Marian said in a soft, demure voice. "I don't know quite how to begin."

"Perhaps you'd care for some water? Tea?"

"Please."

Pritchard stepped through the side doorway and returned a moment later with a tray holding a silver tea set and cups. Placing it on the edge of the desk, he poured a cup each for Marian and the banker. Then he retreated to the corner beside a tall oak filing cabinet. *Where he can watch my face*, Marian thought. *Call him whatever kind of vice president you want to, he's still a policeman.*

"Maybe you'd better begin with the note you sent in," Pritchard said. Grove shot him an annoyed look but said nothing. "You say you have information about a robbery?"

Marian sipped her tea. Grove had the big office, but Pritchard was the one in charge at this meeting. She put the cup down and nodded.

"I understand there's a reward for information about the robbery and killing here. Is that right?"

"There's a reward for information leading to the capture of James Lockhart and the return of the stolen banknotes," Thaddeus Grove said. "Can you help us with that, Miss Hartley?"

"Is the reward only for Lockhart, or for the identity of the real criminal?"

"What?"

"Lockhart escaped custody in California," Pritchard cut in. "It's probable he's killed at least one lawman since then. I'm satisfied he is the real criminal."

Marian looked directly at him. "You didn't think so at first. Your report to the police didn't even mention him. It wasn't until you heard about the other robberies that you changed your mind."

"How do you know that?"

"Is it true?"

Pritchard didn't answer. Thaddeus Grove cleared his throat.

"Young woman, we know that George Stanhope met Lockhart that night. Then, later, George returned to the bank, where he was murdered and the notes stolen. Except for Lockhart, no one outside the bank knew about the delivery of the notes. And no one has suggested any reason George might have returned unless he was forced to."

Marian smiled, trying to watch both men at once. "That's why I'm here. I know the reason."

Grove stared at her, waited. "Well?"

"About the reward. Is it just for information about Lockhart? Or are you interested in the truth?"

"We know the truth!"

"Wait, Thad," Pritchard said. He took a step closer to Marian, trying, she thought, to use size and nearness to intimidate her. He wasn't as good at it as Marshal Doom. "Lady, I want your truth. And the bank will back me on that. Won't it, Thad?"

"I'm not so sure about that."

"Won't it?"

"Why, of course."

"Very well." Marian put down her teacup. "A few weeks before Mr. Stanhope was killed, he made improper advances toward one of his female customers, a young woman seeking a loan."

"How dare you!" Grove was on his feet. "I knew George Stanhope for twenty years. I won't sit here and listen to you defile his name."

Pritchard waved a hand. "Sit down, Thad. We both knew George. Who was this woman, miss?"

"A young woman, I say, in straitened circumstances. I think I won't tell you her name just now."

"Maybe you'd tell it to the police."

Marian shrugged, though she felt cold all over. "If you wish. It was my thought you'd prefer to avoid having this become public."

"That's blackmail."

"Leo." Grove swallowed, slowly sat down again. "Miss Hartley is quite right. No more talk of the police."

"I think we should."

"No."

Pritchard looked unhappy. "All right. Let's hear the rest of it."

"The young lady says that he promised her an extension on her loan in return for certain favors." Marian looked down, hoping the men would take her disgust for ladylike reticence. It was one thing to make such a proposal to someone like her. For making it to Nellie North, Stanhope had deserved killing. "He arranged to meet with her at the bank late one night to consummate the arrangement. The lady agreed, but didn't keep the appointment."

"Hell," Pritchard said. "So she says. So *you* say. What does that prove, even if it's true?"

"One of the things he told her is that hers was not the first such case." Marian looked from Pritchard to Grove. "May I ask if anyone has investigated to see whom Mr. Stanhope might have been meeting that night?"

Grove took a handkerchief from his pocket, shook it out, wiped his forehead. "Miss, are you a newspaper reporter?"

"I am not."

"Let me seal a bargain with you, Miss Hartley."

"What bargain?"

"Mr. Pritchard and I will do a quiet investigation within the bank. May I have your word that you will neither say nor do anything to jeopardize that?"

"All right."

"Then, if you will return here to my office tomorrow afternoon, we will discuss the matter further."

Marian remembered to be predatory. "And the reward?"

"In due course."

"If this leads us anywhere," Pritchard added.

"I shall return tomorrow afternoon."

"Very well." More musing. "But should I need to contact you in the interim, where might I send a message?"

She thought of the Norths, of the danger she had already exposed them to. "I'm staying at the Ginnochio Hotel," she said, then wished she'd thought faster. It was one of the places the troupe had used when they'd played Fort Worth.

Pritchard made a note. "Don't get lost, Miss Hartley," he said. "We'll find you."

Not likely, cousin! "I'll be back for that reward," she said.

Neither Grove nor Pritchard offered a hand as she left the office. Feeling as if she'd just escaped being burned at the stake, she made for the front door, arriving just as a tall, pale man opened it from the outside. Removing his hat, he stood aside for her.

"Thank you." The words froze in her throat as she looked into a face she knew. It took her an instant to find the name. *Edward Givens, I think. One of Jim's friends. Good God.*

"My pleasure, ma'am." If Givens recognized her, neither his face nor his harsh voice gave any hint of it. He inclined his head to her and went inside the bank, leaving Marian staring.

What the hell's he doing here? Just following his route? Coincidence? Hard to trust coincidence, but he couldn't be looking for me and not recognize me when he saw me.

Recovering herself, she hurried away. In her confusion, she did not see at the far end of the block a large man holding a folded Denver newspaper.

13

Little China was not marked with a sign, but Rags seemed to know his way. Lockhart wasn't worried about finding the place. What worried him was the rider he had glimpsed paralleling their trail.

Rags had been expecting someone to meet him, either close to the railroad or at the Roost. He'd been visibly disappointed that morning when his expected reinforcements didn't arrive. He'd tried a dozen arguments to delay starting for Little China. Finally, Texas Bob had reared up in the blankets where he slept on the saloon's plank floor.

"Cap'n, if'n you can't get that little sidewinder moving, you just give me and Matthew a chance. With him caterwauling that way, can't an honest man sleep."

Matthew Quint thrust a shaggy head from his own blanket roll. "Nor a thieving one neither. One more peep out of you, Rags, and the King of China won't find enough of you to say grace over."

Still protesting, though not so loudly, Rags had led the way out of the Roost. But he'd kept on looking back, obviously hoping for help. Lockhart wondered if the distant rider was it.

Of course, there was no more reason to think the other rider was headed for Little China than to think he wasn't. He might be anyone—a drifter passing through, a fugitive outlaw looking for the Roost, an Indian cowhand searching out a lost calf. *Or he might be Marshal Doom, complete with handcuffs, all set to drag you in and watch you hang.* Lockhart smiled. That was foolishness; Henson might have gotten back to

Denver by now, but he could hardly pick up the trail so quickly.

Whoever the stranger was, he kept his distance. In No Man's Land, nobody was eager to crowd anyone else. Giving up on the question, Lockhart gave his attention to the narrow and rocky trail Rags swore would take them to Little China.

More than once, Lockhart thought he sensed the presence of lookouts, but he never saw any. Then, at a point where the trail seemed to end against a stone wall, a tall, thin Chinese man materialized in the trail. His black hair was done up in a long pigtail that swung behind him. He wore a brimless red brocade cap and a black robe like a light, loose-fitting duster without buttons. A wide red sash secured it at his waist. In his hands he held a factory-bright Winchester repeater, and Lockhart could see at least two revolvers and a long knife thrust into the sash.

"You stop," he said, raising the rifle just enough to give Lockhart a clear view down its bore. The Winchester was cocked and ready. Lockhart stopped, folding his hands over the reins on the saddle horn.

Rags had jumped in surprise when the sentry appeared. Now he raised his hands. "Us friends," he proclaimed in a high, hurried whine. "No shoot. Us want see number one big boss man, makee talk-talk. Got muchee big business. No shoot."

The thin man spoke to Lockhart. "The small noisy one is known to me. You are not known to me. What do you want?"

'It's my first visit to your country. I want an audience with the King."

"Wan Lo, he means," Rags said. "We got to see Wan Lo. How come you never talked real American to me before now, Ran Sing?"

"My esteemed master Wan Lo, whose illustrious name

should not be defiled by the tongue of a foreign devil, does not expect you today, small one. Your companion he does not expect at all, unless in the company of another."

"What other?" Lockhart asked. Then he held his tongue as Ran Sing's eyes swung his way, but he had to fight down a surge of excitement. He was on the right road! He might learn the answer he wanted, if he could avoid getting shot by the sentry. *Or crucified by the King.* But it was too late to worry about that now. He was pretty sure Ran Sing wasn't the only one with a gun pointed their way.

Composing his face into a mask as expressionless as the sentry's, he said, "Nevertheless, we are here. Tell your master I have a shipment of banknotes I wish to sell. Sixty thousand American dollars."

Ran Sing looked interested. "If so, they are well hidden."

"Yes."

"I will see them."

"No. I'll show you one of them if you'll allow me to remove it from my pocket." Getting no reply, Lockhart put his left hand inside his coat and produced a folded note, then held it out to the Chinese man.

Rags said, "Take it, Ran Sing. Won't bite you."

Whether relieved of any fear on that account, Ran Sing took the note and stared at it with the shrewdly appraising eye of a man who cannot read but can recognize familiar patterns. "One," he said, waving the paper note in the air. "Where are the many?"

"I will explain that to your master."

Ran Sing thought about it. "You will leave your firearms here," he said at last. "You may reclaim them should the generous and benevolent Wan Lo graciously permit you to return alive."

"Hey, listen—" Rags began, then broke off when the Winchester swung his way. "I ain't got no gun," he growled. "This Moneytree–Smith–Cap'n feller done took mine."

Ran Sing raised his eyebrows in polite acknowledgment. "A most wise precaution. You, then, will have more than one revolver to leave with me, not so?"

"So," Lockhart admitted. "Thanks, Rags."

He added the little man's Colt and the ancient hideout Navy to the pile. Ran Sing nodded and thrust out a bony arm.

"Go through there. Li Woo will do you the undeserved honor of escorting you the rest of the way."

"There" turned out to be a narrow fissure in the rock wall, the place from which Ran Sing must have emerged. Lockhart and Rags squeezed single-file through a passage some sixteen or eighteen feet long and barely wide enough for the horses. Looking up, Lockhart could see dappled patches of sunlight high on the walls, but overhanging rocks shut out any direct view of the sky.

At the far end, a young Chinese woman waited for them, sitting sidesaddle on a prancing black mare. She might have been anywhere between fifteen and thirty for all Lockhart could tell. Her fine-boned face was beautiful and delicate as a porcelain doll's. She was dressed in the same garb as Ran Sing, but her long mane of hair flowed unbound and black as a raven's wing. Her hands were folded inside the long black sleeves of her robe.

"You will please deign to accompany this ignorant and unworthy person," she said in a low, musical voice.

Rags looked at her in alarm. "What about the blindfolds? Ain't you gonna give us blindfolds?"

"No blindfolds will be needed."

"My God, no blindfolds! I ain't going!"

The young woman withdrew one small hand from her sleeve. She held a Smith & Wesson American revolver. Its ugly shape and long barrel seemed too harsh and heavy for her, but the muzzle was steady on the little man's chest.

"That would be most regrettable. Please to follow."

"No blindfolds," Rags whimpered to Lockhart. He was

sweating and his eyes showed white. " 'We'll just us go see the King ourselves,' you said. 'We can make the deal without Sim or nobody else,' you said. No blindfolds!"

Lockhart tried to ignore him, but the little man's fear was contagious. The path led along what had once been a narrow streambed. High gray-black rock walls, scoured and polished by the floods of centuries, seemed to meet somewhere overhead. The canyon wound and twisted, branching as it went downhill. Even without a blindfold, Lockhart was far from sure he could find his way in again.

Or out. If we have to run for it, there had better be another way out.

Little China, when they reached it, looked like a bigger Roost. Lying at the foot of steep cliffs in an apparently blind side canyon, it consisted of a scatter of wooden buildings surrounding a spring. A long, low, many-windowed hut was probably a barracks. The big square log building from which woodsmoke and the smell of boiling cabbage arose was obviously the cookhouse. The others might have been anything— dwellings or storehouses or even a saloon like the one at the Roost. Lockhart, staring into the smoky gloom where the sun seemed unlikely ever to penetrate, saw nothing in the structures that suggested any influence from Chinese architecture.

The pool around the spring, though, was different. Its border had been paved with tiny green tiles. Flowers that Lockhart couldn't identify grew everywhere, though the first freeze of the year must have been a month past. As he dismounted, following Li Woo's lead, he caught a glimpse of orange and golden carp swimming languidly in the clear water.

"This way."

Tying her horse in front of the largest building, Li Woo waited for Rags and Lockhart to dismount, then led them to the steps. At the doorway she stopped, glided to one side, and bowed.

"Please to honor this insignificant slave by entering. The illustrious Wan Lo will see you."

"Oh, God. God help us," Rags moaned.

Lockhart said, "After you," with the thought that the smaller man might be a more welcome and familiar visitor. Rags didn't see it that way. He hung back. Lockhart could smell his fear. "All right, I'll go."

Pushing aside the heavy canvas flap at the doorway, he went inside. On the threshold he halted to blink in disbelief. If the outside had been pure American shanty, the building's interior was China. The walls seemed to throb and shimmer with tapestries rich in gold embroidery. Dragons wound their sinuous length from panel to panel, unicorns pawed and stamped, a fierce-eyed demon gathered men in a basket for some purpose Lockhart suspected wasn't benevolent. Heavy rugs, bright with flowers and winding geometric patterns, covered the floors. Gilded statues and polished bronze shields reflected light from a hundred flickering oil lamps.

"Please to proceed," Li Woo prompted.

Lockhart shook himself, half expecting to awake from a dream. Two muscular Chinese, looking at first like two more statues, stood on either side of the doorway. They wore a shorter, tighter version of Li Woo's sashed wraparound, but theirs were in red with black sashes. They didn't seem to have guns, but each held a long, straight broadsword upright in his hand. Firelight gleamed on the naked blades.

At the far side of the room, an even larger and heavier man sat in a massive wooden armchair which Lockhart immediately took to be his throne. A slender youngster of fifteen or so stood behind his right shoulder, and four more guards towered at the sides of the throne. Li Woo led Lockhart and the cowering Rags to a place directly before the seated man. Bowing from the waist, she spoke to him in rippling Chinese.

"So."

Wan Lo's single word seemed to echo from inside a gigantic bell. He rested one hand easily on the broad arm of his chair and leaned forward, stroking his pointed beard with the other. Without apparent interest, he gazed at Rags and Lockhart. Not knowing what was expected, Lockhart kept silent, but Rags gave a hasty bow and burst into an apology.

"It ain't none of this my doing, your majesty, I wouldn't never have thought to bother you off'n my own hook, but this here Moneytree threatened my life to make me bring him here the which I wouldn't never've done but what I thought he might have something you'd want because—"

Wan Lo raised one finger of the hand that rested on the chair arm. The guard nearest to Rags stepped forward. Almost too fast for Lockhart's eye to follow, his great broadsword swung in a whistling arc. Lockhart closed his one eye and waited to hear the little man's head bounce on the floor. Instead, Rags let out a squeal, trying without moving his head to look down at the bright blade that poised an inch from his throat.

"That will do." The bell in Wan Lo's voice tolled mild amusement. "Brutus was to come with you. Where is he?"

Brutus. In spite of himself, Lockhart strained forward, bringing a sharp look from Wan Lo. *Brutus. What's his last name? Who the hell is my Brutus!*

"Well?" Wan Lo said. Rags gulped, his bobbing adam's apple almost touching the raw-looking sharpened steel along the blade's edge. Wan Lo raised the finger again. "Be brief."

"I—I don't know, your highness. He didn't meet us where he was supposed to. I was all for waiting, but this one would come!"

"But instead, you saw fit to ignore my order and bring a stranger among us. I am displeased." The Chinese frowned, and Rags shut up with an apprehensive glance at the guard with the sword. Wan Lo turned black eyes on Lockhart.

"You have heard my name. This inconsequential

stripling"—he gestured at the tall young man behind him—
"is my son, Wan Chan. My worthless daughter you have met
already. You may speak."

Lockhart bowed as Rags and the woman had done. He
wondered at the difference in names if Li Woo was a daughter, but it didn't seem the right moment to ask. "Thank you,"
he said. "I am honored to be in the presence of the great
Wan Lo, whose fame has spread far beyond the bounds of his
most honorable kingdom."

"It is an honor few of your race seek." Wan Lo rubbed
his mouth, whether to hide a smile, Lockhart couldn't tell.
"What is it you want?"

Lockhart hesitated long enough for the King to notice.
His thin cover story about stolen banknotes had made everyone suspicious, Rags and Sim Janks and even the sentry at the
gate. He suspected it would be fatal to rouse Wan Lo's suspicions.

"I ask a favor. I am prepared to pay for it."

The hard eyes narrowed. "It was my impression you
wished to sell me something. Banknotes."

"That's what the bastard told me, your grace, I swear it."

"That was a lie," Lockhart said, "to fool your agents and
get into your presence. I would not think to pit my insignificant wits against those of the brilliant"—*that's Marian's
word*—"Wan Lo."

"Only once would you think thus. Who are you?"

When in doubt, tell the truth. Lockhart took a deep breath.
"My name is James Lockhart."

Wan Lo's reply was no more than a polite hiss of breath,
but Rags turned white. Heedless even of the sword that hovered before him, he turned to stare at Lockhart.

"Lockhart! My God Almighty, if these heathen don't kill
me, Sim will sure for not killing *you!* But first he'll about pull
your guts out and hang 'em in a tree for what you done to his
onliest brother!"

Wan Lo tapped the arm of the chair. This time, the blade nicked the sagging skin of Rag's throat, bringing a drop of blood. The little man rose on tiptoe, leaning away. He seemed to have forgotten what he wanted to say.

"These interruptions grow tiresome," Wan Lo said in a mild tone. To Lockhart, he said, "A favor, you say. What favor do you ask of Wan Lo?"

"The name of the man who robbed the banks in Denver and three other cities, who killed two of my customers and put the blame on me."

A smile tinted Wan Lo's round face. "Simple enough. What would you pay to gain such knowledge?"

"Anything I can. For openers, the banknotes. I don't have the sixty thousand I baited your helpers with, but I do have about two thousand from my sample case. It's yours for the name."

Prince Chan leaned down to whisper something to his father. The King stroked his beard, looking at Lockhart.

"Blockhead though he is, my son yet poses a perceptive question. If I agree to your bargain, would you be satisfied with this knowledge?"

"I would."

"Then you would gladly give up your life the moment it came into your possession?"

That caught Lockhart by surprise. Rags moaned.

"Not gladly," Lockhart said. "Not willingly. I seek the knowledge so I can spend it elsewhere."

"And your knowledge of the way to my kingdom—how and where would you spend that?"

Now we come to the problem, Lockhart thought. It was a direct and obvious question. He wished for an equally direct and obvious answer. "I wouldn't," he said, knowing that wasn't the one Wan Lo would accept.

"Mr. Lockhart, I believe you have some familiarity with your poet, William Shakespeare?"

Now what in hell does he know about that? "Some. I'm learning more all the time."

"I surmised as much. Learning can be quite pleasant with the right teacher." Wan Lo gave Lockhart a moment to wonder what else he knew. Then he waved a hand in a gesture that took in his throne, the building, all of Little China. " 'To be thus is nothing but to be safely thus.' Has your education extended so far as that?"

"No. But I take your meaning."

Wan Lo indicated Rags without looking at him. "This one will not reveal our secrets to your lawmen. He fears— quite rightly—that my agents would slit that scrawny throat before his last word was out. His ugly friend with the ugly name, Janks, will not betray us because he has his own sort of integrity." The King leaned forward, resting his elbow on his knees while he stroked his beard. "I detect no such fear in you, Mr. Lockhart. Do you have the integrity to keep our secrets?"

He's playing with you. It's a trap. But trap or not, Lockhart still had to answer. Would Wan Lo believe a ringing protestation of loyalty? *Of course not. That's what he'd get from Rags.*

"I can give you my word, Wan Lo, but you don't know what that's worth. You'll have to decide if you can trust me to keep it."

Wan Lo raised his eyebrows. Leaning back in his chair, he frowned. The young prince again leaned to whisper something, but Wan Lo waved him away.

"I perhaps know more than you think, Mr. Lockhart. Strange to say, your offer tempts me. It would be novel to do business with an honest man."

For one dizzy moment, Lockhart thought he was going to get away with it. Somewhere out in the real world a gun boomed, awaking echoes in the outer canyon. Other shots followed. Lockhart heard Rags take a breath, felt the armed giants move in to close a ring about the two of them. Li Woo had disappeared somewhere at the first shot. Lockhart hoped that whatever swamp he'd blundered into had a bottom, but he felt as if he were in over his head and sinking like lead.

"I have perhaps misjudged your honesty," Wan Lo remarked, apparently unconcerned though the noise was clearly getting nearer. "Is this your work?"

"It's him, your worship, I swear," Rags yelled, pointing a shaking finger at Lockhart. "It's all his doing! I got no part in it. I'm your friend!"

"We're alone," Lockhart said. "Your man has our guns." He held out his hands with upturned palms as the guards closed in more tightly. "I don't have any idea what's happening out there."

Wan Lo nodded. "I believe you. However, coincidence is confusing."

He raised his hand. The guards raised their swords.

"Wait, your lordship!" Rags cried. He bowed deeply. His oversized cap fell off. He reached for it and came back up with a vicious little four-barreled Remington pistol in his hand. "Stand back, you heathen! I ain't got any part in this."

One of the swords whistled down. Lockhart heard the shot and solid *chunk* of an ax splitting firewood at the same instant, but he didn't see what had happened. He had dived to the side as another blade slashed his way. Immediately, another and larger gun roared from the doorway. The guard pursuing Lockhart fell. The deep bell of Wan Lo's voice pealed an alarm as the big gun boomed again, filling the room with acrid powder smoke.

Lockhart kept on the move, dodging swords and dreading bullets, until he found a corner to get his back into. Obscured by the smoke, some sort of scrambling conflict was going on at the other end of the room. Before he could decide whether to stand his ground or run, Lockhart found Wan Lo looming through the haze.

"You!" Wan Lo's eyes were bright as polished coal, but

the long knife in his hand shone even brighter. Lockhart grabbed his wrist as the blade started down. For a moment, the two grappled, but Lockhart knew it was a losing fight. Wan Lo's superior weight and leverage told, forcing Lockhart to his knees, driving the knife downward until the shining point touched the lapel of his leather coat.

"Stand back!"

Even in his confusion and his fear for his own life, Lockhart recognized the bellowing voice. *Nightmare. This whole thing's been a blessed nightmare. I'll wake up in a minute safe in bed in the hotel with Marian beside me.* He felt the knife slice through the leather and draw blood over his heart. *But it had better be soon!*

One last gunshot crashed out. Wan Lo shuddered. He stared down at Lockhart; his eyes were still implacable, but his knife arm seemed to lose its strength. A trickle of blood came from the corner of his mouth, dripped down onto the breast of the silken robe. Slowly, the King of Little China fell to one side.

Lockhart had but one thought. He knelt beside the stricken King. "The name. What is his name?"

Wan Lo focused on his face with some difficulty. Then he smiled and shook his head slightly. "You presented no merchandise," he said.

A tall man with white hair materialized through the smoke, pointed one of his heavy revolvers at Lockhart, then looked down. At his feet, a dead guard lay on top of Rags. Lockhart looked only once, saw what the sword had done to the little man, and turned away. He had seen enough of that to last out his lifetime.

His back to Henson, he fumbled in his coat for his other samples, found them, fanned them out before Wan Lo's eyes. The dying man said, "So. You did not lie."

"I did not. Tell me the name. *Please.*"

Wan Lo looked past him. Henson was bending over

them now, listening. The King's black eyes came back to Lockhart.

"Two . . . names. Brutus and . . . his companion." He smiled. "You of all people should know," he said. Then he was dead.

"If that's not just like a Chinaman," Henson said. "Invented gunpowder back before Noah's Flood sometime, and still can't think but to put some damned big knife up against a Colt." Holstering one of his guns, he reached down and hauled Lockhart to his feet. "Move along. Won't those guards of his stay spooked long, and likely they'll next time come shooting."

"You heard him," Lockhart said. "He knew the name of the man who stole my banknotes. You heard him, didn't you?"

"Heard and saw enough to hang you another time over, if any more evidence was needful. By rights, I should've let him slice you up, but I won't have it said I lost a prisoner that way."

"But he gave us the man!"

Henson was prodding him toward the doorway. "Move, I say! Less'n you still want to end up carved like an ox, that is. Those guards won't be playing. Up on that horse and ride ahead of me, pronto!"

Back on his own horse, Lockhart spurred out in the direction Henson pointed. The marshal was close behind, bellowing orders and firing back over his mount's tail with one revolver. A few bullets followed them out. Lockhart didn't think the Chinese would try to pursue, but Henson wasn't taking that chance. He forced a gallop until both horses were streaked with sweat and breathing in great heaves. At last, he allowed Lockhart to drop back to a walk.

"Then there really is another way in," Lockhart said. "How'd you find it?"

"Would've found the road to Hades, did I know you were headed there. When I found out who you'd been seen alongside of in Denver, wasn't any question where you were headed."

So much for all our careful disguise. Lockhart slumped in the saddle, the reaction from his escape just beginning to hit him. *And so much for proving my innocence. Any hope of that died with Wan Lo.*

"Pull up."

Henson drew one of his revolvers, shucked out the hulls, and began to reload it. "This time I'm not going to chain you. All I'm going to do is shoot you right out of the saddle if you do anything funny at all. Understood?"

"Understood."

"Then turn and ride."

Lockhart turned and rode. Glancing back, he saw Henson listing in the saddle. The marshal's face had lost its normal reddish flush and now showed patches of gray.

"Marshal? Is anything the matter?"

"Nothing for you to fret over. You want to worry, worry about the hangman. Ride, I said."

"Wan Lo could've proved I was innocent. He tried to tell me with his last breath who the real killer was. Didn't you hear him?"

"Heard gibberish. Saw you trying to deal with him. For banknotes. Stole some we didn't know about. I guess."

"Marshal?"

"Ride."

"Marshal." Lockhart reined in, half-turned in the trail. "What's the matter?"

Henson lifted his pistol. He tried to train it on Lockhart, but the barrel wavered downward. Hunching himself over the saddle horn, Henson made another try. This time, the black muzzle centered on Lockhart's chest.

"Won't. Tell. You. Again."

"You're hurt."

"Don't." The pistol drooped in Henson's hand. He jerked it up again. "Count. On."

Before he could finish, his eyes rolled up to white. He slid sideways out of his saddle, landing in the trail like a sack of grain. Only then did Lockhart see that the back and left side of Henson's gray coat was dyed a sodden reddish-black with blood.

14

"That's a bad cut," Doc Odum said. He clucked his tongue, examining the deep straight slash under Henson's left arm more closely. Then he looked at Lockhart. "What in tunket made him wait so long to do anything about it?"

"I don't know. I guess he figured it would stop bleeding on its own."

Doc snorted. "Would've done that, certain sure, just so soon as he ran plumb out of blood. His well's pretty nigh dry now. You didn't get that bandage on him none too quick."

"We were busy."

Henson lay on the rude bar in the Roost's saloon, his coat and shirt sliced away to reveal the wound. He was unconscious, and Lockhart devoutly prayed he would stay that way. Bringing him to the Roost had been a desperate idea, but it was the only place Lockhart knew of within a day's ride that might have a doctor—or someone who could pass for one.

"Busy, was it? This feller's lucky to still have an arm. Or

a head, either." Doc spat on the floor. "Well, the bleeding's as stopped as it'll ever be. Get me my needle and thread, Bob."

"You want your bonnet and thimble too, Auntie?"

"Don't recollect you being so snippety when they brought you in with a bullet under your short ribs and blood every time you went to the privy. Back last February, was it?"

"March," Texas Bob said. "I'll get your tools."

"Bring my little round glasses, too. I'll stitch him up as tight as a quilt from the Ladies Missionary Society."

Lockhart hadn't met Doc Odum on his first visit to the Roost. Evidently, the place had a larger population than he'd suspected. At least a dozen men he hadn't seen before had heard about the wounded man and come to watch the fun. One of them toward the back of the crowd caught Lockhart's attention. Among the shaggy and bearded denizens of the Roost, he was cleanshaven and looked as if he'd seen a barber within the last month. His face was strikingly handsome below the wide brim of a white sombrero. Though he wore the same rough trail clothes as the rest, he wore them awkwardly.

Like a man playing a part. Something in that nagged at Lockhart's mind, but he shrugged it off. *Well, hell, why should I be the only one here pretending to be something I'm not?*

"I can tell this is Chinese work," Matthew Quint said. "Keep them big swords stropped sharp enough to shave. How'd you get out there without them nicking you, Cap'n?"

"Lucky."

"What about Rags?"

"He wasn't."

Doc took a pair of wire-rimmed spectacles from Texas Bob and perched them on his long nose. "That's better. Could you bring me that lamp over here? Good. Now bring me some whiskey."

"He won't know you give it to him."

"Not going to."

Doc took the bottle that one of the men held out, pulled the cork, splashed a dollop of the raw amber liquid into Henson's wound. Even in unconsciousness, the marshal heaved himself half upright and let out a groan. Pushing him down, Doc repeated the process until the cut was thoroughly clean.

"Don't know why you always do that," Texas Bob said.

" 'Cause I've found out only about half my patients die when I do."

" 'Stead of all of 'em, like before," Matthew Quint murmured. "Waste of good whiskey."

"I wouldn't do it with good whiskey, only this coffin varnish of yours." He took a deep pull from the bottle himself, then set it aside and squinted to thread his needle. "Wish I'd knowed that trick back when I was sawing off arms for Gen'l Lee."

Texas Bob steadied the old man's trembling hand. "Thought you was with Bragg's army, Doc."

"Him, too. Can't get this consarned thing to hold still."

"And Kirby Smith's."

"I got around some in them days. There!" Doc took another drink from the bottle. "Now you'll see some fancy stitching. Hm, not so much of a cut really, not hardly worth the thread. I mind I once sewed up a greenhorn in Californy—"

"You never been to California."

"—or Kansas or someplace had tangled with a grizzly bear. Counted three hundred thirteen stitches up to the knot. Tied the loose end onto another spool and went on till I ran right out. That's good whiskey. Where've you had it hid?"

Lockhart at first wondered if he was endangering Henson's life even more by letting this half-crazy old coot get at him. But while Doc's cracked voice rambled, his fingers were expertly pulling the raw edges of the cut together with neat, tight stitches. Reassured, Lockhart watched without looking while his thoughts washed over a hundred grislier scenes

from his Army days to sweep up like waves against the wall
of Wan Lo's death.

*The son of a bitch could have told me my enemy's name. In-
stead, he laughed at me while his men were chopping up my companions and while Henson's bullet was chewing at his heart.* It
had not earlier occurred to him that Henson's presence could
have sealed off the whole matter. *Why hell. Had the King told
me and had Henson heard him say the name, I'd be cleared. Instead, the villain did me more harm than good. He all but made it
sound as if I were the man myself!*

"Cap'n, what's the matter with you asleep in your tracks?
I was asking you who is this old man?"

Lockhart looked into Matthew Quint's beady eyes. "Said
his name was Henderson. Don't know what he was doing at
Little China, but it wasn't for no Sunday School picnic.
Them guards with the shiny knives would've had me for hash
if it wasn't for him."

"Henderson." Quint scratched his head. "Don't sound
right."

"May not be. I've heard that not every man in this territory uses his own name."

Two or three of them laughed. "That true, Cap'n
Smith?"

"He puts me in mind of somebody."

"Everybody puts you in mind of somebody, Matthew,"
Texas Bob said. "You're getting as bad as Doc here."

Quint smiled like a good-natured bear. "Reckon that's
so. Why, just today I was thinking I'd seen—"

"Henson!"

The man in the white sombrero had been talking to another of the crowd. He moved away, while the second man
pushed toward the bar.

"What's that you're saying, Curly?"

"He ain't no Henderson. That there's U.S. Marshal

Rance Henson, and I'm to be damned if I don't believe he's got a warrant in his pocket on half the men here."

Lockhart said, "I believe you're to be damned all right," to make the rest of them laugh. "But I'll swear he's no law-man, the way he cleaned out that bunch at Little China and shot down the King."

"Wan Lo's shot? Why hell, I heard bullets wouldn't pierce him."

"Hear that? Cap'n says the top Chinaman's dead."

Curly wasn't to be distracted. "Come to that, I don't know *you*," he growled at Lockhart. "Could be you're an-other one in cahoots with him."

Matthew Quint turned. He still looked like a bear, but no longer a good-natured one. "Well, I know the Cap'n. And I'll vouch for him, even if I did remember it wrong."

"I'm telling you true I've saw this man and he was a damned marshal of some kind, and by our law we should rightly hang him. I'm going through his pockets, and if I find a badge, we *will* hang him."

That was all right with Lockhart. He'd already been through Henson's pockets. The marshal's badge was safe in his own coat, and nothing else with Henson's name or pro-fession remained to be found. His saddlebags had indeed been crammed with warrants and other documents. Lockhart had kept the material relating to him and Marian and, after some hesitation, had burned the rest.

"Go ahead. Just be sure what you take from his pockets doesn't end up in yours."

"Just a second," Doc said. "Don't disturb the master at work. There!" He tied a final knot. "Good a job as you'll even see."

"It's a wonder you don't sew your fingers together, you old drunk."

"What?" A look of concern came over Doc's face. He

held up his left hand with the fingers cupped tightly together. "Why, I just believe I did!"

When Curly bent forward to look, Doc waggled the fingers in his face and laughed thunderously. The others joined in, and Curly's face went red. Bending over the wounded man, he rapidly and roughly searched his pockets. Halfway through, Henson stirred and tried to sit up.

" . . . going on?" he muttered vaguely. "Stand back . . . name of the . . . "

"He's in pain, Doc," Lockhart cried. "Give him some of that whiskey."

"Barely enough left for me," Doc complained, but he tilted the neck of the bottle to Henson's mouth. The lawman gurgled, choked on the raw liquor, lay back again.

"Stop! Name of . . . "

"There! You hear that? I say we hang him."

"I didn't hear nothing."

"Curly's right. We can't afford to take the chance."

"I heard that there Henson's a ring-tailed roarer. This white-haired old billygoat don't look the part."

"Don't matter. We ain't had a good hanging for nigh three months."

Lockhart took a step aside to put his back to the bar. *Hell. This wasn't the way I meant to die, keeping somebody from hanging the man that wants to hang me! Sorry, Marian, but the bastard did save my life.* Slowly enough not to attract attention, he drew one of the marshal's Colts. When he cocked it, he had everyone's attention.

"Listen," he said. "I don't care if this man's a criminal or a marshal or General Sherman hisself. He saved my life, and anybody hangs him will have to hang me first."

"Sherman," Henson said. "General." Lockhart hoped he wouldn't start singing "Marching Through Georgia."

"We got two ropes."

"You got three, Curly?" Quint asked, moving over beside Lockhart.

Doc Odum burped. "Better make it four. I wasted half a spool of good thread and half a bottle of the worst tarantula juice I ever saw on this patient. Wouldn't be professional to let some yahoo hang him now."

"You old fool."

"Didn't get this old by being a fool, Curly."

Lockhart held Henson's Colt steady on Curly. He wished he knew where the man in the white hat had gone, but he didn't have time to look. The crowd was wavering, some in favor of Curly's side, some undecided.

"You got two lives?"

"Hell's fire, Captain."

"That's right. You ought to see the gate to hell yawning at you right about now."

Doc cackled. "He's right. I smell the sulphur burning."

"He can't shoot us all!"

"Now, gents." Texas Bob's voice was soft, but it was punctuated by the sharp snick of metal. Lockhart glanced his way to see him holding a big-bored double shotgun. "Let's keep this thing polite."

"Listen, Bob!"

"You listen, Curly. I got a little to say about what goes on in this wickiup, and I ain't figuring on any hanging today, less'n it's you."

"Our law says hang him."

"Our law says a man that makes trouble gets banished. It says you kill a man here, you hang—no self-defense, no circumstances, no nothing. We bury the loser and hang the winner, savvy? Back off."

Curly backed off.

"Cap'n?"

Lockhart holstered his gun.

"All right. I'm glad we got that settled. Cap'n, probably it'd be best if you and your friend spent the night in the back room. Me and Matthew will help you get him there."

"Thanks."

"*Por nada.*" Texas Bob glanced back to see that the others had gone back to their drinking. In a quieter voice, he said, "Nothing against you, but I'd take it a kindness if you'd ride out soon's your friend can sit his horse."

"We'll be gone before daybreak."

"I'll have Cookie fix you some biscuits to take along. And I'll see Curly and his buzzards don't follow after you."

"Right."

Scooping the half-conscious Henson up in his arms, Matthew Quint chuckled.

"I swan, Cap'n, if that weren't just like the old days. You ain't changed a bit." Then he frowned. "Shows how your mind can play tricks, though. The more I thought on it, the more I was ready to swear it was your other eye you lost that time."

Sergeant Quint's last remark assured Lockhart of a sleepless night, so he was up and ready to leave early. He saddled and bridled the two horses, collected his and Henson's gear, stopped by the cookhouse for the promised biscuits and a cup of coffee.

"I wrapped up a mite of fatback and some grits in there, too," the cook told him. "Mind you stop to eat it before the grease soaks through."

"Just like the Army."

"Pardon?"

"I will. Thanks."

Henson had either slept well or fallen unconscious for much of the night. He looked better than he had the day before. Though he was still deathly pale, his eyes focused on Lockhart and he seemed to know what was happening. He leaned heavily on Lockhart's shoulder as they went out to the horses. Lockhart said, "Can you get up?"

Henson nodded, then leaned against his horse. Lockhart helped him get a boot in the stirrup and boosted him into the saddle. The marshal said, "I'll have my guns."

"Maybe." *Quick recovery!* "As soon as we're clear of this place, we'll talk about it."

"And my badge."

"Don't even talk about that badge."

Leading his own horse, Lockhart walked beside the marshal. As best he could, he retraced the route along which Rags had brought him into the Roost, back down the dry riverbed and along the sandy creek bottoms. It was hard going for a man on foot, and apparently not much better for Henson. The marshal was still weak. He swayed in the saddle, and he tended to slide off into sleep, much to his own annoyance. Doc Odum had strapped his left arm up and put it in a sling, and Lockhart could see that bothered him, too. But he wanted to talk.

"This is the second time you've stole a gun from me. Not counting that hideout pistol the woman took from my saddlebags. Nor my Winchester. Nor that twenty-eight dollars."

"I gave the first gun back," Lockhart said. "Didn't you find it?"

"By the ghost of Julius Caesar, you admit it! God knows Lucius Martin was a poor excuse for a lawman, but that doesn't justify your killing him."

Lockhart shook his head. "Martin was a better excuse for a lawman than you know. He saved my life, and Marian's." Then he looked up at Henson. The marshal was watching him narrowly. "You're being tricky again, Marshal. You know by now that Lucius wasn't killed with your gun."

"Doesn't matter whose gun killed him, if you and Phineas Janks were throwed in together."

"Have it your way. But keep your voice down. There are guards with rifles up along the rim, so don't rile them."

They were well along the trail back to Liberal when Lockhart deemed it safe to stop. He found a gully with a thread of creek running down it and ample grass for the horses. Henson had been silent for some time. He muttered something when Lockhart helped him down, then sank into what seemed an exhausted sleep. Lockhart stretched him on a blanket and hobbled the horses to graze. Then he carefully unwrapped the marshal's arm.

The wound had bled just enough to stain the bandage. Lockhart could see no sign of infection. Doc Odum's sewing job might not win prizes at a county fair, but it seemed to be what Henson had needed.

With the bandage changed and the marshal still sleeping, Lockhart sat down at the edge of the creek to eat his breakfast. He had finished and was wondering if it would be safe to boil up a pot of coffee when his horse suddenly threw up its head and whickered a greeting to some unseen animal. Lockhart was instantly on his feet, reaching for the marshal's right-hand Colt.

Winchester's still on the saddle. Stupid. Think you were safe here, did you? Just trusted Texas Bob when he said he'd handle Curly? Damn, Lockhart, act your age!

"Who's there?"

Getting no answer, he ran west along the creek, bending to stay below the edge of the cutbank. After thirty yards, he threw himself at the southern bank—*whoever's there will come from the south*—scrambled up, and poised on the rim, gun in hand.

A black horse shied at the unexpected sight of him. The rider fought for control, one hand on the reins, the other clawing for the saddle horn. He lost his white sombrero when the black reared, but managed to hold his seat. By the time he got the horse calmed and could think about anything else, Lockhart was standing flatfooted in easy range with the Colt trained on him.

"Stand and deliver, you carpetbagging Yankee bastard. One move and I'll blow you to hell!"

His visitor threw back his head and laughed. Hat and all, it was the same man he'd seen in the Roost just before Curly had decided to hang Henson. Lockhart had first tagged him as handsome. On closer inspection that label still held. He looked a little younger than Lockhart, his thick wavy black hair showing just a distinguished tint of gray. He had a square, manly jaw, a high-bridged nose, and frank brown eyes beneath bushy brows.

"Very good, Mr. Lockhart. The real Captain Ross couldn't have done it better. And your performance at the Roost was every bit as convincing."

Lockhart tried to keep his expression from changing, but he'd never had a poker face. "Lockhart?" he growled. "Who's that?"

"Come, Mr. Lockhart, don't play games. You were quick enough to reveal your identity in Little China, or so I'm told." He made a gesture toward his fallen hat. "May I get down? We could talk more comfortably."

"Maybe you should throw down your pistol first."

"I don't believe so. But you're free to shoot if I make a questionable move." Without waiting for an answer, he swung down from the black and bent to recover his hat. Brushing its crown with his sleeve, he said, "It's contrary to your interest to shoot me, just as it's contrary to mine to shoot you. Shall we go down to your camp, Mr. Lockhart?"

Lockhart thought about it, then shrugged. "All right. But you have the advantage of me."

"Yes, and I intend to keep it for awhile. If you need a name, you may call me—"

"Brutus," Lockhart finished.

The man paused, turned to look at Lockhart. "Very good, Mr. Lockhart." His tone was still light, but there was a new and more cautious look in his eyes. "You're clever."

"Thanks." Lockhart gestured with the Colt. "Down there. And you haven't yet convinced me it's contrary to my interest to shoot you."

Leaving the black tied to the ground, Brutus scrambled down the bank. He was awkward at it. *City boy.* But what could he make of that? He wasn't exactly an intrepid scout himself.

Henson's eyes were still closed and he was breathing in a rasping half-snore. Lockhart worried about him. What had Doc said? "*. . . only about half my patients die. . . .*"

Brutus also seemed worried about Henson. After a searching glance at the marshal, he moved several yards downstream, motioning for Lockhart to follow.

"I don't want to be overheard, Mr. Lockhart." Brushing off a spot on the grass, he sat down. "As for your self-interest, there's this: I can clear you."

Lockhart caught his breath. "What?"

"Oh, yes. I know who stole the banknotes you're accused of taking. And I'm willing to help you clear yourself. In return for your help."

Lockhart squatted opposite him, keeping the Colt ready. "You know all this because you were in on it. You're the one who brought them to Little China to sell."

"That's right. But the game has become much too hot for me. For one thing, the King is very angry."

"The King is dead."

Brutus smiled. "The King is dead; long live the King. *King* Wan Chan has put a price on the head of his father's killer. And on yours, too. He was inclined to execute me."

"Too bad."

"But I convinced him I could make amends. The other thing is that many of my employer's helpers are dying suddenly. I don't want to join them."

"You mentioned my help."

"Yes." Reaching carefully inside his coat, the man withdrew a long thin cigar. He lighted it with a scratch of the match against a fingernail and puffed with maddening deliberation. "Your help in return for mine." He blew out a stream of smoke. "You see, we'll have to kill my employer. Then I can testify to your innocence, and there'll be no one to tie me to the notes."

"How about Sim Janks?"

"Janks would never talk. Rags would have, but"—a shrug—"that's attended to."

"I see." Lockhart tried to look like he was thinking it over. If he could jump the man, get him disarmed without damaging him, he would have something concrete to show Henson. He suspected the marshal could convince Brutus to tell what he knew.

Brutus stood up suddenly, his hand going to his pistol. Lockhart raised the Colt.

"I hardly think you'll shoot, Mr. Lockhart. We have much in common. More than you know. I can make your life easier in several ways."

My life. What life? Reputation ruined, people's trust shattered, everything gone. You can give my life back, you bastard!

He cocked the Colt. "I could break your leg."

"Dangerous. I might bleed to death. Gangrene might set in. I might even draw and beat you to the punch, or force you to hurry your shot and kill me."

Lockhart hesitated. "Suppose I agreed. Then what?"

"There's just one more thing." Slowly, keeping the muzzle pointing away from Lockhart, Brutus drew his gun. He walked down the creek toward the place where Henson lay. "I have to placate the King of China. And there's only one way to do that."

With a cold shock, Lockhart realized what he meant to do. He rose, bringing the Colt up.

"No."

"You must see there's no other way. Marshal Doom will

simply disappear, and no one the wiser. You and I will bring the real bank robber to justice, clear your name, collect the rewards, and go our separate ways."

The heavy revolver shook in Lockhart's fist. He wrapped his other hand around the grip and leveled it. "No!"

On the ground, Henson seemed to wake suddenly. Seeing the figure looming over him, he half-rose, cried out, fell back. Raising one foot, he tried to kick at Brutus. The man jumped back, brought his gun around to fire.

"Don't!" Lockhart said. *He was on the battlefield at Franklin. Dead Rebs, still ranked in regimental order where they'd fallen. Dead Federals where the outlying picket had been overrun. Lockhart walking under a leaden winter sky, looking for a friend. A movement ahead—a man—scavenger, stripping the bodies. Robbing the dead.*

"Halt. Stop that!"

Snaggled teeth in a grin. Tatters of uniform, maybe blue, maybe gray.

"It's all right, mister. They be Rebs. Still some life in this one, but I'll tend to that."

A white hand reaching up from the ground, trying to fend off the knife. A cackle.

"Stop!"

Lockhart fired.

The bullet slammed Brutus back against the bank. He turned, red staining his brown vest, stared incredulously at Lockhart. "You . . . fool!"

"Drop the gun."

But the gun was coming up, the wild vindictive light in Brutus's eyes showing he didn't care now, and there was no choice. At the second shot, he doubled over and fell across Henson's legs. The marshal pushed at his body, staring at Lockhart.

"Good God Almighty!"

"Yeah." Lockhart thought of trying to explain it all to

Henson. No point. He'd had his bird in hand, and he'd shot it. No point. "That's how it was at Franklin, too."

"What?"

It had been the worst moment of the war for Lockhart. He'd knelt over the bony corpse of the scavenger, sick that the man had been reduced to robbing the dead, sick that he'd been reduced to killing him. And all for nothing, because the young Confederate was too badly wounded to move, too badly wounded to live, and Lockhart could do nothing but leave him there.

"Lockhart, what was that about?"

"Go to hell, Marshal Henson." With savage force, Lockhart drove the pistol back into its holster. "I'll help you on your damned horse. Liberal's that way. You'll make it, if you go slowly. I'm taking another trail."

"You saved my life."

"Clever of me, wasn't it?"

Henson frowned. "Can't figure why you took my side. Can't figure you at all." He shook his head. "I'll still see you hang, but I'm damned if I'll enjoy it half as much as I ought."

15

- - - - - - - - - - - -

Marian Taylor returned to the City National Bank well before it opened. Posting herself where she could watch front and side entrances at the same time, she opened the morning paper and read it without interest while the bank's staff arrived. By the time the front blinds went up and the tall doors opened, she knew that neither Marshal Henson nor Edward Givens had gone inside while she was watching.

Grove and Leo Pritchard might be laying a trap for her—she especially distrusted Pritchard—but she would handle that if it happened. Meanwhile, the curtain was rising. She started across the street, carried along on a wave of confidence and excitement. She knew she would give a good performance.

Before she had time even to give her name, Leo Pritchard came across the lobby to meet her. Taking her arm, he led her aside, his dark head bent close to hers, a bank employee giving confidential advice to a customer.

"We'll need more time, Miss Hartley," he almost whispered. "But what we're finding confirms your story. It appears Mr. Stanhope had been indiscreet on more than one occasion."

"I see." Marian was grateful for the low tones. It helped her keep her voice steady. With just the right trace of eagerness, she asked, "What about the night he was killed? Was he meeting someone then?"

"That's what we're trying to determine. You'll understand, these inquiries have to be conducted with great caution. Tact, as Mr. Grove would put it."

"Of course."

"We'll have to delay our appointment. Can you come back at, say, two o'clock the day after tomorrow?"

"I'd rather settle this sooner."

"So had we. But I'm afraid that's the best we can do." A quick, hard look. "We sent word to your hotel, but apparently you didn't get the message."

He's good. "I made other arrangements."

"I don't think you trust us, Miss Hartley."

She could smile at him without acting. "Of course I don't, Mr. Pritchard. Do you trust me?"

He returned her smile with a grudging grin that made him seem younger and considerably less grim. "No. But we're both interested in the same end."

"The reward," she said quickly.

"The truth." He smiled, reassured. "But it comes to the same thing. Until then, Miss Hartley."

He took the hand that she offered. As she turned to go, a bank employee came up to Pritchard. "Leo? A Mr. Lysander Thompson to see you. I told him to wait in your office."

Thankful that Pritchard couldn't see her face, Marian practically fled from the bank. Outside, she went straight to the post office, too rattled even to notice if she were being followed. No letter from Lockhart. By the time she emerged, she was calm enough to watch her backtrail as she sauntered along Main looking idly in the store windows. As soon as she was sure she was alone, she caught a horse car back toward the northern part of town.

Sitting alone in a back corner of the rattling car, she tried to get her emotions under control. The delay at the bank concerned her. The sudden appearance of Givens and then Thompson worried her. What frightened her so desperately that she could hardly breathe was the lack of a letter from Lockhart.

Where are you, Jim? What's happening? Are you still alive?

She drew a long breath, willing herself to calm. Deep inside, she was quite certain she would know if Lockhart had died. Aside from that, she could do nothing about him, nothing to speed along his return. *Leave that to heaven*, she thought, but adapting the quotation was no fun without Lockhart to enjoy it with her.

The bank, then. She was doing what she could about that. Cover her tracks. Be careful. Be doubly careful when she went back in two days.

"The fighting was easy," Lockhart had told her once when he tried to talk about the war. "Waiting. That was hard."

First Givens, if indeed it was he. Now Thompson. What are the two of them doing here?

Remembering something half-seen earlier, she rum-

maged in her bag for the newspaper. A small article, down toward the bottom of a page, something the reporter hadn't
taken too seriously—There! KENDRICK AIRSHIP ON MAIDEN
VOYAGE; AIR TRAVELER TO CALL AT FORT WORTH. Marian
stared at the headline, not needing to read the rest.

"Opportunity Knox," she said.

When she returned to the North cottage, Marian Taylor
brought bags of food, matching dresses for Nellie and Ellie,
and a soft cloth doll with a china head.

"Oh," Ellie cried. "Is it for me?"

"If you like it."

"She's lovely." She hugged the doll and turned a circle or
two as if dancing with it. "I love her."

"What is her name?" Nellie asked.

"I shall call her Marian, if you don't mind, Mother?"

"I think that a very fine name," Nellie said. "Why don't
you show her around?"

"Of course. Come, Marian."

Nellie North closed the door quietly behind her daughter. "Thank you so much," she said to Marian. "But please, I
never meant for you to buy us things."

"Nonsense," Marian interrupted briskly. "It's only right
that I pay my way. Especially since I have to ask you a great
favor. My business is taking longer than I expected. Would it
be an imposition if I stayed until Friday?"

"Why, that was just what I was going to ask you! The
lady who sometimes looks after Ellie is sick, and I have to—
to go out tomorrow. If you could watch her . . ."

"I'd be pleased."

"Oh, thank you. Thank you so much!"

Nellie North pressed a lilac-bordered handkerchief to
her eyes. She seemed much more grateful than the small
favor deserved. Suspecting she still hadn't come to what she
really wanted to talk about, Marian waited quietly. Sure
enough, Nellie blew her nose, then looked up shyly.

"Marian, I wondered if I might—well, if you would advise me in a rather delicate matter?"

"I'll be happy to help in any way I can."

"Well, you were so understanding about Mr. Stanhope, and what he said to me, that I thought you might tell me . . ."

She broke off long enough for Marian to feel a sharp stab of conscience. She'd been understanding for her own reasons, for the use she could make of Nellie's problem. "Go on, my dear."

"I didn't tell you the full truth about our trip to California," Nellie said. "I was visiting my late husband's family. They didn't approve of the marriage. I was hoping they might help, but they want nothing to do with Ellie or me."

"Figures," Marian said under her breath while Nellie used the handkerchief again.

"The little money he left is almost gone. Our church has helped out, but I can't live on their charity forever. I've been looking for work. There's not much I know how to do, just cooking and sewing and the like, and there's Ellie to consider." She stopped and took a breath. "I think that if someone like Mr. Stanhope were to make that offer now, I would be compelled to consider it."

Someone has. Marian went to sit beside Nellie, putting an arm around her shoulders. She'd heard this kind of thing before, but it had always been the come-on for some sort of shell game. This time, she had no doubt it was real. *Damn all men anyway! Except Jim. Maybe.*

"And Marian, I can see that you're—well—a woman of the world, used to making your own way. And I know it would be wrong, a sin. But would it be *very* wrong? I mean with Ellie to think of and all?"

I didn't have anybody to ask. I was sixteen, with a father who'd run off and a drunken stepfather I had to get away from. And he—what was his name?—said I had talent, that he could get me on the stage. And he did. I know it was wrong. Was it very wrong?

Nellie was waiting for her answer. "I had a similar problem once," Marian said. "For a long time, I didn't regret my decision." *Until I met Jim.* "I think now that I made the wrong choice. But I didn't have a child to think of, so I can't answer for you. Maybe you should look for another way until you're certain you won't find anything else."

Ellie came back into the room with her new doll, sensed an adult conversation not meant for her ears, and sat down to listen intently. "Are you talking about me?"

Nellie dabbed at her eyes again. "In a way, dear."

"Do I make you cry?"

"Of course not." Marian's voice was husky, too. "We're just having a good cry together, sweetie. Would you like me to stay with you for a day or so while your mother does her errands?"

"Oh, yes! Can she, Mommy?"

Nellie smiled and stood up. "Yes, Ellie, that'll be fine." Then she put her hand to her mouth. "Oh, Marian, can you begin this afternoon? I just remembered an appointment."

"Certainly."

"It's odd, after our conversation the other night." She glanced at Ellie as if half afraid the girl would understand. "But a man at the bank sent word he wants to see me. A Mr. Pritchard."

"I see," Marian said.

Jim, wherever you are, get here fast! This is getting out of hand.

It was good to have two eyes again. Devoid of any disguise except dirt and his battered trail clothes, James Lockhart huddled on a seat in a crowded second-class railcar bound for Kansas City. Despite what he'd told Henson about taking another route, he'd cut back and ridden hard for Liberal as soon as he was out of the marshal's sight, confident he could move faster than the wounded man. Once there, he'd sold his horse and gear for half what he'd paid.

"Lucky to get that," the liveryman said. "Market's really gone down since you were in last."

"That was three days ago."

"Can't tell about the market. Changes fast around here."

The gunsmith was equally glad to see him again.

"Ain't the same Winchester you started out with." He assessed it with a hawk-eyed glare. "Selling this one, be ye?"

"No. I'd like you to hold it for awhile. There'll be a big, loud man with white hair and a shiny badge in to retrieve it. Here's a dollar for your trouble."

"Ain't my proper trade. S'posing I was to just keep it?"

"Suit yourself. But I think you'll want to give it to him."

From where Lockhart sat, having two eyes was the only good thing he could say about his situation. He'd bought a ticket on the last train out of Liberal that day, but that wouldn't keep Marshal Doom off his trail for very long. Marian was in Fort Worth, possibly followed by Janks, probably in all kinds of trouble. He needed to get to her and he had his ticket, but he couldn't use it yet. He'd have to mislead Henson somehow, lose his trail in a tangle of connecting railroad schedules.

Kansas City. That's it. I'll hit the terminal there, duck out for a bath and shave—a favor to my fellow passengers—then head to Fort Worth. Let Doom figure that out.

Kansas City was far out of his way, but it was a hub from which at least eight different rail lines radiated. Henson would probably have no trouble tracing him that far, but that should be the end of it.

Even if he knows I'm checking up on the crimes, he'll think I've gone to Hannibal. So much for that!

He would send Marian a letter telling her that he would be late reaching Fort Worth, and warning her to look out for

Janks. He could mail it from the train. That was the best he could manage.

The plan seemed a good one, but he took no satisfaction in it. Try as he might, he couldn't fight off the sick knowledge that he'd let one chance after another get away. The King of China had known—how much?—more than he'd let on, obviously. Henson had killed him. The man who called himself Brutus had known everything—the identity of the real criminal, the way Lockhart had been framed, where the money had gone. And he had been willing to tell.

You shot the man who could save you to save the man who wants to hang you. Brilliant!

Marian's word again. She had tried to warn him that what he'd planned was impossible. How could he have believed he could follow up the robberies and find the true criminal with Marshal Doom on his trail? It was hopeless.

Hopeless. I could pick Marian up in Fort Worth, break for the border. We could get into Mexico and hide out there, probably even make some kind of living. No. What kind of life would that be for Marian? If he were going to run out, better to leave her and go alone. *Go alone? Leave Marian? Might as well turn myself in and let Henson hang me.*

For no reason he could think of, Lockhart saw in his mind the face of the wounded Confederate from the Franklin battlefield. No more than a boy, really, maybe seventeen. Lockhart had saved his life, then left him to die in the mud.

What else could I do?

The question fit Henson's case as well as it fit the other. He could no more have let Brutus kill Henson than he could have left the scavenger to slit the young Rebel's throat. Now it came to him that the pain of making a bad choice was not lessened by the knowledge that it had been the only choice available.

* * *

Marshal Rance Henson hit Liberal like a tornado swirling up off the southern prairie. He was as dizzy and weak as a man recovering from a two-week drunk and his arm hurt like Satan's own pitchfork was stuck through it, but the marshal was angry enough to outweigh all that.

Left alone by Lockhart with the fancy man's body, Henson had put in a little time gentling the black horse. Then he'd heaved the corpse of its former owner up across its saddle and tied it in place. He always liked to know the name of a man who tried to kill him. This one wasn't anybody he recognized, though his face was tantalizingly familiar—from a poster, maybe. Maybe he was known in Liberal.

What should have been a minute's work getting the body across the saddle had taken him nearly an hour, with stops to rest whenever the walls of the gully started to turn red and swirl around him. By the time he was able to ride, he realized what Lockhart meant to do. *Should've known it sooner, but I was too busy wondering why he hadn't let that handsome devil kill me. Still can't figure that out.* Then he'd pressed on as fast as he could—maddeningly slowly, for all his efforts—to find he'd hit town fifty minutes after Lockhart and the last train of the day had pulled out together.

"Yep, sounds just like him," the clerk at the depot said. " 'Cepting he was wearing both his eyes when I saw him. Dirty, rough-looking devil." He looked past Henson, toward the two horses standing near the platform. "Uh—say, that feller on the black. Tied across it that way, I mean. Is he—is he dead?"

"If he isn't, he'll be damned uncomfortable by now. Where'd Lockhart go?"

"Lockhart? No, that's not right, gave his name as Henson, Rance Henson."

"That son of a—"

"Bought a ticket to Hutchinson, but that don't mean nothing. He can connect up to anyplace there, even Kansas City."

"Then that's where he'll go. You sure there's nothing going out of here tonight? A local, a freight, anything?"

"Nope. Not a blessed thing till tomorrow noon."

"Dam-*nation!* Can't the damned railroad put on enough damned trains to satisfy its"—Henson remembered then that he was well into his second six months of profanity—"paying customers?"

The clerk drew himself up to his full five feet. "Be a train tomorrow noon, mister, take you anyplace you want to go. Proper connections, you can get plumb to Boston, if that's what suits you. Can't do a bit better'n that. We ain't got a shop here makes locomotives to order."

"You got a telegraph key?"

"Why, sure, mister, we got all the latest gear."

"Give me a message pad."

Henson scribbled a wire to the Kansas City police to watch for Lockhart. *Not that that'll do any good. Don't know when he'll arrive, what he'll look like by then, or where he's likely to head out to. KC Police'll laugh at me.* The marshal tightened his jaw. He did not like the idea of being laughed at.

"Get this one out. I'll have the other in a minute."

"Listen, mister, I don't know."

Wordlessly, Henson laid his badge on the counter. The clerk looked at it, picked up the form, and rattled the telegraph key while Henson considered the wording of his second message.

Deputy Marshal Chet Archer, Federal Court House, St. Louis: Alive. Lockhart slipped through. Forward latest developments here immediately. Henson, Marshal.

Gnawing at the point of his pencil, Henson frowned at the blank. That was all he needed to say. Maybe more, because Chet would guess the message meant he was alive. But he wasn't satisfied.

Marshal Rance Henson was not a stupid man. He knew

his mind didn't work as fast as some, but he also knew its bulldog persistence always got to the answer in due course. His slow, painstaking investigations, more than his bluster and force, had put many a smart outlaw behind bars or under a headstone. Now the bulldog was growling at him.

He wasn't happy about Lockhart. He'd done his investigative work, connected together four seemingly unrelated crimes, found enough evidence—circumstantial, to be sure, but good enough for a jury—to hang a dozen James Lockharts. And nothing that had happened since had changed that fundamental picture.

Lockhart was a thief. The Janks brothers, with Rags and the man across the black, were his go-betweens and henchmen. They quarreled over the spoils, and Phin Janks was dead. Lockhart went to Little China in person because he needed more money now that he was on the dodge.

It all made sense. Except. Twice now, Lockhart had been within a trigger-squeeze of putting Henson off his trail for good. The first time, back in the shack in the Sierras, Henson could discount. But out on the prairie, Lockhart had to know that Marshal Doom would dog him to the death. And the cold-blooded killer who'd murdered two helpless bank employees shouldn't have hesitated to remove that threat.

"Hell," Henson said.

"Yes, sir, got that one sent. You finished with the second message?"

Henson glared at the clerk. Then he scratched out his signature and added, in bold block letters: GATHER ALL DOCUMENTS RE LOCKHART TAYLOR. REVIEW FOR DISCREPANCIES. GATHER ALL DOCUMENTS RE THOMPSON GIVENS KNOX BAKER. CHECK ALIBIS. HOLD FOR MY REVIEW. HENSON, MARSHAL.

"That's a heap of words."

"There'll be an answer. Is there a hotel here?"

"You bet, mister. Like I say, we got all the latest conveniences. Over by the Drover's Palace Saloon there, one flight up. All the latest conveniences. Even get a bath in your room, meaning no offense to you."

"Bring the answer there."

"I ain't no messenger service. Got responsibilities. Can't leave the station. What if a special was to come through?"

"Then it would damned well be lost!" Henson roared. "You bring me that telegram, hear?"

Stalking out of the depot, Henson grabbed the reins of his horses and led them across to the town constable's office. He was not happy. Backtracking on an investigation he'd finished upset him. Lockhart's latest escape—*That's three times running I've lost that same son of a bitch!*—made him furious every time he thought about it. And his encounter with the depot clerk led him to believe people here didn't have the proper respect for a federal marshal. Clomping across the uneven boardwalk to the constable's door, Henson felt he would explode from sheer frustration unless he found a release soon.

A lanky deputy was on duty in the dusty office, tilted far back in a wooden chair with his feet crossed on the desk. He pushed his hat up off the bridge of his nose and peered at Henson.

"Help you?"

"There's a dead man tied over that black horse outside. Killed out on the prairie about fifteen-twenty miles south."

"Out of our jurisdiction."

"Get out there and see if you recognize him. If you don't, see if anybody else does. I want to know who he is."

The deputy pushed his hat back a little more and looked full at Henson. "*You* want that, do you? Well, who in the hell are you, mister?"

With a quick glance of thanks to the Almighty, Henson

said, "I'm the man who's going to kick your lazy, insubordinate ass right out in the middle of Main Street in front of everybody unless you rouse yourself up and help a brother officer."

The front legs of the chair hit the floor and the deputy bounded up, reaching for the Colt that hung too low on his hip. "Listen, you old bastard."

Henson's hand flashed down and up again. The deputy froze, his gun only halfway out of its holster. Instead of a pistol, Henson held his shiny badge in front of the young man's nose.

"Move that gun another inch, and I'll tie it around your ears," Henson said pleasantly. "Now that you're up, go have a look at that body."

An hour later, Henson made his way to the hotel. The deputy had been pretty cooperative, once Henson had gotten his attention. He didn't know the dead man, nor did the two or three people he'd summoned from the saloon. But there was a photographer in town. Henson made arrangements to have the corpse cleaned up, photographed, and buried, then went to find himself a room and a bath.

"Henson. Feller been asking about you," the desk clerk said. "Right over in the parlor, there."

His hand on his revolver, Henson stepped into the parlor. A man was bent over a small table beneath the one oil lamp in the room, furiously scribbling on a pad of yellow paper. After a moment, he looked up and saw Henson.

"Marshal!" He bounded up, offering Henson a damp hand. "You remember me? Clyde Darrow."

"I can't say I do."

"*Sacramento Daily Union.* On roving assignment now, covering the Lockhart case. Do you have news?"

"No."

"Now, don't be modest, Marshal. A bit of favorable publicity never hurt anyone. I've heard you've been off to break up some Oriental gang. How is Lockhart involved? You wouldn't want me to print guesswork. What happened to your arm?"

Henson considered. The best course of action would be to clout Darrow with a singletree. But the newspaperman might be useful.

"Maybe we can help each other, Mr. Darrow. I'll tell you what I can if you'll do a favor in return."

Darrow gave a smile that Henson could have used to grease a windmill. "Of course, Marshal. Always delighted to help the law."

"You go over to the constable's. Tell the deputy you want to look at the man I brought in. I'm going to clean up, and then we'll talk."

"We'll meet for supper."

Henson would rather have shared a meal with a flock of vultures. "That'll be just fine. I'll see you in about an hour."

When someone tapped on the door just after he emerged from his tin bathtub, Henson feared it was Darrow. Pulling up his long johns, he took his pistol in one hand and opened the door with the other. The clerk from the depot blinked up at him.

"Ah—sorry, Marshal, but you said you wanted an answer to your wires right away. Is your arm all right?"

"Sure enough! Come in."

Henson tossed the Colt on the bed and eagerly took the two yellow slips. *Sim Janks, Robert Smith not seen Denver since 13th inst. Whereabouts unknown,* said the first. Robert Smith was Rags, and Henson knew his whereabouts.

"Heaping up coals for the devil's furnace," he murmured, "and stealing half to sell in Purgatory."

Woman answering description Marian Taylor reported Fort Worth. Contact Leo Pritchard, City National Bank.

"Fort Worth!" Henson grabbed the startled clerk, pumped his hand in congratulations. "And Lockhart'll go to her like a bee to honey! Listen, mister, get me a ticket on the fastest thing going to Fort Worth!"

16

▬▬▬▬▬▬▬▬▬▬▬▬▬▬▬▬▬▬▬▬▬▬▬

"I believe we'll go downtown today, Ellie. Would you like that?"

"Downtown? Golly! Could I really? I've been wanting my whole life to go downtown!"

"As long as that?" Marian asked, giving the child a wistful smile. "Well, then, it's time your desire was gratified."

"Huh?"

"That means we'll go this very afternoon. Let's pick you out a frock."

Nellie North had found an advertisement in the *Fort Worth Democrat* for someone to do domestic work for a well-to-do Lakeview family. That morning, she'd set out by horse car to inquire.

"I have another appointment at the bank today," Marian had told Nellie. "What should I do if you don't return before then?"

"Maybe that'll mean I got the job. Wouldn't that be wonderful?" Nellie had placed a thin hand on Marian's arm. "Could you take Ellie with you? If it wouldn't be too much trouble, I mean."

"That would be fine," Marian said, "if you think she'll be safe."

"I'm sure you'll keep her safe, right here or downtown. Thank you, Marian."

Marian Taylor wasn't delighted with the idea of taking Ellie along. She'd stayed close to the North home for two long days, not even venturing to go to the post office. If Lockhart had reached Fort Worth, he would have found her letter for him and come to the North house. Since he hadn't shown up, she was afraid to check for a message, afraid of what continuing silence might mean.

Ellie picked out a blue and brown gingham dress, almost too thin for even the mild fall day. Marian saw that she was warmly wrapped in her coat, then started the walk down the sandy lane to the corner where they could catch a horse car.

"What will we do downtown?" Ellie asked.

"I have to keep an appointment or two."

"Appoint?"

Marian laughed. "I must see some people."

"What people?"

"A man at the post office and a man at the bank."

"The bank? That's where they keep all the money. Are we going there?"

"Yes. And you'll have to sit very quietly and be good while I talk to the man there."

"What man?"

Marian laughed again. *And to think I've been wanting to have children!* "You'll see, my dear. Here, don't go in the street. We'll wait right here for a car."

Although she had no real reason to worry, she took Ellie for a stroll before going into the post office. She was anxious to learn whether by some miracle Lockhart had found a way to send her a letter, but she was still cautious. *Just to see whether anyone is watching. I won't put this child in danger.* But Ellie, as it seemed, marked Marian as a mother and thus changed her identity as well as one of her more elaborate disguises.

"Now," she told Ellie, "we'll see the man at the post office."

Ellie nodded. "What's his name?"

They went into the post office, where Marian looked carefully at each patron until she was satisfied none of them had any interest in her. Then she stepped up to the window. A different clerk was on duty today, a lanky, bushy-haired man.

"Do you have any mail for Miss Mary Hartley, General Delivery?"

"I'll see." Busy sorting through a stack of envelopes, the clerk barely glanced at her. "Be a minute."

Ellie crowded up to the counter, craning her neck to see the clerk. "What's your name?"

To Marian's surprise, the man's mask of indifference broke up into a smile which showed his discolored teeth. "My name is Tom," he said. "And what is your name?"

"Ellie."

"Well, you're a fine young lady!" The clerk began looking through the General Delivery box. "Hartley, did you say? Yes, as a matter of fact, I do have something for you." He handed her an envelope. "And may I say you have a lovely daughter?"

Marian grasped the letter with both hands as if afraid it would fly away. Staring at the bold, black strokes of the address, she realized she didn't know Lockhart well enough even for his handwriting to be familiar. But no one else would have known to write her there. *Jim. You're alive!* Almost unable to speak, she managed to whisper, "Yes, thank you."

"She's not my mommy," Ellie explained. "Who's your letter from?"

"A friend," Marian said. She went to a table at the front wall, tore open the envelope, and unfolded the single sheet of paper.

"What friend?"

Marian said, "Jim," without taking her eyes away from the page.

"What does he say in his letter? It must be very sad, since you're crying."

I am not! But she was, foolish as it seemed. She took a handkerchief from her sleeve and pressed it to her eyes. *Gone again. Gone on another damned man!* This time she didn't believe it herself.

"What does he say? Did he say hello to me?"

"He doesn't know you, dear. I'll tell you about it in a minute. Let me read it all first."

Dear Marian,
Written from the train en route to KC. It's possible that a man named Sim Janks is following you. Big, almost a giant. Wears checked lumberjack shirts and heavy boots. Be careful of him. He is very dangerous, and you are very dear to me. Our friend Doom caught me again, but I escaped. The trip into No Man's Land was not as productive as I had hoped. Two men there might have cleared me, but they are both dead. ~~I now—~~

Here most of a line was blotted out in vicious strokes of black ink. Marian frowned at it, then read on.

I must detour north to throw Doom off our trail, but will join you according to our plan as soon as it's safe. Again, take care, my Love

Yours, Jim.

Marian read the last line again, smiling. Then she held the paper to the light, peering closely at the sentence Jim had begun but had scratched out. A few words showed through the black crosshatching. *I now fear . . . no hope . . . that we . . . come clear . . . this.*

"Oh, no," she whispered. "No, Jim, don't quit. Whatever you do, don't give up!"

"I knew it was sad," Ellie accused. "Now you really are crying. He's a bad man, to make you sad that way."

Marian looked at the child, crumpled the letter in her hand. "No, Ellie. He's a very good man." *And he scratched out that passage. He went on to make plans to come to me.* "I hope you can meet him soon."

She took Ellie's hand, looked around the post office again. No one seemed interested in her, and no one seemed familiar. *Sim Janks—he's the one I saw in Denver, and again on the train. He was following me. But I haven't seen him since. Where is he, and what's his part in all this?*

"Where are we going now?"

"We have a little time before my appointment at the bank. Let's walk around and look in the shop windows and pretend we can buy anything we want."

"All right."

Janks. But he wasn't the immediate problem. She had to get ready for the bankers again. From what she'd learned about Nellie's talk with Pritchard, she knew the bank was investigating her allegations against the late George Stanhope. But she still worried that she was walking into a trap.

"If we work this right," Leo Pritchard said, "she'll be walking into a trap."

Marshal Rance Henson looked across the bank lobby. Clyde Darrow was talking to an uneasy Thaddeus Grove, learning all about Marian Taylor and her visits to the bank. Darrow had shared the train ride from Liberal with Henson, causing the marshal to draw on another six months in his profanity account. Henson hoped he could keep the reporter out of the way when things began to happen.

He tried to shift his arm in its sling so that the stitches didn't pull quite so tightly. That drunken sawbones at the Roost might have saved his life, but he'd certainly drawn up his thread so that the healing wound would be as painful as possible.

"We don't want her to know it," Henson said. "The idea's to watch her, see where she goes, wait for Lockhart."

"Yes, sir. I'll have a man on each door, ready to follow her when she leaves. You might want to take a post in the lobby."

"I'll be outside. Want to be able to see her when she comes in. Lockhart may be here already."

Pritchard nodded. "I'm afraid I picked us a bad day for it. If I'd known in advance about all the commotion, I would've tried to find some alternate plan."

"I thought you had a lot of people moving around. What's the occasion?"

"Everybody wants to see the airship." At Henson's wondering look, Pritchard went across to a table and brought back a copy of the *Democrat*. "Here you are, see?"

MARVEL OF THE AGES the headline read. KENDRICK AEROBAT ON DISPLAY AT COLEMAN'S FIELD!

Beneath a fuzzy woodcut of something that looked like a gigantic sunfish were a dozen paragraphs of type about the aerobat and Professor Kendrick and the way the two of them were about to change the world of transportation. Toward the bottom, Henson spotted a name that annoyed him instantly.

"Opportunity Knox."

"Pardon?"

"Poppycock! The Almighty never meant man to fly."

Pritchard pursed his thin lips. "Expect you're right about that. The bank certainly isn't lending any money on airships." He hesitated a minute, then said, "Funny thing. That Taylor woman put us onto the right track. We've determined that George Stanhope had some hanky-panky going on, both with the bank's female customers and with the bank's money. It's entirely possible that he met someone besides Lockhart the night he was killed."

Henson glared at him. "Do you have proof of that?"

"No. Not yet."

"Well, that banker in Denver, Murdock, was as strait-laced as they come, and Lockhart was the last person seen with him, too."

"I know." Pritchard chewed his lip. "I'm still convinced Lockhart is the one. It's just . . ."

"What?"

"I'm nowhere nearly as convinced as I was."

An hour early to intercept Marian Taylor at the bank, Henson sauntered down Main, glanced in for a moment to be certain neither of his birds was silly enough to be at the post office, and walked slowly on back toward the bank. His eyes were alert on the crowd of passersby, but his mind was on what Pritchard had said.

He's beginning to wonder. Somebody might have seen Stanhope alive after Lockhart left. And if that happened, the case against Lockhart for the Fort Worth crime falls apart.

Not only that. Henson had been the one to see the similarities in four apparently different cases, to trace down the one man that fit all four crimes. But if Lockhart were innocent of one robbery, he might be innocent of all. *Like hell!* Henson thought. *Anyway, that's for a jury. My job's to bring him in.* But he wasn't happy with that.

Across the street, a smartly shaped woman stood with her little girl looking into a store window. At that distance she reminded him of Amy Robbins, whom he'd once thought of asking to marry him. But then, she'd beaten him to the draw by marrying another man. God damn all women, anyway!

Forgive me, Lord. Call it an even two years, then. But you got to admit it Yourself, You never would have made women but as an afterthought.

He was a block past before he remembered who had caused him to think of Amy Robbins after all these years. He whirled, retraced his steps, looked across the street again just in time to see Marian Taylor without disguise. The girl

might be hers or might be a stage prop for all he or any mere
man knew, but of the woman he had no doubt.

He waited. She turned the corner, looked back. *Has the
saucy trollop seen me?* He was patient. She held the girl's hand
and towed her on. Still Henson waited. They couldn't out-
run him. He knew that. The woman was his now, and Lockhart as well, if only he were willing to be patient. He made
himself wait, and his patience paid off.

The woman did not come back round the corner. From
down the street a very large man turned the same corner on
the other side of the street and began to follow her. Henson
moved. He wished he could talk with Pritchard, could get the
help of his two detectives, but there was no time left. He'd
come for the woman and she was about to get away and make
a rendezvous with another of her criminal consorts. He had
to stick with her.

He crossed Main and made it to the corner very quickly.
On the far side, the big man had stopped to look in a window.
On the near side, the woman and child had disappeared. The
man was Sim Janks from Denver, alive and in the flesh. Henson knew what Janks did for a living, and he knew the big
man's brother had been killed in the El Paso shooting. Thus,
Janks was involved in the Lockhart business right up to his
eyeballs. Why he should be in Fort Worth following Marian
Taylor wasn't clear. *But you can bet your heirlooms it has something to do with those banknotes!*

Figuring Janks knew where the ladies were, Henson fell
in behind him, following from across the street. *Most men
don't recognize their own trick when it's played on them.* The big
man turned from the shop window and strode down the
boardwalk and into an alley. Henson stopped to look at the
toy display in a store window. If he showed his hand now, he
might ruin the whole thing. All patience, Henson waited.

* * *

Marian led the child out of the post office and walked a block or so along Main before she stopped to look in a shop window. No one had emerged from the post office to follow them. After a few minutes she crossed the street and walked back past the post office and toward the bank. Ellie still had many questions and Marian forced herself to answer, to give every appearance of a mother with her child. Across from the bank they stopped to look in another window. Reflected in the glass, a man came along the far walk in a ground-eating stride. He carried his left arm in a sling. Marian caught her breath as she recognized Marshal Rance Henson.

Henson! Jim said—but Jim didn't know. That snake Pritchard must have telegraphed Henson. That's why he asked me to return today! In the glass she saw the marshal walk on past.

It is a trap! But for Ellie by my side, Henson might have recognized me on sight as I recognized him.

"Marian, why did that man have his arm in a sling?"

"What man, dear?"

"The one you were watching in the window."

"Perhaps he hurt it." Marian wondered what part Lockhart might have played in that injury. She turned and led the child away along the walk.

"Are we going to the bank now?"

"No. I think I saw a shop you'd like just around this corner."

"But isn't that the bank over there?"

"I really don't need to go to the bank after all."

"Why?"

"Because I'd rather look in the window of that shop I told you about."

"I want to see inside the bank."

"Another time we will."

"No." Ellie's shout was loud enough to startle Marian. "I want to go now!"

"But why?"

"I want to see all the money. Mommy says we need more money. I want to go in the bank and get her some money!" The child drew back, tugging to get her hand free of Marian's grasp.

"Come along." Marian tried to keep her own voice down, tried to control the suddenly frantic little girl, tried not to look across where Henson might even then be. But Ellie was determined. At last Marian knelt beside the child, looked quickly at the bank, and spoke softly. "My appointment in the bank is not for an hour yet. Right now, I thought we'd look in that shop where I saw toys and things for little girls."

Ellie stopped struggling. "All right."

For heaven's sake! Why didn't I try reason to begin with? "Come along, then." She got to her feet, still holding tightly to Ellie's hand, and continued along the walk. When they turned the corner, she glanced down the street and saw a large man standing beside the door of the post office. If he was looking at her, she could not tell it at that distance. She could not be certain at that distance if he was the man from Denver.

She hurried along to the toy shop, all but dragging Ellie. "Here it is."

"I want to look in the window."

"First, let's go inside. We can see even more."

"Can we see what's in the window?"

"Yes. Let's hurry."

"Why?"

Inside, Ellie looked at the toys in the window display while Marian fended off a pushy sales clerk and looked through the window to see whether the large man would come around the corner following them.

The clerk came back. "Weren't you in here yesterday?" she asked Marian. "Bought one of our dolls."

Marian nodded. Ellie asked, "Is this where you found Marian?"

"Yes," Marian admitted. "But let's look at other things."

"We have other dolls somewhat like that one."

"Not like Marian," Ellie said. "No doll is like Marian!"

"We'd like to just look around if we may," Marian said.

"Very well, just help yourselves."

Ellie ran from display to display, tugging Marian's hand to show her each new thing. Marian had lost track of Janks, and she hoped Henson had lost track of her, if indeed he'd ever seen her. *No one's come in the shop. They're still out there somewhere.* Working her way back to the window, she looked out. The man she thought must be Sim Janks had gone along the walk on the far side of the street and stopped to look in a window half a block away. In all likelihood, it meant nothing.

Still, she could not afford to place Ellie in any danger. The child was holding up a toy china tea set with teapot and cups and sugar bowl.

"Oh, look, Marian. If I had this, Marian and I could give tea parties for the other dolls. And for Mommy, too."

"Good idea. We'll take one of these," she said to the clerk.

"Of course. That's our very nicest one. Forty cents. Would you like me to wrap it?"

"What I'd like is for you to let us leave by your back door."

"I beg your pardon."

Marian worked at looking embarrassed. "My daughter and I are playing a game."

"Are we?"

"Yes, dear, don't you remember?" She winked at Ellie and hoped the child would be quiet. To the clerk she explained, "It's rather like moving pieces on a game board."

"I'm afraid I don't understand."

Marian adopted a conspiratorial tone. "Then I must take you into my confidence," she said softly. "I want you to walk up to the window and look out to your left. You'll see a very large man across the street. I believe he's looking in the bakery window. He is an enemy of my husband and has been trying to kidnap our Ellie."

"If that is true, I'll send for the police."

"No!" Marian said.

Ellie said, "That would be fun!"

"If you'll just go look, you'll be able to tell what I mean. Then we can decide about the police."

"All right then, I'll look, for pity's sake. But it all sounds very odd to me." The clerk turned and hurried toward the front of the shop.

Immediately, Marian took Ellie's hand and led her around the counter. They slipped through a curtain, dodged around the cartons and debris, and found the back door. Within the shop the clerk was calling after them.

"Here, wait! You can't go back there! Besides, there isn't any man looking in the bakery window."

Marian wrenched the door open. She plunged into the alley, drawing the child after her. If she went to her left, she would come out on Main within sight of the bank. That wouldn't do. She hurried along the alleyway to the right, came to an intersection, and stopped to look each way. She saw no one ahead of them, no one to their left. Behind them the clerk had come into the alley, brandishing a broom and shouting. Some distance away to the right, a large man stood at a corner from which he could see both the alley intersection and the front of the toy store.

To avoid being within his vision any longer than necessary, Marian took the child across the narrow, cluttered intersection and stopped short to peek around the corner. The big man was picking his way between carriages, crossing the street, coming straight toward their alley. Marian picked up Ellie and ran. At the next street, too tired to continue in that manner, she put Ellie down and turned to her right in the hope of confusing her pursuer. *Of course, I don't even know that he's following us!*

Nearing the next corner, having looked back several times, Marian felt better. But she would have to get Ellie home quickly. Then they came to the corner and she bumped smack into the large man in the tan duster.

"Well now, ladies," he said. "I'm mighty glad to catch up to you at last." He took Marian by the arm in a grip like a blacksmith's vise.

Marian said, "I'll scream."

The big man leaned down to whisper harshly in her ear. "Go right ahead. But you don't want the police no more than I do." He smiled down at Ellie, showing big square teeth. "And I can break this here little girl's neck faster'n you could kill a chicken."

Ellie smiled back at him. "Hello. Are you Marian's friend?"

"That's just who I am, little lady." He put a big hand lightly behind her neck, looking at Marian.

"No!" she said quickly. "Don't hurt her. I won't make trouble."

"Smart. You lead on out. Get us a carriage. I've a mind to do a spot of searching out at that little place where you're staying."

James Lockhart got off the local from Fort Smith at noon and went straight to the Fort Worth post office on Main. He claimed the letter Marian had left for James Merri-weather in care of General Delivery. As much as he wished to tear open her letter and read it at once, he put the envelope in his pocket and went out the door as if under no urgency from any quarter.

Then he walked until he came to a park, where he sat on a bench to read his cherished letter. Marian detailed what she'd learned in Denver and mentioned her hopes for an interview at the bank in Fort Worth. She still had money. On the train she had met a young woman and her daughter. She was staying with them.

Lockhart frowned. He didn't know that he liked that. Still. She told him how to find the Norths' home. Last, she committed to him on paper a feeling he enjoyed as much as a twenty-year-old might have. "It's happened just as I told you on the handcar it would. I love you." Simple, brief, beyond misunderstanding. He folded the letter with care and put it in his inside pocket.

Now. I must find her. Get out of Fort Worth. Janks could be looking for her. Could have her this minute! Then there's the real killer. I'm not just sure what to do about that, but I can't let her face it alone!

He thought of returning to the post office to leave her a note outlining the dangers and setting up a place to meet. Then he decided that wasn't needed. After all, he knew where she was staying.

He crossed the street through carriage and wagon traffic and walked rapidly to a corner some distance away before he stopped to be certain no one followed him. No one did. *No one should. Rags is dead, Janks doesn't know where I am, Henson is probably still sniffing for a trail from Kansas City! I'm home free.*

The idea didn't lead him to relax. Stealth had become a part of his consciousness by then. He ducked into an alley, went along it for a few steps, waited. The only person he could see was an unkempt man who seemed to be examining the trash bins behind a saloon. Lockhart waited.

When the man was out of sight, Lockhart walked along the alley away from Main and the post office and the crowds in the street. He'd made up his mind to find the North home.

He walked past a couple of carriages for hire, considered the convenience, then forgot it in favor of stealth. When he had gone half a mile, being certain no one was following, he turned back to the south looking for the street Marian had mentioned in her directions. It was not far from the point he expected.

The North home, as he understood it, lay two or three miles out along Alice Lane in the direction he was going. From her description, he would recognize the house when he saw it. He settled in to those long strides in which he felt comfortable. The bag was no burden to him, the air cold but pleasant, the ground a mere space to be consumed, the sky wide and blue and inviting. The world was his, except for the never entirely still anxiety that he was a wanted and pursued man.

Three-quarters of an hour later, he'd found the house, or thought he had. No one answered his knock at the door. After a moment, he walked round to the side and finally to the back door, where he knocked again. It was a fine, tight, well-kept house, needing a fresh coat of paint but still in its prime. Lockhart saw four newly planted oaks, a sign of the inhabitants' intent to remain, persevere, homestead. Across the backyard ran a hedge planted like a boundary to keep out the wilder country beyond. It needed trimming. He liked the place, figured he would like the people. Since they'd been kind to Marian, he wished he had time to help with the hedge and painting the house.

But they were not at home and he was not at leisure. He didn't think he ought to be seen hanging around the property, especially now that his description had been made public. Although he saw no one, he could not be certain. He left the North property and walked on up the hill as if he'd only stopped to smell the flowers in the beds all around the house. There seemed to be no one in the area to dispute him.

At the top of the hill, four hundred yards above the house, he looked back. Most of a mile away, a carriage was struggling up the hill. Its horse wore a bright blue plume bobbing above his harness. The carriage stopped in the lane at the cottage. Three people got out. At the distance, Lockhart could not determine anything more than that the three people were quite different in size. *The little girl, the mother, the husband. Is that it? Looks so. I might as well go meet them and have a cup of coffee while we're waiting for Marian.*

He gathered up his things and went back onto the road where the going was easier. He changed hands with his bag and slowed into the last fifty yards of his descent. Within the house someone screamed.

17

Marshal Rance Henson watched Janks come together with Marian Taylor and the little girl at the corner. He saw that the woman did not show surprise or cry out or try to run. She was expecting the man, just as Henson had supposed. Janks hadn't been stalking her; he was meeting her. And tied up someplace in it all were Lockhart and those missing banknotes.

Hell. I'd halfway got myself believing Lockhart might be innocent. But he's just another smart crook like the rest of them, and I'm getting stupid in my old age.

The three, now looking like a family group, started along the plank walkway in front of a hardware store. Janks, the attentive husband and father, held Marian Taylor's arm. His other hand rested lightly on the child's shoulder. Henson moved with them. When Janks suddenly stopped and looked back along the street, Henson stepped under an awning and gave his full attention to a window display of Dr. Strong's Tricora corsets.

I could go collar them right this minute! God knows Janks is guilty of enough to hang him, this deal aside. Proving it would be another matter. But if I pick them up now, they'd die without telling me where to find those notes! Better to follow along and let them lead me to Lockhart. But I wish I had another man to help out.

Janks, still looking back, raised a long arm and waved. A smart-looking cab wheeled to the side of the street and stopped. "Hell," Henson muttered. He broke into a run, but had not covered half the distance when Janks herded the other two ahead of him into the cab. The driver whipped up his horse and the carriage rolled across the intersection as if they were going to a fire. Henson treated himself to another six months of perdition while he watched the bobbing blue plume on the horse's harness disappear up the street.

"Cab! Hey, you! Halt in the name of the law!"

Another carriage, this one black and battered, pulled to a stop, the driver gawking at him. Henson held up his badge.

"Follow that cab."

"What?"

A plump, balding man stuck his head out the window. "See here, sir, I've hired this conveyance."

"And the government of the United States thanks you for its use," Henson said as he pulled the door open and assisted the occupant to dismount. It took quite a bit of assistance. The man was still protesting when Henson swung up beside the driver.

"That way," Henson said. "I'll give you a dollar gold if you can find a carriage up that way was here a minute ago's got a blue plume on the horse."

"Eddie Swell's rig?"

"Could have been Eddie Swell's rig. I didn't get close enough to read the lettering. You know it?"

"You bet. For an extra dollar, I'll *find* it."

They were already moving; then they moved faster. The carriage rattled south along Main, dodging in and out among buckboards and buggies and horse cars, made a hard turn onto Eleventh and passed through a section of saloons and brothels. It was the kind of place Henson would have expected to find Janks, but there was no cab with a blue-plumed horse.

"Maybe went out to Coleman's to see that aero-whatever-it-is," the driver suggested. "Seems like everybody's talking about it. I even heard they're selling tickets to ride it east."

"Won't work. The Almighty never intended man to fly."

"That's just what I was telling the missus last night. 'If He'd intended us to act like birds,' I said—"

"That's not where they went, anyway. They're hid out someplace."

"Well, we ain't finding Eddie very fast. How's about I pull over to these other drivers and ask who's seen him?"

Henson looked at a couple of other cabs parked in front of a place called the Red Light. "Ask them," he said.

The driver stepped down, looked up at the marshal. "May I offer a dollar to him who knows?"

"By God," Henson said, "offer ten! I want the people in that carriage, and I mean business. And I'll jail the bunch of you if you don't cooperate!"

The driver went over to the others, stated his case. The others looked at Henson, made up their minds, and drove their carriages off in different directions. Henson's driver climbed back up to the high seat.

"One of them'll catch sight of Eddie, or we will. The bunch of us is to meet in a quarter-hour's time at the Trinity bridge." He clucked to his horse and started back north.

"Hey, mister, I ain't complaining about that dollar you promised me, but if it's worth ten for Eddie's rig, I ought to have it."

Henson waved an impatient hand. "The government'll look after you, son. Find that carriage."

They met one of the drivers in less than ten minutes and learned that Eddie Swell had gone off north on Alice Lane.

"That don't go anyplace, just sort of runs out over by the stockyards. He's bound to come back down in a few more minutes," Henson's driver said, "I could take you to the bottom of that road where we could meet him quicker and he could tell me how to get where he's went."

"You take me *up* that road to meet him quicker, and then he'll take me back." They made it no further than the bottom of the road before Eddie Swell's rig rolled down to meet them. Henson gave his driver more than enough money, then got into Swell's rig and demanded to be taken where Eddie had just been.

"Busy place, for such a little house," Eddie commented. "Friends of yours?"

"Like my own family. I just missed them in town, or I'd have rode out with them."

"Might've been a trifle crowded. That big fellow took up most of a seat by himself. Surly customer he was, too."

"Get rolling. We'll discuss all that on the way."

Lockhart was startled at first. Then he remembered that little girl's scream. He remembered when his own daughter had been small. It hadn't mattered whether she was elated or terrified—she screamed. Children were like that. Then the child in the North home screamed again. He didn't think she was elated.

Even though the chances were nine in ten that none of it was his business, he left the road to come up to the rear of the house, using the hedge to keep himself as much out of sight as possible. As he neared the back door, feeling more and more foolish, he heard Marian's voice inside.

"You leave her alone, you ruffian. I'll—"

"You'll damn well shut up, lady. Ow!"

"Take—"

The sound of a slap silenced Marian. The little girl let out another short scream. Though he had heard the man's deep voice only once before, Lockhart recognized it. It belonged to Sim Janks.

Lockhart took out his gun. He tried the kitchen door gently, found it locked. It went through his mind to run around to the front door, but he knew it might just as easily be locked, too. One round from the big Colt would have shattered the flimsy lock, but he didn't know where the people inside were, where his bullet might end up. He measured the door, hoping it was no stronger than it looked. Then he stepped back, holding the Colt up out of harm's way, lowered his shoulder, and lunged.

Trouble with living in a place like this. Never had to lock the doors at the farm. Anybody that came by was welcome to—

He hit with a tremendous crash. A stabbing pain went through his shoulder. Wood splintered as the upper panel split lengthwise. The door buckled, sagged on its hinges, held. Recoiling from his first try, Lockhart kicked it solidly on the lock and went in fast when it crashed open.

Against the far wall, a blond girl of five or so was trying to stuff both hands into her mouth. Her eyes seemed to be the biggest thing in the room. Sim Janks had turned to face the door. Almost lost in his huge hand, a long Army Colt was coming up into line on Lockhart's gizzard. And Marian Taylor, her own eyes wide and bright, her lip bleeding and her cheek swollen from Janks's slap, was grabbing for the first thing she could find on the kitchen counter and swinging it with all her strength at the big man's wrist.

The first thing she found happened to be a cast-iron frying pan. It hit the giant's gun with an echoing clang that was immediately lost in the roar of the pistol. Lockhart felt something tug at his right boot. The gun clattered on the floor. Janks bellowed like a wounded buffalo and belted Marian aside as if she'd been the child's rag doll. Teeth bared, he wheeled to face Lockhart.

"Hold it!"

Lockhart pointed the gun at the big man, but Janks didn't seem to notice. He was staring at Lockhart's face with almost comic puzzlement. Then recognition dawned in his close-set eyes.

"You! Moneytree! Where's Rags?"

"Hands up."

"Like hell!"

Once before, Lockhart had been surprised by the giant's speed. This time he was ready. Janks put his head down and charged, muscular arms outstretched. If he was afraid of Lockhart's Colt, he didn't show it. *Mister, I been shot, stabbed, cut at with an ax . . .* And Lockhart didn't want to shoot; there were too many people in the small room, too much chance of the bullet going astray.

As the powerful hands closed around his throat, Lockhart pivoted, swung with all his weight, slammed the big revolver against the side of the giant's head. Janks blinked, stepped backward, looked at Lockhart with injured surprise on his face.

"Damn," he said, lifting a hand to his ear. "That *hurt.*"

Then he leaned toward Lockhart. His eyes rolled back and he kept right on leaning, sliding like a loose-limbed avalanche down to the floor and dragging Lockhart with him. Her frying pan poised to strike, Marian Taylor hovered above his shoulder.

"Jim? Is that you? Are you all right?"

"I'm okay."

"Has he hurt you?"

"No, I'm all right. Here, help get him off me. That's better."

With Marian tugging at the big man's belt, Lockhart scrambled out from under his limp body. The little girl, hands still in her mouth, stared at him.

"Hello," he said to her. Then Marian caught him in a hug almost as tight as the giant's.

"Oh, Jim, I was so scared and so worried about you and I was afraid that big ape would hurt Ellie and he thought we had the banknotes and I saw your letter where it sounded like you were giving up but you can't because you're the only damned thing I've—"

He kissed her, as much to keep her quiet as anything. At least, that was his first idea, but he quickly got involved in the project for its own sake. She threw her arms around his neck and her body seemed to blend into his, and for a time, he forgot everything else. Then Janks stirred on the floor and let out a deep groan, and Marian sprang away. The little girl, watching them as if they were a puppet show, giggled.

"Hello," Lockhart said again. He knelt to pick up the giant's gun. "What's your name, young lady?"

"Ellie." She wiped damp fingers on the front of her skirt. "Are you Marian's gentleman?"

"I suppose I am. My name's Jim."

Ellie bobbed a curtsey. "I'm very pleased to meet you. Did you hurt that bad man?"

Lockhart bent over him. Janks had settled back into what seemed a peaceful sleep. "Not much, I think."

"He made a mess of Mommy's clean house. I don't like him."

"Then we'll move him outside." Lockhart glanced up at Marian. "Are you all right?"

"Fine."

"I'll just be a minute."

Hooking his hands under the giant's arms, Lockhart dragged Janks out to the rear hitching post and used his own belt to strap him firmly to it. Then he went back into the house.

He hadn't noticed before that the kitchen floor was strewn with items from the open cabinet. In the bedroom off the kitchen other things had been thrown about. *All my fault. Janks thought Marian had the imaginary banknotes!*

Marian and Ellie were on the horsehair sofa in the sitting room. Ellie gave Lockhart a big smile.

"Do you have any little girls like me?" she asked.

"I did. I had a little girl very much like you."

"Where is she?"

He knelt beside her. "She grew up. She's quite a woman now."

"Henson's here," Marian said.

For a moment, the words didn't register. Then Lockhart stared at her. "What? No, he can't be. I threw him off my trail in Kansas City."

"Then he got here some other way. Maybe Pritchard sent for him."

"Who's Pritchard?"

"From the bank. Anyway, I saw Henson, just before Prince Charming out there grabbed Ellie and me and brought us back here." Her eyes filled with the memory of that, and Lockhart thought she was going to cry.

"Did he see you?"

She didn't cry. "I don't know. Want to bet that he didn't?"

"No." After a moment he stood, went to the front window, and looked out down the road. At the bottom of the hill a carriage was just turning their way. *A cab, that same one with the blue plume. An odd coincidence? Sure.*

He looked again toward the carriage. It wasn't likely to be headed anywhere else but the North house. "Could this be Ellie's mother?"

Marian shook her head. "I don't think so, but that's the same one we came in. Henson could have seen us in it and had the man bring him to the same place."

The carriage was moving slowly up the hill, a shadow across it so that the passenger or passengers could not be seen. *I'd give ten dollars right now for my field glasses!* But that really didn't matter. Knowing for certain would not give them any more time.

"What about your things?" he asked Marian, but she had already left the room, drawing the girl after her.

"Come in here," she called. She was stuffing a last item or two into her bag. It reminded him that his own bag was behind the hedge.

Ellie said, "You're not going!"

Marian took time to kneel beside the girl. "We'll come back to visit you very soon, Ellie," she said. "But right now, there's something very important I need you to do."

Lockhart closed her bag and cinched it shut with the straps. "Listen," he said, but Marian ignored him.

"In just a moment, a very nice man wearing a badge is going to knock at your door."

"Really?"

"Yes. You'll like him."

"Is he your friend?"

"In a way. We've been very close to him for the past few weeks. But what you must do is invite him into the house. Then tell him that you've been kidnapped. After that, tell him that the bad man is out in the backyard."

"The great big man?"

"Yes. Then the marshal will arrest the bad man."

"But where will you be?"

"I'll be thinking of you and what a brave girl you are and what a dear friend."

"And you'll come back soon?"

"I promise."

"All right."

Lockhart said, "The carriage has turned up the drive."
He patted Ellie on the head, then took Marian by the arm
and carried her bag out the back. Janks was beginning to
moan.

Lockhart collected his own bag and took them both to
the far end where the hedge turned to grow sporadically up
the side yard. He saw Marshal Rance Henson leave the carriage, speak to the driver, and head up to the quiet house. If
the marshal was alarmed or anxious, he did not show it. The
driver was turning his carriage around.

As soon as Henson was on the porch and out of their
sight, Lockhart and Marian hurried to the low, scattered end
of the hedge for a better look. Henson was just opening the
front door, looking straight down at someone not nearly as
tall as he. Then he went through the doorway in a rush. The
door banged behind him.

Lockhart didn't need to urge Marian or explain his intention. If she hadn't read it in his thoughts, she'd come up
with the same plan herself. They ran to the carriage, threw
in their bags.

The driver said, "You the two passengers the marshal
said he'd be adding?"

"We are," Lockhart said. "Let's go."

"Got to wait for the marshal."

"No. We'll go now."

The driver grinned. "Can't do that. That old man's got
a badge bigger'n—"

Lockhart took out the Colt and pointed it at the driver's
prominent nose. "Bigger than this?"

Eddie Swell blinked at the gun, straightened in his seat,
gripped the reins. "Where to, sir?" he asked brightly.

Lockhart got up in the seat beside him. "We'll decide
later," he said. "For now, just go."

Releasing the brake, Eddie Swell slapped the reins on

his horse's rump. The carriage began to roll. Lockhart looked back. Because the house sat at an angle to the road, Henson did not have to run all the way around to see the carriage moving. He cried out at them but did not shoot.

Whether it was beneath Henson's dignity to run after the cab or whether he knew he'd never catch it on foot, Lockhart didn't know. All he knew was that the marshal didn't try. Instead, he stood for a moment watching them roll away down the hill, then gave in to a little girl who was tugging at his hand.

Looking back at Marian in the rear seat, Lockhart said, "Now what?"

"I know the very thing," Marian said.

Having told Eddie Swell to wait, Marshal Henson had strode across the lawn and tapped on the door of the North home. He had his hand on his pistol, ready for anything except the small blond girl who opened the door and looked up at him with complete trust.

"I'm Ellie," she said.

"Is your mama in, Ellie?"

She shook her head, eyes solemn. "Mister," she said, "please help me. My mommy's not here and there's a wicked giant out in the backyard."

"Wicked giant?"

"Like in *Jack and the Beanstalk*. He was going to hurt us. Marian said you'd 'rest him. But he's resting already, by the hitch rail."

Not knowing what to make of all that, Henson drew his gun and followed her. The house was strewn with things as if someone had been throwing them. Henson kept his eyes open and his Colt ready, but there seemed to be no one else at home.

"Where's the woman brought you up here?"

"That's Marian. The wicked giant caught her, too."

"Did he?"

"Then her gentleman saved us. She and her gentleman wented away."

Henson looked out the back door and saw Sim Janks slumped against the hitching post. He was just beginning to complain about his situation. "What gentleman's that?"

"Jim."

Henson went through the door silently using up another six months' worth of his soul. "I know you," he told Janks. "What're you doing here?"

"Sitting on my hands feels like."

"Get up."

"Can't. Tied like a dog to a post."

"Where's Lockhart and the woman?"

"Lockhart? Wish I knew. He's the scoundrel killed my bud. Don't know any Lockhart."

Henson gave verbal vent to his hostility and frustration. Behind him Ellie said, "Uh-uh, that's ugly." Further behind him Eddie's rig began to roll.

Henson sprinted around the corner of the house just in time to bring his gun to bear on the bouncing carriage. *It would be just my luck to hit the woman and have to listen to that the rest of my life.* "Well, I'll just be"—the girl tugged at his arm—"doggoned!" he said with real venom.

"I want to see my mommy."

"Well, I don't know what I can do about that. Where *is* your mother?"

"Don't know."

God have mercy. "When will your mother be home?" he asked.

"Later."

"Surely she doesn't leave you here by yourself?"

"Oh no. I stay with Mrs. Sykes sometimes. But today I stayed with Marian."

"You got a horse?"

"No."

"Well, that's just fine!"

Ellie curtseyed. "Thank you."

Saddled with a girl he couldn't leave and a prisoner he didn't want, Henson watched the rig take Lockhart and the woman out of his reach again. With a new restraint, he let the girl lead him back to Janks.

"Say, lawdog, can you get me loose from this?"

"I could, but I intend to leave you here awhile."

"I wish you'd bring me my hat, then. Sun's hot as hell."

Henson looked at the bloody gash above the man's ear. "What'd he use on you?"

"How'd I know? Feels like it was a flatiron, or maybe an anvil. If I'd seen it, I'd've stuffed it down his gullet instead of giving him leave to whang me with it."

"What were you looking for in the house?"

"Cookie jar."

Ellie brought out a hat and set it on Janks's head. "The cookie jar was on the shelf. You broke it."

"Sorry, kid."

Henson took Ellie into the house and began picking up some of the things. Ellie smiled at him. "Marian was right. You're a very nice man."

"She told you that?"

"Yes. She said I'd like you. And I do."

"Well—" Embarrassed, Henson shrugged. "Well, I'm glad to hear that, miss. Say, is that a carriage coming?"

"It sounds like one. Can we go for a ride?"

Henson didn't believe it, but in a moment he heard a horse's hooves on the front drive. Eddie Swell's rig pulled up and stopped with its blue plume waving in the wind.

"Thought I'd better come back for you," Eddie called.

"Why didn't you wait like I told you?"

"That jasper with the gun talked me out of it."

"Hold on. I've got a couple of passengers to get."

Three minutes later, Henson had the girl and the giant seated in the carriage. "Take me where you took the ones that hijacked you."

"It's a big day for that," Swell said, but Henson did not hear him. They drove down the hill at a brisk clip, swerved onto a wider street, and came to a stop a half-mile further.

"What the hell?" Henson wanted to know, without a thought to his indebtedness.

"Paul'll have some news for us, I'm bound."

"Paul? News?"

"This is where I took'm before they changed to his rig."

"Changed?" There weren't human words to express Henson's thought at that. "Where did they go?" The mildness of his tone surprised him himself. No curses to the Almighty.

"Coleman's Field," the other said. "It ain't more'n a couple, three miles up past that corner of the stockyards."

"Stockyards?" Henson looked at the stretch of pens defined by heavy board rail fences as high as a man's head and stretching out in every direction. "Which one?"

Eddie said, "I know where he means."

"Use your whip!" Henson said.

Sitting in a twist with his hands over the side rail, Janks said, "These damned handcuffs of yours is too tight, Doom."

"Good. And watch your language in front of Ellie."

"I want to see my mommy."

"Use the *doggoned* whip, Swell."

Up ahead, beyond the tangle of rail fences and posts and lowing cows, Henson saw the land open out. There was a big crowd of some kind ahead, carriages and buggies and horses everywhere. The ground was black with people on foot. Squinting into the sunset, he saw something huge and brown towering above them, festooned with ropes and netting.

"What's that?" he called to the driver. "Tent meeting of some kind?"

"That's the airship," Eddie Swell said. "People been coming out all day to see it."

Sim Janks spat over the side of the cab. "Blamed foolishness," he said.

Reluctant to agree with Janks about anything, Henson still had to nod. "Almighty never intended—" he began.

Before he finished, the huge tentlike contrivance slowly rose, swung toward him, came directly on east, blocking out the sun. Too large to fly but flying, too heavy to rise but rising, it swooped over the cab like a bird without wings. Ellie gave a delighted whoop and waved at it. Janks gawked. Henson and Eddie Swell gawked. The horse reared and tried to run away.

It was like a sunfish, Henson saw, or a big cigar. A sort of basket or car swung from ropes beneath it, and some chuffing unseen engine drove a windmill-like wheel to push it along. It slid gracefully over them, gradually gaining height and speed, seeming as big as any train Henson had ever ridden.

"Lord of mercy," Eddie Swell breathed. "Who'd've thought it!"

"Wheeeee!" Ellie said.

Henson, certain as anything that his quarry was up in that silly-looking gondola speeding away on the wings of the wind, said nothing. But he did realize the Almighty still had a trick or two up His sleeve that He hadn't shared with Rance Henson.

18

For months on end, crossing the country with Opportunity Knox and the other drummers, Lockhart had heard the young salesman sing the praises of Professor Kendrick and his marvelous invention.

"The *Air Traveler* will be the transportation of the future," was one of Knox's favorite phrases. "You'll have to tell your grandchildren what a Pullman car looked like, because they'll never see one! Here, let me show you our prospectus."

He hadn't known if Opportunity believed his own sales pitch, or if he was only doing his best to hustle another worthless stock. Lockhart himself had never for a moment thought there was anything to it. Even now, standing at the edge of the crowd on Coleman's Field with the great brown bulk of the thing puffing and straining in readiness above him, he had trouble believing the *Air Traveler* was real.

The line drawings in the prospectus had been accurate, so far as he could see, but they did no more justice to the real item than a toy train to the real one. Once or twice during the war, he'd seen observation balloons, but this was something entirely different. Long—more than a hundred feet, he was sure—tapered and rounded at its ends, the billowing bag looked more like some nightmare fish than anything else. The illusion was strengthened by a broad, cross-shaped tail at what he presumed was the back. Below the gasbag, an insubstantial-looking cabin dangled from a rat's nest of ropes and webbing. Lockhart heard the soft chuffing of a steam engine from someplace inside. A thin black drift of coal smoke eddied back toward the tail.

Beside him, Marian hung back against the pressure of his arm. She was staring up at the thing like a child seeing her first elephant.

"Whose idea was this, anyway?" she said.

"Yours."

"I was crazy. Can that—that—*that* really fly?"

"I don't know. But they got it here some way."

"No," she said. "We can't. Not on that. I was crazy."

"Well, Marshal Doom will be along as soon as that cabbie can get back to tell him where we went. You'd better pull your alternate plan together pretty fast."

She looked up at him, and her hand tightened on his arm. "Serves me right for getting mixed up with another damned man. Let's go."

They walked then toward the machine, which loomed more enormous at every step. The crowd was heavy. Half of Fort Worth seemed to be there, with ladies in their finest and men in all kinds of clothing. Kids hawked programs and peanuts, and a beer wagon from the Red Light was doing a brisk business over in one corner of the field. But moving toward the airship was easier than Lockhart would have expected. In the crisp fall breeze, the *Air Traveler* panted and quivered and surged against its mooring rope as if it were alive. Nobody seemed eager to get too close.

Almost in the ship's shadow, a five-piece band was playing "The Yellow Rose of Texas," its members occasionally missing a note as they glanced nervously back at the bulk of the gasbag towering above them. Still closer to the center of attention stood a small group of people, crowded together perhaps for comfort as they moved slowly toward the ship's gangplank. Lockhart noticed that some held tickets in their hands. Then, just at the foot of the gangplank, he saw a table where young Opportunity Knox was taking tickets and apologizing to those he had to turn away.

"Sold out," he said, half in relief. "Come on. We can lose ourselves in the crowd, slip off before Doom—"

"In a pig's eye." Marian pulled him into the line. "Slip off from that son of a—bloodhound?" she murmured just loud enough for him to hear. "Play up."

"What?"

They had moved behind a well-dressed elderly couple. The woman was looking up at *Air Traveler* with a certain amount of trepidation.

"I'm sure there's no danger, dear," the man was saying, not sounding too convinced himself. "The paper says it's the transportation of the future."

"But it isn't the future yet. What about right now?"

"Well, I don't know."

"I hope they've solved that problem with the steering," Marian said brightly to Lockhart. "We wouldn't want to hit a mountain, like that one in Pennsylvania did."

"What?" Lockhart said. Marian dug him hard in the ribs with her elbow.

"And with all that hydrogen. Just imagine—*boom!* No one would find any pieces big enough to put you back together for decent burial."

"Burial?" the woman in front said.

"Uh—yes." Lockhart cleared his throat. "But they don't always explode, you know. That airship in California didn't."

"Oh, that's right! Its inventor was very lucky. It fell into the ocean, so he drowned instead."

The man in front turned to look at him. "Say, mister, you seem to know a lot about these things. Do you think they're safe?"

"Oh, sure. That gas will explode all right, but it's perfectly safe as long as there's no fire near it."

"Like that fire in the boiler, you mean?" Marian asked.

"Or as long as no one smokes, or strikes a match, or there isn't any lightning—"

"It looks like rain, don't you think? We'll have a thunderstorm later."

"—and nothing rips that cover, and all the stitching holds, and the steam boiler doesn't explode, and—"

"Howard," the older lady said. "Howard, I told you we shouldn't go."

"Now, Betty, we've already bought our tickets."

"—and the cabin doesn't break loose in the wind and fall—"

"Oh, I envy you!" Marian said. "We couldn't get tickets, and I wanted so much to take the flight!"

"Did you? But I thought you wouldn't want to."

Marian touched her arm and leaned closer. "Suicide pact," she whispered. "We'll just have to find another way."

"Oh! Howard, they seem such a nice young couple. Maybe we could let them have our tickets."

"Oh, we couldn't," Marian said. "Then you'd miss it all."

"No, no, it's all right."

Howard said "Let her have them? Do you know what those cost?"

"I'll pay you what they cost," Lockhart said. He fished in his pocket, found his wallet. "Can't disappoint the little woman. And we won't be needing the money anyway."

"Hundred dollars. For the two."

It strained Lockhart's finances, but he counted out the bills. Howard took the money and shoved the tickets at him. Then he and his lady began immediately to move away.

Marian said, "Oh, you must stay and watch it take off. Even if it falls, it probably won't land on the crowd."

They didn't answer. Marian nudged Lockhart. "Little woman?"

"You're a great actress," Lockhart said. "You made that thing sound terrifying."

"What makes you think I was acting?"

"I really admire you."

She looked up at him from the corners of her eyes. "Admire?"

He bent to kiss her in front of her ear and whispered, "Love."

"Thank you."

"And when we get out of this, I'm going to make an honest man of myself."

"Yes?"

"By paying you back all the money I owe you."

"How *very* nice."

"What?"

"You heard me."

"What've I done now?"

Opportunity Knox said, "What you've done is purchase tickets to adventure, tickets to sights and wonders never before known to mortal man."

They had come to the head of the line without noticing. Lockhart held out the tickets, his eyes downcast. Knox took them, glanced up at the passengers' faces. He froze, the tickets still in his hand.

"Lockhart? Jim!" His face broke into a happy grin. "Jim, it's great to see you." He looked at Marian. "And it's—ah—Mrs. Taylor," he finished more softly.

"Marian."

Knox pumped Lockhart's hand. He didn't seem to know just what kind of expression to put on his face. He settled for the grin again.

"So you've come clean of that business in Sacramento, both of you. What happened?" He looked at the crowd behind Lockhart, then waved a hand toward the gangplank.

"You'll have to tell me all about it later. Better get on board. We cast off in five minutes."

They climbed the swaying walkway, Lockhart uneasy at its flexibility and tendency to quiver, Marian holding tightly to his arm. It led them onto a narrow railed deck that seemed to go all the way around the boxcarlike cabin. Neither deck nor railing was half as solid as Lockhart would have liked.

"Doesn't give us much time to change our minds," he said quietly to Marian.

"Other things don't give us any choice at all." Her voice was flat.

Lockhart looked at her. *Like Doom chasing us? Like your husband, whatever's become of him?* Before he could put either thought into words, Opportunity Knox came bounding up onto the deck beside them. A burly young man in a blue uniform pulled in the gangway.

"Had to get rid of the rest of them," Knox confided. "We can only carry a dozen passengers, and we're running so late we can't do any more excursion rides. Got to head for Little Rock." He raised his voice. "Captain York!"

"Aye, sir," came from somewhere forward.

"It's time. We are ready to cast loose."

"Aye, aye," York replied. "Crewmen, stand by."

The youth in the blue uniform dumped the rolled-up gangway in a locker and hurried to the front of the cabin. Lockhart saw another crewman come out of a door further back and head for the stern.

"All ready."

"Let go aft."

The ungainly craft gave a lurch that made Lockhart drop his suitcase and grab for the rail. Marian's fingers dug into his arm.

"Let go forward."

Another lurch. And then, while the deckhands were nonchalantly coiling up the long ropes, Lockhart saw the ground

begin to fall away beneath them. All in a second he realized
that they were rising instead. His stomach gave a swoop like
a hawk diving on a rabbit. Marian screamed.

"Engaging the screw. Full power."

The steam engine speeded up and took on a deeper, laboring note. Behind the cabin, a cross between a ship's propeller and the business end of a windmill began to turn with
a steady *whup-whup-whup*. The *Air Traveler* nosed forward
like a balky horse, turned into the wind, and suddenly was in
its element, a fish in water, sliding through the air with
smooth, quiet ease.

"My Lord," Marian Taylor whispered. "It works!"

Daring a second look over the rail, Lockhart saw Coleman's Field already an incredible distance below, a plain
of upturned sunflower faces. A few bleating notes of "The
Yellow Rose of Texas" rose to follow them on the wind,
and then they were past the edge of the field, skimming
above the track of a dirt road, soaring over a toylike carriage from which thrust the goggle-eyed face of Marshal
Rance Henson.

While Janks and a delighted Ellie waited with Eddie Swell at
the edge of Coleman's Field, Henson picked up a brochure
showing the *Air Traveler*'s proposed route and a schedule of
its stops. He saw he would need wings himself to catch up to
it, but he meant to have his try.

"Downtown," he told Eddie. "Marshal Courtright's office."

"It's only that I feel like I know you, you being such a
steady customer and all, makes me ask, but you ain't planning
to arrest that thing?"

"Just a man that's on it. Him and his ladyfriend."

"That's Marian. And her gentleman. They said you were
nice," Ellie said.

Eddie thought that over. "Seems to me you're in for quite a chase if he stays with the aero-thing."

"Chase him across hell in a rowboat, if that's what it takes," Henson growled. "I'm getting good and"—he caught Ellie's reproachful look—"dadgummed tired of this."

"Bet it gets harder before it gets easier," Eddie said. "Use your whip."

At the marshal's office, just down from the county courthouse, Henson herded Janks inside. Ellie skipped along with them, clinging to Henson's hand. The officer on duty, a heavy-jawed man with a drooping mustache, glanced up from his paperwork. Recognizing Henson, he straightened suddenly, his hand reaching toward the holstered Colt lying on the desk beside him. Henson waved his free hand.

"Relax, Jim. I'm not after you this time."

"You sure about that, Rance?"

"Word of honor. You haven't got that New Mexico business cleared up yet?"

"Depends on who you talk to. But I'm downright shy of federal lawmen. What the hell's happened to your arm?"

"Nothing much. All I've got for you is a prisoner."

The lawman rose, taking his hand off the Colt and offering it to Henson instead. He looked at the handcuffed Janks, then smiled at Ellie.

"Which is your prisoner, the big one or the little one?"

"The big one. This little one is Ellie. Ellie, meet Marshal Courtright."

"Pleased." Courtright offered his hand to Ellie, who touched his fingers and put two of her own in her mouth. "But I'm not but a deputy now, Rance. What's the big one done?"

Henson had been considering that. He was pretty short of witnesses to convict Janks of anything. "Whatever he could think of, I expect, but the only witness we have for his business here is Ellie, and I don't think we want to put her in court."

"Suppose you take these damned handcuffs off me, then," Janks suggested.

"Thing is, I'd like you to keep him out of circulation for awhile. I have a complicated investigation going on, and he keeps tracking up the middle of it."

Courtright's mustache twitched. He rubbed his mouth. "I read something about that. Newspaperman name of Darrow, I think."

"That—" Henson looked at Ellie, bit his lip, forced his face into a smile. "That's right. Think you can help?"

"Oh, I expect we can hold him a month or two." Courtright took Sim Janks by the arm and tugged him toward a side door. "Come this way, friend, and we'll get you settled for the night. My, you're a big one."

Janks held back. "You can't do this. What's the charge?"

"I think we'll start with felonious ugliness and go from there. Move along, or you'll be resisting an officer. Rance, stay around and we'll have a drink."

Henson felt Ellie's tug on his hand. "Like to, Jim, but I have to get this young lady home. Her mama will be worrying."

In fact, Nellie North was close to frantic. While Henson was paying off Eddie Swell and adding a big enough tip to buy his horse a fresh plume, Nellie rushed out on the front porch to embrace her daughter.

"Oh, my Ellie!" she cried, looking at Henson with a reproach that startled him. "Where have you been?"

Not knowing what else to do, Henson showed her his badge. "I ain't meant the child any harm," he said. "I found her here in the company of felons and worse, so I took charge of her and kept her safe. It seemed best to take her with me."

Nellie put her small hand over her mouth. "Felons! Oh my lands! What about Marian? Is she all right?"

"Oh, yes. She's just fine."

"They flewed, Mommy." Ellie made swooping motions

with her hands. "Ellie and her gentleman. They flewed like the sparrows."

"*Flew*, dear." Nellie kept her hand to her mouth, gazing at Henson uncertainly. Henson thought it made her look like her daughter.

Ellie said, "Mr. Henson is a nice man."

Henson liked that. He couldn't remember the last time anyone had said it of him. And it seemed to decide Nellie North about him. She swung the screen door wide.

"Please come in, Mr.—Marshal Henson. I want to hear all about it."

Henson turned his hat in his big hands. "Well, ma'am, I'd better be moving on."

"And I've waited supper for Ellie."

Henson sat at table with them and listened to the girl say grace and partook of their hospitality as hungrily as a bear just out of hibernation. Besides a warmth of feeling he recognized but couldn't remember, he enjoyed the home-cooked pot roast. He got his tongue tangled trying to find words to tell Nellie about his felons. Finally, he told her about the *Air Traveler* instead.

"It was the most wonderfulest thing in the world!" Ellie said. "There were people on it, and it flewed—flew."

Nellie, too, was fascinated by the talk of the airship, but soon she wanted to know about Marian. Cutting his story to fit her ears, Henson told—more accurately than he knew—how Janks had kidnapped Ellie and Marian, how Marian's friend had subdued Janks, how he himself had come to find the house suddenly empty.

"Finding Ellie here worse than alone," he said, "I had cause to wonder where her daddy is."

Ellie said, "My daddy's in heaven."

Henson said, "I'm sorry to hear that." He felt his face getting hot because he was lying and because he'd made it sound like he wished her father were in hell. "That he's passed, I mean. May I ask what happened?"

He listened to the woman's explanation only to hear her voice and watch her mouth move. When she'd finished, he hadn't heard a word but knew from her demeanor that her husband had been dead long enough. When he had planned out the speech well enough to give it clean, he told her what a fine dinner it was.

She blushed, he thought, while he was telling her. For whatever reason, she got up immediately and turned her back on him to fidget around with some pans on stove. Finally, she said, "Thank you."

He even enjoyed the dessert, though he seldom chose them in the hotels where he usually took his meals. There was nothing he wanted more than to stay for another cup of coffee and visit in Nellie North's parlor, but he knew he'd have to catch the night train, and he knew he was up to his chin in uncharted waters. Still, he couldn't bring himself to leave until he'd worked out a last speech.

"I was wondering," he told Nellie. "I often find myself in Fort Worth. Would it be too much of a bother to you if I was to drop back by, to check on Ellie, when I've wrapped up my business with Miss Marian and her friend?"

It didn't go the way he'd planned it, and he felt himself the fool, but he got through it at least. The woman did not avert her eyes or hesitate. "It would be a pleasure," she told him, "to see you again."

He remembered those words and went over them in his mind all the way to Texarkana. *She could have said she wouldn't mind. She could have said it would be all right. Hell, she could have said straight out she'd rather I didn't. But she said, by God, it would be a pleasure to see me again.* He marveled at it.

* * *

"Professor, I thought we had a stowaway," the young crewman said, "but I must've been mistaken. I've checked the engine room and looked at all the tickets again."

Professor Augustus Kendrick broke off what he'd been saying to Lockhart. "Eh? A stowaway? Ridiculous."

"Yes, sir. But a man was fooling around with the aft netting just before we ascended. I thought he might be trying to get aboard."

"Ridiculous!" The professor jutted his white beard toward Lockhart. "A man like myself—a true scientist—shouldn't be bothered by such nonsense. I told Mr. Knox it was too early for a public test, but he insisted."

"We're grateful he did," Marian Taylor said.

They were seated at a flimsy table inside the gondola under Edison lights generated by the engine. Opportunity Knox had seen to their luggage, hurried them in to meet the professor, then left them for the moment to tend the other passengers. Most of them were talking, sampling the airship's cold supper table, peering through the forward windows to watch Captain York at work in the wheelhouse. Outside, to Lockhart's continuing astonishment, the bleak moonlit sky slid effortlessly past.

"Professor, do you want me to look again?"

"No, no." Kendrick waved a blue-veined hand. "Go about your duties, young man. Stowaway, indeed! I should be perfecting my work on the aerobat!"

"It seems pretty perfect to us as it is, sir," Lockhart said.

"What? Oh, I grant you it functions. But the power plant is the problem. You know hydrogen is safe as long as it isn't exposed to a flame."

"Like that fire in the boiler, you mean?" Marian asked. She had said that earlier, to the people on the ground, but it hadn't impressed Lockhart in exactly the same way.

"Precisely, young woman. The *Traveler's* steam engine is

the most powerful for its weight in the world, but the boiler is the heart of the problem. I fear the aerobat will never be truly practical until I devise a more efficient engine."

Opportunity Knox paused beside Kendrick. "Now, Professor, don't discourage your investors. Why, the *Air Traveler* is a great success already."

"We think so," Lockhart agreed. Suddenly, he was tired of the talk, tired of being in the stuffy cabin when the night outside was a magic carpet ride. "Excuse me, but I think I'll take a turn around the deck, if that's all right?"

"Oh—ah—yes," Knox said. He started to follow, but Kendrick caught his arm, wanting to argue. "Go right ahead, Jim. I may come out in a minute, to talk about things."

"Fine. Marian?"

Marian gave him a lazy smile. "I think the excitement is getting to me. Maybe later."

Lockhart wondered if she'd read his mind again and knew he wanted a moment alone. He didn't doubt it. "Bring a wrap if you come. It's cool out."

It was more than cool out by the railing on the open deck. A strong, steady breeze came from the ship's blunt bow and whispered off the stern behind the churning propeller. The bulge of the gas envelope blocked off most of the stars, but Lockhart could see a limitless distance out and downward. Some unimaginable distance below, moonlit trees and an occasional lonely light glided past. Hills rose up toward the airship but couldn't touch it. It soared above them like a great sailing ship bound for the stars, driven by the music of its faithful engine. For the moment, Lockhart could forget Henson and the unknown killer and all his other problems and rest content in this new world.

He felt the walkway quiver and turned to see whether it was Knox or Marian who had come to join him, hoping for Marian. Instead, a stranger was swinging down like a monkey from the tangle of rope netting that held the gondola to the big balloon above it. Dropping lightly onto the decking, he faced Lockhart.

"You're the stowaway," Lockhart said.

The man leered and reached inside his flapping coat. "And you're ten thousand dollars on the hoof, mister." He pulled out a gun and pointed it at Lockhart. "Big day for me. Collect from the gov'ment, collect from the King of China, collect from the big man. All for the same scalp."

"The big man? Janks?"

The other laughed. "Janks! Why, mister, Sim is short for simple. You don't think he planned this?"

"Who then?"

"Told me your galfriend would lead me to you. But you might' near shook me, dodging around that damned lawdog."

"Who is he? Who's the big man you're talking about?"

The stowaway looked surprised. "You don't know? Not a heap smarter'n Sim, are you?" He chuckled. "Well, it won't fret you none from here on, you being dead and all."

"Wait! You'll be dead yourself if you shoot me."

The man looked quickly around. "Nobody here. And nobody'll care anyway, you being wanted and all. Who's gonna kill me, you?"

"You're going to kill yourself and me and everybody else on board if you pull that trigger." Lockhart gestured upward. "That bag's full of hydrogen gas. One shot and it'll go off like a Roman candle."

Unwillingly, the other glanced up at the vast black shadow of the bag. He brought eyes and gun back to Lockhart. "Lying."

"You don't see me going for a gun, do you? No firearms on board. No smoking, no matches, no cooking fire, no kerosene lamps."

The stowaway looked at the lighted cabin windows,

looked at Lockhart. Holding the gun steady, he moved forward. His left hand dipped to a pocket.

"Just have to get in close—"

Lockhart never found out how he'd proposed to finish that sentence. Almost at the man's elbow, the cabin door opened and Opportunity Knox came through, saying, "Jim, are you—hey, what the hell?"

Startled, the stowaway swung toward him. His left hand came out holding a folding knife, not yet opened. He swatted at Knox with the back of his hand, trying still to keep the gun on Lockhart.

Lockhart leaped. He plowed into the man and the two of them caromed into the rail. Wood cracked and splintered. Lockhart felt the rail give, felt them leaning far out, but he had time and thought only for the gun. He got his hand on it, going for the hammer, knowing that if it fell Marian and Knox and the old professor and the magical aerobat would all melt away in flame as if their spell had been broken. Knox yelled something and the other man gave a strangled scream and Lockhart was rewarded with a stabbing pain in the ball of his left thumb. He'd caught the hammer.

"Jim!"

Then the rail gave. Lockhart felt himself and the stowaway launched together out into the air. He opened his mouth to cry out, but something brought him up with a jerk. Inches from his own, he saw the moonlit face of the stowaway, hair streaming in the wind, mouth agape, eyes wide and filled with terror. Then the face fell away like a stone dropping down a well, and Opportunity Knox, one hand twisted in the rope webbing and the other grasping Lockhart's coat, hauled him back to the safety of the deck.

"How—how high are we?" Lockhart gasped, his cheek against the cold planking.

"Don't know. Seven hundred, a thousand feet from the ground. Jim, my God!"

Panting. Lockhart pushed himself up until he sat with his back against the cabin wall. "Opportunity," he said, "we haven't exactly told you the truth, Marian and I, about our situation."

19

Opportunity Knox offered his hand at the rail. "Take care, Jim. Good luck."

"Most unscientific," Professor Kendrick muttered, but he too shook Lockhart's hand. "I enjoyed our discussion, young man. I trust you'll find a path out of your predicament."

Lockhart, who didn't feel like a young man by anyone's measure, smiled. "Thank you, sir. And thanks for the unscheduled stop. I'm sure Henson will have somebody watching for us at Little Rock."

"No trouble at all, Jim," Knox said.

That wasn't quite true. Tethered by her nose, the *Air Traveler* bucked and surged against a strong breeze. Treetops loomed from the darkness now and then, uncomfortably close. Knox cleared his throat and looked toward the rope ladder.

"I don't want to hurry you, but the captain's not sure how long he can hold her. Can you handle the ladder all right?"

"No trouble at all," Lockhart said. He grasped its sides and lowered himself, trying not to look at the broken railing. "So long."

The ground was only a dozen feet below. At the bottom, the burly young crewman stood in the center of a beam from the searchlight. He steadied Lockhart, looking at him with intense curiosity. Then, acting the part of a man who could do his job without asking questions, he turned to hold the ladder for Marian.

"Your bags are right over there, sir. Are you and the lady all right?"

Lockhart planted his feet on the solid, unmoving ground. "Fine," he said.

"Then I'll be going."

With a last quizzical look, he scurried up the ladder and hauled it in behind him. "Lights out! Take in the anchor!" Captain York's voice bellowed from above. "Engaging screw. Full power!"

The light blinked out. For one moment the *Traveler*'s black shadow hovered over them, menacing as the pall of doom. The next, the *Air Traveler* was rising like a ball of thistledown against the stars. Lockhart caught a glimpse of Opportunity Knox waving from the rail, heard the beat of the engine and the whupping of the propeller, and then the airship was gone and he and Marian were alone in the peaceful darkness.

"Was that real?" Marian asked, still staring at the sky. "Any of it?"

Lockhart remembered the stowaway's face in that last instant. "I hope not," he said.

"Where in heaven's name are we?"

"Arkansas. There's a road over there that leads to some town, Opportunity said." Lockhart turned, uncertain in the darkness. "Or was it over there?"

"Brilliant." Marian Taylor picked up her bag. "Come on. I can see I'm going to have to get us out of this."

The road, at first little more than a track where the stumps were cut shorter, led to a town and, finally, to a hotel. Marian slumped on a settee while Lockhart registered them as Mr. and Mrs. Hartley. The elderly clerk peered at the names and then at Lockhart.

"Traveling late."

"Yep. We'll have a hot bath. Two hot baths. Right away."

"A hot bath? Now? Mister, do you know what time it is?"

"Yes, and I don't want it to be much later before we get those baths. Where is this place, anyway?"

"Where? What town you mean? Why, this here's Fulton." He scratched his head. "Ain't been a train nor a stage through since sundown. What'd you folks do, drop out'n the sky?"

He was still staring after them when they went down toward their room, clearly without the slightest idea why they'd both dissolved into such helpless laughter at his civil question.

"There's a railroad here," Lockhart said.

"Um!" Marian was already in bed, an anonymous mound under the covers.

"We can get out tomorrow."

"Wonderful."

"I think we should go to Hannibal. I want to ask Aaron Porter why the hell he thinks I robbed him."

"I think you should come to bed. Do you know how long it's been since we've slept?"

"I know how long it's been since we slept together."

Marian sat up. "I guess you'll need me tomorrow. To go see your damned banker for you."

"You could disguise me."

"If he knows you well, he'd probably recognize your voice."

Lockhart tried an old man's voice. "Even like this?"

She laughed. "You'll need me!" she said. "Would you like me to play the old woman or the concerned relative or the tart?"

Lockhart stretched out beside her. She smelled of soap from the bath and freshness and Marian. "Do you mean with Aaron," he asked, "or right now?"

It was a long ride to Hannibal. Lockhart had plenty of time to tell the story of his own adventures and to hear the account of Marian's.

"The strangest thing is all the others showing up there," Lockhart said. "You're sure about Ed Givens? I didn't think Fort Worth was even part of his territory."

She nodded. "Very sure. I only heard Thompson's name, but I saw Givens. And don't forget Knox dropping out of the sky like that." She giggled, remembering the desk clerk the night before. "Sorry."

"The only one missing is Mel Baker."

"Maybe it's suspicious that he *wasn't* there."

Lockhart tried to find some place to fit that in, then waved it aside impatiently. "Opportunity had a great chance to kill me on the *Traveler* if he'd wanted to. And somebody in Fort Worth hired that thug who fell over the side."

Marian put both hands around his arm and squeezed hard. "That was scary," she said softly.

"Your getting waylaid by Janks was scary. I should never have left you alone that way."

With a squawk of laughter, Marian released his arm and sat up. "Damned if that isn't just like a man! You walk in among two dozen Chinese swinging swords at you, and then you get in a wrestling match with some stray murderer a thousand miles up in the air, and then you tell me *I'm* not fit to be left alone?"

Lockhart stared, then laughed along with her. "Guess you're right, at that. Maybe I'm the one not fit to be left alone. But I worry about you."

"I worry about you—and with lots better reason! I could've handled that Janks ape."

"I didn't handle my part of it very well. When I shot Brutus, I killed the goose that might have laid the golden eggs."

"Brutus." Marian frowned. "More Shakespeare. Maybe. What was he like?"

"Well-spoken man, younger than me, lots of black hair. He looked like he belonged in St. Louis or San Francisco instead of the Roost. He kept hinting about the things he knew, but he wouldn't come out with anything definite."

"Sounds almost like an actor." The train lurched around a curve, throwing Marian against him again. She started to move away, then settled her head on his shoulder instead. "You seem youthful enough sometimes, James Lockhart."

"If I'd waited, talked to him some more."

"If you'd waited, he would have killed Henson. You couldn't have done that, much as I might like to myself."

Though he'd never meant to mention it, Lockhart found himself telling her about the field at Franklin and the scavenger he'd killed and the young Confederate.

"It was dark, I remember," he finished. "I remember the torches. And we were pulling out for Nashville—my regiment was in the rear guard. There was nothing I could do but leave him."

"Maybe his own side found him. Maybe he didn't die."

"It was all useless. Like the business at Little China. No use at all."

Marian said softly, "Don't worry so. We'll find the answer."

Like hell. Weeks of chasing back and forth. No telling how many people dead, the latest that poor bastard who fell from the Traveler. *And we're not an inch closer than we were at the start.*

He started to say as much. Then he looked at Marian, at the weariness in her face and the indomitable strength in her eyes and the set of her mouth. He felt ashamed.

*No. We'll find the answer in Hannibal. Or we'll find it some-
place else. But I'm damned if I'll quit until we get this sorted out!*
"Hannibal," he said aloud. "The answer's in Hannibal."

When Marian started for the bank in the guise of Lockhart's
elder sister, he stayed behind at their hotel with her copy of
Henson's notes on the Hannibal theft. Lounging in a chair,
he read through the marshal's version of the crime and what
each of the other drummers had said about it.

Opportunity Knox had been in Hannibal on that day.
He'd drunk a cup of coffee with Lockhart before going on to
call on a potential investor. Knox told Henson he thought
Lockhart seemed a bit nervous, not quite himself, thought he
didn't know why. Yes, he'd seen Lockhart go in the bank
shortly after it opened. They hadn't met again until the train
pulled out that night. Yes, he'd sold a hundred shares of stock
in the *Air Traveler* there. (*Idiot!* was Henson's somewhat
harsh comment.)

Mel Baker had been there but definitely had not seen
Lockhart until they got on the train together. (*What time
was that?*) One of those dreary night trains. Ten o'clock, he
thought. Maybe later. (*Would have given plenty of time.*) Baker
supposed that was true, but he didn't know. If the robbery
had happened in the middle of the night, Lockhart couldn't
have done it. (*Breakin aft 4:30, bfr 10:00. Bnkr's idea of midnight or ltr must be wrong.*) No, Lockhart didn't seem nervous
or different, but of course Baker never guessed his friend
had launched upon a career of crime, nor that he'd already
murdered a man in El Paso.

Thanks, Mel. Lockhart frowned at Henson's spidery
writing. *Career of crime! And why don't you sound like yourself here? Are you hiding something? Something like theft and
murder?*

Lockhart tried to picture Mel Baker as a killer, failed

completely. But that didn't help. The same was true of Knox and Givens and—no.

It's not true of Reb Thompson. He could kill someone. And I could. I have.

He leafed through the notes until he found what Thompson had told about the incident in Hannibal. He'd known nothing of it until the marshal brought it up. No, he had no special memory of Hannibal or of that date, though his calendar showed he'd been there. He might have seen Lockhart go in the bank, but what of it? Lockhart had been in a thousand banks but it didn't mean he'd robbed or killed anyone. (*V. dmd uncooperative!!* Henson declared.)

It turned out to be Ed Givens who couldn't remember being in Hannibal at that time. He couldn't even remember the others getting off the train there. Maybe, yes, he *had* been detained an extra day in St. Louis while the others went ahead.

But I remember his being there! We talked about—but no. That was Mel. Ed wasn't there. I even remember his telling us all that he would catch up to us on down the line.

Lockhart ruled out Opportunity Knox and concentrated on the others. Their testimony about the crime in El Paso was no more helpful. This time, they'd all proceeded by different routes, leaving Lockhart behind. Givens had gone on to Denver, Thompson to Tombstone where the market in guns was suddenly strong, Knox back to Fort Worth. They'd crossed paths again in Cheyenne, or maybe it was Kansas City, a week or so later—none of them was sure just when, and neither was Lockhart.

He shook his head in frustration. He could make nothing out of that, and nothing more of the notes on Denver and Fort Worth. The one thing that stood out was that he was the only one who'd definitely been in all four towns and all four banks on the right day. He had spoken with each banker before the crime, and he'd left on that same day.

No wonder Doom thinks I did it. Maybe I did!

He gave it up, tucked the notes away, went downstairs to find a paper. Three men had their heads together in the parlor, talking about Mark Twain's new book on the Mississippi.

"It's a disgrace, that's what," one of them was saying. "That Sam Clemens was idle enough as a boy, but for a grown man to waste good work days writing claptrap is just pure shiftlessness."

"Well, Sam never could hold a regular job," another defended. Lockhart wanted to hear the rest, but a suspicious look from the clerk sent him back to his room.

Suspicious look! He mocked himself. *The wicked flee—* But no, he couldn't use that with Marian. It was from the Bible, not Shakespeare.

The newspaper he'd found was from St. Louis. There was no mention of a body falling from the sky to land in some farmer's potato patch, and Lockhart supposed there never would be. A thing as small as a man would be easy to lose that way. Lockhart worked hard to keep his thoughts off that subject. He probably didn't succeed too well, because he was a page past the big story when its headline registered on him. Then he turned back, still thinking he must have read it wrong.

HEROIC LAWMAN CONFRONTS YELLOW PERIL! Then, running along in progressively smaller type: *Hell in Little China! Marshal Henson Escapes Carnage with Life and Honor! Famed Thespian Slain!* Lockhart wasn't surprised by the final entry, Clyde Darrow's byline.

Lockhart began to read the only news he already knew. Marshal Rance Henson, it seemed, that eagle-eyed protector of all that was good in society, had charged into the outlaw fastness of No Man's Land in search of a desperate criminal. There he'd encountered a nefarious plot hatched by the almond-eyed Sons of Heaven. Beset by vast numbers, Henson had shot his way out, sustaining a grievous wound. His action had certainly prevented dark but unspecified crimes, might even have saved the republic as Darrow knew it.

I'll have to cut this out and save it for Henson. Give us something to talk about the next time he catches me. The most obvious thing to Lockhart was that his own name didn't appear anywhere in the piece. That was clearly Henson's work, and Lockhart wondered why the marshal had left him out. *Maybe he's starting to believe me. But more likely he doesn't want to admit he had me and lost me again.*

Darrow wasn't through. *"This reporter,"* Lockhart read, *"has only now learned the identity of one of those slain in the fierce battle that raged in the heart of outlaw country. The dead man, who gave his life in valiant service supporting the cause of justice, was noted Shakespearean tragedian Junius Brutus Taylor . . . "*

"My God," Lockhart said aloud. "Brutus." Slowly, he reread the last part.

" . . . Junius Brutus Taylor, known to his loyal public as the Hamlet of the Golden West. The circumstances of Taylor's death are unclear, but Marshal Henson, like a Spartan warrior of old, bore home the body of the fallen hero when he returned to Liberal for treatment of his own desperate wounds."

There was more, a lot more, much of it about Taylor's distinguished career cut short just as he stood on the verge of greatness. Lockhart couldn't read it. He let the paper fall. Its pages had not settled when Marian Taylor opened the door, sighed, and came into the room smiling at him just as if he weren't guilty of killing her husband. She stopped in the act of removing her hat.

"What's the matter with you?" she asked. "You look as if you'd just killed someone and hadn't had time to hide the body!"

"I haven't."

"Good. It went very well at the bank. No posse behind me, no need to run for our lives."

"I haven't had time to hide the body."

"What?" She looked at him. "Are you all right?"

He shook his head. "Nor ever can be again." *For you'll hate me when you know. There'll never be any way of getting past your husband's corpse between us.*

"I'm afraid for you."

He laughed, picked up the paper, handed it to her. Unable to find the words to tell her himself, he pointed to the article.

"Darrow again. Who taught that man to *write?*"

She waited for him to join in her laugh. When he didn't, she looked into his face, then sat on the bed and began to read. Lockhart saw her eyes go wide, saw her stop and back up as he had done, saw her read the rest slowly and white-faced. The paper fell from her hand and she collapsed onto the bed with no sign of acting out a part.

"Marian," he said.

"God forgive me"—the words came out muffled by the pillow, choked with what he heard as a sob—"but I just can't help it."

"Marian, I'm sorry."

"I'm so grateful!"

"What?"

She rolled over, gazing at him. "It was a prayer."

"What?"

"It's June and that newspaper article. June would have loved it. It's the best review he ever got. He would have died a dozen times for a notice like that."

She wasn't crying, he saw. Her eyes held tears all right, but she was laughing and trying not to. *Hysterical? Her reason unsettled? Should I slap her? Call a doctor?*

"Marian?"

"Jim, I'm so happy. And for so many reasons. It's wonderful!"

"I don't think you understand."

She laughed. "I don't think *you* understand."

"I've killed your husband."

She sobered immediately. "Oh, Jim, I'm so sorry. I'd forgotten that. For a moment, I'd really forgotten. I'm sorry it had to be you. It must have been awful for you, finding out who he was." She sat up and reached out for his hand, but then her voice hardened. "And if you could have brought him in, I'd know how to make the little weasel talk. I could teach Henson a few things about interrogating June Taylor."

"But I killed him. I'm sorry."

"Sorry he's dead? Me? Not likely! My husband wasn't just an unfaithful rogue. He was mean. Evil."

"You must have loved him once."

"Must I?" She laughed. "Maybe you're right. June is—was—such a beautiful man. And his voice. You've heard it. He could charm birds out of trees, backers out of their cash, angry theater managers out of closing the show, women"—she swallowed, but went on—"women out of their bloomers whenever he put his mind to it. But after awhile, it lost its charm."

"He must have loved *you*. He must have been jealous, must have wanted you back."

"Oh? Did talking to him give you that impression?"

Lockhart thought back. The man he'd known as Brutus hadn't seemed jealous. He'd seemed amused, mocking. *"We have much in common,"* he'd said. *"More than you know. I can make your life easier in several ways."* Lockhart understood suddenly.

"That son of a bitch," he said. "He was talking about *you!*"

"What about me?"

Lockhart told her, filling in as much of the conversation as he could remember. Falling back on the pillow, Marian began to laugh again.

"If I'd had any doubts, that would settle them. That was June, all right. *Now* do you understand how I feel?"

"I'm starting to."

"And he was in on it all along. Our mysterious drummer stole the banknotes, gave them to June when their paths crossed, and June passed them along to Janks or directly to the King of China. I knew June was booking the troupe into some odd places, but I never imagined why."

She stopped, looking at Lockhart. He wondered if she could read his thoughts in his face.

"He had to meet with the killer," Lockhart said. "Didn't you ever see him with Thompson or Givens or Baker? Didn't you ever suspect anything?"

"I suspected plenty." Her voice had that hard, flat ring again. "But not what he was really doing. I didn't see much of June when we weren't on stage. He was always finding a fresh card game or a new woman to while away the hours."

"I see."

"Do you?"

"Yes."

"Except that you think I might have been in on it with him." She closed her eyes. "Serves me right. Another damned man!"

"No," Lockhart protested. "Of course I don't." *But it does fit together very well.*

"Listen, idiot. If I'd known anything at all, June would never have dared to run out on me. I could've hanged him higher than Haman. Don't you see that?"

"Of course I do."

He lay beside her, tried to take her in his arms. She stiffened and turned her face away.

"Careful. I may be armed."

Now she was crying. Lockhart patted her shoulder, got no response. In as normal a tone as he could manage, he said, "Maybe he helped with the actual robberies. He might have been the brains of the whole thing."

"No." She hiccupped. She still wouldn't look at him.

"The dates are wrong. We were never playing in the same town when there was a crime. I looked at that in Henson's notes." Her voice stopped. She finished in a different tone. "I looked at it first, to be sure."

"Then you did suspect him."

"Oh, *damn!*" She burrowed her face into the pillow. "Yes! Yes, I suspected him, because we played those towns and June would have skinned his grandmother for a dollar. But I knew he didn't plan it, because he was too stupid, so when the dates didn't match I didn't say anything to you. And now you don't believe me."

"I believe you. Especially the part about his being stupid."

She turned her head far enough to bring one dark eye to bear on him. "Why?"

"Because any man who would set aside a woman like you for a bushel or a hundred bushels of banknotes has to be stupid." He bent and kissed the corner of her eye. "I'm pretty stupid myself, sometimes. Forgive me for doubting."

She didn't answer, but this time she turned toward him when he put his arms around her. They lay there, neither speaking, for a long time. Finally, Marian raised her head.

"Jim? What now?"

He didn't know if she meant between the two of them or in their race with Henson and the unknown killer. He chose to answer the easier question.

"We're running out of money. Just like in the war, we'll have to regroup and resupply before we can fight another battle. We'll go home."

He felt her stiffen again. "Where's home?"

"Ohio. A place called Loveland, not far out of Cincinnati. We can afford the train fare, barely. My daughter and her husband have a farm there."

"Oh."

"Zack's a good man. They'll help us."

"They'll help you," she said. She burrowed closer to him. "We could rob a bank instead."

"That isn't funny."

"I wasn't joking. Can we afford a night's rest first? You've already paid for it."

It was in his mind to say that they needed to hurry, that Doom would be coming along their track before long. But he felt the tension in her muscles, heard the desperate appeal in her voice. "Sure." he said.

Yes, I've paid for a lot, he thought, holding her while she didn't cry, *and there's more left to pay for.*

20

They took the morning train to Springfield. Lockhart stared at the railroad bridge across the Mississippi, gazed into the swirling brown water below the mass of girders and pilings, turned back to look into the sleeping face of Marian Taylor. It made him feel a bit younger and stronger to think she trusted him that much. She was sleeping on the morning train because she had lain awake most of the night worrying or lost in reverie. He hadn't known if she was thinking of their predicament or her dead husband or of meeting Ann and Zack. Nor had he thought it right to ask.

Marian stirred in her sleep and said something Lockhart could almost understand. Then she put her head against his shoulder and began to breathe again in long soft sighs. *Is she dreaming of him? How do I know she really meant it when she said she didn't love him?*

Lockhart caught himself. It was easy, and getting easier, to slide off into someplace he had never known existed, a horrible, inverted world where every innocent word or glance had a double meaning, where every other human being was an enemy waiting to strike.

Has that smiling woman with the baby seen my picture on one of Henson's circulars? Did she report us when the porter stopped to compliment her on her daughter? That man who keeps reaching for his pocket—is he really looking at his watch, or does he have a gun hidden there? Did the conductor notice anything suspicious when he took our tickets? Will the law be waiting at the next station?

Before he knew it, he found the skin along the nape of his neck tightening, sweat breaking on his forehead, his heart racing with a rapid, painful patter. He drew a deep breath, willing his muscles to relax. He wondered how the real outlaws had survived with no one to trust, no safe place to lay their heads. Then he laughed. By Darrow's account, anyway, Lockhart was as real as the worst of them.

PHANTOM JIM LOCKHART ESCAPES FORT WORTH MAN-HUNT, the last headline had read. *Killer and Paramour Elude Marshal Doom; Henchman Captured after Titanic Struggle.*

Jesse James had been hunted for years. He'd finally been shot down by a man he'd trusted, a relative.

Zack and Ann. Can I trust them? What will my Ann say when she sees me with a woman at my side? It came to him that he might leave Marian in a hotel in Cincinnati while he went out to visit the daughter. *Surely Ann would be happier not to know until we come back married?* But that was wrong. He had nothing to be ashamed of. *Not much!* Of course Ann would never understand. *A man my age taking up with any woman at all, let alone a younger woman. A younger woman whose husband I killed!*

"Where are we now?" Marian's drowsy voice asked.

"Well into Illinois."

"Springfield?"

"Not far ahead."

"Jim? Do you want me to stay in Cincinnati while you visit your daughter?"

He looked at her, saw the doubt in her eyes. "I wouldn't want to go much of anywhere without you."

They got off the train in Cincinnati less than a mile from Lockhart's home office. "I need to go there right now," he told Marian, "to see Mr. Tanner and tell him the truth."

"He's your old boss? I'll go with you."

"You mustn't. If he should turn me in." A thought struck him. "If he turns us in, we wouldn't get to see Ann. I have to see Ann first."

He was picking up their bags from the platform when he saw on the train moving out east a face he knew. Reb Thompson neither smiled nor turned away but watched Lockhart without recognition until the train took him out of sight.

"What is it?" Marian asked.

"Reb Thompson."

"Did he see us?"

"I don't know." He picked up the bags. "It doesn't matter," he said, although he was sure it did. "We'll have to hire a rig. It's an hour and some to Loveland."

"Do we have enough money left?" In her voice were injured feelings, anxiety at meeting his daughter, sudden frailty of spirit.

"I think so."

"I thought you were keeping careful record." That reminded him it had been *her* money after all, money he'd promised to repay.

"I am."

He rented the buggy without further talk, choosing a fast-stepping gray horse and paying two dollars extra over the nag the stableman had first offered him. Marian shared his silence until they were clear of Cincinnati's busy streets and out onto the tree-shaded lane to the east.

"That's a nice name for a town," she said then. Her voice offered to make peace. "Did you really grow up in a place called Loveland?"

"No." Then to make peace, he said, "My daughter and her husband live on a farm out from there. We'll turn off before we get to Loveland."

"Oh."

"We might see Loveland later, if you'd like."

"It doesn't matter."

He heard that, knew he deserved it, and flicked the reins across the horse's rump. "Get up," he said. They made the turnoff in less than an hour. Then he slowed the pace, anxious to see his daughter but fearful of how it might turn out. Ann would surely have heard that her father was an accused murderer escaped and loose to wreak havoc across the country. Would she take him in or turn him away or have Zack shoot him on sight?

The miles went by quickly, and too soon they reached the gate. "This is it," he told Marian, though his stopping to unwire the gap had made that obvious. It was not a large farm. They could see the house from the road. He even saw the young woman come out onto the porch and shade her eyes with a hand to peer at the buggy. Then, when they were still forty yards from the house, the young woman stepped off the porch and gathered up her skirts. She ran awkwardly toward them, her pregnancy hobbling her.

Lockhart stood down from the buggy, started walking in his own long strides, then broke into a run to meet her halfway. Ann was laughing, tears running down her cheeks. Father and daughter met on the grass between the ruts and embraced as if they hadn't seen each other in years.

"Thank you," he said at last, "for taking me in."

"Taking you in?" She kissed his cheek again. "This is your home!"

He touched her rounded belly. "Are you all right?"

"Wonderful! I'm sure it's a granddaughter."

"I imagine you've heard."

"About your being arrested? It was in the paper. Sheriff Sanders came out to ask a lot of questions some marshal had wired him to ask."

"And you don't mind my coming here? Is it safe for you?"

"I'm ever so glad to have you here! I know Zack will be, too. Who's that in the buggy?"

Shall I say a colleague? Another orphan of the storm? The widow of one of my victims? A fellow escaped felon? "My lady friend," he said instead. "I've brought her to meet you."

Ann said, "Oh, she's lovely." They went to the rig arm-in-arm looking up at the handsome woman who sat holding the reins.

"Marian, I'd like you to meet my daughter, Ann Grier. Ann, this is Marian Taylor."

Tying off the reins, Marian stepped down and put out her hand, but the younger woman embraced her instead, skewing her veil. Lockhart held the horse at the bit and watched while the women began first to talk, then turned toward the house arm-in-arm as if neither of them remembered or had further need of him. Left alone, he led the horse at a slow walk all the way to the barn, to get the rig out of sight.

When he came into the kitchen through the back door, Ann was feeding kindling into the coals of the big wood cookstove and Marian, having set aside her hat and veil, was pumping water for the coffeepot. He visited with them a moment, saw they were all right, asked about Zack.

"He's working on the fence down behind the barn."

Lockhart went back outside, heading for that stretch of fence which had always been hard to keep up, surveying as he went the shed and hog lot and garden plot. He heard hammering before he dropped beneath the low ridge and caught sight of the far fence.

His son-in-law was a sturdy man with a shock of black hair, arms like a blacksmith's, and trousers that never seemed to fit. Though not quite as tall as Lockhart, Zack Grier was broader and easier in motion.

Lockhart went on without hailing him until at a break in his work, Zack heard the older man's boots in the long dry grass. He turned, already half-smiling a welcome, then saw Lockhart and stared.

"Is that you, James?"

Caught up in the joys of homecoming, Lockhart said, "It is! And how are you, my man?" He held out his hand.

Grier took it after a second's hesitation. His grip was as strong as ever and acceptance almost as quick, but he was not as happy to see Lockhart as he might have been. After a moment he said, "We heard you'd had trouble."

It was a question. Lockhart saw he would need an hour and a pound of fresh-churned luck to explain it all to Zack's satisfaction, for in that hard son-in-law of the land there was no simple or complete acceptance like Ann's.

"Have you come clear of it?"

"About halfway. The law's still looking for me, if that's your question."

Zack nodded, spat tobacco across his new fence rail, waited.

"I didn't do any of it. I regret it's likely brought you shame among your neighbors. But I've been caught in a trap and I'm dragging it by the lame foot until I catch up to the son of darkness that set it for me."

"Where's he at?"

"I don't know."

"What's his name?"

"I don't know that, either." Lockhart looked at the unbridged gap between the new section of fence and the ruins of the old one and realized that he would need more than time and luck to explain to Zack. "He's one of four, but I don't know which, and I have precious little room left to find out."

The younger man spat again, failed to clear the new rail. "How'd he set you a trap?"

"He followed along right after me like the rooster beating the hens to the mash. He went in and stole the notes I'd just delivered and when he had to he killed the men who trusted me."

"How then can you hope to find him?"

"I'd need to be as shrewd as a son of darkness, too."

His son-in-law's eyes went narrow, darkened against the evening sun. "Let's pick a starting place, then, and outfigure the nasty son. How'd you know him?"

Lockhart was amazed at the spectacle of Hercules ready to tackle the wizard on his own ground. "We traveled together, were friends on the trains."

"But you don't know which? Four of the sons, you say? Not counting you?"

"No. Make it three, leaving out the one who lately saved my life."

"No more but three? Why, hell. Which one liked you best?"

"Mel Baker. Known him since, well, since long before Ann's mother died. Why? You think he'd be the one or the one to eliminate?"

"Hard to say. I've knowed both kinds. Any of them seem not to like you much?"

"Ed Givens is pretty distant to everybody. Reb Thompson's friendly enough."

Zack spat out his cud of tobacco. "And all three of them was at every place it happened?"

"Not by their word. Could have been one of them said he wasn't at this place and another at that."

"Say then they was always one of them absent. One not at Hannibal and another not at Fort Worth, and the other not at El Paso." Zack had clearly studied the accounts and thought about it.

"All right, say that."

"Then you'd be left to figure none of them done it."

Lockhart nodded, frowned. He had often been left to suppose that.

"Else you could figure *all three* of them done it and schemed it up together to make you figure none of them done it."

That's very shrewd indeed, Zack. "Trouble is, the killer had a helper or two, now dead, who could have filled in when he was absent."

The younger man gathered up his tools. "That's too thick to chew," he said, "without a good strong cup of coffee. But it'd be my guess one of them did the killings and the other didn't."

Amazed at Grier's avenues of thought, Lockhart asked, "Would you figure the boss or the helper?"

"Done the killings?" He bit off a small fresh plug of tobacco to last the short walk. "The boss done the killings."

"Why would you think it?"

"Because he's still alive. The quick and the dead."

Zack's thought might not pass many tests of logic, but it held a truth of its own. Without logic, Lockhart found himself agreeing.

In the kitchen, Lockhart introduced Marian to his son-in-law.

"We're glad to make your acquaintance at last," Zack said, leaving it clear to Lockhart just how closely he and Ann had been keeping up with the news of the man and woman on the run.

"Aren't you a little afraid?" Marian asked him.

Zack looked at her then and seemed to approve in her a

directness that matched his own. To Lockhart's surprise, the sturdy man smiled. "I am," he replied, "for the sheriff checks by here now and then. But James says your rig's hid in the barn, and we could hide you two in the loft if it come to that." He gestured toward the corner where a ladder leaned against a wall joist.

"Zack Grier, you don't talk that way," Ann scolded her husband. "No one's coming out here to search our farm. Sheriff Sanders doesn't more than half-believe those tales about you two."

"Doesn't matter," Zack said. "Rex Sanders would arrest his mother if that's what his duty called him to." He looked steadily at Lockhart. "I'm just as pleased it's not me in his place."

"Zack!" Ann cried, but Lockhart raised a hand.

"No, Ann, it's all right. Zack and I understand each other very well. But I hope you didn't even half-believe it."

Ann hugged him, glancing sideways at her husband. "We never believed it for a minute," she said.

"It might be," Zack said to Lockhart, "that you'd got the link between your killer and his helper, else you wouldn't know he'd helped."

"This is the best coffee I've had in two months," Lockhart declared. He turned so as to put his back to the ladies and shook his head slightly at Zack. "There's not a restaurant in the country makes coffee like my Ann."

Ann smiled mischievously. "Your Marian made the coffee."

Decked by Marian and Ann in a drooping and battered high-crowned hat and a snowbound forest of white hair and whiskers, Lockhart went into Cincinnati just as dawn was coloring the eastern sky. A bit doubtful at the disguise, Zack drove him in the farm wagon, tying it up near the produce

market. While Lockhart huddled on the seat and appeared to
doze, Zack went to see R. K. Tanner, president of Western
States Engraving. After half an hour, Zack returned, looking
about himself in awkward stealth and obvious enjoyment of
his part in such an intrigue.

"He knows you and trusts you, for I told him he must.
He's already gone to meet you down by the war cannon in
the park."

"Did you mention the money?"

"I did and he said he'd bring it."

"I don't know that I've thought to tell you, big Zack,
what a good man you are."

Zack Grier looked around for a place to put the compliment. Not finding one, he spat between the wagon's shafts.
He glanced at Lockhart and looked away. "Well, you'd better hie because he'll be waiting."

Lockhart turned and walked slowly in his old man's disguise down through wagons of produce and off along an alley
toward the quiet park. He saw the trees above the old cannon
and wondered whether Tanner would have brought the law
or a shotgun. As he came closer, he saw his man sitting on a
bench near the cannon eating a sandwich Lockhart would
have bet was ham on rye. Tanner saw him coming but made
no sign either to him or to others who might be hiding in
wait. Lockhart went on to the bench and sat beside his boss.

"Jim. Is that you under that haystack?"

"It is. R.K., I'm grateful for your trust."

Mr. Tanner didn't look at him but said as if to the pi-
geons, "I'm grateful for your trustworthiness. I'd love to
know the story. If there's anything I can do to help you catch
the son of darkness that brought it on you, say the word."

Lockhart heard the echo of his own thoughts in the
words Zack must have chosen for his speech to Tanner.

"I've brought the money. Zack said you can't go to the

bank." He nudged a cloth bag across the bench toward Lockhart.

Though he'd only cried once since he wiped off his sword after Chickamauga, and that at the death of his Martha, Lockhart had to look away from the cloth sack to save his reputation with himself. "I thank you," he managed to say. "I'll gladly give you a draft on my account to cover this."

Tanner leaned back on the bench and laughed. "Jim, you had a better head for tactics back when we were younger and you were my best company commander. View this as an advance on future wages. I'd look silly getting arrested for passing a check signed by the Attila of the Plains."

"You've been reading those damned newspaper stories."

"They'll have a dime novel about you next. I'm saving a file of them to blackmail you after you've waded through this swamp and come back to work."

Lockhart groaned. "Work! Have you hired a man to replace me?"

"I've got Hoggard on the road. He's not worth a warm spoon of spit, but he's out there trying. Thing is, Jim, I really need you back."

"You mean you'd have me? After all of this?"

"Son, I've never given you up."

Lockhart smiled grimly. "I'll dare to ask one further favor of you, then."

"Whatever's in my power I'll surely do."

Lockhart made his request, thanked Tanner, took up the sack of bills, and walked back toward the market. Halfway there, he passed the square. Sheriff Rex Sanders was standing in the middle of a knot of men giving instructions. Horses stood ready, laden with gear.

Lockhart didn't have to study that situation to understand it. They would be looking for him. Henson must have sent word. Or Tanner hadn't trusted him after all.

*   *   *

It was noon and Zack had the horse hitched to ride out in an adventure quaintly foreign to his quiet rural existence. "You get it?"

"I got it." Lockhart wondered what he had. "We have to move. The sheriff's gotten up a posse."

He covered the baskets and took his place on the seat. They drove amid questions from Zack's friends and found the road toward Loveland. Lockhart was happy. He had money enough to repay Marian and to pay the freight for the rest of their hunt. He had a friend in his boss. Or did he? Perhaps he had a poke of paper and a posse on his trail?

Half a mile along the road at the draft horse's petty pace, Lockhart was wondering again when he heard a bee sing past his nose and touch Grier on the sleeve. Lockhart saw that the bee left blood at the same time he heard the sound of the rifle. Grabbing for his Colt, he leveled it toward the puff of white smoke from the rider off to their left and emptied the gun while Grier whipped up the horse. The rifle spoke only once more, but Zack was driving like a madman set loose. The stolid draft horse ran like a thoroughbred, while the wagon creaked and cracked and groaned in its agony.

"Is he after us?" Zack asked.

"Don't see him. I might have dropped his horse."

"Who was it?"

"God only knows. Another son of darkness."

They reached the turnoff with Lockhart holding the reins while Grier wrapped a piece of sacking around his wounded arm.

"There's our proof," Grier said as he pulled the knot tight.

"What?"

"The son of a whore's still out there in the dark or he wouldn't be shooting at you."

Lockhart set the brake and got down and opened the gap. Then he got back on the seat and took the reins and drove to the house without closing the gate. Zack wasn't bleeding badly, but his face was pale and damp. Lockhart recognized the symptoms. Strong or weak, it didn't do anyone any good to be shot. Worried about the younger man, he flung the wagon up nearly to the porch, helped his son-in-law down, and got him into the house where Ann was waiting as if she'd known what to expect.

"I'll make it up to you," Lockhart said with more conviction than he felt capable of fulfilling.

Then he ran out to the barn. Marian was backing the rent horse into the rig shafts. "I'm ready," was all she said. He saw the bags in the back and knew she wouldn't have left anything. He strapped the harness and led the horse out of the barn with her on the seat. Then he leaped to the step and clambered in place beside her.

The hooves of the posse were pounding on the road to remind him he hadn't closed the gate when he lashed at the rented horse and drove it beyond the barn and over the ridge toward that gap between the new fence and the old. The rig bounced and wavered but hung behind the fast gray horse as they flew through the gap and across the shallow creek and over the sloping rise. Lockhart looked back once to see the posse milling between house and barn. Then he kept his attention on the horse and the way he was choosing across Miller's field toward the road where there was no fence.

They bounced onto the road heading north. *Running into the heart of Ohio instead of toward any border!* But borders wouldn't matter to a posse. And Henson was probably with them or hot on their heels to give them the authority to follow Lockhart into Illinois or Pennsylvania or hell itself. He whipped the horse because it was all he could do.

On the level road, then, Marian was busy loading his revolver. He took it from her and stuck it in his belt and whipped the horse. The posse would not be stopping to bind Zack Grier's wound. They would be after him along the only path leading to him. But the horse was running. A big strong gray. If he could make it to Hamilton ahead of the posse, Lockhart and Marian Taylor might be lucky enough to catch the train to Dayton. It was the best Lockhart could hope.

He flinched at the first side road, thinking to throw them off, but kept to the main track because it was faster and speed was his only hope. In Hamilton, they abandoned the rig on the square and half-ran two blocks to the depot, swinging their bags. With his own real money he bought two tickets to the next stop. He urged Marian on board, gave his tickets to the conductor, and found empty seats. There was no need to look back. Either they'd made it or they hadn't.

21

The bed wasn't actually still warm when Marshal Rance Henson fetched up in the Hannibal hotel room, but it hadn't yet been made nor the room tidied up. It didn't matter. Lockhart and the Taylor woman were as gone as could be, leaving behind not even so much as a hatpin. The manager's wife, who did the cleaning, appreciated their neatness.

"Rightly thoughtful of them. You seldom ever find people so considerate any more. You should see the way some folks leave these rooms—the drummers, especially. It's a scandal."

Henson growled something vaguely like agreement, longing for the sort of clues other criminals had left for him to find in their hotel rooms. Among the litter of empty bottles and cigar butts and discarded papers, he'd turned up letters to sweethearts or accomplices telling when and where the fugitive might meet them; sheets of ciphering where a gang had split up their loot, complete with the names of the members; once, even, a railroad timetable with the train his man was taking and its destination marked in red ink. That was the kind of behavior Henson thought was considerate of outlaws; but Lockhart couldn't get even the simplest thing right.

Henson had changed his mind in mid-chase after the *Air Traveler*. Along toward Little Rock, it had come to him that Lockhart and his woman were backtracking the scenes of their crimes. He'd heard of such things but had never seen it before. They'd been to the other three, so Henson had himself and his horse switched onto a mixed train for Hannibal. It had been a good guess, but once more he was a few hours late.

"Remember them? Certainly," the desk clerk told him. "Remember them well. Handsome couple. Mrs. Hartley very attractive for her age."

"When was that?"

"Checked out right after breakfast. Maybe eight o'clock, that was."

"Do you know where they were headed?"

"Said they had to hire a rig at the livery and drive to Palmyra. Said the lady had relatives there."

Maybe, but I wouldn't bet my aunt Fannie's corset stays on it. But Henson couldn't afford to pass up the trail. He got the name and location of the stables and went straight there. The proprietor was busy but finally stopped his work when Henson showed him his badge.

"Merriweather?" He didn't seem very interested. "Never heard the name. Nor Lockhart nor Hartley nor Moneytree. Say, mister, how many folks are you chasing, anyway?"

"Just answer the question."

"Did. Never heard of them, and never rented any rig this morning. You might ask Oscar over to the stockyards."

Oscar didn't know any more. Hannibal also offered two railroad stations and a steamboat wharf, but at least there were no dadblamed airships darkening the sky. At the second of the railway depots, Henson found a ticket agent who remembered selling a middle-aged couple tickets on the morning local to Springfield.

"That's the one in Illinois, not the one in Missouri, mister. Should be pulling in about now."

"Thanks. I need to send a telegram."

Relieved of the need to warn the Springfield police, Henson wired Chet Archer, his deputy. *In Hannibal. Forward developments. Lockhart headed east into Illinois. Where in hell going query. Advise.*

"I'll stop back by for the answer. Got an errand at the bank."

Aaron Porter's office was small and unimposing. Its simple furnishings were comfortable and comforting to Henson, and he thought Porter himself looked the way a banker ought to but seldom did. Henson laid his badge on the scarred wooden desk and introduced himself.

"I'm on the track of a pair of escaped felons. At least one of them is known to you. James Lockhart."

"Yes. Sit down, Marshal. Cigar? Well, it's an odd coincidence. Just lately I've had occasion to reconsider Lockhart's situation."

"Have you?"

"A lady came to see me, yesterday it was. Lockhart's sister. She asked some questions that made me think."

"Lockhart doesn't have a sister. He had a younger brother, died of typhoid in 1853."

"What? Are you certain? Then who was the lady?"

"In her thirties? Brown eyes?"

"That isn't much to go on."

"The rest of her changes."

"This one had dark eyes, all right, but I would have thought her older. Fifty, perhaps."

"You would have thought her Methuselah's grandmother if that's what she wanted you to think. What did she have to say for herself?"

Porter hesitated, drew a circle on the desk with his fingertip. "Well, it wasn't so much what she said. Some of the times didn't match up quite right, never had. You remember when I gave my statement to your deputy?"

"I've read it." *Should have questioned him myself. But by then I had the goods on Lockhart anyway, figured this one would fit right in. Sloppy.* "Have you changed your mind about it?"

"No, sir. But you might remember I said we had an audit going on some assets the bank had just acquired. We had people in and out of the offices until quite late that night."

"I believe I will have that cigar after all, if you don't mind." Henson took it, made a business of lighting it while he thought back over Porter's testimony. "Yes, sir, I recall that. Your first thought was that the robbery was done after midnight." *After Lockhart was on the night train with Baker and Thompson, that would be.*

"That's right. Then your deputy asked if Lockhart—or someone—might not have found his way in earlier, and I said of course, that we hadn't had people here every minute. If he knew where the notes were and had the combination, he'd've had time to slip in and get them."

Henson took a puff on the cigar, then laid it aside. He leaned forward to look more closely at Porter. "So the Taylor woman—Marian Taylor's her real name, near as we can tell—suggested it might have been different?" he asked.

Porter blinked at him. "Why, no, she didn't do that at all. She just asked me a question." He paused, waited for Henson to ask, then said, "She asked how Lockhart could have known he'd have that much time."

"Did she?" Henson took out his notebook and pencil and scribbled a note. "Did she, now?"

"I hadn't thought of it like that before, Marshal. I must say it raised a doubt in my mind." The banker shrugged as though reluctant to hurt Henson's feelings. "I—I thought it was a good question."

Henson snapped the notebook closed and rose from his chair. "You're right about that, Mr. Porter," he said, not feeling that this time should count against him. "I think it's a *damned* good question."

Chet's reply was waiting when he got back to the depot. *Air Traveler arrived and departed Little Rock. Why in hell Hannibal query. More follows.* A second telegram was more helpful. *Lockhart daughter Ann Grier Loveland Ohio. Contact Sheriff Rex Sanders Cincinnati. Good luck.*

"Cincinnati," Henson told the clerk. "I need passage to Cincinnati and a stall for my horse. And I need to send another wire."

Henson felt sure enough of his man to wire ahead to Cincinnati. He asked Sheriff Rex Sanders to have a posse ready to ride when he arrived. During his wait for a train out of Hannibal, he found a doctor who clucked his tongue at Doc Odum's needlework, removed the stitches from the healing wound, and put a clean dressing on it. Henson wasn't ready to wrestle anyone, but he figured the arm would do for most purposes.

He was uncomfortable on the train, nervous and expectant in a way that was rare for him. He fumed at the train, which wasn't going fast enough to suit him and wasted time stopping in every wide place along the tracks.

Getting old. Never had the jitters before. But I would've been too old for Lockhart when I was young. That man would make a deacon cuss!

Every couple of hours he went back to check on his horse. Like Henson, the animal seemed cramped and overfed and as anxious to be out and moving in the real world off the tracks as Henson himself. By the time the train pulled in, Henson had the horse saddled and ready. He checked his gun and rifle, rode down out of the car as soon as the workmen got a plank in place at the door, and went to find Sanders.

Sanders was mounted and waiting when Henson led his horse down the planks. The rest of the posse stood idling nervously on the road behind the depot. Though he wasn't very interested, Henson took time to look at the men in the posse and the people lounging around the station. *It would be just like that pair to be sitting here waiting for me to ride off on a snipe hunt while they bought tickets on the next train!*

"You seen them?" he asked the sheriff.

"No. One of the boys saw the son-in-law trying to sell tomatoes down to the market, but he's gone now."

"No unusual folk around? No strangers to wonder at?"

"No. They may have an accomplice, though. Was a man went out that road not five minutes ago riding like he was the head Indian in Colonel Cody's circus. Craig Estes from over to the livery told me 'cause he'd just rented him that horse and was plenty sore to see him treating it that way."

"What'd he look like?"

"Long-legged black with a diamond on his forehead and one white stocking. Best horse he has, said Craig."

Henson swallowed another month's worth of swearing and spoke softly. "The man. What did the man look like?"

"Oh, well, tall enough and lean as a rail. Said the liveryman, it was hard to tell about the face behind his scraggly old beard."

"Damnation," Henson said. He hoped it counted in the same six-month period he'd already marred. "That'll be Lockhart in disguise. Let's ride!"

They were four miles out of town with Henson taking the lead when they found Craig Estes's best horse dead in the road. He'd been shot once in the middle of the blaze on his face.

Sanders said, "Where in hell's the man was riding him?"

"They's tracks here. Must've took to the grass, made for that grove in the hilltop."

"No." Henson pointed. "He's ahead of us. Ride." Henson was already moving again. He had his eye on a faint cloud of dust still hanging over the road some distance beyond the downed horse. It didn't make any sense to him that Lockhart would have shot his own horse out from under himself. But he figured he'd worry about that later.

I'll ask him once I've got him chained to a locomotive. Have to chain the blamed woman by her waist—would be the only spot where she couldn't wriggle loose one way or the other!

He came to a side road, saw the dust, made the turn without slowing more than necessary. Here the dust was thicker, heavier in the air. It made a rough job for him and the horse, breathing more dust than air with every step they gained on the wagon. It ended at last where to one side of the road a wire gap was open.

Henson reined the horse back on its haunches, heard the posse pounding up fast behind him, headed down the lane toward a white farmhouse with a picket fence around the garden. A wagon stood by the front porch, its tired plow horse cropping at the rosebush that grew beside the steps. Henson drew his gun, waited for the bullets that might start seeking him out at any time.

But the bullets did not come. *They must not have a rifle!* Ready to shoot it out face-to-face, he stood down from the still-moving horse, and ran onto the porch. The door was open. He went in, gun moving, ready to shoot. A pregnant woman stood at the kitchen table wringing out a bloody rag in a bowl. In a chair beside her sat a young man with arms like a railroad spike driver, Henson thought. Neither of them paid him any particular attention.

The man's head lolled back and his big arms lay loosely on the tabletop. An ugly cut or burn had slashed across the right bicep, which still oozed blood. As Henson watched, the young woman poured something on the rag and wiped it across the cut. The man drew in his breath sharply and opened his eyes. He looked at Henson.

"Who're you?"

"Name's Henson, United States Marshal," he told them, holding his gun on the young man. "I'm after James Lockhart, and I mean to have him. If you've got him hid, tell me now. Else I'll arrest you along with him and the woman."

"Zack Grier," the man said. He turned over a hand to point without raising his arm from the table. "Sorry not to get up for you. James was headed that way the last I saw of him."

The young woman never stopped her work on her husband's arm but said, "My father isn't here just now. Would you care to take a seat and wait for him to return?"

Henson didn't for a moment doubt that Lockhart was gone. Whatever idiot had shot or been shot off the horse had surely alerted him and the Taylor witch. He heard the horses of the posse approaching. Footsteps sounded on the porch.

"Thank you just the same, ma'am," he said, "but I suspect that would amount to right smart of a wait. I believe I'll have my look out back instead. Be best if the two of you were to stay right here and not cause a lick of trouble till I come back."

Holstering his gun, he went out the back door. The posse was making enough noise for a herd of buffalo, but he thought he heard a wagon off in the distance. He went back in the kitchen. "Your father sitting behind a fresh horse?"

"Yes."

Henson looked out the window. His horse had found the water trough. For the time being, the horse was done in. He considered the situation and found it unworthy of further invective. "I think you got that wound clean pretty much right down to the bone," he told her. "I was you, I'd now put a little of that carbolic acid on it and tie it up. I'd judge it to be a bullet track."

"It is," the young man said.

"Lockhart give it to you?"

"It was give to me by the real son of darkness you ought to be chasing instead of my father-in-law who he was trying to kill when he shot me."

Henson blinked while he thought that through. "Son of darkness?"

"The one that really robbed from those banks and killed those men."

"You know who he is?"

"Not by name. I'm morally certain that twenty minutes ago he was riding a tall black horse and chasing us on the Cincinnati road."

"Black horse! With a white diamond on its face?"

"I was driving and didn't have that long to look. But the man riding it was shooting at James Lockhart and just happened to miss him and hit me."

Well, I will be dipped and damned! Which may not count against me since not said aloud. I've got Lockhart out ahead of me running for the railroad and what could maybe be his accomplice or the real killer out there to hell and gone behind me!

Henson strode out onto the front porch and began shouting at the men. "Sheriff Sanders," he said, "I wish you'd take half your men and go back where we found that black horse was down. Fan out and find the man was riding it."

"Why?"

"Because I'd like mightily to ask him when he was last in Fort Worth and some other places and what he was doing there and why he was doing it. Leave me five or six men with good horses. I'm going on after the other wagon."

"Other wagon?"

"And leave one good man to sit with these nice folks. I'd hanker after a cup of coffee and a chat with them, providing we don't catch up to Mr. Lockhart."

Henson knew he wasn't going to catch up the wagon, but he hoped to stay close enough to find out where it went. The horse surprised him by holding a steady pace without lathering unduly. He followed the tracks right up to the wheel of the rented rig where somebody had left it on the square in Hamilton. The big gray horse stood in the traces with his head hanging and his flanks flecked with drying foam.

"Couple of you take this animal over to the livery. Get it tended and find out who owns it and where did it come from. Rest of you stay together, look around for a man and a woman don't belong. I'll be up at the depot."

Ten minutes at the depot was all it took. "They're gone to Dayton, and the Almighty Himself probably don't know where from there," he told his posse when they reassembled. "By the ghost of Julius Caesar, I haven't thought this Lockhart customer was any too bright, but he's got the devil's own stopwatch when it comes to catching trains. I'd say we might as well ride back to where we started and talk this over."

Sanders had not found the rider of the dead horse, nor any sign that he'd been wounded, nor any living soul in the county except Zack Grier and the liveryman that had as much as seen him. The Griers were willing to tell Henson anything except where they thought Lockhart might go next. Henson threatened, badgered, cajoled, and bullied, all without denting Zack Grier's stolid determination to keep his mouth shut. Inside himself, Henson admired the young farmer and envied him his pretty wife and coming family.

Must be some business I can find to do in Fort Worth, and Lockhart and all his kin and kind can go to hell. But he knew he wouldn't give up on a chase while the fox was still running loose.

It was going on midnight before Henson finished at the Grier home and nursed his tired horse back to town. Disgusted with himself and Lockhart and everything connected with law enforcement, he ate a heavy supper and went to bed at his hotel. At four-thirty the next morning, he awoke, lighted a cigar, and sat up to put his thoughts in order.

So far, he'd relied on the usual way of doing things, following Lockhart's trail and waiting for his chance. That hadn't worked for sour apples. From Little China to the Grier farm, Henson was always one jump behind with Lockhart headed for the king's row. In Fort Worth, Lockhart had literally flown away from him. Somehow, Henson had to find a way to get ahead of the game.

He leafed through his papers until he found the *Air Traveler* brochure. The foolish name "Opportunity Knox" leaped up at him. Henson admitted to himself that he hadn't taken the young man seriously during the interview in Sacramento. Now it was very difficult to overlook the incredible coincidence of Lockhart's meeting Knox in Fort Worth and the two of them flying away together. *Is there any connection between the Fort Worth and Hannibal stops on the circuit? Is there some tie I don't know about between Knox and Lockhart?*

Henson didn't think so, but he couldn't be certain. So far as Lockhart had established a pattern in his running, it was to go back to places he'd been before. Maybe he would do that with Knox. No gambler would have covered a bet like that, but Henson had learned over time to trust his instincts and intuition.

The way he saw it, this was his one last good shot. It might be worthwhile to have someone look in on the other drummers, provided he could locate them, but Opportunity Knox he would handle personally. What he would need to do was waylay the *Air Traveler* at its next stop. He flipped through the circular and found the airship's schedule. Unless an offended deity took note of the abomination and blasted it with a lightning bolt, the *Air Traveler* would be in Springfield in two days' time. Henson would meet it there, then stick to Knox like a cockleburr to a coyote's tail until Lockhart came to him. It would be as simple as that.

22

- - - - - - - - - - - - - - - - -

The train ran on toward Dayton as if no one were yearning after it to pluck up James Lockhart and Marian Taylor and drag them off to decorate a hangman's noose. Lockhart stood on the rear platform of the last car, looking back into the gathering darkness. He didn't turn when Marian came out to stand beside him.

"Expecting to see Henson pumping after us on a handcar?"

He didn't smile. "Knowing our friend the marshal, it wouldn't surprise me a bit."

"We almost cut this one too close."

"More than almost." Lockhart gripped the railing. "Henson's probably got Ann and Zack. He can arrest them if he wants to, charge them with aiding a fugitive."

Marian put her hand on his. "Fugitives. But I don't think Henson will do that."

"How do you know what Henson will do?"

She fought the impulse to draw back her hand, to answer in the same sharp-edged tone. "Because he seems to be a decent man," she said.

"He's a hypocritical white-haired son of a bitch and I wish I'd let your husband kill him."

He stopped, but not before the words hit her like a blow from his fist. He turned toward her, his face filled with concern.

"Marian, I'm sorry. I didn't mean it that way."

Who do I need to be for him? Lady Macbeth's too scornful. That isn't what he needs. But not Ophelia or Desdemona—too weak and clinging. Maybe I just need to be Marian. If I could decide who that is.

"You didn't mean it at all." There, she'd kept her voice calm and level. "If you did, you wouldn't be the man I'm in love with. What is it, Jim, really? What's the matter?"

A flaw in the wind blew coal smoke back across them. Lockhart coughed, cleared his throat before he could answer.

"The matter's I almost got Zack killed."

"He's all right."

"I've seen them take off a hundred arms for no better reason than a streak of blood poisoning."

"That was a long time ago."

"And I've put Ann in danger. Suppose the man on the black horse had come to the farm instead of trailing us on the road. Suppose he'd come while you and Ann were alone."

Marian felt the weight of Henson's small hideout pistol in her bag. *Then he'd have to be damned quick to be still alive*, she told herself. But maybe not. Fear for Ellie North had kept her from trying anything like that with Janks.

"He didn't," she said.

"We can't take that kind of chance again."

"We won't." Then, to steer him away from his guilt, she asked, "Who shot at you and Zack? Was it one of Henson's men?"

Lockhart shook his head. "Could've been anyone. I'd first thought it was our killer. But it might have been one of Rex's deputies, or a bounty hunter, or just a farmer looking for the reward." He stiffened. "If I happened to hit him, there may be a real murder charge against me."

Marian shivered. Then she realized that couldn't be so. "But you were in disguise!" she said. "How could anybody possibly have recognized you?"

Lockhart blinked. He straightened, released the handrail, turned to look at Marian. "That's right. Then it wasn't somebody hunting the reward."

"No. It was the man we're after. Or the one that's after us."

"More than that. He had to know R. K. Tanner was my boss. Had to figure I'd come there eventually. Had to be watching." He stared at her, and seemed suddenly to see her. "You're cold."

She had been. It was freezing in the rush of air that whipped around the end of the car. But the rush of relief that she felt at the change in his tone warmed her.

"I was."

"You'll catch your death." He put his arm around her. "Come on inside. We'll get you some coffee in the dining car."

"No time. We'll be in Dayton in a few minutes. But we can get a cup there while we plot our next step, unless Doom has the police waiting on the platform."

Nobody was waiting at Dayton, but Lockhart didn't take any chances. He bought tickets to Toledo with connections to Detroit, then spent some time asking the station agent about Canadian railway schedules.

"Aren't you headed the wrong way?" Marian asked as they left the counter.

"Depends on where we're going. From Detroit into Canada, across to Vancouver, and then catch the first boat to Australia. Think Doom would come looking for us there?"

"I think Doom would come looking for us in hell and figure he could shoot his way out once he'd caught us. Stop being so damned smug and tell me what you're up to."

Lockhart led her outside. Two tracks away from the platform, a long special lay panting as the tender took on water.

"Immigrant train," he said. "I heard the stationmaster talking while you were fixing your hair. Germans and Poles, mostly, headed for Chicago by way of Indianapolis. Come on."

"Chicago?"

"Indianapolis. Every through train in this part of the country goes there or Cincinnati, and I don't want to go back to Cincinnati." He was boosting her up the steps to one of the cars. "We'll pay our passage on board, then turn our tickets in when we arrive."

"And Marshal Doom?"

Lockhart grinned. "Maybe he really will go looking for us in Australia."

Marian Taylor awoke, cramped and sore, to the smells of garlic and sauerkraut and cooking sausage and strong tobacco. She sneezed, thinking drowsily that she must be back in the Palace and wondering why June had signed to play in Denver again. Then the slow swaying of her bed and the muffled click of the wheels told her where she was. She sat up in the hard berth, not surprised to find Lockhart gone.

Straightening her clothes, she swung her legs carefully over the side. The cars of the immigrant train were creaking with age, some of the earliest excuses for sleepers ever devised. The berth was more like an overhead luggage rack than a bed, separated by wooden partitions from those in front and behind. The seats immediately below her were crowded, as was the entire train.

"Ah! *Gut morgen*—morning, is it! Please."

The man below untangled himself from his family and reached up to help her down. Marian thanked him, then smiled at his wife. In a few moments, she found herself rocking a sleeping blond two-year-old. In the opposite seat, the young woman unhooked her blouse to feed his little brother and explained in a mixture of German and English how they had come from Krakow to find a new home.

"Minn-e-sota. Is buffalo and red Indians, yes?"

"Not so much anymore, I think."

The woman looked disappointed, then concerned. "But is good land, yes?"

"Yes. Is very good land."

"Hello."

Marian looked up. Lockhart was standing in the aisle, staring down at her with an odd expression. She was suddenly intensely conscious of the child in her arms.

"Jim." She sat a little straighter. "This is Helga and Karel. And their family. They're going to Minnesota."

Lockhart shook hands with Karel, which delighted the young man. Still with that peculiar expression, he said to Marian, "We're here. Indianapolis. We'd better go." He lifted his left hand, which held a greasy parcel. "I've brought us some breakfast."

Passing the boy back to Karel, Marian got up and gathered their bags. "What next? After breakfast, I mean. I'm ravenous."

They sat on a bench on the station platform while Lockhart opened his package. Breakfast was some kind of spicy sausage wrapped in an odd flat piece of bread and still warm.

"This is wonderful. Maybe we should go on to Chicago with them."

"We might. I'm waiting on word."

She swallowed. "What word?"

"Here, there's some coffee, too. I place our best hope in

learning which of our suspects is still on the job and which one abandoned his regular calls to chase after us."

"Brilliant. Except how could you ever hope to learn that?"

"I have my best man working on it right now. Oh, something else."

"More riddles?"

"No." He reached into his coat and took out a cloth bag, offering it to her. "Here. It's the money I owe you. Every cent."

The bread and sausage seemed suddenly too dry to chew. Marian put it aside on the bench. She didn't reach for the bag, didn't want to look at it.

"So. Then we're all even, is that it?"

"What?" He frowned, clearly puzzled by her lack of enthusiasm. "I don't know what you mean. It's your money."

Damn you. How did you stay married so long if you don't know the first damned thing about women? Your Martha must've been a saint. She turned her face away. *And I'm not even close to that.*

"I don't want it."

"But it's yours."

"I don't need it," she said, "not apart from you."

He frowned again. "You're not apart from me, God knows. We're in this together."

"You don't sound like it. *My* money. *Your* money." She bit her lip. "Whose damned bed have we been in, yours or mine?"

"Ours." He pushed the bag across to her. "Carry it for us, then. We'll need it soon enough." He paused. "What was the baby's name?" he asked.

She hadn't expected the question. "What? Which baby?"

"The one you were holding on the train."

"I don't know." She stopped, got hold of herself, shrugged. "Something I couldn't pronounce. Why?"

"No reason. But I think you liked it."

"What?"

"I think I'd better see if my telegram's been answered. Finish your breakfast."

TO W. T. SHERMAN, INDIANAPOLIS. BAKER ON ROAD LAST REPORTED OMAHA. KNOX ON ROAD WHERE-ABOUTS UNKNOWN. GIVENS WHEREABOUTS UN-KNOWN. THOMPSON LEAVE OF ABSENCE REPORTED BOUND FOR PROVIDENCE, KY. PRAYING. GRANT.

"Grant?" Marian raised her eyebrows. "Sherman?"

Lockhart shrugged, feeling like a kid playing cowboys and Indians. "Code. It's from Tanner."

"Brilliant." She studied the telegram again. "We know about Knox. That leaves Givens and Thompson."

"And Thompson's in Kentucky. His home, I think."

"Well, that's easy. How do we get to Providence?"

Providence was nowhere near a railroad line. They crossed the Ohio River at Evansville, then caught a local to a place called Slaughters.

"Encouraging name," Marian commented, looking around at the forested hills that surrounded the station. "Where's the *Air Traveler* when you need it?"

"I'll see about hiring us a rig. We have about enough daylight to drive to Providence."

"Has it occurred to you that nobody on earth knows where we are?"

"Has it occurred to you that anyone who did would probably arrest us?"

"Hire your buggy. I'll watch our bags."

Joggling along a narrow hillside road behind the tired brown horse, Lockhart tried to picture Reb Thompson as the killer. *It never figured*, he told himself. *It never figured that*

Reb should have taken to me. He knew I'd campaigned right op-
posite him in the war. And now it comes clear. He sidled up to me
only to use me, only to destroy me. Only to make me the particu-
lar recipient of his general revenge on the Union.

Marian said, " 'Why so pale and wan, fond lover?' "

"I was thinking about—Brutus."

Her face showed concern. "Jim, you're not still fretting about that? You know you had to do it."

He shook his head. "It's not that. The name. I thought it was a clue, something in the way the King of China talked about it. Brutus and his friend, his colleague, something like that. But it turns out he was only using his middle name."

"Jim, the killer had to know Brutus—to know June. How would Thompson have met him?"

An owl, or some big bird a lot like an owl, swooped across the road in front of them, startling the horse. Lockhart tightened the reins, but the animal's fright didn't amount to much more than a twitch of the ears. Still, it reminded Lockhart how dark it was getting. The sun was still fairly high in the sky, but here among the pines it was far into dusk.

"How would any of them meet him? Of course, we all attended your shows at one time or another."

"Givens was on the stage once. He told Henson so."

"Really?" Lockhart thought about it. "Hard to picture that. But I saw Reb on the train, remember, just before all that business with Zack. It's got to be him."

"I like your daughter. She's very sweet. She'll be a wonderful mother."

Lockhart agreed. "I don't even know if Reb Thompson is married."

"Will it matter?"

"No."

'Do you think he's done all this? That he had people try to kill us?"

"The thing to remember is that we may not've run out of people wanting to kill us."

In Providence, they found the blacksmith shop. The smith was on his way home to dinner, but for a good Yankee dollar, he agreed to postpone his meal long enough to tend their horse and put away the buggy.

"You'll be wanting a room," he growled. Lockhart couldn't decide if he sounded unfriendly or if that was his normal tone. "The widder takes in boarders sometimes. She's a passable fair cook, too. Third cabin down toward the holler."

They found the place guarded by a long-eared yellow hound that raised a tremendous fuss until Lockhart knelt and offered it the back of his hand. It nudged at him with a wet, broad nose, snorted once, and went to curl up beside the porch.

"I guess he thinks we're harmless," Marian whispered.

"Hope everybody feels that way."

"What do you intend to do when you find Thompson?"

"That depends."

"Oh, that's marvelous! You had me worried there for a minute before you laid out the logic of your plan."

He knocked at the door until an old woman came in her robe and slippers to let them in. Yes, she had a room. Yes, she'd be right proud to hire it to them. Might not be as fancified as they were accustomed to, but it had a washbasin and a bed and a down comforter she'd sewed her own self in case the night blew up cold.

"I'm sure it'll be just what we need."

"Breakfast at six, if you hanker for it. Be right proud to have you."

The room was small, cramped, stuffy. But it was so clean that Lockhart was almost afraid to touch anything, and the featherbed and comforter were all anyone could have asked.

"This is heavenly," Marian sighed, wrapped to her eyes. "After that bed of nails on the immigrant train, it's too good to be true."

"I wish you'd learned the baby's name."

"Go away. I'm asleep."

Over ham and gravy, eggs and biscuits and grits and honey, Lockhart asked the old woman whether she'd ever known any Thompsons in the area.

She turned from the stove, looking at him with bright shoe-button eyes. "That's laurel honey, from the bees down at old Seth Thompson's place." she said. "They's a right passel of Thompsons. Them and their kin's all about the woods hereabouts, and then there's the Shady Grove Thompsons over west a smidgen."

"I was thinking of one I used to know. Lysander Thompson, though he pretty often went by Reb."

"Lys Thompson? Seems I remember him. Went off to fight for the South in that awful war, and him just a slip of a boy then. Hardly knew the Lys that come back from it. Was you in it?"

"Yes, ma'am."

"Hm! Federal, I be bound. Well, each had to do right as the Lord showed him. We was divided here in Kentucky, you know."

"So I've heard. Do you know where I might find this Lys Thompson?"

"Out to his pa's old place on the Shady Grove road, be it he was home. Down that road about six mile, then off'n to the right at a big pine's been struck by lightning. Here, have a little more of them eggs."

"Thank you."

"Don't know as I was you I'd go out there without he

asks you. I'm told Lys don't welcome company much, not even such nice folk as you and your lady."

Marian smiled at her. "Thank you."

"At least sample them grits, honey. They's not always to northerners' taste, but you might be surprised."

"Maybe we'd better not call on Mr. Thompson, then, dear," Lockhart said to Marian. "We'll drive on to Shady Grove instead and finish up our business there."

"Yes, I think that's best. Dear." She took a spoonful of the grits. "You're right. These are very good."

"I'll just go down to the blacksmith's and see about our rig." Lockhart rose and nodded to the woman. "Thanks. You've been a big help."

Two or three men stood in the coal-smoked gloom of the smithy watching the blacksmith shoe a mule. They noticed Lockhart right away. *Stranger in a small town*, he told himself. He would have preferred being lost in the crowd of a city. *Probably Thompsons, every one of them. Better not ask any more questions about Reb.*

He went into the shop to quell their suspicions. "Morning," he said to the smith. "When you get the time, I'd like to get my horse and buggy."

"Be done directly," the blacksmith said. He stood with a red-hot iron shoe in his large pincers. Then he laid the shoe atop his anvil and began to beat·it into shape. When he had dipped the shoe into a bucket of water to temper it, he put down his tools, took off his gloves, and said, "Rube, you keep this old mule quiet. I'll tend to the gentleman's horse. Rented it over to Slaughters, did you?"

"That's right."

"Probably overcharged you, did they, you being an out-lander and all?"

One of the idlers who had been watching and listening with interest said, "Going back that way today, are you?"

"I'm not sure. I have some business in Shady Grove."

Rube, holding the mule, spat tobacco juice. The others nodded, pursed their lips, thought it over.

"What's your name, stranger?" the first man asked.

The question was direct enough to worry Lockhart. He supposed this county had a sheriff somewhere, that posters on him and Marian had been circulated. Maybe Henson had even warned the local law to watch out for strangers asking after Reb Thompson. *But I didn't ask for Reb here.*

Merriweather came to mind first, but he'd used that often enough. "Moneytree," he said.

The men stood, moved in closer. The vocal one asked, "Well, Mr. Moneytree, what might be your business in Shady Grove?"

Lockhart saw that the blacksmith had come back without the hired horse. *That's it! They know me—they're after the reward!* He looked at the smith's great bulging right arm, looked at the small-town stubborn meanness in the eyes of the rest. The weight of the Colt was heavy at his waist, but he didn't reach for it. *No. I could threaten them with it, but there would be at least one who wouldn't threaten. And I can't shoot even such a gang as this.*

"I don't know that my business need concern you," he said.

Rube laughed. "Listen, boys, don't he talk just prettier'n a hand-colored Sunday School tract?"

"Talks like a Yankee."

"You do concern us, mister. I think we'uns will just ride out toward Shady Grove with you and your missus, since that's where you're so anxious to go."

Rube tied the mule off to the anvil and stepped out toward Lockhart. "What we'll do is take you to Lys's place to see whether he wants to hang you or shoot you or throw you to the hogs."

"I don't think so."

"You don't need to think."

He was close enough. Lockhart hit the man on the angle of his jaw with a quick upward jab that felled him on the spot. The gun was in his hand before the rest could react. He hoped Rube was the one who wouldn't threaten.

"I've explained to you as carefully as I know how that I don't want to go see your friend. Now I'll ask you to stand over against that wall."

Behind him an old woman's voice said, "I'll ask you to let go that little gun of your'n instead. This here old shotgun'll about saw you in two if'n you don't."

Lockhart hesitated. He heard the sharp clack of the hammers going to cock, but that wasn't what decided him. *I might have brought myself to shoot Rube. But the old lady who fed us eggs and biscuits?* Defeated, he tossed the Colt on the dirt floor beside Rube.

"What have you done to Marian?"

"Ain't done her a mite of harm. Being the two of you's so interested, we'll all us ride on out home to pay my boy that visit you had in mind."

23

Lockhart and Marian Taylor lay back-to-back, trussed in rope like a pair of packages wrapped by a child who didn't know when to stop but used the whole ball of string. The heavy jolting of the hay wagon tossed them back and forth painfully, but there was nothing Lockhart could do about it but swear. He did that only in his mind, not wanting to underline for Marian their complete helplessness.

At the tailboard of the wagon perched their luggage.

Lockhart supposed the woman had taken it from their room to avoid leaving any evidence of them in town. Next to them, the still-unconscious Rube showed no interest in where he was or why. It had already occurred to Lockhart to wonder what the man would do when he came to his senses. There being as little he could do about that as about anything else, he allowed his mind to rest on the gentler horns of how Thompson would dispose of him and Marian. Would he kill them in the presence of witnesses or would he dismiss the rest so that he could dispatch them at his leisure? Neither option seemed appealing.

"*Has it occurred to you that nobody on earth knows where we are?*"

He'd ridiculed Marian's question the day before. Now it didn't seem quite so funny. Nobody on earth would ever know. It would be a good joke on Rance Henson, but Lockhart wasn't yet prepared to laugh at it.

Lysander Thompson's mother was in no hurry to drive the six miles she'd spoken of. Nor was she in a mood to chat about it with the other two men who went along in the wagon. Instead, she drove the team at a pace matched to the mournful tune of the ballad she sang to herself.

> "*Cold wafts the wind o'er my true love.*
> *Full gently drops the rain.*
> *I've never had but one sweetheart*
> *In the laurel he lies slain.*
>
> "*I'll grieve as much for my true love*
> *As any fair lass may;*
> *I'll mourn and weep upon his grave*
> *For a long year and a day.*"

Lockhart had to wonder what joy she took in delivering him over to her son. *Will this bring mother and son back to-*

gether? Maybe she's his partner in the robberies. Does she know he killed two of the bankers? Would she care that George Stanhope wasn't even a Yankee?

He wanted to talk to Marian, to apologize for getting her into his mess, to apologize for getting her killed, to apologize for not having had leisure to marry her, to tell her again how he loved her. He struggled with the festoon of ropes until he found her hand with his own. He touched her fingertips and hoped she would understand.

"She has a nice voice," Marian Taylor said a little above a whisper. "We could have used her in the show."

Lockhart twisted his head toward her. "I'm sorry I got you into this."

"I wish she'd sing something a little livelier, though."

"I wish I'd married you when we had the chance."

"Just like a damned man. Anyway, when did we have the chance without having Doom show up to be best man?" Her hand squeezed his, and he realized she'd gotten free of some of her bonds. "How's your plan coming along?"

"I'm still working on it."

> *"I asked my love to take a walk*
> *And have with me a little talk,*
> *Down where the waters gently flow,*
> *Along the banks of the Ohio."*

"That's better."

> *"I thrust my knife into her breast*
> *As in my embrace she pressed."*

"I had to ask."

> *"Oh Willie dear, don't murder me,*
> *God knows I'm little fit to die."*

"Does Shakespeare have anything helpful to say?"

"I can't think what. This is more like *A Tale of Two Cities.*"

"Marian."

She squeezed his hand again. "Shut up."

It was a crow day. Lockhart had noticed the phenomenon before. Some days were hawk days when hawks hunted in pairs, mates, he'd always figured, the one skimming a pasture in close-at-hand search of what the other looked for from the height of a nearby tree or telegraph post. But this was a crow day. Crows were working the fields, in groups and alone, now walking, now hopping. Crows were on the telegraph wires and fences, a few individuals standing at a rakish slant with one foot on the rail and the other on a post. Here and there cattle ranged the pastures, ignoring the crows as the crows ignored them. Lockhart believed that crows had more humor and therefore more fun pound for pound than any other creature. *Unless it were man at his leisure.*

From her spot on the wagon seat, the old woman said, "It's a buzzard day."

Looking ahead, Lockhart saw the dozen or more buzzards soaring on the air to form the vortex of their search for whatever they smelled or suspected or knew was coming their way. He could not find in their waiting anything to comfort him. He touched Marian's hand again and felt her limited response among the ropes.

"Do they know something we don't?" she asked.

"The buzzards are just playing. It's their way." Very softly, he asked, "Any luck with the ropes?"

"Maybe by Tuesday."

"Do people up here read minds?" Lockhart asked to take his mind off the buzzards. "How did those apes in the blacksmith shop know I was asking for Thompson?"

Marian sighed. "I can help you with that. Good old Rube was on the back stoop, listening while you talked to Mama.

She mentioned that while she was wrapping me like a fly in a spiderweb."

"Gran Thompson. They's talking."

"Don't matter. How's Rube?"

At the sound of his name, Rube rolled his eyes, rolled up to a sitting position, came back to the world of the living. He sat for a moment, staring at Lockhart, trying to remember how he had gotten in the back of a hay wagon. Then an awareness keened in his dark eyes.

"Aren't you . . . ?" he asked of Lockhart.

Lockhart ignored him.

"By God, you are!" the man said. He struggled up onto his knees and crawled across the wagon bed to focus on Lockhart close at hand. "You hit me," he accused.

Lockhart looked him in the eye. "I'll hit you again," he said, "if you'll cut this rope so I can reach you."

The man appeared to think it over, to be struck at last by the absurdity of it. He started to laugh, grimaced, cradled his jaw in his hands. Then he leaned back to gather strength and momentum before he plunged a heavy fist against Lockhart's cheek just below the eye. Lockhart felt his head rock back and thump against Marian's. Then he didn't feel anything.

"Here, you, Rube!" the old woman said. She turned from her team to lash the man across his shoulders with her whip. "You'll do no more of that. We're not riding all this way to deliver my boy a bill of damaged goods."

The man lifted a bloody fist toward her but found neither voice nor words to challenge her. In their net of ropes, Lockhart and Marian Taylor slumped with their heads down, bouncing gently with the wagon. Asleep.

Lockhart came out of it when the wagon stopped. He was aware of someone getting off the seat, heard him open a gate, felt the wagon surge off the road onto an even rougher track. When he opened his eyes, he saw around him a pasture stocked with scattered red cattle. The gate closed behind them, the springs creaked as the man got back aboard, and the wagon moved again along a rutted lane across a grassy cleared pasture.

Rube sat with his arms resting on the side rail, staring at Lockhart with the promise of further business between them. No one spoke. He couldn't tell whether Marian was alert or not. He tried touching her hand, but his own fingers were too numb to be certain whether he succeeded.

When at last the wagon crawled to a stop before a small log house with a wide front porch, Lockhart saw Reb Thompson sitting in a rocking chair with a blanket over his legs. At least two dozen others, men and women alike, gathered in knots here and there on the porch and under the big shade trees. Saddle horses and buggies and farm wagons filled the side yard.

"It really is *A Tale of Two Cities*," Marian murmured. "Where's the guillotine?"

"I haven't read that. How does it end?"

"Badly."

Thompson stood with an effort, put a hand to the porch post, and said, "Well, what do we have here?"

He limped down the steps, leaning heavily on a hickory cane. By common impulse, Marian and Lockhart struggled up to a sitting position. Lockhart had a hard time seeing out of his left eye. Thompson reached the wagon, grasped its side rail, and stared at them.

"Jim. Lord of mercy, how'd you ever get yourself into a fix like this? And Mrs. Taylor, isn't it?"

"Your mother and her friends invited us to supper," Marian said. "We didn't see how we could refuse."

"Looks like they pressed the invite pretty hard." He looked at his mother. "Sheriff know they're here?"

"Not likely. But he's liable to, do any of them Shady Grove Thompsons hear of it."

"Best we be quick, then." Reaching to his back pocket, Thompson brought out a huge clasp knife and snickered the blade open. "Waste of good rope," he said.

"Listen," Lockhart began. Then he stopped, not even breathing as Thompson slid the blade up between Lockhart's ribs and forearm, then pulled it back sharply to cut through several strands of rope.

Deliberately, he sliced through several other rounds until the man and woman were left sitting all but free of each other. He cut the rope on Lockhart's wrists, then put the knife in his hand. "See can you get the ropes off your lady's wrists."

But Marian Taylor had freed her hands earlier. She stood and began brushing hay off her dress. Thompson lowered the tailgate and helped her down. "I'd like it," he said, "if you two would go on up and sit in them chairs on the verandy. You climb down, too, James Nathan, and stand up there behind them."

That last was addressed to the younger of the men on the wagon seat. Looking at him, Lockhart saw the resemblance around the eyes and mouth to Reb Thompson's face. When he turned back, Reb was holding out his hand for the knife.

Lockhart gripped it, looking around him. Everyone was watching. All the men were armed, and some of the older boys, probably some of the women, too, for all he knew. He saw revolvers, shotguns, a couple of old squirrel rifles, Winchesters, a slide-action Colt Lightning. Carefully, he folded the knife and handed it back to Thompson.

The old woman said, "What're you doing, Lys?"

Thompson hobbled back up to the porch and settled himself in his chair. "Well, by the leave of Elder Randolph over there, I'm fixing to preach me a sermon," he said. He nodded toward Lockhart and Marian. "And these two Yankees are the text."

Marian Taylor laughed. Nobody else did. Lockhart

didn't know why Thompson was delaying whatever he had planned for them. He decided to be grateful for the reprieve.

"First off," Thompson went on, "the rest of you in the congregation make yourselves comfortable wherever you'd like. My Corrie and some of the other women have tea and lemonade and the like. I figure this'll be pretty dry."

"They're making a party out of it," Marian whispered. "What happens at the end?"

Lockhart shook his head. He'd felt more at home in Little China.

His mother said, "Son, let Corrie bring you a glass of water. Speeches did always dry your throat out."

"Nope. Later. Right now I want to tell you a story. Most of you's heard bits of it before, but this is the whole thing." He paused to smooth his mustache and gaze moodily at Lockhart. Then he said, "Some of you remember when Bedford Forrest's men came through in the fall of 'sixty-four and I and cousin Elijah and Lemuel Blessingwell from down at the Forks went off to fight for the Confederacy."

"I remember," an old man said. "That very day, Hezekiah and Alvin Thompson from Shady Grove enlisted for the Union. Said you Providence Thompsons wouldn't have the better of them."

Reb Thompson smiled. "That's so, and they picked a better way to go soldiering than I and Lije and Lem. We ended amongst Granbury's Tennessee brigade of Hood. By and by, we come up to Franklin, the generals arguing among themselves fit to fight. The National troops couldn't ford the Harpeth, and they'd forted themselves up in the town to fix the bridge."

Lockhart noticed that Thompson's drawl became more pronounced as he talked. The congregation was listening intently. The speech stirred Lockhart's own memories, but he couldn't imagine where Reb was going with it.

"Old Hood, he threw us out in line of battle. We looked at them Yankee trenches, and the greenest one of them knew what was coming. General Cleburne—oh, but he was a fine-looking man—rode along our front. 'Boys,' said he, 'if we're to die, let us die like men.' So in we went."

Lockhart closed his eyes, his own position forgotten. He remembered those gray lines forming up along the Columbia Pike, rolling forward, smashing Wagner's advanced brigade, coming on. Nobody could storm entrenchments. Both sides knew it. But the gray lines had charged straight into the concentrated fire of two divisions.

"My Joe was there." A woman stood up and pulled her shawl about her. "He never knew a day's peace afterward, not to the day he died."

"Joe was a rank behind us. Lije was on my right hand, and Lem a few files down. We came up along the Pike and scattered the first outpost and French's brigade of Stewart chased them into the main line and broke that, too. They was fighting around the cotton gin. When we went to help, the Federals hit us front and flank. Our line rippled like a row of corn under the scythe and the next I knew it was dark. Lije was dead beside me and I couldn't move for the pain in my innards and I never knew what happened to Lem.

"I knew, as a man knows, I was hard hit. Couldn't crawl, couldn't holler out, couldn't hardly breathe. There was torches moving on the field. I thought they was souls going to glory, and I tried to shake loose and go with them, but the Lord wasn't ready for me."

A murmur went through the crowd. Two of the women were crying, either from Reb's story or from some memory of their own. "Amen," intoned a tall bony man whom Lockhart took to be Elder Randolph.

"Somebody bent over me, fumbling in my breast. I thought he meant to help, but what he had was a knife. Weak as I was, I tried to fight him. He was set to cut my throat, and then there was a flash and a bang and he fell dead across me."

Marian's hand gripped Lockhart's with agonizing force. He hardly noticed. He stared at Reb Thompson, trying to see in him the bloody, thin-faced boy from the Franklin battlefield.

"Then a National officer was kneeling by me. I was muddy and covered up with blood, and he looked clean-shaved from that very morning, I reckon, so I seen his face clear as a tintype. He asked how was I doing, and I tried to answer with my eyes that it would be a mercy was he to shoot me as well. And I believe he understood what I meant. What he done instead was to give me a drink of the finest water I ever tasted. Then he put his own overcoat across me and left me his canteen." Thompson pointed so that all would see a battered old tin canteen hanging above his doorway. "That there's the canteen, over my door's a welcome sign to whoever comes to it hungry or thirsty or half killed. And to remind me about loving my enemies, whoever they be."

"You didn't tell me about the overcoat," Marian whispered.

"I didn't remember."

"Some of you's heard that part. But God give me the chance to come across that Yankee officer in this life after that death. I've rid trains with him and drunk with him and played cards with him. And when the damned Federal laws took after him for what I knowed he never done, I took a leave from my job and set about to find the one had left it to look like his work."

He pulled himself to his feet again and held out a hand. "This here's the man. Name's Captain James Lockhart, and it's as proud a moment as I've known, to have him and his lady at my home."

The tall youngster behind Lockhart put a hand on his shoulder. "You's the one I'm named for, I reckon," he said.

"Want to thank you for my pa's life. Mine, too, far as that goes."

Lockhart couldn't think how to answer. He was saved from having to try when Thompson held up his hand. "Which brings us to another matter. My one question is who laid his hand to my friend's face? Jim?"

Lockhart said, "I don't remember."

Rube stepped forward and said, "I'm proud to say I done hit and would again 'cause I was told he was your enemy!"

Thompson thought about it. Then he smiled. "I was told that same thing once about him and his."

"You going to hang me?" Rube asked.

"Not if you'll shake Lockhart's hand and tell him you're ashamed you've forgot the manners you was once raised with. Your jaw looks to me like you've done been compensated for your meanness."

Rube kicked the ground, glared, marched up and held a hand out to Lockhart. "I'm rightly sorry, stranger."

"Call it even, Rube."

Then the others were gathering around, the men crowding to greet Lockhart, the women making much of Marian Taylor. Lockhart smiled and mumbled, his face burning. He was relieved when the group around him parted like the Red Sea and Reb Thompson stumped up to him.

"Before God, Reb, I never suspected that was you. I didn't think that boy would live through the night."

"Wouldn't've, but for that coat of yours. There's lots of better men died." He clapped Lockhart on the shoulder. "Corrie and them's got the fatted calf cooking. It's only for me to ask if there's any little thing at all I could do to make you and your lady happy?"

"I'd admire to hear what you've learned looking into my case. But, with the lady's agreement, there is one thing I'd like most in the world."

"Name it."

Lockhart whispered in Marian's ear. She smiled, nodded, kissed him on the cheek. "What we would like most is to be married here and now."

Reb looked surprised, then broke into a broad grin. "Married! Well, by thunder! James Nathan, you get your mama and sisters out here. Elder Randolph! We've got a couple of customers for you, and a better reason yet to have a feast."

Lockhart was never afterward sure just what happened after that. He had scattered memories: Elder Randolph, long and bony as a garfish, towering like a prophet under the arched branches of a blackjack oak. Corrie Thompson pressing her grandmother's ring into his hand, "to use until you can find something store-bought." Marian, her hair covered by a white veil Lockhart had never seen before, escorted between rows of standing Kentuckians by two small Thompsons. The Elder's deep voice: " . . . whom God hath joined together . . . " And a party with music and dancing and eating and drinking and praying for continued blessings all mixed together until Reb and Lockhart could find a minute alone.

"Hate to take you away from your wife, but there's some things you'd best know."

"Sit down and tell me, Reb. What's the matter with your leg, anyway?"

"Lead poisoning. That snake we're after put a bullet in me. Thought I'd best come here and fort up, like you all did at Franklin."

"You've seen him? Do you know who it is?"

"That's just what I haven't done. Has to be one was on the road with us, Givens or Knox or Mel Baker, though it's beyond me what one of them would do with the notes when he had them."

"I can answer that. But go on, what did you get?"

"Went to the bankers first. Knowing me, and knowing I

knew you, they thought nothing of talking about it. I learned precious little there. Then I got to spading up Baker's garden, and that's when I got myself shot."

"Mel Baker shot you?" The disbelief in Lockhart's voice was so intense that Thompson laughed.

"Not that I know of." He rubbed his leg as though that helped him recall the event. "Went clear to Boston to see about him. I was on my way back, meaning to see why he spends so much of his time in Omaha, when some son took a leg out from under me. Upset the Boston police no end."

"We saw you passing through Cincinnati. I thought you were the one that turned us in."

Reb Thompson put down his glass and stared. "Lord of mercy. That's what you're doing here." He pointed a finger at Lockhart and began to laugh. "You thought it was me!"

"I'm ashamed to say I did."

"Lord of mercy."

"You've been a loyal friend, the best I've ever had."

"No better than you were to me, and not even knowing who you were doing for." He pushed to his feet again. "I don't much touch hard liquor these days, but I'm bound we ought to drink on this. Lord of mercy, wait till I tell Corrie what you all was thinking."

"Lys! Lys Thompson!"

Rube came riding hard up the road toward the house. "Halloo the house," Rube shouted. "Posse's coming!" He reined the horse up short at the porch steps. "Lys, they're coming. Sheriff and a dozen men."

Thompson said, "How far back?"

"Maybe half a minute. They's at the gate last I looked back. Best hurry, less we want this party to end in a hanging."

24

James Lockhart ran to the oak tree to claim his bride from a group of ladies. "Quick," he said. By the time he turned, Lysander Thompson was leading two horses toward him on the trot. Their leather bags were tied on behind the saddles.

"Go!" Thompson said. "Rube'll guide you. Down that backtrail, across the crick, then up right through the woods. You'll come to a road. Take the left and don't quit riding till you get free!"

Already in the saddle, Lockhart said, "I'd like to thank you."

"Another time. We'll hold them here long's we can!"

Rube led, riding all out through the scattering members of the festive wedding party, down the backtrail toward the creek. There wasn't much water in it, and Lockhart figured that might be their best piece of luck. Once he thought he heard shouting back at the house. After that, they were out of earshot. He hoped they could stay out of rifle range as well.

The woods were thicker than he'd expected, but Rube threaded his way among the trees as if he were enjoying a canter in the park. Lockhart gave his horse its head, hoping it knew the way better than he. He lost some time looking back to be certain his new wife was following. He needn't have worried. Riding astride at considerable cost to her dress, Marian clung to his flank like a trooper. It gave him a new pride to see that she could ride as well as most men. *I'm the*

*luckiest damn man in the world. I just hope I live to enjoy a little
more of it!*

Probably their best luck was finding no fence at the dirt
road which they suddenly crossed and had to come back to.
Rube reined up there and pointed.

"Off to the left, just like Lys told you. The Pike's a mile
or so yonderways, take you straight south to Princeton. They
got railroad trains there to anyplace."

"What about you?"

Rube started to grin, then put his hand to his jaw and grimaced instead. "Aw, if anybody be following, I'll lead them
on a little chase up through the hills. You all take care."

"Thanks, Rube. You've been a friend."

"That goes for me, too." Reining her horse close, Marian leaned in the saddle to kiss Rube's bearded cheek. "Take
care of yourself."

"Ain't nothing so much," Rube mumbled. He half-lifted
a hand. "Best get on, give me time to mix your trail a mite."

At any other time, Lockhart might have thought the road
an enchanted lane lying beneath trees whose ancient limbs
overhung it from both sides. At the moment, however, he felt
more as if they were lost in an endless tunnel from which
they could not escape and at the end of which another posse
might be waiting for them.

Still, they rode as hard as they dared drive the horses. He
would never afterwards remember how long they were in
those woods, but he remembered coming out of them at last
into a cold clear moonlight. His idea of resting the horses
was to allow them to come down to a walk without stopping.
But he disliked lingering too long in any open spaces along
the road, just in case he and Marian were targets for some
sharpshooter, and especially because the posse might at any
moment burst into sight behind them.

They came into the outskirts of Princeton before they'd

realized it. At first it was only a scattering of cabins. A dog barked. They pressed on toward the dusty square, leaving a string of barking dogs in their wake. No one came out to shoot at them, and no one followed.

People may've had more cheerful honeymoons, but no one's ever been luckier. So far.

The business block was dark. In the moonlight, a lone Confederate soldier atop a tall pedestal stood guard in the center of the square. The only light in town, a sputtering yellow kerosene lantern, hung by the door of the ramshackle freight depot. From it, gleaming silver tracks reached east and west, away from the posse.

Lockhart's pounding on the door brought an elderly, sleepy, unshaven clerk to the door.

"When's the next thing through?"

The man scratched himself, yawned, gestured to the notice board on the wall.

"Ain't nothing scheduled regular till day after tomorrow. But they's a mixed local comes through in nigh an hour, don't stop less' it's flagged."

"That's good. Two tickets on that, then."

The stationman opened his eyes a little wider. "Where to, mister?"

"Far as it goes."

They waited, the horses saddled and ready to run, hoping the train would arrive ahead of the posse. When it did, they left the animals at the depot with a dollar and instructions to contact Elder Randolph about them. The train, drawn by a locomotive that had been ready for retirement when Lockhart fought at Chickamauga, was no more than a couple of boxcars and a mixed baggage and passenger car. Except for a surly baggageman who awoke long enough to take their tickets, Lockhart and Marian were the only living things on board. The car was dim and smelly and cramped, but Lockhart thought that, next to Marian, it was the most beautiful thing he'd ever seen.

"Which way is it going?"

He pointed along the tracks. "West, looks like."

"Where will it take us?"

He remembered Rube's words. "To anyplace."

"Good enough."

He swung their bags up into the rack and helped her to a seat. "I never knew you could ride like that," he said.

She laughed. "One of my few remaining secrets. We played *Mazeppa* one season, so I had to learn."

"Oh." He frowned over that for a few seconds. "Isn't that the play where the heroine rides off the stage . . . "

"Naked?" She grinned at him. "More or less."

"I don't like that very much."

"Tights. Pretty pink tights. I'll show you sometime."

Four hours later, having slept most of the way, they got off the train in the flat muddy river town of Cairo, Illinois. They checked into the Little Egypt Hotel and went straight to bed with no thought of consummating their marriage. At four o'clock in the afternoon, they went out to eat. After their late breakfast, Lockhart said, "We really ought to do a little shopping."

"Whatever for?"

He opened the door to a jeweler's shop and guided her in ahead of him. An old man pushed his thick glasses up on his forehead and peered at them with watery blue eyes. Leaving aside his work, he turned to greet them.

"Help you folks?"

Lockhart was looking at a display case. "You can. My lady wants to choose rings."

The old gentleman smiled. He stood down from his tall stool and moved with arthritic difficulty over to the counter across from them. Then he slid a tray of rings out and placed them on the glass countertop facing Marian. "Do any of these please you?"

"They're lovely," she said.

Lockhart thought she sounded like a girl in her joy.

"May I try this one?"

The old man took the ring out of its velvet snug and held it out toward her so that its small diamond caught every imagination of light and refracted it in sparkles. "You couldn't try a nicer one," he told her. He looked at Lockhart. "And will you be wanting a band to match?"

"He will," Marian said.

"Definitely," Lockhart said.

Back in their room, Marian removed her hat and sat on the bed. Holding up her left hand, she turned it so that the diamond caught the light. "We'll have to get Corrie Thompson's ring back to her," she said.

"I'll send it to Reb care of his home office. That'll reach him all right."

She leaned back on the bed, propped on her elbows. "Well, what now?"

"There's a train out in forty minutes. I've sent for tickets to Omaha."

"Omaha?" She sat straight and opened her eyes. "Forty minutes? Why Omaha?"

"That's where Mel Baker has been spending his time. Reb was looking into Baker's business when he got himself shot up."

"Well, sure, but forty minutes. I mean, can't we spend one night here?" She looked up at him hopefully. "I could show you my pink tights."

"What do you think?"

She pondered it, then sighed. "Omaha. But this time."

"What?"

"This time could we at least splurge on a damned Pullman berth?"

* * *

"I think it's Ed Givens," Marian said.

She was sitting up in a darkened compartment of a Pullman sleeper, her arms wrapped around her knees. They'd done even better than a berth, catching the Midwest Flyer out of Poplar Bluff and booking a compartment through to Omaha. Outside the little room's drawn blinds, the sunlit landscape of Missouri or Nebraska or someplace flashed past.

"You've always thought that. Because he called you a harlot."

"Because he was on the stage, and might have known June. Because he doesn't have a regular route to cover. Because he kept defending you when Doom was making all those charges. The others were all surprised and not too sure, but he kept saying you didn't do it."

"That makes him a villain, all right."

"All right, damn it, because I don't like him. And you don't seem to care that he called me a harlot." She laughed. "Even if I am acting the part today."

"You ought to get up. The porter has knocked three times wanting to make the bed."

" 'One turf shall serve as pillow for us both; one heart, one bed, two bosoms and one troth.' "

"What's that?"

"*A Midsummer Night's Dream.*"

"We should get something to eat."

She patted the berth beside her. "What you should do is come back to bed. Or isn't it fun anymore, now that it's legal?"

Lockhart laughed and began to unbutton his shirt. "Nothing we do is legal," he said.

They were up and dressed in time to disembark at Omaha, knowing less than they needed to. Lockhart had an address and the word *Backer* scribbled on a tag of paper

Thompson had given him. He assumed the word was intended to be *Baker*. To have a safe place to stow their luggage, the newlyweds took a hotel room.

"We might ask around, see what we could learn about Baker. Thing is, he doesn't live here and wouldn't have any reason to be here. Baker lives in Boston."

"Are you certain?"

"He told me more than once. His wife's name is Marie."

She frowned. "Well, since we're here, we might as well find out what Reb got shot for."

He laughed. "Let's aim at a different outcome."

"Then maybe we ought not to ask around. Isn't that what Reb was doing?"

"I see your point. If we ask questions, we're just as likely to sound the alarm as learn anything useful. You're thinking we ought to hit it straight on?"

"I agree."

He smiled at her tact, looked at her face, and thought he was beginning to see the real woman. "Let's go get him."

Not knowing the length of their trip, they took a carriage. Lockhart gave the driver the address from his piece of paper. To his surprise, the ride didn't last long. The carriage stopped across from a snug house on a quiet residential street lined with windswept shade trees. There being then nothing else for it, Lockhart paid the driver, helped Marian down, and went across to the house.

"Any ideas?" he asked her.

"We're friends of Melvin Baker, hoping to visit with him."

"And if he answers the door?" *With a gun in his hand?*

"Then we shall have found him."

"I think I'll leave all the planning to you from now on."

He knocked at the door. Presently they heard footsteps within. A brisk, gray woman reminding him of a mouse opened the door to peer out with quick, alert eyes. Lockhart expected her nose to twitch at the sight of them.

"Yes?"

Marian said, "Good morning. We're sorry to disturb you without any warning. We're Mr. and Mrs. Merriweather."

"How nice. Won't you come in?" she said as if she welcomed any visitors at all. "I'm Harriet Baker."

They went in. Lockhart took off his hat, and they sat on a tired sofa in the front room. "Actually," he said, "we don't know whether we've come to the right place. We're looking for a friend we haven't seen in some time. Melvin Baker."

"Oh," Harriet said, "you've just missed him. He went down to the office to catch up on his bookkeeping. He'll hate it he wasn't here to greet you. We so seldom have company."

"Office?" Lockhart asked.

"Yes. Of the Good Sense Dry Goods Company. It's just a branch office of course."

"The home office is in Boston?"

She brightened. "Yes. Melvin is a very important man in the company, you know."

"So we've heard."

"My goodness, I'm forgetting my manners completely. Could I fix you a cup of tea?"

Lockhart shook his head, but Marian said, "That would be very nice. Perhaps I could help." She rose and went into the kitchen with her hostess. "You have a lovely home. Have you lived here long?"

"Seven years. Since Mel and I married."

Lockhart felt his mouth drop open. He closed it, sat on the sofa, and pondered Mel Baker. It wouldn't be the first time his memory had failed him. But he had the rest of it right. Perhaps Melvin Baker had said Harriet rather than Marie. Probably so. Maybe Baker had been transferred to this branch office. *But the woman said seven years.*

He heard but did not pay much attention to Marian plying the woman with questions and mixing in a bit of her own life. "Jim and I are newlyweds," she told the woman. It strengthened him with a sense of pride.

Then it sobered him in consideration of the cloud hanging over them. He put a hand on his gun to remind himself that Melvin Baker was quite likely a man capable of treachery and even murder or conspiracy involving murder. Baker could easily be the man who had shot at him and Zack in Ohio.

The gun comforted him, but he had no intention of killing Baker. He thought he might break a few of his bones, but he definitely needed Melvin alive to tell the story and clear the newlyweds of the mountain of charges against them.

He drank the tea and ate a stale sugar cookie and listened to the women talk. Harriet Baker turned to him. "Where did you say you knew Melvin?"

"On the trains," he said. "I'm a traveling drummer myself. Mel and I have customers in some of the same cities all across the country."

"Oh, he tells me such stories about the places he goes. Boston, of course, to the home office. Sometimes he has to stay up there months at a time. Then he may be off all the way to California. Such stories he tells me." She turned up her hands. "But I guess you know all about that, Mr. Merriweather."

"Yes. Do you know where Mel stays when he's in Boston?"

"Oh, he has family there. He stays with his sister Marie."

"Would you like to go with him one day?" Marian asked.

"Oh yes. More than anything. Of course, I'm needed here. I keep the home fires burning, as Melvin puts it."

Marian looked at Lockhart. "A woman's place," she murmured.

"He tells me about his friends on the train!" Harriet said brightly.

"Does he?"

"Yes. I'm trying to place you, Mr. Merriweather. But I can't recall. Melvin sometimes mentions a James, but his name is Lockhart, I think. Do you know him?"

"Passing fair," Lockhart said. *Though lately he's sometimes a stranger.*

"Oh, it's so exciting! This Mr. Lockhart is a fugitive from justice now, the most wanted man since Jesse James, the newspapers say. Why, just this past week, there was a big article on his escape from a farm in Ohio after a tremendous battle with the lawmen. The reporter just made me feel I was right there on the spot amidst all the gunfire and bloodshed!"

"Clyde Darrow," Lockhart said.

"Pardon me?"

"Mrs. Baker, do you know any of Melvin's other friends?"

She smiled. "Well, he sometimes travels with a Mr. Thompson. A Confederate soldier, he was. Melvin was in the Union Army, you know. Sells firearms! 'Not entirely civilized,' Melvin says."

"That's the one," Marian said, "but his appearance is deceiving. He's really quite a fine gentleman."

Lockhart looked out the window. "Do you think I might go down to the office to visit Mel?"

"You could, but you might miss him on the way. He'll be back with his work done and his newspaper to read."

"But you don't know just when, I expect."

"I know exactly when. He'll walk up on the porch a minute on either side of eleven! Regular as the railroad."

Lockhart looked at his watch. He had eight minutes. "I believe I'll step out for a minute, if you ladies will excuse me."

"Of course." Harriet Baker patted Marian's hand. "I'm sure we'll find plenty to talk about. I'm just so eager to hear about your wedding, my dear."

Leaving Marian to handle that, Lockhart went outside

and down the walk to the street, where he turned toward the taller buildings. Walking slowly, checking his gun, deciding what he would say, he made his way to the corner, stopped, and waited.

In the distance he saw a man approaching with an unneeded umbrella hooked over one wrist and a newspaper tucked under the other. If Melvin Baker recognized Lockhart, he gave no sign of it. Lockhart turned his back and waited. As Baker crossed toward his corner, Lockhart said, "Nice to see you, Mel."

Mel Baker turned automatically, his hand starting to come out, a smile of pleasure forming on his face. Halfway along, he froze in place as if a passing Medusa had turned him to stone. Finally, he gulped and dropped his hand, making no move for a weapon.

"My God, Jim," he said, peering at Lockhart through his rimless glasses, "is that you?"

"Just about is. We need to have a talk, Mel."

"Well, of course." Baker darted a quick look toward his house. "We could go to my office. Nobody much there this time of day. How did you find me? I mean, what is it I can do for you?"

"You can tell me about those robberies and killings. But not at your office. You want to do it here or up at your house in front of Harriet?"

"No!" Baker stopped. "Then you know about Harriet?" He stepped toward Lockhart, and suddenly he looked as dangerous as Lockhart thought he might be. "You haven't harmed her?"

"No. Nor told her anything. But you'd better come up with the truth."

"The truth." Baker chuckled. "All right. We'll talk here." He offered Lockhart his hand. "I haven't heard anything further about your—the—crimes. Except of course that you'd escaped." He looked nervously up toward the house. "With that Taylor woman."

"My wife," Lockhart said.

Baker looked startled. "Your wife? But wasn't she married?"

"You may not be the one to ask about that. Harriet tells us you stay with your *sister* Marie when you go to Boston."

Baker's face went pale. "For God's sake!" he cried, but then he looked at Lockhart more calmly. "All right, Brother Lockhart. You've caught me out. Always knew it had to happen, but I confess this wasn't how I'd expected it."

Lockhart hadn't wanted to believe it. "You have two of them?" he asked.

"Don't be envious," Baker said. "Worst trap ever a man was caught in."

Lockhart didn't doubt that. "Should we go talk that over with Harriet?"

"What is it you want of me?"

"I'm sought for my life, and I believe you ought to be in my place."

Now Baker looked genuinely puzzled. "Your place? Why? What are you talking about?"

"I believe you knew my appointments pretty well."

"We all knew each other's business, right enough. And I never believed what they said of you, Jim. Still don't. But I don't see what you're getting at."

Lockhart watched him closely. Was Baker that good an actor? He wished Marian was there to judge. All he himself could see in Mel Baker was surprise, a touch of guilt and concern, and a growing bewilderment. All natural enough as it seemed to Lockhart.

"I'm saying you went along behind me like a jackal stealing the goods I'd delivered and killing my customers. My friends."

"As God's my witness!" Baker said.

"As He was at your weddings?"

"Jim. There's a difference. Marrying too many women's the kind of fool I am. Can you see me bashing in Elvin Murdock's head? Elvin was at Gettysburg, same as me."

"You needed money. It can't be easy, paying for two households."

Baker raised his eyes to heaven. "God knows that's gospel true. Do you mean to kill me?"

Lockhart let the gun show at his belt. "I haven't come to a conclusion. I'd rather hear your confession."

"You know the most of it already. I married two women. It just happened. I met Harriet afterwards."

"Save that. I want to hear about the robberies."

"Then I can't help you. If I knew who did them, I'd tell you. I swear it on our friendship, on my wife's honor." A glint of wry amusement came to his eye, and for a second he looked like the Mel Baker Lockhart remembered. "On both their honors. But I can't do more than that."

Against all rational judgment, Lockhart believed him. "That leaves no one but Ed Givens," he said. "You think you could help me find him about now?"

"Ed Givens?" Baker stared at him. "I guess on the run— I mean as busy as you've been—you don't get much news."

"News?"

"It happened in Missouri, over by Jefferson City just a few days back. Don't know what he was doing there. Out of his usual territory."

"Whose territory?"

"Ed's. But you don't know. It was an accident, run over by a train and cut nigh all to pieces. Ed Givens is dead."

25

"Two?" Marian Lockhart said.

"I suppose you're envious!"

"No."

"Then you feel sorry for him having twice the woes you have!"

"I feel sorry for the wives," he said.

"Good! You certainly should." She began to respect his quickness, perhaps even his perspective.

"That isn't the worst of it."

"You mean there's a third one!"

"Ed Givens is dead."

"What!"

"An accident, Mel said. In Missouri. But that doesn't figure. I think whoever's done all this has killed him."

She put her hands to her cheeks. "So that's on our balance sheet as well?"

"On the killer's, not ours. But it makes our job all the easier. There's nobody left but Opportunity Knox. That baby-faced bastard's been the one all along."

"It couldn't be. He had chances enough to kill us on the airship. You, especially."

"And I can't think why he held off. I'll have to ask him about that. But we've eliminated the others. He's the only one left."

Marian bit her lip in uncertainty. But it was true. Even she couldn't imagine Mel Baker as the killer, quite aside from the fact that Harriet in all ignorance had given him a perfect alibi for the El Paso killing.

"Why, yes, that was our anniversary! Melvin spent the whole week here."

"Knox," she said. " 'We'll sift him!' " *But that was Claudius's line. No matter, I'll play the man if needs be. It'll need a better costume is all.*

"Do you still have the *Air Traveler* schedule?"

"I don't know. In my bag, perhaps. I'll see."

Two days later, they sat waiting in St. Joseph, Missouri. "Are you listening?" she asked.

"Certainly, yes. What did you say?"

She smiled. "I said that the ship is nearly a day behind schedule."

"What will we do?"

We could stay in our room in bed and never put on our clothes until time to come back here. "I could look at your scars again, tell you about the ones you can't see. On your back."

"Do you have any scars I haven't seen?"

He was quicker than she'd thought. "Some. I don't know that you could see them. But you might look."

"I'm your man."

"You'd better be." She smiled at him, sitting with his long legs strung out to full length, his hat tipped down over his eyes. "Perhaps we might look around town first."

"A stroll?"

"I'm your girl," she said. She stood, tugged at his arm, and took it when he rose.

"You'd better be."

They walked slowly along the riverfront, he waiting now and then while she bent to pick a flower or watch a boat or raft passing with the current, she clinging to his arm as he pointed to some water bird. At three o'clock, they went back to the fairgrounds to check on the *Air Traveler.* Nothing of certainty could be said, but the latest telegraph suggested the ship would not arrive before sunset. After that they returned to their room to salve each other's scars.

She awoke a little after five when Lockhart got out of bed. In the faint light through the curtains she watched his naked form as it moved to the dresser. He looked at his watch, turned toward her. "Come back for a moment," she said. "Get warm."

He came back. "We'll have to go."

"When you're warm."

She walked beside him toward the fairgrounds, the nickeled Colt in her purse, a soft flutter in her heart. If it came to it, she could shoot Opportunity Knox. *And I will. But I know Jim needs him alive. In the end, that'll be up to Knox. If it works, fine. If it comes down to his life or Jim's, I'll kill him, even if it means we live on the run the rest of our lives.* "What?"

"You were shivering. I asked whether you were cold."

She smiled and hugged his arm against her side. "I'm still warm."

"Are you?"

"Glowing." Ahead, she could see lanterns already lit against the possibility that the ship would be late. "If it doesn't come until dark, could it land?"

"Well, it did for us. The lanterns are mostly for the crowd, I think. Captain York can use those big electrics in a pinch to light his way."

At the gate he paid a dollar to get the two of them in to see the landing up close. To her surprise, a crowd of hundreds had already gathered to watch. She and Jim mingled in among them and waited.

Then, just at sunset, she saw it, heard the murmur of the crowd about them. Too big to fly, too big to believe, the bulky body of the *Air Traveler* caught the last rays of sunlight. Dark against the sky, it swooped over the fairgrounds, turned to put its blunt nose into the wind, and whupped its way back to where men waited to grab its mooring ropes and reel them in. As the black shadow covered the field, a child screamed, broke loose from his mother, and ran in terror away from the group The woman ran after him, calling his name to no avail.

Moments later, the ship hovered before them as if it were about to unfold its feet and perch. Instead, men at the rails threw down long ropes to those on the ground. They wrestled with its buoyancy, wrapped the ropes around pylons, and began to take up slack a turn at a time. As the ship was being forced to the ground against its will, Marian looked up at the passengers gathered along the rail. She might catch sight of Opportunity Knox, give them an advantage before he knew they were there. But instead—

"Oh, my Lord," she said.

"What is it?"

"There, just back from the wheelhouse, the big man with the white hair."

"Damnation."

They turned their faces away and worked back through the crowd, hoping they looked as if they were frightened of the ship instead of its passenger. "Do you think he saw us?"

"I'd be afraid to think he didn't. Keep moving."

She kept moving all right. She clung to his hand and followed as he drove through the throngs who were in a poor humor to part for their passage. When they finally broke free behind the moving crowd, she looked over her shoulder. If Henson wasn't looking straight at them, he was a better actor than June had been. Off to their right, the mother had caught her son and knelt beside him drying his tears, holding him tightly, reassuring him. *I would do the same for you, my Jim. I would, if only you were a child.*

"This way," Lockhart was saying. "I don't see another gate anywhere. We'll have to climb the fence."

Behind them the *Air Traveler* strained, tried to rise, slowly let itself be borne to earth. It hadn't touched. She couldn't see Henson anymore, guessed he would be shouting at the captain or the crewmen or anyone who would listen to lower the gangway or drop a rope ladder. She looked hopefully for a gap in the fence but saw none. Jim was right. If they went all the way back to the main gate, they would put themselves within Henson's reach.

Lockhart had made up his mind. He put his foot on the lower support rail of the fence, hauled himself up the splintery boards, reached down for her. She ignored his hand. Hoisting her skirts up to her waist, she scaled the fence as nimbly as any boy. Behind her, she heard laughter and an appreciative shout, but then they were over and sprinting into the dark woods beyond the fairgrounds.

"Listen," Lockhart panted. "I don't like you showing your bloomers to that crowd!"

"They weren't looking at us. Run."

They ran. Inside that dark forest perimeter, they stopped, hid behind a tree, looked back. All they saw was a throng of people around the tethered ship. Lockhart pulled her to his chest and kissed her. "Idiot," she said.

"Right enough. It was something about watching you scale that fence."

"Better than pink tights?" She pulled his face down and kissed him. Then she tugged at his hand and they moved further into the trees. "Do we dare go back to the hotel?"

"Got to have our bags. If we hurry, we can beat him there, even if it's the first place he looks."

She was panting, trying to keep pace with his long-legged trot, fighting for breath. "If he does look there, he'll know."

"You going to leave a note?"

"No." Pant. "The last poster I saw on us gave the name *Merriweather* as . . ."

"What!?"

She was all but done in. "Alias."

He stopped to let her breathe. "Glad you happened to think of that."

"Thank you."

"More than halfway wish you'd mentioned it earlier."

"Just be grateful."

"What?"

"That you don't have two of me."

He sat down and crossed his legs and laughed.

"Get up," she told him. "You can laugh when we're clear of this."

He got up on one knee, still laughing. "Maybe not. Might not live that long!"

"Sure as hell won't, you idiot, if you don't get a move on."

They walked quickly back toward a point between the fairgrounds and their hotel. She hoped that Henson would be caught up in the festivities surrounding the *Air Traveler*, at least long enough for them to get their things. Not the least of those belongings were her notes on the crimes. *If we lose all that now, it will be as if someone went into our room among our things to sort through them. To steal things which are ours. Ours in union as man and wife!*

"Look. We're too late."

In the distance a tall, vigorous, white-haired man was striding across the street, obviously bound for their hotel. Beside him, young Opportunity Knox struggled along like a two-year-old trying to keep pace with his grandfather. Knox did not look at all pleased to be separated from his ship and the adoration of the multitude at the fairgrounds. Henson didn't look like he cared. Neither of them noticed the Lockharts.

"We can't go back now." *Our things!*

"Don't look so guilty," he told her. "I paid them in advance."

"It isn't that. I hate to leave our home."

"I hate to leave our bed."

"That most of all."

They turned and walked away from the hotel. She followed along for a time, not wanting to ask where he intended to go. She figured when he knew, he'd tell her. Until then, she'd better leave the leading to him. A man had his pride.

"Where do you think we might go?" he asked of a sudden.

She liked that, his willingness to share that pride. "I'm yours," she replied. "We might try a rooming house out of the way somewhere."

"Thought of that. We could say our luggage is coming later. But the real thing is we need to go right back and watch to see where Knox goes. He's got a day and half layover here."

She wasn't sure she liked the idea of going back, especially the half a mile they'd walked out of the way. She didn't like it because she was afraid. But she was his and she would follow where he led. "Let's go get him, then."

Lockhart looked down at her with what she interpreted as a possessive pride in her. "Let Henson be damned—though I doubt that the devil would have him. Knox is our only hope."

She nodded. "Yes. But how can we get to him?"

He stopped to think about it. "It would help if we knew what room he's in."

We could try every door. "I'll go in and ask."

"Wouldn't that be pretty! A married woman asking after a handsome young bachelor."

"I don't have to be a married woman. Hotel clerks are accustomed to such things." She saw the look on his face. "Remember, I'm whoever I need to be to get the job done. And he isn't handsome. You're handsome. He's a baby-faced kid."

"They'd know you at the desk."

He was reluctant. She couldn't help laughing.

"You know better than that." Her hands went to her hair, removing her hat, unpinning, pinning up in a different style. "I wish I had a mirror." *And my things from the little blue trunk. And a quiet home in Ohio, with Jim's granddaughter on my knee.* "But I'll manage."

"It's too risky."

She reached in her bag. Lip rouge, powder. Did she have a beauty spot? "So is not knowing."

"All right. We'll wait, watch for our chance."

Their chance came an hour later when U.S. Marshal Rance Henson came out of the hotel, stood at the top of the wooden steps to light a cigar, then walked away toward the restaurant in which they'd had dinner. She wondered if Henson was hungry, or if he was following their trail through the town. *It doesn't matter. We haven't much time either way.*

"Now," she said.

"I can't let you do it."

"Don't get all manly and protective. It's now or some other lifetime."

"I'll go myself, then."

"And I'd be glad, but I want you to have the best chance. I pray you, let me go in as a stranger, get the number, and come give you a signal. Like this." She gestured, holding up different numbers of fingers in succession. "I won't come back here to you." *I know you have to do this thing alone.* "I won't risk drawing them to you just in case someone's recognized me."

"If you're not out in two minutes, I'll come in after you."

She kissed him, lingered a moment, then went across the street and into the hotel without looking back.

At the doorway, she paused to adjust her gait and her expression to the part. *Harlot, just as Givens thought. Getting too old for the job. Brassy and bold about it. Show it in the walk.*

She glanced at the people in the lobby but didn't study them. It was crucial that she get to the desk, get the number, and get out.

"Evening, mister," she said to the clerk. "I wonder, do you have a certain party staying here who asked me to call on him?"

The man looked up at her, raised his eyebrows. "I haven't seen you before."

"Never too late." She gave him a smile. "New in town, but always interested in making new friends. About that guest."

"Name?"

"Opportunity Knox."

He stared at her. "Does it?" She recognized the leer, the desire, that old look men had given her ever since she was sixteen. As she'd learned to do almost as long ago, she played up.

"Not tonight, but maybe later. That's his name. Mr. Knox."

"Oh." He looked at his records. Then in a voice much too loud to suit her, he said, "Mr. Knox is in room two-one-three."

"Thank you very much."

"Shall I send up for him?" The leer again. "Or would he rather your visit be in private?"

She waved a hand. "Don't trouble yourself, sweetie. Not at all. I'm to meet him for dinner down the street. I'll wait there."

She turned, walked back toward the front door feeling as if the whole world were staring at her and knowing who she was. She determined to stare them down. But she saw only a middle-aged couple talking earnestly in the parlor, two young bucks nudging one another and grinning her way, a gaunt older man giving her the merest glance above his newspaper.

She went outside. Lockhart was little more than a shape among the shadows by the alley near the rear entrance. Standing beneath the light so that he could see, she held up two fingers, a fist, one finger, a fist, and three fingers. She was about to repeat it all when she saw him mingle into the shadows as he moved along toward the rear entrance to the hotel.

Staring then into the darkness where he had been, she saw in her mind a pair of eyes on the train to Sacramento, a pair of eyes glancing at her above a newspaper, a pair of eyes watching hungrily from the audience in a dozen theaters.

"Yon Cassius has a lean and hungry look . . . "

Cassius, the friend and fellow conspirator with Brutus. And she had just seen them again not a minute earlier. She understood all in a flood of memory and awareness just whose eyes they were. *Oh my dear God, I should have known!* She put her hand in her purse, took a grip on the small revolver, and dashed back into the lobby. Cassius was gone.

My God, Jim, it's a trap and you don't know. It isn't Knox! I must send him a note by the clerk! No, it's too late for that. With her hand still in the purse, she raced past the goggling desk clerk and started for the stairs. Just as her foot hit the first step, a pair of strong arms circled her in a grip she couldn't hope to fight, lifting her off the floor.

"By the ghost of Julius Caesar," said the voice of Marshal Rance Henson in her ear, "I've got you at last!"

26

Lockhart stood at the corner of the alley and waited. Just when he had decided to go in after his wife, she came to the light at the front corner of the hotel.

345

She looked his way, made the hand signals she had promised. *Two—one—three. All right, Knox, you son of a bitch, I'm coming for you!* He went in the back door and up the back stairs without so much as a glance along the lower hall. The second-floor hall was not as well lighted as he might have wished, but he figured it was better for him. He was not the game, after all, but the hunter. Moving softly but with as much speed as he could manage, he worked down the hall until he reached the last door on the end: room 213.

He listened a moment, heard a noise, knocked quietly enough at the door. In a voice betraying an exhaustion not fitting his usual enthusiasm, Opportunity Knox said, "Come in."

Lockhart cocked his gun, tested the knob, and turned it. He opened the door into complete darkness, the dim light behind him throwing his shadow onto the floor and etching him as a perfect target. Half-expecting a bullet, he came inside fast and low, slamming the door behind him.

Instead of firing, Knox let out a moan. There was a noise of something heavy falling, bed springs creaking, the heavier breathing of someone suddenly between Lockhart and the door.

Lockhart started to whirl, but the other presence thrust a gun muzzle against the small of his back. Another hand snatched his own gun away from him, withdrew, turned a key in the lock.

Lockhart said, "I'd like you to hear you say you did it before I die."

A dry, throaty chuckle came from behind him. "It won't make much difference to you, Lockhart, but I'll say it. I stole the notes, killed those two meddling fools at the banks, fixed it up so it would fall on you. And it has."

The voice didn't belong to Opportunity Knox. It didn't seem to belong to anybody, but Lockhart knew what the answer had to be.

"They said you were dead."

The chuckle again. "I am. A man run over by a train is as dead as they get. Sometimes the only way to identify him is by his clothes." The gun nudged Lockhart's back. "Over there."

Lockhart moved in the darkness, straining his eyes for a sight of something, anything. "You were hard on your helpers, Ed," he said. "Do you have any left?"

"Don't need any more. I'm done now. I can pull a trigger for myself."

"Have you done for Opportunity, too? What did he ever do to you?" Lockhart felt the hesitation. "What did I ever do to you, Ed?"

Givens snorted. The dry voice held real malice. "I did it to you because I hate your arrogant ease. Officer in the Army. Trusted deliveryman for real goods."

"Hell."

"And that stripling Knox. Him and his big plans and big ideas and his big mouth. And I a better man than either of you."

Someone tapped at the door, rattled the knob.

"Jim," Marian's voice cried through the door. "Jim, let me in. Jim! I've seen him. Edward Givens isn't dead! He's the one. It's Givens!"

"Hist!" Givens said. The gun ground into Lockhart's back. "Careful what you say. Get her in here!"

Lockhart didn't have time to take it in, but he understood enough. He understood who was holding a gun to his head and who would need to kill Marian now that she knew he wasn't really dead.

"Get her in! Or I'll shoot her right through the door!"

Lockhart felt the gun's muzzle shift and knew he'd never have a better chance. With no last prayer for his own soul, he cried out, "Run!" He got out one syllable of the word *Henson* before the world fell in on his skull.

The carpet scraped the side of his face raw and he knew that he wasn't out. Givens kicked him in the ribs. Lockhart had the feeling that the broken ends of those ribs must have caved in to touch his backbone. But the fresh pain brought him around so that he was able to take hold of the boot when it came at his head. He hung on, rolled over with the one clear thought that Givens couldn't afford the noise his gun would make, and toppled him onto the floor with a crash.

Lockhart struggled up enough to launch a blow at the other man's face, but Givens struck at him with the gun, missed his head, hit his shoulder. Lockhart's left arm went numb, but with his right he took hold of the gun, wrestled for control of it, kneed Givens in the gut, got in a blow to the side of his head. Finally, he pulled the gun free. Givens came for him, and he struck his enemy down.

He pulled himself up on the dresser, went to the window, tried to open the curtain and yanked it down onto the floor instead. Light from the street lamp let him see what he needed to know before he lit the lamp on the dresser.

Opportunity Knox lay still but moaning softly on the bed. Edward Givens had pushed himself off the floor with one hand. He sat in that position apparently staring at his own blood dripping slowly from his mouth onto the carpet.

Someone hammered on the door with the sound of thunder. Almost as thunderous was the voice of Rance Henson.

"Open up in the name of the law! Lockhart, open this door! What's going on in there?"

Lockhart looked down at Edward Givens. Givens looked pale, shrunken, sick. His mouth was smeared with blood, but Lockhart didn't think he'd hit him there.

"All right, Ed," he said, "I figure you've got about half a minute."

"To live?" Givens wanted to know.

"That'll be up to you."

Givens gave a thick laugh. "I've got the consumption and half a dozen killings pulling at my life. A gun doesn't frighten me."

Lockhart saw his life passing before his eyes. "That's why you did it? Because you were going to die?"

"Worked that route for years. Deserved something for my trouble. Deserved some money to die on. No trouble to open a safe. No trouble to get in a bank. Just took what was mine."

"You took what was *mine!*" Lockhart said. "My reputation. My life. Now you're going to give them back."

"Or you'll shoot me? Then what? That lawdog's here to arrest you, not me."

Something thudded against the door, loosened the hinges. "Lockhart!" Henson shouted.

Givens smiled with bloody lips. "Think I'll clear you? It was too hard a job putting your neck in the noose." He reached into his coat, came out with a pocket gun. "You wait for me in hell, hear? I'll be along soon."

He had begun to lift the gun when Lockhart shot him through the chest. Henson slammed against the door again. It flew loose from the jamb and fell at Lockhart's feet. Lockhart threw down the gun and waited.

Henson walked it like a gangplank until he stood right in Lockhart's face. Marian was close beside him. The marshal looked at Edward Givens lying on the floor, at young Knox who had just begun to sit up.

"Well, you dumb bastard," Henson said to Lockhart, "you couldn't open the door when I had her call you, so that I could have nabbed him more or less alive. And you couldn't wait just another second for me to get here but that you had to kill him."

Lockhart said nothing.

"I'd half have believed it of Givens that he done it, but

that you had to go and kill him so I'd always have to think you done it to shut him up."

"Shut who up?" Opportunity Knox said. His speech was slurred, his pupils big as black olives.

Marian said, "We can get you the proof now. I know we can. Jim didn't do it. Givens was the one." But in her voice Lockhart heard a certain resignation at what he'd done. She knew as well as he that they would never be free, even though they'd found the killer.

Knox said, "Shut who up?"

Henson went across to the bed to look at the gash on the young man's head. "To shut Givens up," he said. "You don't look too good. You just lie back and don't flail around so."

"Jim didn't shut him up," Knox said. "I heard it every word. His confession. Givenses's." He put too many syllables in the word, laughed foolishly, then put his hands to his head. "No, listen. I heard him."

"Hell," Henson said, "everybody's loyal to Lockhart. You don't know a thing about it. You was out on your face on the bed when I come in."

"I was on my face because I didn't want to get killed. That man was crazy. But I did hear it. Listen."

Thickly and with some false starts, Knox spent the next several minutes giving in fair detail the elements of the conversation he'd overheard. Lockhart couldn't find much of it to disagree with, so he kept quiet. He stood with his arm around Marian and waited. Marian said, "There, isn't that enough for you?"

"Damnedest motive I ever heard of. Didn't like these two because you were too—too what? Because things were too easy for you, he thought?"

Marian shook her head. "It wasn't that. Not really." Softly, she said, " 'He hath a daily beauty in his life that makes me ugly.' "

"What's that?"

"Poetry."

As if that explained it all, Henson nodded, and went on writing in his leather book.

"Can we go then?" Marian asked him. "We have a room of our own. You can find us if you need us."

"I know you do. I've had a man waiting in it for you to come back. You can about go, I reckon. Hell, I'll even apologize for all the trouble it's cost you. All right?"

Lockhart said, "All right."

"I'll even thank you for saving my life a couple of times."

"And I'll thank you for saving mine," Lockhart said. They shook hands. "You're a good man, Marshal Doom." Then he took Marian and walked out into the hall.

Henson said, "Just a damn minute, both of you."

Lockhart was not really surprised. It hadn't all been answered. There was still a better than even chance the marshal would hold them for one of the murders along the way. If not that, then there was kidnapping an officer, escape from custody, any number of little things.

"All right, Marshal. What else?"

"You still owe me twenty-eight dollars."

Get caught reading.

Jake Lloyd reading ENDER'S GAME.

A Message from the
Association of American Publishers